SPIRITUAL WARFARE

SPIRITUAL WARFARE

EAGLE FEATHER

SPIRITUAL WARFARE

iUniverse books may be ordered through booksellers or by contacting:

iUniverse
1663 Liberty Drive
Bloomington, IN 47403
www.iuniverse.com
1-800-Authors (1-800-288-4677)

Because of the dynamic nature of the Internet, any web addresses or links contained in this book may have changed since publication and may no longer be valid. The views expressed in this work are solely those of the author and do not necessarily reflect the views of the publisher, and the publisher hereby disclaims any responsibility for them.

Any people depicted in stock imagery provided by Getty Images are models, and such images are being used for illustrative purposes only. Certain stock imagery © Getty Images.

ISBN: 978-1-5320-4010-8 (sc)
ISBN: 978-1-5320-4011-5 (e)

Print information available on the last page.

iUniverse rev. date: 04/02/2018

TO THE READER...

This novel is completely unedited...completely untouched by professionals. What you are about to read is my voice... a voice in it's purest and rawest form.

SUMMER
1988

The second Kevin stopped screaming was the second the evil voices began. Every horrible detail of that very second had etched itself into the heart of the child... engraving... burning. It was at the age of 8 in the year of 1988 when this story began. Joshua Lone Wolf stood looking towards the cloudless sky... a sky tinted blood-red from the sunset. Afternoon shadows crept over the city of Omaha like a sinister cat creeps through the glade. The faint sent of BBQ drifted on a gentle breeze as the sound of children laughter and rap music fills the air.

"What's on your mind, Little Wolf?" Kevin asked his younger brother. Kevin stood on his front porch, along with thee of his fellow gang-members. They were all drinking and smoking herb, listening to N.W.A.'s latest hit on a boom box.

"You gonna walk me home?" Lone Wolf asked as he walked towards the porch.

"You only live three blocks away, lil' nigga. So gets to walking," Rex said. He was one of Kevin's friends.

"Shut up, punk bitch!" Lone Wolf cried as he launched towards Rex with his tiny fists clenched. But Kevin was able to grab his younger brother before he was able to do anything stupid.

"Is you crazy, lil' sucka?" Kevin asked as he started to laugh. "Go fight a lil' dude," he laughed as he playfully pushed his brother towards the house.

"Yeah," Rex said, "mess with me and get crushed," he said causally as he lit a joint.

"Fuck you!" Lone Wolf cried, trying to launch another attack on Rex, but again the child was saved by his older brother.

Key-Low, another friend of Kevin, had a low and croon voice, "One day, lil' cuz gonna jack you up," he said to Rex in his slurred voice.

Rex simply rolled his eyes.

"Yeah, I'll walk you home," Kevin said as he grabbed his younger brother. "You got food at the crib?"

"No. why? You gonna buy some?" Lone Wolf said as he acted like he was trying to get away.

"You got a little smart mouth on you, huh?" Kevin said laughing as he picked the child up and placed him on his shoulder. Setting him back down he said, "Go and eat before we go," then he playfully pushed the child towards the house.

Kevin was only 16 years old, but he lived by himself. His mother had abandoned him two years earlier... vanishing without a trace. Not a phone call... a letter... or even a good-by.

Both he and Kevin shared the same father... but had different mothers. But the child's mother wasn't any better than Kevin's. She was never active in the young child's life... neglecting him at every point. She was more into partying and getting drunk... often leaving the child to fend for himself. But when she was there... the many men that came with her were brutal to the young child... leaving both physical and emotional scars.

Kevin only lived three blocks from Lone Wolf... but to the child it seems like miles. The young child was always left alone at night, and would often call Kevin when he was afraid. Kevin was always there to comfort him. They would talk and laugh until the child was too tired to be afraid. For as long as the child could remember... it has always been Kevin who was there for him... to care for him... to love him. And because of this... Lone Wolf loved and cherished his only brother with a sense of loyalty beyond measurement. The cruelty they had endured had brought these two tortured souls closely together... creating an unbreakable bond. The constant struggle to survive the rigors of family drama and life on the streets had only reinforced this bond. A bond that somehow brought peace and meaning to the child's otherwise meaningless and foul existence.

After Lone Wolf finished eating, he slowly made his way to the front door, stopping just inside the screen so that he could listen as his brothers and his friends conversed.

"Ah, Krump Dawg," Key-Low said in his usual croon voice, "word from the birds, that slob ass fool T-Roy starting his own hood. 'Murda 8' or some bull like that."

"Man, forget that nigga, Cuz!" Kevin said as he started to reach for his pistol... but instead he leaned back shaking his head, as if resisting his call to combat. "'Murda 8?' Psst, please."

T-Roy was Kevin's arch enemy. Although T-Roy belonged to a rival gang, this feud had started long before colors got involved. The hatred and the resentment generated by years of war has caused the two to forget how this war even started... but it was an open state of war nonetheless.

"I heard that fool got heat now, so see careful, cuz," Cocaine said looking at Kevin with genuine worry lurking within the depths of his eyes.

Seeing this worry tugged at the child's soul.

"Psst, cuz, I ain't going no where." As Kevin said this, Lone Wolf emerged from the house, then sat down next to his brother.

"You straight?" Kevin asked the child.

"I'm coo," the child answered. Just then, from within the house, the phone began to ring.

"Who the hell..." Kevin asked as he made his way into the house. No sooner that Kevin was gone, Rex started in with the child again. Rex leaned towards the child and whispered; "Say sum-um, and Imma fuck you up."

Lone Wolf watched with a cold kind of dread creeping through him as the wolfish grin expanded on Rex lips. The child knew Kevin wasn't around to save him from Rex... but he knew he had to say something.

"Shut up," the child said in a weak and frail voice.

"Uh-oh," Cocaine said laughing... Key-Low began to laugh as well. Rex stood up and stepped forward... towering over the small child. The name "Rex" was short fro Tyrannosaurus Rex, due to his huge and intimidating size.

"What you say, lil' nigga?" Rex said in a growl, causing a strong surge of fear to race threw the child's body. He wanted to run... he wanted to hide... but this fear-induced state wouldn't allow his legs to move.

Just then, Kevin stepped from the house. A wave of relief washed over the child, allowing him to breath once again. With a new sense of courage, and with a wide smile across his face, Lone Wolf looked up towards Rex and said, "I said 'shut up' punk bitch!" Then the child turned and ran towards Kevin.

Everybody on the porch howled with laughter.

"What's going on?" Kevin asked as he sat down.

"Rex messing with your brother again," Cocaine said as he took a long hit from the joint.

"Why you always messing with lil' Wolf?" Kevin asked grinning at Rex.

"Cos', the lil' sucka gotta smart mouth," he growled, leaning towards the child.

"Didn't I say shut up, punk bitch?" said the snickering child. The porch roared with laughter again.

Kevin wasn't nearly as big as Rex... and Rex knew he could easily defeat Kevin in hand-to-hand combat. But in the eyes of Lone Wolf, Kevin was the giant who was both feared and respected by all... including Rex.

"It's getting late," Kevin said as he looked towards the west. "Let's ride out ya'll." As he said this he hopped from the porch and began making his way down the street... the rest followed behind.

As a unit... they all began walking down the street. Night had already fallen upon the streets of Omaha... patches of clouds darkening the full moon as it stood high and proud in the nighttime sky. Rex was carrying the boombox, which was again playing N.W.A.

Kevin and the rest of his gang all had blue bandanna hanging from their back pockets. Cocaine had one tied around his right leg and another hung across his left shoulder. They would each take turns dancing, and as they did, they would throw up gang signs that would tell a story. Kevin couldn't dance, thou... he wouldn't even try. He would simply throw up his set, and keep on walking.

* * * * * *

Lurking in the shadows less than a block away... four men sat in a red '73 Fleet-wood. The car reeked of the stale smell of alcohol and weed as they sat there with the lights and engine off.

"Ah, T-Roy, ain't that that crab ass fool, Krump?" the driver asked as he pointed to a small group of men.

"Fuck yeah, that's him," one of the men in the back sat said.

Sitting in the passenger seat, T-Roy turned to the two men in back and asked, "What's up, ya'll? Ya'll ready for this 1-8-7?"

"Murda 8," one of them said... the other simply took another drink from his bottle, then patted the shot-gun that laid across his lap. Now talking to the driver, T-Roy asked, "You ready, dawg?"

"For sure thou," the driver said as he started up the car.

Under the cover of darkness, the car slowly crept threw the street... tightly hugging the curb. The three men began to load their small arsenal of weapons. This arsenal consisted of a sawed-off .410 pump action shot-gun, a .380 semi-automatic SL and two Colt .45 Pythons. As the car continued to crawl, they began wrapping red bandanna's around their faces.

Rolling down the windows, all but the driver stuck half their bodies out and took aim.

* * * * * *

"Krump Dawg! What it B like, blood?!"

As Kevin heard his name being called, he turned around, only to be greeted by a spray of lead and buck-shot. As bullets continued to rain, the gruesome sounds of ripping flesh etched itself into Lone Wolf's memory... sounds he will never forget.

Immobilizing fear struck the young child with a vicious force. As if in slow motion, the child watched as Kevin gaped... terror was written in his eyes. The empty thud of his broken body hitting the pavement echoed in the child's ears. Frozen in the icy grips of fear, he watched as Kevin's gang disappeared into the shadows... echos of their fleeing footsteps fading into the night.

The squealing tiers left a strong scent of burning rubber; it mixed with the heavy smell of gun powder and blood... the blood of Kevin... the blood of his brother. Lone Wolf looked around helplessly for Rex and the others... but they were nowhere to be found. A numbing sensation fell upon his body as he slowly knelt beside his brother.

Kevin looked up at the child... despair shone in his hollow eyes. The wetness of blood on his body began to grow. Seeing a blue bandanna laying beside him, Lone Wolf picked it up and tried to apply pressure to one of his many wounds.

Kevin screamed... but only briefly.

"Kevin?" the child said in a small, frail voice. "You gotta take me home, now." Lone Wolf watched as his brother's life slipped away... the child could scarcely breath.

"Kevin, please..." the child plead, "please take me home." Blood seeped threw his little fingers as he tried his very best to apply pressure with his small trembling hand. It's amazing how at times like these the eye and the mind finds it easy to avoid accepting the obvious.

Sitting down on the pavement... he placed his brother's head onto his small lap and held him... doing his young best to comfort his big brother... just as his big brother had comforted him countless times before.

SUMMER 1996

DAY ONE

"Lone Wolf! Is that you?!" Murdah Man asked as he stepped from the house.

"What's cracking, cuz?" Lone Wolf said as he made his way up the driveway.

"Damn cuz, you got big. Give a nigga some love." Meeting Lone Wolf half way, Murdah Man grabbed him in a bear hug, lifting him off his feet. "When they let you out?" Murdah Man asked, setting him down.

"Psst, they didn't," Lone Wolf said with a smirk.

"Oh snaps, again?"

"You already know."

"So the police on ya ass, huh?" Murdah Man asked as he looked up and down the street.

"Naw cuz, I left them up in Pleasant View. They probably *still* in the projects looking for me," Lone Wolf said as he started to laugh.

"Aw man, you know them fools gonna be pissed off."

"I don't give a fuck, buck them nigga'z. This Tré Seven," he said as he twisted his fingers in the air.

"Psst, you on the AVE now, best calm that down, cuz," Murdah Man said smiling as he put a hand in the air with a finger bent.

"Look, we can set-trip later, right now, I'm hungry as hell," Lone Wolf said rubbing his stomach.

"I know you are," Murdah Man said laughing, "from the projects to here? Damn, that's a long ass walk."

"First off, walk? Fool, please. You know I got the key to the city," Lone Wolf said as he produced a flat-head screw driver. "Second, you know what I mean when I say I'm hungry. I need to be fed."

"Aw shit, cuz. You ain't saying nothing. You came to the right place." Turning and walking towards the house, Murdah Man said, "Come on in and I'll make that call."

As the two made their way to the house, Lone Wolf could hear a baby crying through an open window next door... then a plaintive lullaby sung in a soothing voice. A little further off in the distance he could hear a couple arguing... the broken glass that littered the streets shinning in the hot summer sunlight. There was nothing Lone Wolf loved more than the sounds of the city. The sounds of car systems booming three blocks away... the sounds of children laughing as they played their little ghetto games... the constant barking of the neighborhood dogs.

Stepping into the house, Lone Wolf was greeted by the sound of Bone Thugs-N-Harmony as it played softly on the stereo system. Immediately he began to sway with the music. Closing his eyes, he began to rap in sync with his favorite music group. He knew every word... every utterance... every subtle intonation by heart.

"Let me make that call, sit tight," Murdah Man said as he walked towards the back. Looking over his shoulder, he added, "And keep ya hands off my cousin."

"Your cousin?" Lone Wolf asked, opening his eyes. A movement from the other side of the room tugged at his peripheral vision. Turning towards it, he found himself looking into the eyes of a beautiful woman. She sat on the black leather couch with her long slender legs crossed at the ankles. Her hair was placed elegantly in a bun towards the back, while her long bangs drifted softly down the side of her face. Her soft dark complexion seemed radiant in the light of the sun as it poured into the living-room through the open curtains.

With beautiful almond-shaped eyes, she looked at Lone Wolf and said, "You're quite the performer," then flashed him a flirtatious smile. "I'm Lady," she said in a soft, soothing voice. "And you?"

He stood silently for a moment... eying her suspiciously. He knew who she was, for she was known to all the local drug pushers simply as "The One." With her unparalleled beauty, she was untouchable to any man who couldn't support her extravagant lifestyle. He had seen her quite a few times... but never approached, for he knew her beauty was worth more than he could ever afford.

"I'm known as Lone Wolf," he said finally.

"Is that your real name?" He nodded. "You Indian?"

"Native? Yeah."

"I can tell by your hair, you have some beautiful hair. What else you mixed with? Black and white?"

"Naw, just African and Native, no white," Lone Wolf said as he sat down opposite of Lady.

"Who's Indian? Your mom or dad?"

"My mother."

"What tribe she from?"

"Damn, what you want? My family tree?" Lone Wolf asked... inadvertently sounding stand-offish. "You know you can be apart of it," he said at a feeble attempt at humor, wanting to defuse the situation.

"Apart of what?" Lady asked, looking confused and not at all afflicted by his harsh tone.

"I make beautiful babies," he said grinning.

Catching on to what he was saying, she began to laugh seductively. "I would, but you know what?" Lady said as she leaned towards him, her voice now whispering softly, like a gentle breeze, "You ain't got enough money."

"Psst, I got some," he said anxiously as he began to empty his pockets out onto the table. She began to laugh as she watched the small coins bounce around on the square coffee table. "Let's see... I got a dollar seventy-three. So what's cracking?"

"Boy, you s silly. So cute."

"Look, I just escaped from juvie, this all I got. But if you're willing to accept an IOU..." he said as he suppressed a laugh.

"A what?"

Just than, Murdah Man entered the room carrying a black duffel bag. "Ah cuz," Lone Wolf called to him, "I need to borrow some money, NOW!"

As he said this Lady laughed even harder.

"What? Ya'll got jokes? Ya'll making fun of me or something?" Murdah Man asked looking down on the two.

"Naw, I'm messing with you. Just a little inside joke between me and Lady. All bull aside though, what's up?"

"You remember Snook'ums?"

"Snook'ums? With the pistols? Yeah, remember O.G. Snook'ums."

"He got two of those thangs for us, so lets mob out," Murdah Man said as he tossed the duffel bag to him.

* * * * * *

After the two got into Murdah Man's blue 95' Ford Probe, Lone Wolf causally flipped threw the CD collection that was sitting on the seat. "Put this on, cuz," Lone Wolf said as he handed him a CD.

Murdah Man read the title, "'The Show Soundtrack,' Damn! Let me guess, you wanna hear track 7, huh?" Murdah Man asked as he placed the disc in the system.

"You already know," Lone Wolf said, placing the remaining CD's in the back seat.

After flipping the engine and slowly pulling away from the curb, Murdah Man asked, "When the last time you did some dirt?"

"The last time I escaped from juvie."

"About four months ago?"

"About that." Just then, the sound of Bone Thugs-N-Harmony began to seep through the speakers.

Turning the volume down a little, Murdah Man continued. "Yeah, I heard you escaped. Why didn't you come holla at a thuggsta?"

"I was only out for three days, not enough time for anything."

"I asked 'cos I got this lick and I wanna know if you 'bout it."

"Psst, cuz, stop playing."

"A-ight. We can get two G's apiece and some work. You down?"

"Lone Wolf, down for whatever," he sang in rhythm with the music.

"It's that nigga G.C."

"G.C.?!" Lone Wolf said in shock. "Young ass G.C. From Hill Top?"

"Yup," Murdah Man said causally. "Young fool got chips. He stupid, thou."

"So now we jackin' Locs too, huh?"

"Like you said about them fools from Pleasant View, 'Buck um.'" With this being said, Murdah Man turned the volume back up, then took a left... heading east on Ames st.

* * * * * *

Murdah Man pulled his Ford Probe into the driveway... parking behind a Lincoln Continental. After stepping from the car, they made their way to the door. "You said you know him, but does he know you?" Murdah Man asked Lone Wolf.

"Maybe too good."

"Why you say that?"

"My every pistol came from him. He taught me everything I know."

"Oh," was all Murdah Man said as he knocked on the door.

"Who is it?" a muffled voice called from behind the door.

"Open the damn door," Murdah Man yelled in a hostile manner.

"Go to the side door," the same muffled voice demanded. Once there, Snook'ums let them in, then lead them up a short flight of steps which lead to the kitchen. The small kitchen had the smell of a wet basement... and for the most part was empty, save the small metal table and two folding chairs placed under it. The kitchen was dimly lit. The only source of light was that of the sun as it was being filtered threw a thin orange curtain.

Snook'ums himself looked a lot older than Lone Wolf remembered him. The years has been hard on him. His thin and frail body belied his 45 years of living. Lone Wolf watched him as he sat in one of the folding chairs... Murdah Man sat in the other. Stepping forward to lean on the dirty counter, Lone Wolf noticed the two pistols laying on the table... his heart raced with evil excitement.

"You remember Lone Wolf?" Murdah Man asked, waving a hand towards him. But Snook'ums kept his eyes focused on Murdah Man.

"So, wheres the work?" he finally asked in a deep raspy voice.

What? Lone Wolf thought to himself in disbelief... completely taken aback. *O.G. Snook'ums a crackhead? A swerve?*

"How do we know these pistols even work?" Murdah Man asked the old man.

"How do I know this yay ain't gank?" Snook'ums replied.

"Lil' Wolf," Murdah Man called out. "Check and make sure they're a-ight."

Lone Wolf stepped forward... picking up the first pistol... then he took it apart. Lone Wolf had an intimate knowledge of weapons... thanks to Snook'ums.

After completely breaking down the pistol and seeing everything was in working order, he put it back together then placed it before Murdah Man. ".32 HNR Magnum, fully loaded with NATO round ammunition. The coil seems a bit old, but it'll still put a hole in a nigga'z chest."

Then he picked up the second pistol and immediately said, "9mm Star. Cuz, this strap ain't worth it."

"What? It won't work?" Murdah Man asked.

"I'm not saying it don't work. I'm just saying it's a cheap design, and it won't last long."

"Will it shoot tonight?"

"Let's see," Lone Wolf said as he began to disassemble the weapon. Holding the pistol and eye level, he squeezed the trigger. "Yeah, it'll work," he finally said. Murdah Man pulled a vial of crack from his pocket and placed it on the table... Snook'ums reached his hand out hungrily to grab it. After inspecting the vial, he said, "I trust this is an eighth?"

"I trust these straps work," Murdah Man snapped in reply.

Slightly taken aback, Snook'ums smiled and said, "Oh you can trust it, young blood. Psst, my trust in these pistols is as strong as my trust in my right hand." As he said this he held up his thin, frail hand. Lone Wolf simply laughed at the old hand as it shook.

* * * * * *

Before stepping back into the Probe, Lone Wolf had to remove the 9mm from his waist band. "You knew you had to sit down, so why didn't you simply stick the strap in your pocket?" Murdah Man asked when he saw the pistol laying on his lap.

"Why don't you stick this cheap piece up ya ass?" Lone Wolf replied hastily, still upset from Murdah Man claiming the .32 HNR Magnum. Murdah Man simply chuckled.

Lone Wolf knew Murdah Man was nothing less than a vicious killer who had killed in the past for less than what Lone Wolf had just said. But such unfortunate souls wasn't considered a friend like Lone Wolf. So he knew he could get away with such statements.

The two rode in silence as "It's an Every Day Thang," played repeatedly on the car system. After reaching 30th and Lake St., Murdah Man took a right, heading north.

"Cuz, G.C. stay just outside where Hill Top used to be," Lone Wolf said pointing west.

"I know. But you see that big ass ball of fire up there?" Murdah Man said sarcastically as he pointed at the sun. "That thing is notorious for helping victims identify people," Murdah Man said as he chuckled to himself.

"Yeah, that's cute," Lone Wolf said. "Real fucking gangsta."

"When night falls we gonna get that nigga, don't even trip. We might even have to kill a nigga. So get cha mind right."

As Murdah Man said this, he reached under his seat and pulled out a purple Crown Royal bag. Tossing it on Lone Wolf's lap, he said, "We have a few hours to kill, so blaze up."

* * * * * *

Back at the house, the two sat in the living-room on the black leather couch. As Lone Wolf swayed to the rhythm of the music, Murdah Man sat rolling one blunt while smoking on another. "Are you high yet?" Murdah Man asked.

"Naw, cuz, you got me smoking on some bull," Lone Wolf said opening his eyes.

"Naw, this is some real shit, cuz, trust-n-believe," Murdah Man said as he took another long pull on the over-sized blunt. "You gonna be high."

"Where's Lady?" Lone Wolf asked looking around.

"Psst, ain't no telling."

"I need a drink." As Lone Wolf said this, he slowly raised from the couch. Now standing, he noticed the room started to spin. He squeezed his eyes shut and shock his head, trying to clear his mind. But when he opened them he noticed the floor was rushing up towards him. It happened so fast that he didn't have enough time to close his eyes before he felt the impact as he fell face flat on the floor. "Okay," he said, talking into the floor, "maybe I'm a little high."

* * * * * *

The time slowly crept by as the two sat smoking another blunt. "I guess this is some good shit," Lone Wolf said after a few minutes of silence.

"Told you," Murdah Man said with pride. Suddenly and for no apparent reason... Murdah Man bursted out laughing.

"What's so funny?" Lone Wolf asked as he began to grin.

"I got this funny ass joke. Peep game, what did the saggy tit say to the other?"

"What's a tit?"

"Titties, man. You know, breasts, yum yumms, knockers..."

"Knocka'z?"

"Motha fucka, you wanna hear the joke?"

"My fault, cuz," Lone Wolf said. "Let me hear it."

"What did the saggy tit say to the other?"

"Other what?"

"Other tit."

"Tits talk?"

"Damn!" Murdah Man said in discuss.

"I'm just saying," Lone Wolf said as he raised his hands in protest. "I didn't know tits talked. Then again, I'm not a very good listener."

"It's a fucking joke, so shut up and listen, a-ight?"

Lone Wolf nodded.

"A-ight, what did one saggy tit say to the other saggy tit?"

"What?"

"We better get some support before people think we're nuts!" As Murdah Man said the punch-line, he began to laugh hysterically... while Lone Wolf sat there looking confused.

"I don't get it," Lone Wolf said tapping on Murdah Man's shoulder. Murdah Man went from laughing, to giggling, to looking confused as well.

"You know what, Lil' Wolf?" Murdah Man said, speaking slowly and rubbing the back of his neck, "me neither."

"What?" Lone Wolf said as he began to giggle. "Why would you tell it if you don't get it?"

"Cos, when I tell it, people bust out laughing. And because I don't get it, sometimes I feel dumb as hell."

As he said this, Lone Wolf busted out laughing. In between breaths, he said to Murdah Man, "Yous a stupid nigga."

* * * * * *

Lone Wolf found himself standing on a mountain ridge... engulfed by a radiant light. The warmth of these rays seemed to penetrate his flesh... proving a warm soothing sensation to his soul. Closing his eyes... he felt a warm and gentle breeze as it lightly brushed his face. Walking on clouds of spiritual and emotional bliss... he traveled from the mountain tops to the heavens. Opening his eyes... he found himself looking upon the place we all want to dwell. A place with a freedom from the daily hostilities of this evil world of the flesh. In a state of tranquility and harmony... he felt his soul being drawn even deeper into the realms of a peaceful existence... a place where he knew he would find his brother.

"Lil' Wolf," the familiar voice called out.

His heart lept with joyful anticipation as he searched the heavens for his big brother. "Kevin!" Lone Wolf called out into the calmness. "Where are you?"

"Right here, lil' dummy," the voice said as it chuckled softly.

The bond that he and Kevin had shared through misery was that of the physical plane... but here in the spiritual realm... they were connected only through love and peace.

"Right where?" Lone Wolf asked. Slowly, the faint image of a man began to materialize in front of him. "Kevin?"

"Don't you recognize me?" The face... vaguely familiar, kept appearing and disappearing in a murky mist. "It's been awhile, huh?" Kevin asked.

The shadowy image slowly drifted towards Lone Wolf. "Do you like it here, Lil' Wolf?"

As the shadow continued towards Lone Wolf... he felt a darkness slowly creeping over him... like the coming of an eclipse. "It's because of you I'm here!" the harsh words rang out... feeling alive in their anger... powerful and relentless in their wicked torment. "Come and join me," the shadow said.

Suddenly... a wicked laughter pierced the air. Lone Wolf stood in a state of speechless and mortal fear as he watched the sinister shadow expand... growing. The tremendous beauty of heaven turned on Lone Wolf with a fury that set his soul ablaze. "Don't you want to join me, lil' bro?" the gathering darkness asked as it inched towards him. The evil laughter became chantings... songs of the dead. Lone Wolf gritted his teeth against the agonizing pain as he felt his soul being burned. He was immersed in tortuous pain as the shadow engulfed him.

Lone Wolf screamed as only the truly hell-bounded could scream.

* * * * * *

"What the hell?!" Murdah Man yelled as he stood over Lone Wolf. "What's wrong with you?"

Opening his eyes... Lone Wolf's vision was blurry. Looking up, he saw the shadow as it loomed in front of him. Fear gripped his racing heart as he reached for his 9mm Star and took aim.

"Cuz!" Murdah Man yelp in shock as he jumped back... throwing his arms up in defense. "Cuz, you tripping!"

Slowly Lone Wolf's vision began to clear, and he saw Murdah Man as he stood on the brink of panic. His face was distorted by odd angular light and shadows cast by the floor lamp that stood beside the couch... but it was his friend, nevertheless.

The adrenaline rush caused his body to shudder. His hand began to tremble as he held on tightly to his pistol. His chest heaved with labored breathing... the air seemed hot in his lungs. He felt the icy sweat as it slowly rolled down his face. He slowly lowered his pistol. Closing his eyes and leaning back... he let his head fall on the couch. Drawing in a deep breath, he felt the tension as it slowly drained from his body.

"Cuz, you a-ight?" Murdah Man asked as he looked across at Lone Wolf.

"Yeah, I'm coo," Lone Wolf replied as he wiped the sweat from his face. "It was just another dream," he said in a weak voice... trying to convince himself more than he was trying to convince Murdah Man. Just another messed up dream."

* * * * * *

The two sat in silence as they drove south along Fontenelle Boulevard. The full moon was slowly crawling across the nighttime sky. Taking a left on Lake Street... they were headed to the drug spot belonging to G.C.

R&B music played softly on the car system. Murdah Man was the first to speak. "There was a rumor a few years back that you went crazy." Lone Wolf didn't respond. "They said you started talking to yourself and seeing things. Ended up in a nut hut."

"Three," Lone Wolf said as he turned his head from Murdah Man.

"Three what?"

"I've been in three separate mental hospitals. But that was back when I was 12."

"Do you hear and see things?"

"No," Lone Wolf lied. "Sometimes I just have messed up dreams about my brother. That's it." He was only able to recall but flashes of what had occurred in these dreams. But the display of unbridled aggression was truly felt.

"So you straight for this 2-11, right?"

"Oh, for sure," Lone Wolf answered.

After a moment of silence, Murdah Man said, "That was some strange shit, cuz. One second we getting blazed. The next second you dozing off... then all of a sudden you started screaming and I got a strap stuck in my face. That was some strange shit, for real."

Lone Wolf wanted to apologize... he wanted to explain... but how could he ever explain his demented way of thinking? Not even he truly understood it.

Two blocks away from their destination, both Lone Wolf and Murdah Man stepped from the car with their pistols in hand. "Why we park so far away?" Lone Wolf asked as they made their way up the street.

"Cos they know my ride."

Less than a block away, Murdah Man ducked into a shadowy nest of bushes... Lone Wolf quickly followed behind. "Damn!" Murdah Man grumbled. "I think he saw us."

"What?"

"He's sitting on he porch. He was looking this way when I saw him. He got three other people with him."

"Who?"

"I'm not sure. But one of them looked like Trigg."

"You talking about Trigg from 40th AVE? Your hood?" Lone Wolf asked in disbelief.

"Look like."

"So what we gonna do?" Lone Wolf asked, staring at the molten moonlight pouring through the layers of leaves above their heads.

After a moment of silence... Murdah Man finally said, "Fuck it, lets get them nigga'z," and pulled his ski-mask from his back pocket.

"I never liked that fool anyway," Lone Wolf said as he did the same.

Under the cover of darkness... the two darted across the sidewalk, then made their way to the house... creeping from shadow to shadow. Lone Wolf was aware of his heart rate picking up. He followed Murdah Man as he made a wide arc so that he would approach G.C. From behind the house.

Finally... standing with their backs pressed against the side of the house, he two head-hunters could hear the sound of their conversation come to them now and again on the gentle breeze... along with brief bursts of laughter, the clink of bottles and the smell of marijuana.

Murdah Man looked at Lone Wolf and nodded his head... then he cocked his pistol... Lone Wolf followed suit. He felt his heart pumping wildly in his chest as the two circled the porch... pistols aimed directly at the group.

"What the..."

"Move and die," Murdah Man growled. Walking up the six steps, he pressed the barrel against G.C.'s temple. "You know what we want."

"I ain't got..." G.C. Tried to protest... but he was cut short by a forceful blow that Murdah Man delivered to the side of his head. The sickening sound of heavy metal on soft flesh caused Lone Wolf to shudder with wicked delight.

"Imma try this one more time, where the shit?" Murdah Man snarled menacingly.

"Man, I don't..." But again G.C. was cut off by the heavy hand of Murdah Man.

Under his mask, Lone Wolf began to grin as he watched G.C. Crumble to the floor. Holding the other three at bay with his pistol leveled... Lone Wolf watched as Murdah Man drugged G.C. into the house... G.C. too weak to put up any resistance, dropped his head and allowed himself to be hauled off. With his pistol causally aimed at the remaining three, Lone Wolf said, "Now I want cha'll to empty ya pockets."

Well aware of what could happen... they willingly rendered their possessions. But for the sake of his own personal pleasure... he struck one of them with a powerful blow.

* * * * * *

"How much we get?" Lone Wolf asked as he struggled to catch his breath. Murdah Man sat slumped over the steering wheel... gasping for air. Too exhausted to answer, he pushed the duffel bag towards Lone Wolf. Opening the bag, his eyes lit up in greed. Inside laid a key of powder cocaine, about seven ounces of rock cocaine and close to 65 hundred in cash... along with three pistols.

"Damn, cuz!" Lone Wolf said, unable to control his excitement. "Now that's a motha fuckin' lick!"

"Told... you," Murdah Man said in between breaths. "Now it's time to paper chase."

* * * * * *

In the soft glow of the street light, Lone Wolf stood on the corner of 24th and Lake St. The busy intersection was crawling with activities as he tried his best to make drug sells. Call-girls of every assortment seductively strolled up and down the street... calling out to passerby's. More often than not, a car would pull over to the side... allowing the women to fight for his attention. Anywhere from 3 to 8 women would rush to the car at once... each trying to entice the driver with ample cleavage or a gentle sweep across his face with the back of her hand. Whomever is chosen would throw her hands up in triumph... then provocatively walk to the passenger's side. Within an hour's time she would return with her ill-gotten gain... ready to make the purchase of rock-cocaine.

Lone Wolf watched as other local drug dealers made sell after sell. The only business he had gotten were from those trying to sell broken car stereos, or CD's, or the occasional opportunity to rent the car itself. Very little money was made.

"Fuck!" Lone Wolf growled to himself as he watched the exchange of drugs and money. His gaze fell upon a petty drug dealer by the name of B.G. Slope... a 17 year old member of Hill Top who is known for being slow and illiterate... but even he was making money at a pace of which Lone Wolf found envious.

"I can't believe this shit!" Lone Wolf said out loud. A few heads turned his direction... but they quickly lost interest. "This slow ass nigga..." he grumbled to himself... shaking his head. "These punk ass nigga'z gotta go," he said as evil thoughts filled his mind.

At that very moment... as if on some kind of sadistic cue, Murdah Man pulled up in his blue Ford Probe. "Get in," Murdah Man called out to Lone Wolf as he turned the car stereo down. Just then, a swarm of call girls rushed the car... each performing their own routine of seduction. Murdah Man causally patted the pistol that was placed on his lap. Lone Wolf laughed as he watched the prostitutes tripped over each other as they scrambled.

Stepping into the car, Lone Wolf asked, "Whuz crackin'?"

"We got another lick," Murdah Man said as he pulled away from the curb. "Got a call from that nigga Ra Roz. He wanna hit them nigga'z from Jaynes Street. He told me to bring the choppa."

"Jaynes Street? Man, is you crazy? Them fools is ruthless."

"Motha fuck them u-lobs, cuz. They bitches."

"Ain't Ra Roz from Hill Top?" Lone Wolf asked. "Yeah."

"So why didn't he call his homies from 33rd? Why'd he call you? A nigga from the AVE?"

"I don't know, he didn't say. Does it matter?" Murdah Man asked as he looked at Lone Wolf. "The nigga said he wanna rob um. He said he got a couple of homies there, but he needed heat. He told me if I wanted a piece, to bring the choppa. I know you're trying to come up, so that's why I got you. You wanna roll?"

"Them Jaynes Street nigga'z is scandalous." Lone Wolf said in a strangled voice.

"Them nigga'z is bitches. Besides, them nigga'z got keys. You think that G.C. lick was somethin'? Nigga we comin' away with 10 G's a piece at least."

"Damn," Lone Wolf said avariciously. "They doin' it like that?"

"You don't know? Them nigga'z doin' it real B-I-G like. So what'z up?" Murdah Man asked sadistically.

"Who's with Ra Roz?"

"He didn't say."

"Fuck it," Lone Wolf said in excitement. "It's time to get paid, huh?"

"Yup. How much did you make on the strip?"

"Twenty."

"Twenty what? Twenty G's."

"Twenty funky ass dolla'z. All I sold was a dime and two nicks."

"Nickles?" Murdah Man asked as he began to laugh. "Nigga you been out here for an hour and a half and all you sold was a dime and two *nickles*? Psst, cuz, stick to robbin'."

"There's too much competition out here."

"It's part of the game."

"Fuck that," Lone Wolf said as he turned towards the window. The two sat in silence... listening to the stereo system as it played softly. Lone Wolf watched as the houses flew by.

How the fuck can I eliminate this competition? Lone Wolf thought to himself. *B.G. Slope and the rest of them nigga'z is well protected by Crime Boss,* he continued to think.

Crime Boss was an O.G. that moved to Omaha from California. As a member of the CC Rida'z, he had an endless supply of cocaine. Crime Boss was the master-mind behind the drug trade and the crime syndicate... he also played a major role in the activities of all the local Loc sets. With the protection of Crime Boss... the Y.G.'s and B.G.'s from Hill Top, Pleasant View, 40ᵗʰ AVE and Small Street became prosperous in drug trafficking. Other Loc sets, such as Tré Seven, Murda Town, 4-4 AMG, Deuce Nine and Camden Block were all left to fend for themselves... which caused resentment and animosity towards those under Crime Boss protection.

Pulling into the driveway, Murdah Man switched off the ignition. Turning towards Lone Wolf, he asked, "You ready for this?"

"What?"

"I mean, shit, nigga we does this shit daily. It ain't no thang to pump slugs. You on the other hand, you ain't around this type of shit all the time. Yous always locked up, surrounded by coward ass white folks."

"Nigga, fuck you," Lone Wolf said with a smirk. "I'm still rippin', ain't a damn thang changed."

"Yeah, okay," Murdah Man said sarcastically. "Let's ride out." As he said this, he reached into the back seat and grabbed a sports duffel bag. As he brought it to the front... Lone Wolf could hear the clinging of stainless steal... his heart raced in excitement.

* * * * * *

When Ra Roz opened the door, Lone Wolf could see the rage and hatred in his eyes. Without saying a word, he turned and lead the way into the house. His long uncontrolled hair looked like that of a lion's mane. The front hall was dark... the only source of light was that coming from the living room. The music of Brotha Lynch Hung could be heard coming from his living room... along with the sounds of resentful curses. The smell of marijuana was heavy in the air... almost as thick as the tension.

Entering the living room, Lone Wolf felt his heart lurch painfully in his chest as he looked at the two figures sitting on the couch. His mind began to race and the clammy edge of panic began to set in as he looked at the weapons of which they held in their hands. One had a semi-automatic sporting rifle... and the other, a sawed-off pump. The one holding the AR-15 face was swollen to twice it's normal size. The big gash across his upper left eye was crusted with dry blood... it still oozed a slimy clear liquid. The one holding the Mossberg pump wasn't as bad as the first... but the flesh around his left eye had swelled up terrifically... almost closing the eye entirely. Full-fledged panic consumed Lone Wolf as he looked into the fiery eyes of Trigg and G.C.

Jumping to his feet, Trigg racked the shot-gun and leveled it at Lone Wolf. Lone Wolf was keenly aware of the destructive power of buckshot at point blank range... but he couldn't move. He was paralyzed by the presence of the acute danger.

As his finger pulled at the trigger, Ra Roz reached out and grabbed the shot gun... but it wasn't fast enough. The thunderous blast echoed throughout the room as flames spat from the barrel of the shot gun.

"Motha fucka!" Ra Roz roared as he pushed Trigg to the couch. "Calm down, nigga!" he barked as he threw the shotgun across the room. The shotgun clattered as it slid against the wall. Turning back toward Lone Wolf... who was still frozen in fear, he asked, "You a-ight?" But before Lone Wolf could answer he continued, "Cuz was robbed a few hours ago, so his nerves are a little on edge."

Murdah Man, who too was afraid, now flew into a boiling rage. "Nigga, if you ever...!" he yelled as he shot his fist into the face of Trigg. The hollow thud was followed by a soft whimper as Trigg collapsed to the floor. Murdah Man went to deliver a kick to the curled-up figure laying on the ground, but the clicking sound of the AR-15 stopped him dead in his tracks.

G.C. Swung the semi-automatic rifle under Murdah Man's nose and said quite low, but with so much weight that no one could mistake him, "Back the fuck up."

Murdah Man threw his hands up and slowly backed away. "Nigga, this 4-D's bidness. This ain't got shit to do with you," he hissed out the corner of his mouth. In a subdued, threatening voice, Murdah Man questioned the wisdom of G.C.'s actions, "So why the fuck you in our bizness?"

"Nigga, this ain't about 40th AVE or Hill Top. It's about them oo-lobs from Jaynes Street!" His voice swelled to unpredictable power as he said, "Do you see what them nigga'z did to me?" He pointed towards the oozing gash above his eye. "And to your homie?" he said as he pointed to Trigg, who was just now starting to slowly pick himself up from the floor... wincing in pain as he did so. "That's what the fuck it's about!" After he said this he turned a questioning gaze towards Ra Roz... silently seeking his assistance.

"Ya motha fuckin' right," Ra Roz said as he pushed away the barrel of the rifle. "And we gonna get them nigga'z. But cha'll nigga'z gotta calm the fuck down." Ra Roz was trying his best to keep his own calm... but the anger and rage was evident in his voice. "Now, Murdah Man, you bring the choppa'z?" he asked as he placed a hand on his shoulder.

"Yup, S-K-S and a old ass B-A-R," he said as he swept his hand toward the duffel bag laying on the floor, but his eyes never left G.C.'s.

"Coo. G.C., have a seat. Lone Wolf? You straight?" Ra Roz asked as he walked towards him.

Through life on the streets, Lone Wolf had learned as a child to hide his emotions as he violently attacked life head on. Thus... Lone Wolf acted completely indifferent to the seriousness of his situation.

"Yeah, cuz, I'm straight," Lone Wolf said with confidence. But the truth of the matter was that fear had flare in almost every part of his body. He was still shaking with a mixture of relief and excess adrenaline. "You said Jaynes Street did this too you?" Lone Wolf asked as he stepped forward. "Yeah, like five of them nigga'z." Trigg said as he looked up at Lone Wolf... but he quickly lowered his eye. Not because of the exaggerated lie... but instead because of the guilt. "My fault, cuz," he had whispered softly. "My mind ain't right, cuz. Them nigga'z tried to kill me, cuz. They tried to leave me for dead." Terror glittered in his one good eye. "They was in all black, like you cuz. And one of them nigga'z was tall like you. So when I saw you I thought you was him." As Trigg said this... Lone Wolf felt his muscles contract. "So that's why I'm trippin' like that, cuz."

"Don't even trip. I feel you," Lone Wolf said as he looked behind him to see what devastation from the sawed-off pump had caused. His gaze fell upon a wooden chair that was left in tatters... splinters littered the floor. Seeing the destruction left behind by a single shogun blast caused a chill to run up his spine. *Fuck! That could have been me!* Lone Wolf thought to himself.

Picking up the duffel bag containing the assault rifles... Murdah Man placed it on the coffee table and said, "So whuz up? We robbin' or killin'?"

* * * * * *

Lone Wolf sat off to the side as the other four men plot and schemed... their minds abound in criminal fantasies. G.C. And Trigg wanted to go on a killing spree... but Ra Roz wanted the drugs, guns, and the money. He also knew that killing would involved the police. Murdah Man was simply indifferent to killing or robbing... to him it was all the same.

Ra Roz then spoke of the war that a killing would sure to spark. A war between Hill Top and 40ᵗʰ AVE, against the notorious Jaynes Street. They listened to Ra Roz as he explained the consequences that would ensue an all out war. It took a lot of convincing before they could agree that there will be no killing.

* * * * * *

The night had grown cool as the four marched beneath the pale moon light. To Lone Wolf... the moon had seemed to be laughing at them... the four candidates for the grave. He became angry. Murdah Man's face was set in a lustful, evil grin. He marched at the head of these head-hunters... he looked like the devil incarnate... armed with a fully loaded Browning Assault Rifle (B-A-R). A fully automatic... known for causing destruction.

With his Mossberg pump in hand, Lone Wolf looked over at Ra Roz... who concealed the SKS in his black leather trench coat. Lone Wolf admired his ability to cloak a rather large assault rifle without being suspicious.

Ra Roz well trained eyes darted back and fourth... fully observing their surroundings. Ra Roz was every bit the image of a professional warrior. At the age of 34... Ra Roz has lived well beyond a gangster's life expectancy. His killing talent and tactical escapes from the police had became legendary within the city of Omaha. And although he has lived his life in the fast lane... and fought many street wars on the front line... he had never been shot and has yet to spend a single day in jail. This street veteran's well-honed ability to foresee trouble made it easy for people to follow him. But with Ra Roz... it was more than his leadership and ruthlessness. Ra Roz was a hunter who loves to hunt.

It was easy to convince Ra Roz to leave Trigg behind. The reason Lone Wolf gave was for Trigg's instability... which may cause him to panic once more. But the real reason was because he knew that in time Trigg would see that it was him who had smacked him during the robbery. And maybe next time Lone Wolf wouldn't be so lucky.

G.C. was in the back of the pack... carrying a duffel bag that was being weighted down by his AR-15 and duct tape. The second he stepped from Ra Roz tan colored Suburban, he immediately pulled down his ski-mask... despite the fact that they had a four block trek ahead of them. Murdah Man laughed at his cowardice... but G.C. could care less. G.C. have had many run-in's with Jaynes Street... so he knew of their murderous ways. Too many of his homeboys had fallen victim to this vicious and ruthless gang for him not to be paranoid.

When they reached the block of the intended target... Murdah Man stopped and turned, facing the three men. Raising his assault rifle, he cocked the lever to load a round and motioned for them to do the same. As each man cocked his own weapon... the metallic clicks were amplified in the stillness of the night's air. Murdah Man's eyes glittered in the dark; he gave a venomous smile... then crept into the ally where darkness swallowed him up. The three followed close behind.

* * * * * *

Sounds of laughter and rap music came from the darkness. The four head-hunters stopped dead in their tracks. Just twenty yards in front of them, two figures emerged from a clearing. The ally itself was submerged in shadows cast by over-grown shrubbery... only small bits of moonlight was able to penetrate the heavy leaves. Putting their ski-masks on... the four stood as still as the shadows around them... part of them... only the barking dogs threatened to alert their position.

The two figures causally strolled to a car that was parked in the ally... but they didn't get in. The group could hear them talking in harsh whispers... and when one of them laughed a second time, they realized that one of the dark figures was a woman. Her bright red outfit gave off a soft glow in the light of the moon. The man, dressed in dark maroon Dicki gear, turned the woman around. Bending her over the hood of the car... the man tugged at her jeans then settled in behind her. She gave off a soft whimper as he entered her.

Lone Wolf laughed to himself. He found it funny that the two had not the slightest ideal of the dangers that lay just ahead of them. As the man pounded away... he was completely oblivious to his surroundings. With the sounds of her moans, and the sound of the music coming from within the house... Murdah Man didn't even have to silently sneak up on the couple. He simply walked up to them with his assault rifle glittering in the moon's radiant glow. He tapped the man's shoulder with the barrel.

The man continued to stroke the woman as he turned his head. Even as he looked down the barrel of an assault rifle, he continued to pound away at the woman.

"What, motha fucka?!" the man said as if annoyed... undisturbed by the clear and present danger. The woman, however, gave a startled yelp as she turned to see Ra Roz approaching. When she noticed the SKS, she began to scream and tried to stand up. But the man that was drilling away behind her kept her in place with an iron grip, and continued to drill her. She let out a savage, rattling shriek... but it was cut short by Ra Roz. In one fluent motion... Ra Roz knocked the screaming woman on conscious with the stock of his rifle, then took precise aim at the man's head... the barrel gently pressed against his forehead.

"What, blood? You gonna kill me?" he asked as he continued to stroke the unconscious woman from behind. "You gonna kill me, nigga?" he snarled like a vicious dog... his lips curled up... baring yellowish teeth. His eyes were wide... but not from fright. When he pulled out of the woman, she slumped to the ground. He turned on Murdah Man and yelled, "Crab ass nigga!" then frantically lashed out with both fists.

Before Murdah Man could reposition his weapon to open fire, Ra Roz, with lightening quick reflexes caught the man in the back of the head with the stock of his rifle.

The man turned on Ra Roz. Breaking into insane laughter, he simply looked at Ra Roz with wild, malevolent eyes. Ra Roz delivered another blow with his stock... this time the man collapsed. From deep within the man's throat came strange animal sounds. A final blow from Ra Roz had finally knocked all consciousness from the derange and demented maniac.

Slowly... imperceptibly... Murdah Man lowered his weapon. He gave an inquiring stare to Ra Roz... confusion written in his eyes.

"I told you these mah fucka'z crazy!" Lone Wolf said in a harsh whisper as he stepped forward.

"Naw, he wasn't crazy," Ra Roz said as he lifted the man's face with the toe of his boot. "He was gone off that dank. This nigga wasn't feelin' no pain."

"Fuck!" Lone Wolf said with a frantic gleam in his eye. "I bet all them nigga'z in there is wet up," he said as he felt the sickening tingle of fear crawling up his spine. In the past... Lone Wolf has had a few altercations with people high on the embalming fluid, formaldehyde. He was well aware of the fact that pain, weakness, and fear played absolutely no role in dictating their actions while in this drug induced state of complete obliviousness. While under the influence of this drug... they became fearless... unyielding... indifferent to pain and death.

"How many nigga'z you think is in there?" Murdah Man asked as he looked towards the house.

"Ain't no tellin'," Ra Roz answered. "Let's peep the scene before we jump to conclusions, coo?" he asked the group.

"If them nigga'z is high, it ain't worth it, cuz," Lone Wolf said to Ra Roz.

"I'm already knowin', young cuz."

"Where's G.C.?" Lone Wolf asked as he searched the shadows.

"Right here," G.C. answered in a hushed whispered. He was crouching behind some garbage cans... completely hidden from view.

"Ahhh, you coward ass nigga," Murdah Man said as he walked towards him. Lone Wolf wanted to laugh... but his attention was quickly drawn towards the house. From that angle, they had full view of the back door, which stood in the shadows... lights from within seeped through the curtains. Piercing the darkness like a knife... they saw a vertical sliver of light from within the house. They watched as the sliver grew wider from the door being opened. The gang flew for cover.

"Brazy!" a man standing in the door yelled into the night. "Brazy-B? Ah blood, where you be?" he asked as he stepped from the house. "I know you fuckin' that nasty ass hood rat," he said as he giggled to himself. Making his way to the ally, the man continued to talk down on the woman... laughing to himself as he went.

Hidden from view... the four head-hunters watched... their fists clenched tightly around their lethal weapons.

Once the man saw the two bodies lying in front of the car, he was overwhelmed by sudden terror. As he turned to run, he saw a movement from within the shadows. "Ahhh!" he screamed towards the house in an attempt to warn the people inside. But Ra Roz pounced on the poor man with the swiftness. The man was able to duck away from the heavy blow of the rifle's stock... he was barely nicked. The man fell to the ground, then tried to escape by crawling on all fours... whimpering all the while. Murdah Man kicked him over, then Ra Roz placed the short barrel of his SKS on side of his face. The man was flushed with terror.

"How many?" Ra Roz said as he applied pressure.

"I-I..." the man shuddered. His eyes wild like a sicked animal. Murdah Man kicked him again... he doubled over in pain.

"How many?" Ra Roz questioned again.

"Eleven," the man gasped.

"Are you lyin' to me?" Ra Roz asked as he squatted above him.

"There's eleven, fo' real, blood. I mean... ah... damn man," the man began to whimper.

"Are they wet?" Lone Wolf asked as he drew closer.

"Wet?" the man inquired.

"Are they smokin' wet? Dank? Sticks?"

"A few are. Just Bo Bo, Barlow and Brazy."

"How much shit is in there?" Ra Roz asked.

"I don't know man, fo' real. I ain't even Jaynes Street. I'm Flatlands."

"Flatlands?" Murdah Man growled. "The fuck you doin' way up here?"

"Bo Bo's my relative."

"Ah cuz," Ra Roz called out. "Bring the tape."

After they tied him up, they dragged him to a secure location. They repeated this with Brazy and the woman. As they were doing this... Ra Roz went to spy through the windows... but wasn't able to gather very much intel. The windows were heavily covered by thick blankets. "I can't see anything," Ra Roz told the group. "Ya'll still wanna do this?"

All but G.C. agreed. He simply stood in silence.

* * * * * *

Murdah Man was first to enter the house... followed by Ra Roz and then Lone Wolf... with G.C. bringing up the rear. The back door lead to an empty kitchen. The group stopped so that their eyes could adjust to the bright light. The music was blaring. Cursing men and laughing women could be heard coming from the living room.

Entering the living room... Murdah Man let off a three round burst into the stereo system... causing it to shatter into thousands of plastic fragments. With satisfaction, Ra Roz noted that the explosive roar of Murdah Man's assault rifle had struck them all with terror. The women gave a sharp cry, then hunched their shoulders tightly together in horror. A tall, slender man had thrown his arms and leg up in panic when he saw the four enter the room with their heavy artillery. You could see in his eyes that he wanted to cry out... but the chilling terror was stuck in his throat. Other men cursed.

"Everybody shut the fuck up!" Murdah Man roared. "You know what the fuck this is!"

Lone Wolf had his gauge causally pointed at their hostages... evil excitement sent wave after wave of adrenaline cursing through his veins. He smiled beneath his mask as he watched them all tremble in fear. That was until he noticed a man slowly raising to his feet.

As slow as the walking dead... the man got to his feet. Strangely, the man moved his blood-shot eyes from one to the other of the four head-hunters. The room became deathly silent. Emerging from the darkness of a hall... a second man stepped forward. His unkept hair was wild and his face was hideously scarred. He looked at Lone Wolf with a pair of strange, dead eyes that were set in a malevolent stare.

"Fuck!" Ra Roz cursed. "We might have to kill these two."

Lone Wolf stood gaping at the second man as if he had caught a glimpse of the super-unnatural... something far beyond the scope of his comprehension. As the man slowly stepped towards Lone Wolf... a subtle smile played around his brutal mouth on his scarred face. Lone Wolf shivered... not because of the cold... but because of the blood running like ice in his veins. Icy beads of sweat was being soaked up by his ski-mask... caused by the unpredictable lurch of ill fate.

The first man grinned fiendishly... maliciously. His eyes shone with hatred. He picked up a bottle, the hurled it at Ra Roz. But with the speed and agility of a cat, he sprang out of harms way. The 40oz bottle crashed against the wall in a shower of broken glass... which landed on a small group who huddled in the corner.

In panic, Lone Wolf pulled the trigger. A dazzling blaze of fire leaped from the barrel as the buckshot tore away at the couch, filling the surrounding air with cloth and lose cotton. The three head-hunters jumped in alarm... the two zombies didn't.

The first man continued his attack by launching after Ra Roz... but Ra Roz saw it coming. He planted the stock of his rifle in the man's face, his head snapped back like a coil spring. He yelled in rage and fury as he lashed out at Ra Roz. Ra Roz, a warrior of a thousand mortal conflicts, was excellent at defense and evaded every murderous blow.

The second man... unaffected by the murderous blast of the sawed-off pump, began to walk towards Lone Wolf.

Lone Wolf's hands began to tremble as he reloaded the gauge. Leveling his weapon at the man, he closed his eyes. As he pulled at the trigger, he heard the rapid fire of an assault rifle. It startled him. As the muscles in his body contracted, so did his trigger finger. The buckshot found it's way just inches from where Murdah Man stood.

"Motha fucka! Watch it!" Murdah Man roared with unbelievable strength and anger.

Opening his eyes... Lone Wolf saw the two lifeless corpses sprawled out on the floor... their bodies riddled with holes. The strong smell of gun powder was over whelmed by the sour stench of blood. Terrified whimpers and resentful curses filled the air. The curses of sworn vengeance from the Jaynes Street members.

"Shut the fuck up!" Murdah Man yelled as he aimed his rifle at the crowd... but the women continued to cry and the men continued to curse.

"Let's go," Ra Roz said as he pulled Lone Wolf along. "Bring the bag. We have to hurry," he said as he looked towards G.C.

In less than ten minutes, the three was able to tear apart the house while Murdah Man held his weapon menacingly on the small crowd... keeping them at bay. They found the guns first. They were concealed in the most obvious spot... between the mattresses in the master bedroom. The money was found next... hidden in a brief case in the back of the closet. The drugs were in the basement... hidden behind the rusty furnace.

"That's what I love about stupid nigga'z," Ra Roz said to Lone Wolf as he placed the drugs into the duffel bag. "They are so predictable. Guns under the mattress, money in the closest and drugs in the basement," he said with a smirk lining his voice.

Lone Wolf wasn't of much help during the search. In a haze, he basically stumbled room to room, following Ra Roz with the duffel bag in hand.

I don't understand, he thought to himself. Heartless... paranoid... hostile... criminal minded... cunning... ruthless... these are words that described Lone Wolf. When it came to the heartless... he was completely devoid of any moral value.... for he thought his every action was justified due to the fact that he was victimizing predators. But murder was a force far beyond the realm of his life's personal experience.

"Should I tape um up?" Murdah Man asked Ra Roz as they entered the living room. He was pointing at the hostages.

"We gots to raise up, for real," Ra Roz said as he took the bulging duffel bag from G.C. "Put um in the basement."

Like cattle... Murdah Man began to herd his hostages into the basement. After the door was secured... the four head-hunters slipped out the back door, into the dark of the night.

* * * * * *

As the four rushed through the ally, they heard the first shot. It boomed like thunder through the hushed streets. "What the...?" Murdah Man yelled as he turned to look back down the ally.

Another thunderous shot shook the silent night. Murdah Man blindly let off a few rounds into the darkness behind them. In response, the rapid firing of fully automatic assault rifles came from the opposite end of the ally. Hearing the menacing whine of bullets humming like bees near their ear sent the gang flying for cover. Malignant blue flames flashed from the barrel of Ra Roz SKS as he returned fire. The muzzle flare from the two weapons on the opposite end gave off their position. From Ra Roz calculations, they were right behind the house they had just robbed.

Although at that distance, a sawed-off pump would have little affect on their targets... Lone Wolf let off his last four rounds anyway. This is when he realized the blazing barrels were coming towards them. His temperature rose in the cool of the early morning. The fear of death came slithering over his body... crawling along his spine like a snake... winding it's coils around his heart... contracting. Suddenly, Lone Wolf was in the grip of an iron claw.

"Move, nigga!" Murdah Man roared as he pulled at the terror-stricken Lone Wolf. Murdah Man and Ra Roz continued to return fire as they ducked and dodged from the rain of bullets. And then there was silence. A strange... ominous silence.

"You think we got um?" Murdah Man asked Ra Ros.

"Naw, I think they're burnt up. I can see one of um."

Far off in the distance, a siren started to whine. "We gots to get the fuck outta here," Ra Roz said as he repositioned the duffel bag he had slung across his shoulder. Lone Wolf peered into the ally... searching for any ill-defined shapes within the shadows... but none was seen.

"Where?" Lone Wolf asked Ra Roz without taking his eyes from the ally.

"Look beside that wooden fence. You see um?" Lone Wolf followed, and indeed he saw a slight movement. "I think their burnt up, outta bullets. Let's go," Ra Roz said as he stood up. Lone Wolf waited for the sound of an erupting rifle... but only the sound of a siren could be heard. A siren that began to grow louder and louder. "Let's go," Ra Roz said to the group.

As the police sirens grew to an inferno howl, the group knew from experience that the time had come for them to make their get away, or risk being caught by the police. As if possessed by a band of rouge demons... the group began their three-block dash to the safety of the tan Suburban. The blue and red lights of the police squad car danced in the shadows of the darkness... spinning in it's rhythmic display of violent temper. Lone Wolf felt the adrenaline hit his bloodstream like a great fountain of fire-works... his legs were pumping at full throttle. The sawed-off pump felt more like a heavy, thick solid rod as he gripped it in both hands... the stainless steal and wood felt hot in his sweaty palms.

G.C. Was the first to reach the tan Suburban... followed by Ra Roz. About time Lone Wolf and Murdah Man had reached the truck, Ra Roz had the engine turned and revved up. Lone Wolf slumped into the back seat. His chest heaved... burning. His head throbbed as he struggled to catch his breath.

"I want cha'll motha fucka'z to calm down," Ra Roz said as he slowly pulled away from the curb. "Catch ya'll breath and look coo," he continued as he looked in his rear-view mirror. At that moment, the rest of the group noticed the police car as it slowly crept up behind. Ra Roz was experienced when it came to manipulating the police. He knew that the number one rule when dealing with these fear-sniffing dogs was to always remain calm. Like blood-seeking hounds... the police can always sense fear and nervousness.

Growing up in the system... Lone Wolf too knew how to skillfully manipulate and evade the inquiring eyes of the police... but the thought of catching a murder case weighed heavily on his mind. He grew nervous and tense. He listened as Murdah Man clicked his assault rifle. "Fuck. Empty," he heard him say to Ra Roz. Murdah Man was sitting in the passenger's seat... he reached for Ra Roz' SKS, but stopped when he heard, "That's empty, too."

Murdah Man looked back at the police, who now had his floodlights on the truck. "Lone Wolf?" Murdah Man asked.

"Empty."

"Fuck," Murdah Man grumbled. "G.C.?"

"I... I... um," G.C. stammered.

"Lone Wolf," Ra Roz interrupted. "I threw the duffel bag in the back." Lone Wolf knew what was coming, "I want you to grab that mah fucka. The straps are at the bottom."

As the tan Suburban slowly crept through the night... so did the police squad car. Lone Wolf heart rate quicken as he thought about what needed to be done. Hatred... caused by unyielding fear has always been the driving force in the heart of Lone Wolf. His heart raced and an unpleasant lassitude gripped his already wary body. His hands began to shake uncontrollably as he thought about the certain death that would follow a shoot out with he police. He knew that if it didn't end here tonight... that one day soon the police would indeed have their vengeance.

Lone Wolf was so caught up in the thoughts of his own demise that he didn't even realize that squad car had turned off a few blocks back.

* * * * * *

Thin tendrils of marijuana smoke lifted lazily from the blunt that hung from the corner of Murdah Man's mouth... joining the heavier smoke that hung in thick clouds near the two floor lamps. All but Lone Wolf had blunts in either their mouths or in their hand. Both drugs and money were piled unceremoniously in huge mounds on the small coffee table... along with the pistols. Lone Wolf stood in front of the house system, flipping through Ra Roz CD collection as Nation Wide Rip Rida'z played.

"You ain't got no Bone Thug?" Lone Wolf asked as he re-checked the collection. Ra Roz simply shrugged his shoulders indifferently, then continued counting the mound of money that lay before him. Lone Wolf's mind kept returning to what had just happened less than thirty minutes ago. He tried resisting the welling regret by trying to think of other things. But nothing seemed to work... especially when Murdah Man was bragging about what he had done.

"Them bitch made nigga'z thought they was bullet proof, huh?" he said to Ra Roz laughing.

"You know we gotta melt them guns down, right?" Ra Roz said as he tried to organize the money.

"For what?" Murdah Man asked.

"Cos they was used in a fuckin' murder, that's why. I think I still got some fuel left in my blow torch."

Slowly, Trigg approached Lone Wolf. "That was real fucked up, what I did," Trigg started off. "Like I said, that's my fault. I mean... fuck..."

Lone Wolf fixed Trigg with a cold stare. Trigg instantly lowered his head. The splinted wood from the shotgun blast still littered the floor... a constant reminder of what could have happened to his flesh.

"I want you to hit me," Trigg said as he offered him his chin. Lone Wolf had to suppress a laugh due to the irony of the situation. The side Trigg was offering was the same side Lone Wolf had struck him on earlier. "I really fucked up, cuz. I want you to hit me."

"Nigga, if you don't go on with that bull shit," Lone Wolf said as he turned to sit down on the sofa.

"I'm for real, cuz. I shouldn't of done that stupid shit. I knew it was ya'll, too. At least I knew ya'll was comin'. Go ahead and hit me," Trigg plead.

Murdah Man… who had watched the whole ordeal, had finally lost his patience. In a swift motion… he was on his feet and shot a fist into the jaw of Trigg. The heavy hand of Murdah Man caused his head to snap back. With a gurgle, he collapsed onto the floor… completely unconscious. Trigg didn't even see it coming.

"What the fuck you do that for?" G.C. asked as he stood over Trigg.

"The little bitch was askin' for it," Murdah Man responded. G.C. looked over at Ra Roz… his eyes pleading for help.

Ra Roz gave G.C. an indifferent shrug and said, "He did ask for it."

"Man, that's really fucked up," G.C. said as he went to help Trigg.

"Nigga, shut up befo' I lay you down next to him," Murdah Man challenged… his icy stare boring holes through him. Having good sense… G.C. didn't say a word.

Less than fifteen minutes later… Ra Roz sat back with a heavy sigh, "I split this shit even five ways. Everybody pick ya pile."

"Hold the fuck on, nigga," Murdah Man growled as he made his way to the table. "What the fuck you mean, 'five way's?' There was only four of us there."

"Yeah, but Trigg was in this, too. You know I gots to keep it real for what's right," Ra Roz responded.

"Nigga, fuck that. That nigga ain't gettin' shit," Murdah Man said as he looked at Trigg, who sat on the sofa babying his swollen jaw. Trigg knew there was no getting around his brutal insistence… so he was willing to chalk it up as a loss.

"Naw, man," Ra Roz said softly… shaking his head. "That ain't even right. It was cuz who got robbed in the first place."

"Yeah," G.C. Spoke up. "And how you gonna treat a nigga from your hood like this?"

"See. There the fuck you go gettin' in my business again, you coward-ass nigga. In fact, Imma take yo shit, too," Murdah Man roared. "Your punk ass bitched up. I had to kill them nigga'z," he said as he pounded his chest with his fist. He then grabbed the duffel bag and began to put three piles into it.

"Hold on, cuz," Ra Roz said in a soft voice. "I can't let you do that," he said as he shook his head.

"Nigga, fuck them bitches," Murdah Man replied as he continued to load the bag.

Ra Roz reached out and grabbed Murdah Man by the wrist,. "I can't let you do that, man," Ra Roz warned him sharply.

"Get your hands off me," Murdah Man gave his own warning in a voice steeled with anger.

"I said you're not goin' to do it."

Lone Wolf felt the fire behind the words of Ra Ros.

"Get your fuckin' hands off me," Murdah Man growled... his patience worn dangerously thin. For a moment their eyes locked in a clash of wills. Although Ra Roz was sitting... Lone Wolf could see his muscles tense... like a wild cat ready to spring. His eyes were narrowed in anger. Murdah Man's face resumed his evil snarl... his expression savage... his eyes filled with rage.

With a mighty lunge... Murdah Man threw his fist in the direction of Ra Roz. But being the experienced warrior he was, Ra Roz rolled out of the chair onto the floor... easily evading the heavy hand of Murdah Man. In a swift motion, he wrapped his arms around Murdah Man's legs. Before Murdah Man had a chance to deliver a second blow, Ra Roz had pulled back, completely lifting Murdah Man off is feet. He crashed to the floor with such a force that all the wind was knocked from his chest. In a fraction of a second Ra Roz was straddling Murdah Man's chest and landed a powerful blow to the side of his face. The sound of the impact was heard clearly over the music playing in the background. If Murdah Man had any air in him, he would have cried out in pain.

With every ounce of his energy, Murdah Man pushed up on Ra Roz and sent him flying through the air. Murdah Man slowly struggled to his feet and stood heaving for breath... his eye already beginning to show signs of swollenness. After Ra Roz had landed, he was on his feet instantly. Watching Murdah Man as he struggled to catch his breath, his mouth worked into a slow smile.

Once Murdah Man regained his composure, he let out a savage roar that had completely drowned out the music. Both Trigg and G.C. drew back in fear. Ra Roz stared at him with cold black eyes. There was no fear in them at all... only a deadly look... the way a rattle snake watch's it's prey right before it strikes. This was a battle between pure power and brute strength against superior speed and agility.

It was Murdah Man who launched the first attack. With his fists flying wild, he threw murderous blow after murderous blow... but not one of them had found it's mark. Ra Roz, who easily evaded every bone-crushing punch, delivered his own punch to the jaw of Murdah Man. But the punch only enraged him even more. With a ferocious cry, Murdah Man used unbridled strength in a single wild punch that Ra Roz was barely able to avoid. The punch crashed into the wall... sending plaster chips flying through the air.

Again, Ra Roz was able to grab a hold of Murdah Man... but this time Murdah Man was ready. In an attempt to get Murdah Man in a position to perform a hip-toss, Ra Roz left his back completely open. With supernatural strength... Murdah Man came down with both fists... the monstrous blow to his back sent Ra Roz sprawling to the floor. Trying to capitalize on the situation, Murdah Man went to crush him with his heavy boot. But Ra Roz was able to roll away before the black boot came crashing down. Ra Roz was on his feet once again with incredible speed. But only to be greeted by a powerful blow. The punch had barely nicked the chin of Ra Roz, but it was enough to send him crashing into the stereo system. The music came to an abrupt end. Slowly standing... Ra Roz wobbled for a few steps, then found his strength flowing back as he rushed Murdah Man. With two quick jabs he sent Murdah Man stumbling backwards... grunting barbarically.

From the corner of his eye, Lone Wolf saw G.C. reaching for the SKS, his hands trembling as he did so. His intentions were obvious to Lone Wolf... it was Murdah Man who was threatening to leave him with nothing. Lone Wolf turned on G.C. with a fury that only Murdah Man could match. The sudden movement of Lone Wolf had caught G.C.'s eye and he clawed desperately for the rifle. Lone Wolf was able to cross the room and delivered a blow before G.C. had time to properly position the rifle. The punch had landed in the dead center of his face. Lone Wolf could feel G.C.'s nose collapse under his knuckles. His head snapped back and he howled out in pain. The blood was dripping in steady streams. G.C. bared his blood stained teeth as he tried to level the rile a second time. But a powerful blow from Lone Wolf found it's mark and G.C. collapsed... the sound of gurgling blood resonated deep in his throat.

Lone Wolf turned around in time to see Ra Roz flying threw the air. He hit the wall with a heavy thud, then slid to the floor. The front of his shirt was covered in blood. Blood from a one inch gash under the right side of his chin. Murdah Man stood gasping for air... his face badly swollen from the first punch. Ra Roz stirred slightly... but made no efforts to stand.

Picking up the duffel bag... Murdah Man began to load it again. "You rollin' with me, cuz?" he asked Lone Wolf. Lone Wolf nodded. Turning back towards the money and drug piles, he removed four of the five piles. "That's for Ra Roz," Murdah Man said as he saw Lone Wolf's questioning gaze. "It's them bitches that ain't getting' shit!" he roared at Trigg and G.C. Slinging the duffel bag over his shoulder, he said, "If you want one of those pistols, better grab one now and let's go. Grab the choppa'z and lets ride out."

DAY TWO

Lone Wolf jerked upright from the waist with teeth-chattering force. Drenched in sweat, he forcefully inhaled air into his burning lungs in short raspy drafts. His muscles jumped and popped from the adrenaline rush... his body was tense. It was already well into the afternoon when he awoke... sunlight filtered into the living room here and there between the thick curtains. Outside he could hear the bass-line of a car system... aside from that, all else was silent.

Lone Wolf noticed a blanket and pillow on the floor... the couch cushions were disarray. For a quick moment he had forgotten where he was at. But last night's activities came rushing back when he saw the SKS, the old BAR, and his newly acquired Desert Eagle .357 semiautomatic SL lying causally on the coffee table. Beside it... the black duffel bag taken from Ra Roz.

Lone Wolf laid back on the couch... his mind swimming in the confusion caused by the mysterious visions that had haunted him night after night. They would enter his subconscious mind... feeding it with gruesome images of demonic creatures... impressions of terror... hopelessness and death. Some nights were worse than others. There were times when these nightmares occurred during his waking hours. Such hallucinations were far from illusions of the mind. These experiences were not merely images or visions conceived by an impractical mind, no, for such delusions does not exist outside the mind. What Lone Wolf felt during these horrible moments were true agonizing and unavoidable physical anguishes. Pain not only of the mind... but of the flesh and spirit as well.

Lone Wolf was startled by the knock on the front door. When thinking about his nightmares and daytime hallucinations... paranoia tends to take hold... caused by an irrational fear of danger.

Lone Wolf flinched again when he heard the second knock at the door.

"This shit's fuckin' stupid," he said to himself as he stood up. Making his way to the door, his mind turned to Ra Roz. "Fuck!" he said aloud. He knew that retaliation's a must... but he wasn't sure if he or anybody from Hill Top knew exactly where Murdah Man lived. Lone Wolf grabbed the SKS as a precaution. Just as he was loading the rifle, the knock turned into a pound... the pounding caused his heart to race.

"Marcus?" a voice came from the other side of the door... the voice of a woman.

"Marcus?" Lone Wolf asked quietly to himself. Making his way to the door he held the rifle in a ready position.

"Who is it?" Lone Wolf yelled through the door.

"Who's that?" the woman asked. But Lone Wolf remained silent. "Is that that Indian dude, Night Flier, or something like that?"

At that moment, Lone Wolf recognized that the voice belonged to Lady... the cousin of Murdah Man. Opening the door, he was struck by the tantalizing scent of her perfume. Her hair was let down in soft waves... highlighted by strands of brown. She wore a white blouse and a pair of jeans that seemed to hug her voluptuous curse in the most provocative way. Around her slim neck she wore a gold medallion... embedded with crushed diamonds. From her ears dangled the matching hoop earrings... glistening from the sun's rays. Her soft eyes lit up in concern when she noticed the SKS in the hands of Lone Wolf.

"Where's Marcus? What's going on?" she asked as she pushed passed Lone Wolf. "Marcus!" she yelled into the house as she walked towards the back.

"If you're talkin' about Murdah Man, he sleep," Lone Wolf said as he placed the rifle back on the coffee table. Picking up the pillow and blanket from the floor, he began to fold them and rearrange the couch pillows.

"Oh," Lady said. "You just waking up?" she asked. Lone Wolf nodded his head. "Damn boy, it's almost 3:30."

"It was a long night," Murdah Man said as he stepped from the hallway. "And why the fuck are you yellin' like you the police?"

"Why is he answering the door with a machine gun?" she quickly snapped back.

"What do you want?" Murdah Man asked as he scratched the back of his neck.

"Why is your eye swollen? What happen? Or do I want to know," Lady asked.

"What do you want?" Murdah Man repeated.

"I just came from court, paying for your tickets. So you owe me $600," she said as she approached him.

Lone Wolf watched as Lady walked towards Murdah Man. That's when he noticed exactly how tight her jeans hugged her voluptuous backside. "God damn!" Lone Wolf inadvertently said aloud, meaning to say it to himself.

Both Lady and Murdah Man looked over at Lone Wolf. Unable to think of anything clever to say, he simply said, "Those are the most awesomeness jeans I have ever seen in my life." A mischievous grin lined his lips.

"What the fuck?" Murdah Man grumbled to himself.

"Is he serious?" Lady asked to her cousin.

"I don't know. The nigga gets weird sometimes."

"I'm just sayin'," Lone Wolf said. "I've never seen a better pair of jeans, ever."

"I'm goin' back to bed," Murdah Man declared as he turned away from the two. "Give her six-hundred," he said to Lone Wolf.

Lone Wolf said nothing. All he could do was to keep resisting the overwhelming urge to stalk. *How the hell I miss that?* he thought to himself. He had noticed yesterday that Lady did have nice hips... he could even tell when he opened the door for her and saw the shape of her thighs busting at the seems of her jeans. But never in his wildest fantasy could he ever conceive such a luscious posterior.

Murdah Man disappeared towards the back of he house... leaving Lady and Lone Wolf alone. "And?" she said to Lone Wolf.

"And what?"

"The $600?"

"Oh yeah," he said as he chuckled softly to himself. As he retrieved the duffel bag, he said to Lady, "I'm trippin', right. Cos' I'm like, Damn, I should of noticed that," he said as he softly laughed a second time.

"Noticed what?" Lady inquired.

"How nice those jeans are. Am I bein' weird?"

"A little. But I don't think I wear jeans that well." She must have accurately read Lone Wolf's expression, because then she added, "And I'm not looking for a compliment." Then she added, "It doesn't matter. Nothings going to happen."

"What are you talkin' about?" Lone Wolf asked as if he didn't understand the obvious.

"Ain't nothin'," she whispered in a seductive tone. "Tell Marcus I'll be back." As she said this she stood up to walk towards the front door. The hypnotizing sway of her hips held Lone Wolf captivated as he watched her go.

"Don't go," Lone Wolf said suddenly... surprising even himself. Lady on the other had wasn't.

"And why not?" she said turning back towards Lone Wolf. Placing a hand on her hip she asked, "Give me one good reason why I should stay."

"Um..." **REMEMBER THIS MOMENT!!! 11-28-2014 7:13** Lone Wolf stammered. Looking into her eyes, he couldn't believe how amazingly beautiful this woman was. "I, um, just thought, um..." Lone Wolf continued to stutter. Lone Wolf knew that when it came to women... combining physical impressiveness along with projecting an air of intellectual insightful produces astonishing results. Lone Wolf was indeed charming... but only in short bursts. Which is why he had become a master at making an exit.

"Not good enough," she giggled as she turned to walk away.

"Um. Shopping!" Lone Wolf yelled out excitingly... grateful he was able to think of *SOMETHING*. This had caught her attention. She turned towards Lone Wolf.

"Shopping? What do you mean?"

"Lady, I ain't got shit to wear. This is all I got." As he said this he tugged on his black t-shirt. "If you take me shoppin', I'll buy you an outfit, a-ight?"

"My choice?" Lone Wolf nodded. "A-ight, coo. So, where you wanna go?"

* * * * * *

As the two rode to the West-side in Lady's '97 Lexus, R&B music played softly in the background. Lone Wolf tried to answer the many questions that were asked. He kept his answers short with most of issues concerning his time in the system. But when questioned about his past crimes or family history... Lone Wolf sensibly kept quiet and causally shrugged his shoulders.

"Why you wanna know so much about me?" he asked.

"I just like meeting new people," she said as she passionately placed her hand on his knee. "Is that okay with you?"

Lone Wolf felt himself jump and twitch.

"You nasty," she said as she began to giggle seductively. "I saw that."

Placing his hands in his lap, he asked, "Saw what?"

"You already know," she said as she flashed him a flirtatious smile.

"Let me ask you some questions."

"Okay."

"How old are you?"

"What? That's rude," Lady had said without taking her eyes off the road. "You ain't never suppose to ask a woman her age."

"Why not."

"Because it's rude. But if you have to know, I'm 29."

"Can I ask your favorite movie? Or is that rude, too?" Lone Wolf said chuckling.

"Don't get smacked," Lady said playfully.

"Smacked?" Lone Wolf said in mock anxiety. "I wish you would. You saw what happened last time you put your hands on me." As Lone Wolf said this, he looked down at his lap and forced himself to twitch. "I dare you to touch me," Lone Wolf playfully challenged.

"Oh, you'll like that, huh?"

"I would, actually."

"I know you would." As Lady said this, she allowed her eyes to slowly run along the body of Lone Wolf. He was looking out the widow, which allowed her time to take in every detail.

"Where you takin' me?" Lone Wolf said without turning his head from the window.

"You told me to surprise you. So just relax." After this was said, the two sat in silence. Lone Wolf had never been this far west before, he began to grow nervous.

"How far is it?" Lone Wolf finally asked.

"We're almost there, so just relax."

"You know I'm on the run, right?" Lady nodded her head. "Ain't nothin' but white folks out here." Lone Wolf continued. "I'm surprised one of these racist ass punk police ain't pulled us over yet."

"Just calm down, you'll be alright," Lady said as she passionately caressed his knee. "You're with me now." Lone Wolf didn't have to force himself to twitch this time... it jumped on it's own. "You're so cute," Lady whispered.

* * * * * *

Lone Wolf had never been inside the Oak View Mall before... and he didn't like it one bit. As the two strolled through the many wide passways. Lone Wolf felt the countless pairs of eyes watching his every move... constantly judging him. A mall security guard had even followed the two as they walked from store to store.

"Just ignore them," Lady had whispered. Regardless of where Lone Wolf went, he had always felt out of place... an unwanted misfit who didn't belong. But it wasn't the constant judging of white folks that brought on the feeling of uneasiness, no. It was knowing that the cowardice and nervousness could compel one of them to call the police.

"Let's just go," Lone Wolf said to Lady as they entered a fancy dress department.

"Don't let these fools run you off," Lady responded.

"One of these mah fucka'z might call the police. Let's just go to the Cross Roads Mall."

"Just relax, will you?" Lady said, growing impatient. "If they were going to call the police, they would have done it by now. Now go try this on." As she said this she handed him a causal outfit.

"This ain't my style," Lone Wolf said as he looked it over.

"It'll look good on you. It'll bring out your high cheek bones." As she said this, she seductively grabbed his chin, then rubbed her hand over his cheeks. "So, just try it on."

Walking into the dressing room, Lone Wolf felt the prying eyes of the saleswoman. She stalked from behind a rack of clothing... discreetly casting furtive glances in his direction... wondering what a man like him was doing in such a fine department store.

In his mind, he visualized himself walking over to her with a pistol in hand... a pistol created by his imagination. A pistol that fired glass instead of bullets. Yeah. Glass that tears and peels the flesh into shreds and tatters... ripping at her prying eyes. "What you lookin' at now, bitch?" he would say to the corpse. At the thought he laughed to himself. He knew that in reality there was no such weapon... and if there were, he wouldn't have the heart to use it. At least not on a person who didn't deserve it.

Stepping into the dressing room, he looked at himself in the full length mirror. His reflexion belied who he truly was... or so he thought. The mirror showed a thug... dressed in black, sagging jeans... black leather boots and a black t-shirt. His long wavy hair dropped three inches passed his shoulders. Around his neck he wore a thin gold cross... and swore up and down he believed in God... but loses faith whenever times got hard. Despite his thuggish ways and mentality... Lone Wolf thought of himself as s highly sophisticated individual. Intelligent by nature... full of rage and hatred through conditioning... extremely bright... but oh so dangerously paranoid.

If the truth were to be told... Lone Wolf didn't know who he was... nor where he stood. His attitude and mentality would change often... like the sands of a beach... where the waves would bring and wash away new ideologies and mythologies of sand with each ripple. His life was a ball of chaotic confusion... torn by conflicting ideologies of life and nature. His Native ancestors would whisper ancient wisdom to him... spoken through gentle winds through the tree. The decedents from the land of Africa... his people, would sing to his heart in a melody of hope and love. But neither his Native nor African ancestors could withstand the overwhelming chants of the dead. Chants that brought pain and suffering. Chants that brought misery. Chants that brought rage and hatred.

Lone Wolf jumped in fear when he heard the knock on the dressing room door.

"Sir? Sir? Are you okay in there? Do you need help?" a soft, feminine voice called from behind the door.

"Um, yeah. I mean, um, no," Lone Wolf said as he wiped the sweat from, his brow. "I'm fine. Thank you," he said as he tried to control his shaking body.

"Well, if you need anything, just let me know, okay?" the saleswoman said with a hint of annoyance lining her voice.

"Yeah. Okay. Thanks," Lone Wolf said as he turned his attention back to his reflection. Seeing the perspiration glistening on his forehead caused him to crack a smile, "Nigga, you got serious issues," he said to his reflection.

* * * * * *

"Um-mm, now don't you look handsome?" Lady said to Lone Wolf as he made his way to where she was standing. "Now, don't you like this better than dressing like a wanna-be thug?"

"I see you wanna-be gettin' yo ass whooped."

"Boy, please," Lady said as she looked him up and down. He was dressed in dark tan khaki slacks and a matching tan and white button down shirt. "Boy, pull your pants up," she said as she stood behind him. "More," she said as she watched him lamely tug at his pants. "More," she repeated.

"Any higher, I'll have a camel toe," Lone Wolf chuckled.

"I said higher." As she said this, she gently tugged on the back of his pants. Stepping back to examine Lone Wolf, she said, "Nice," then playfully slapped his butt.

"Girl, you better stop playin' with me. You gonna make me slap you back. But Imma do it harder," Lone Wolf said as he stepped closer."

"Hmm. I like that in you. A little pain brings a lot of pleasure," Lady said with a smile.

"Oh, I'll bring the pain."

"Whatever. Now go try this on," she said as her entire demeanor changed. Lady handed him another outfit, complete with another button down shirt.

"I don't like these shirts," Lone Wolf said as he handed the shirt back. Lady took the shirt from him, then stepped back to view him in whole. She bit at her well-manicured fingernail as if deep in thought.

"Okay, fine," she finally said. "I saw some Rugby's in the other isle."

"Rugby's?" Lone Wolf asked as he wrinkled his nose. "I ain't wearin' them thick ass sweaters. It's hot than a mah fucka."

"No. I'm talking about causal dress shirts by Ralph Lauren. You'll like it, trust-n-believe." As she said this, she lead him through the store by the hand.

Oh, my god, Lone Wolf thought to himself, watching the sway of her hips as she walked in front of him caused his heart rate to quicken.

"Why you playin' with me?" Lone Wolf finally said.

"What?" Lady asked as if she didn't know what he was talking about.

"You know what you're doin'."

"Yeah, helping you shop," she said sarcastically. As she said this, she held a nice Polo shirt up to his chest. "You like?" He did in fact like the pin-striped shirt, but said nothing. "Go try this on," she said.

"You ain't gonna tell me why you playin' with me?" he asked as he took possession of the shirt.

"Ain't nobody playing with you. Besides, if I was, it ain't like you got the heart to do anything about it," she playfully challenged.

"Fuck!" Lone Wolf said in frustration. Lady gave a satisfying giggle.

* * * * *

As the two sat in the food court sharing a taco salad, Lone Wolf was trying to calculate his spending in his head. He was eying the three large shopping bags placed at the side of the table when he realized Lady had yet to collect her dues. Judging from her style, her outfit would cost far more than his three bags combined. But it didn't matter to him. The two robberies pulled the night before gave him the luxury to spend money without worrying.

"Say something," Lady said eying Lone Wolf.

"Like what?"

"I don't know. You like your new gear?"

"It's a-ight." Lone Wolf had completely forgotten about the prying eyes. He didn't even notice the second mall security guard that had followed him for a better half of an hour. He was simply enjoying the company of Lady, the woman with a beauty one reads about only in fairy tales. He felt comfortable around her, now. As they laughed and played flirtatious games throughout the mall, Lone Wolf was wondering why Lady was holding back. True, she would entice Lone Wolf with her ample curves... swaying her hips a little more when she knew he was watching. She would also seduce him with a gentle sweep of her hand. But whenever Lone Wolf advanced... she would withdraw... giving him the cold shoulder.

"What's really goin' on?" Lone Wolf asked her as he pushed the taco salad to the side.

"What you mean?" Lady asked innocently.

"What's with the mind games? I know your style. I know your flava. But I also know you like dick. So what's up?"

"Oh, so you know my style, huh?" she asked. "And my flavor?" Lady paused for a minute... as if debating if she wanted to continue the conversation. Finally she asked, "How old are you? 13? 14?"

"Now that rude," Lone Wolf said playfully. "You ain't neva supposed to ask a nigga his age. Ain't that what you said?"

"I'm serious. How old are you?"

"18," Lone Wolf lied.

"18? You look younger than that."

"Don't be fooled by the baby face." As Lone Wolf said this, he swept a hand across his cheek... then pulled at the peach fuzz he called a goatee. "Besides, what's my age gotta do with anything?"

"What can an 18 year old do for me?"

"I can make you feel younger."

"Please," Lady scoffed. "It's time for us to go."

"What about your outfit?" Lone Wolf said trying to stall. Despite the past few minutes, he didn't want this day to come to an end.

"Here? Yeah, right. I only buy mail-order." As she said this she grabbed her small clutch-purse and started to stand. Lone Wolf mind raced with excuses to stay.

"Wait," he finally said.

"For what?"

"Let me dress in one of these new outfits. I wanna be clean when we roll back to the hood."

"Fine," Lady said as if irritated. "Hurry up."

"Where am I suppose to dress at?"

"The bathrooms are down stairs in the basement. Change there."

"Where's the basement? This is my first time here."

"Come on," Lady said, agitation lining her voice. As Lady lead the way... Lone Wolf was again hypnotized by the sway of her hips. The round firmness of such a big backside like hers comes few and far in between.

I'm about to fuck her, Lone Wolf thought to himself. *But how?*

Lady lead him down an escalator, then to a side door which leads to the basement. The basement resembled that of a business office more than it did a mall. Lady led him down a narrow corridor where there were offices on both sides. The wide windows showed row after row of empty desks and chairs. Finally, she stopped just outside a door with signs that read, "Ladies."

"The men's is right there," Lady said, then disappeared into the women's restroom. Lone Wolf stood in the emptiness of the long hall way... his mind raced.

A little pain brings a lot of pleasure, the soft voice of Lady echoed in his mind.

"Yeah," Lone Wolf said as he cast a sinister grin. "I know what she wants."

Lady was startled when she saw Lone Wolf bust threw the door. She was standing in front of the mirror readjusting her hair. "What are you doing?" she asked him... but he just simply bore an evil grin.

"Get out of here!" Lady said as she bore her white teeth... her eyes were fiery.

Lone Wolf dropped his bags just inside the door... then slowly began to approach Lady like a sinister panther stalking his prey.

"I said get out!" Lady's eyes flashed angrily... but Lone Wolf simply ignored it.

"A little pain brings a lot of pleasure," Lone Wolf said in a harsh whisper. "You said I didn't have the heart to do anything about it. I know what you like. I used to have a girl just like you." As he said this he seized her by the wrists then pushed her back against the sink. Pinning her arms above her head... he looked deeply into her eyes... searching for clues. But he conflicting clues puzzled him. Her eyes were angry... but her bottom lip quivered. She tried to free her arms... yet her legs put up no resistance. She cursed and spat... but her pelvis was trust forward.

"You're hurting me," she said as she angrily thrashed her head... but her body seemed to relax.

Yeah Lone Wolf thought to himself... *this is exactly what she wants.* Using an old wrestling maneuver... Lone Wolf twisted her arms so that her body was now facing away from him. Now standing behind her, he began to grind his stiffness against the firm, yet softness of her backside... letting her know that he's far from the child she sees him as.

"Stop," Lady said in between clenched teeth... as if she were still angry.

"Shut the fuck up," Lone Wolf growled as he bent her over the sink. Letting one arm lose... he waited to see if getting free was something that she really wanted. But it wasn't. With her free hand she gripped the sink's edge and began to push her butt back against the hardness of Lone Wolf.

As he kissed the back of her neck, Lone Wolf reached both hands around her thick waist and unbuttoned her jeans. Even through the thick fabric, she could still feel him twitching and pulsating against her. Her jeans rode up in between her juicy butt, so it took a little work for Lone Wolf to get them down... revealing the firm, smooth flesh. He began to tug at her G-string, but became easily frustrated. He gripped the string by the side and yanked at it forcefully... causing the string to dig into her fleshly thigh. Lady gave off a whimper.

In a fluent motion, he free himself from his own jeans and held it in his hands... slowly guiding it to the warmth in between her legs. After he found the entrance... he only slipped an inch in. With his free hand he grabbed Lady by the back of her head... grabbing a fist full of hair. As if possessed, he plunged into her as hard as he could.

Lady's body wasn't ready for this. As he forcefully pushed inside of her, she felt every inch. Pain shot threw her body as she felt his thickness forcing open her tightness. He held it there... she could feel it throbbing inside of her. On the second plunge, she felt as if she was about to rip open.

"You're going to tear something," Lady shrieked... but Lone Wolf ignored her... forcing himself into the fragile flesh that wasn't quite ready for her. With one hand, he gripped her thick thigh in an iron grip... digging his fingers into her flesh. With his other hand he pulled her hair... forcing her head back. He continued to slam into her as hard as he could... driving as deep as he could go. He loved the sounds of moans... of groans... and the sounds of flesh hitting flesh.

Lady tried to stand up... tried to escape the pain... but Lone Wolf placed his hand on her shoulder... holding her down while pulling her back onto him. After she had gotten lose, Lone Wolf slid in and out of her with ease. He pulled all the way out of her... then slammed it in as fast and as hard as he could. Her soft whimpers turned into a gurgling shriek... so he did it again. Each and every stroke started well outside her body... but ended deep inside her stomach. As if angry, he pounded away at her flesh... loving the sounds of his thighs slapping onto her fleshy backside.

Lady was driven over the edge time and time again... orgasms shooting wave after wave of ecstasy throughout her body. She felt full when he was deep inside of her... like she was ready to burst. When he came, she felt the hot semen burning her insides. She felt the three streams shot off inside her. The heat of his cum caused her body to tremble. When he pulled out, she felt the hot liquid running down her inner thighs.

Slowly, she turned to face Lone Wolf. She had had sex many times with many partners... but never had she felt anything like this. She looked up at Lone Wolf... then fell against him as if the bones in her legs had melted. Her forehead dropped onto his chest, where she could feel the rapid beating of his heart... and he could feel her labored breathing.

* * * * *

The two sat in silence as they rode back to the north side. Slow music again played softly. Lady had sprayed herself with her sweet smelling perfume after the encounter... its sweet fragrance filled the air. Lady kept stealing glances of Lone Wolf. The inner lips of her womanhood still held on to the strong tingling sensation... and the outer lips throbbed... which caused her to have mild organisms even half an hour after the fact.

"Why'd you do it so hard?" she finally asked. But he causally shrugged his shoulders and continued to look out the window. "Now Imma be sore all week," she said as she smiled over at him.

"You know you liked bein' gorilla fucked."

Lady was offended by this comment... but she didn't want to spoil the mood... so she simply sat quietly. The truth was... his body did give off some kind of animal heat... heat that kindled the flame of her own passion... her own lust.

"Lone Wolf, you can stay with me if you want," she finally said. Lone Wolf didn't respond. "I have a real nice apartment. And I know you don't like sleeping on the couch."

Lone Wolf turned to her and smiled. Not because of her offer... but because she had not the slightest clue about the true depth of his instability.

"You wouldn't want the," he said to her as he thought about the look on Murdah Man's face when he pulled his pistol on him.

"Why'd you say that?" Lady asked curiously.

"You just wouldn't."

"Well, would you at least spend the night with me tonight?"

"Shit, I roam the streets at night. I ain't about to be up all night watchin' you sleep."

"I'll stay up, too," Lady protested. But Lone Wolf simply shook his head.

"I see you totally changed your attitude towards me, huh?" Lone Wolf chuckled.

"What you mean?"

"At first I was too broke, too young... this and that. And now..."

"Whatever," Lady interrupted.

"I'm just sayin' that..."

"Whatever," Lady snapped.

"Because that you..."

"Just shut up! Okay, Lone Wolf," Lady said in anger. "Can we just listen to he music?"

"You're the one that..."

In anger and frustration, Lady jerked the volume knob to full blast... drowning out Lone Wolf's comments.

* * * * * *

"Damn, cuz, you didn't let a nigga know you was leavin'. Just uppt and bounced on a nigga," Murdah Man said to Lone Wolf as he entered the house. Lone Wolf noticed the swollenness of his left eye and a lump on the right side of his forehead.

"Damn, Murdah, you got knocked the fuck out!" Lone Wolf said laughing... imitating Smoky from the movie *Friday*.

"We got jokes, huh? We got funnies?" Murdah Man said as he gently pushed on the tender flesh around his eye. "What you got?" he asked as he noticed the shopping bags in the hands of Lone Wolf.

"I needed some gear. So Lady took me to the mall."

"Aw, so you gonna be ready for tonight, huh?"

"Ready fo' what?"

"Nigga, we goin' to the club tonight, nigga," Murdah Man said as he threw his hands in air... as if trying to dance.

"That's so fuckin' gay," Lone Wolf said as he rolled his eyes.

"Nigga, fuck you," Murdah Man said as he continued to dance.

"Naw, cuz, I gotta get my paper right. So Imma try the strip again," Lone Wolf said as he sat opposite of Murdah Man.

"You tried slanging, cuz. You only made $20 in like three hours. Nigga, you ain't shit," Murdah Man said laughing. "You better stick to robbin'. Besides, nigga we got G's off two licks. It's time to floss."

"I gotta stack my chips. I ain't got shit."

"You got half of this," Murdah Man said as he moved the duffel bag from the floor to the coffee table. "There's about 16 stacks, eight a piece. Plus nine and a half bricks. What more we need? It's time to parlay."

"I need a crib, a ride, I need everything."

"You can stay here. We got a ride. You straight."

"Yeah, but I need my own. I was thinkin'," Lone Wolf said as he leaned back. "You know that nigga B.G. Slope from 33rd, right?"

"You talkin' about dumb ass Slope?"

"Yeah. I saw him, K-9 and Hollow Tips last night on the strip. Out there doin' they thing. We should sell them 5 a brick."

"5!" Murdah Man gasped. "Nigga, is you stupid? 5? We should get at least 20."

"We need to get rid of this shit," Lone Wolf lied. "The sooner the better."

"Why?"

"We can't be sittin' on this shit, cuz."

"If we do this ourselves we can easily get 75 G's of each brick. And you wanna sell it for 5?!"

"It's the smart thing to do. If we out there nickle and dimin', we gonna fuck around and get caught up. Let's just push this shit and start again. Off two licks, that's over a hundred and twenty-five G's, cuz. You can't be mad at that, feel me?" Lone Wolf rationalized. "Then we can hit another lick tonight. It's damn near 10 o'clock, now. So you know the streets are crawling right now."

Lone Wolf could tell Murdah Man was flipping the issue over in his head. "Think about it, cuz. In two days we got 125 thousand," Lone Wolf continued. "If we slang it ourselves, it'll take months to get that. Tonight, we might hit another 10G's and some more work."

Lone Wolf was careful to stay away from the fact that B.G. Slope, K-9, and Hollow Tips were all from the same set Ra Roz and G.C. were from. He was also careful to stay clear of the fact that over stepping Crime Boss authority was sure to bring consequences. "Not to mention," Lone Wolf continued, "the time we spend out there grindin' we could be parlayin', cuz. Fo' real."

* * * * * *

The streets of 24th and Lake was crawling with it's usual activities. Sounds of stereo systems and honking horns would occasionally drown out the talking and laughing. Every now and again, one could hear a woman yelling and cursing for one reason or another.

"What's up, ya'll. What cha'll need?" Hollow Tips yelled as he approached a group of call-girls.

"I need you," one woman said as she walked towards him... smacking on her gum nosily.

"I got that A-1 yola, bitch," he said as he reached in his pocket. The woman shot Hollow Tips and evil look.

"'Bitch?'" she asked as she placed her hands on her curve-less hips.

"Shut up, bitch," he said as he causally brushed her off. "What cha'll need," he said as he dangled a baggie in their faces.

"You got 20?" another woman asked.

"I got 30 for you sweet thang."

"Oh really?" she said as her eyes lit up.

"But you gotta do me a favor," he said as he waved a hand towards the first woman. "Smack this bitch."

In the background B.G. Slope and K-9 howled with laughter.

"She ain't gonna do that for you," the first woman said as she got in his face. "Stupid, bitch nigga, you need to…" But before she could finish, the second woman reached around and smacked her with astonishing force that belied her size. With the first woman's mouth open, her gum flew the distance to where B.G. Slope and K-9 was standing.

"Damn!" B.G. Slope and K-9 howled simultaneously with laughter. The first woman had fallen to the ground with a hollow thump. Mildly amused, Hollow Tips simply stepped over her and handed the entire baggie to the second woman. "That was a helluva blow."

* * * * * *

Lone Wolf and Murdah Man sat in silence as they watched the whole ordeal take place. Although the window to Murdah Man's Ford Probe were rolled down… the two were too far away to hear what had happened… but it wasn't hard for them to figure out. They too, howled with laughter.

"These mah fucka'z are silly," Lone Wolf said to Murdah Man.

"You sure you wanna deal with these goof-troop nigga'z?" he asked Lone Wolf, who simply shook his head.

The ally of which they sat in shielded them with a blanket of darkness. Even if one were to try, they couldn't be seen. From this vantage point they could easily observe the happenings of 24th and Lake without ever being noticed. They watched as the call-girls and petty drug-dealers went about their business… wrapped in a blanket of false security.

"You know how easy it would be to snipe these nigga'z?" Murdah Man asked as if reading Lone Wolf's mind.

".308 and a suppressor. Smooth get-away."

"What's a .308?" Murdah Man asked as he turned towards Lone Wolf… who again simply shook his head than continued to sit in silence. "Can you imagine doin' a drive-by with assault rifles and Mac's and TEC's, but they all got silencers?" Murdah Man said slowly… deep in thought.

"Mah fucka'z droppin' all around you and you don't know why," he said as he chuckled.

Lone Wolf was thinking of his immediate situation concerning the upcoming drug deal. But as he listened to Murdah Man, he couldn't help but to think of him. He had known Murdah Man for almost seven years... they met in a group home for "disturbed" children... a place for those who aren't accepted by foster parents. He knew Murdah Man had a split personality... the first being the playful, joking type. The one where a brother's embrace wasn't hard to find. Without question he would open his heart and home to those who were blessed enough to be called his friend... his brother. A home that's full of warmth... and a heart that was devoid of selfishness.

The second was the polar opposite of the first... where he would fight and kill for the sheer love of battle and destruction. Murdah Man was feared by many... including those he wanted to do business with here and now, although they would never admit to it. Especially Hollow Tips. Lone Wolf knew that Murdah Man could easily influence their decision in this transaction... which is why Lone Wolf needed him here.

"So what we gonna do?" Murdah Man asked, breaking Lone Wolf's train of thought.

After a moment of silence, Lone Wolf finally said, "Flash ya lights."

* * * * * *

"What that is?" B.G. Slope said to K-9, pointing at the flashing lights.

"Probably for one of these hoes," K-9 answered back.

"Ah, Tip?" B.G. Slope hollered. When he turned around, he followed the direction of B.G. Slope's pointing finger. "Tell them hoes they got a customer." But Hollow Tips didn't have to say anything. Before he even finished the sentence, a few of the women were already heading towards the flashing lights.

"God damn, these hoes mean business, huh?" Hollow Tips said laughing.

"Why you give that bitch all ya work?" K-9 asked Hollow Tips.

"Cos I can," he said as he approached the two. "Now break me off a fat ass chunk."

"Naw, nigga," K-9 said as he turned away. "Shouldna gave yo shit away."

"Nigga, I'll rob you, nigga," Hollow Tips said as he lifted the front of his blue hooded sweat- shirt... revealing the handle of his 9mm Beretta.

"Now you know that motha fucka is *NOT* loaded!" K-9 said as he smacked B.G. Slope's arm... the two busted out laughing.

"Cuz, you know who I is," Hollow Tips said as he threw up his arms. "I gots a clip full of Hollow Tips. Now break yo-self," he said as he ran his fingers along the handle of is pistol.

"'You know who I is,'" K-9 laughed, mocking him. "Yeah, I know, HOWARD!"

"Nigga, fuck you. Give me some work and stop playin'," Hollow Tips said as he looked around. "And don't be sayin' my name all out loud like that, nigga."

"My fault," K-9 said, throwing his hands up. "How much you need, HOWARD!!" K-9 and B.G. Slope busted out laughing again.

"Fuck both you nigga'z! Am I the only gangsta out here?" he asked in frustration.

"Don't get mad at me," B.G. Slope said as he continued to laugh.

"Yeah, he didn't give the name of a duck!" K-9 said in between laughs.

Turning around, Hollow Tips found the woman he had given his crack to and yelled, "Ah, wanna make another 30?!"

Just then he was approached by a fiend holding two wrinkled five dollar bills in his hand. "You on?" he asked as he grinned... his yellow teeth gleaming in the street lights.

"Come here," B.G. Slope said reaching into his pocket. "I got you."

"I got this," Hollow Tips said as he tugged at the old man's soiled shirt. "Right?" He shot K-9 an evil look.

"Fuck!" K-9 scuffed as he reached into his pocket... retrieving his baggie of narcotics. The larger zip-lock baggie was full of smaller baggies... each containing a certain quantity of rock cocaine. Some held 20 dollars worth, a few held 50 dollars worth... but most of them held 10 dollars worth. With little care of what was given, K-9 handed Hollow Tips half of the baggies within the zip-lock.

"Ah, ya'll," a prostitute said as she approached the three. "Some nigga named Lone Wolf said he wanted to holla at cha'll." As she said this she pointed in the direction of which the flashing lights had been... but now it was only darkness.

"Who the fuck is Lone Wolf?" K-9 asked as he peered into the ally behind the brick building.

"That big Indian nigga from Tré Seven," B.G. Slope said as he too peered in the direction.

"I thought that nigga was locked up," Hollow Tips said to B.G. Slope. "I was just in juvie with that nigga."

"What the fuck he want?" K-9 asked.

"Probably gots some pistols he wanna get rid of," Hollow Tips answered.

"Pistols?" K-9 said. "What kind of pistols?"

"I don't know."

"What if it's a trap?" B.G. Slope spoke up. "You know that nigga loony."

"Naw, it ain't no trap," Hollow Tips said as he started to cross the street. "If it was, he wouldn't of let us know he was there. Make sense?"

K-9 and B.G. Slope followed Hollow Tips as he made his way to the ally.

"What you mean he's loony?" K-9 asked B.G. Slope in a low voice.

"Remember that new nigga that was out here talkin' to himself last night?" B.G. Slope asked.

"That was him?" Hollow Tips asked. "I really wasn't payin' attention."

"Yup, that was him. He's always talkin' to himself. When we was in juvie they made him be in a cell by himself cos he was always bangin'. But even in a single cell that nigga be cussin' and screamin' and fightin' nigga'z that ain't even there."

"That was all an act," Hollow Tips said over his shoulder. "That nigga be fakin' that shit. Ah, K-9, cuz, that nigga a bitch. He only fought nigga'z he knew he could whoop."

As they drew closer to the spot, they all became silent. They saw the outline of a figure leaning against the hood of a sports car. Both K-9 and B.G. Slope had their hands on their pistols.

"It ain't even like that," they heard Lone Wolf's voice call out from the darkness. "I'm here on business." But the two kept their hands on their weapons, nonetheless. As they approached, they were hit with the sweet aroma of a Black & Mild cigar... but they didn't notice that Lone Wolf's hands were empty.

"What's up?" Hollow Tips asked as he stopped in front of Lone Wolf. The group watched Lone Wolf as he reached for a duffel bag that was sitting at his feet. Unzipping the bag... he produced a package, then handed it to Hollow Tips, who played with it in his hands.

"What's this?" he asked as he looked the package over.

"A key of pure cocaine. I got nine of them I want ya'll to buy."

"What?" Hollow Tips asked in disbelief. "First of all, how we know this shit is real? Second, where the fuck we gonna get the N's at?"

"The shit's legit. And I don't care how ya'll gonna pay for it, but you will," Lone Wolf threatened.

"What, motha fucka?!" Hollow Tips said in anger as he took a step closer to Lone Wolf. Pulling his pistol he yelled, "Nigga, I'll take yo shit!" But Lone Wolf didn't budge. Instead, he held his stare firmly with Hollow Tips. Hollow Tips simply held his pistol... pointing towards the ground. Lone Wolf knew he needed to push him a little further, but not too far. For the results could be fatal.

"It ain't even like that," Lone Wolf growled. "But it's gonna get real ugly if you don't back the fuck up. Understood?"

"What?!" Hollow Tips yelled as he raised his pistol... his eyes wild with rage and anger. Just then there was a metallic clicking sound coming from within the car. The sinister sound was amplified in the hollow ally. The three knew it was the sound of an assault rifle being loaded... it was followed by another, even louder clicking. The group stood frozen... hushed and listening... like wild animals when they scent death in the air.

"You got three assault rifle aimed at cha fuckin' chest. And that nigga Murdah Man in one of his moods." On cue there was a growl coming from within the car. Hollow Tips cast a frightening, yet inquiring glance towards the windshield... but he couldn't see inside. His hand began to tremble.

"So," Lone Wolf said causally, "Like I once said, it ain't like that, but if you don't get that fuckin' pistol outta my face, we all goin' to die tonight. And I'm ready, how 'bout you?"

Every feature of Hollow Tips face showed fear of the unknown ahead. He slowly lowered his pistol.

"Like I said, you three nigga'z gonna buy these keys. We want 12 G's a piece."

"12?" Lone Wolf heard K-9 gasp in disbelief.

"The shit is pure. You gonna find none better."

Hollow Tips eyed Lone Wolf suspiciously as he slowly handed K-9 the package. "12, huh? You sure this ain't gank?" he asked. Lone Wolf shook his head.

"I'll give you 2 ½ now. We'll be back in an hour to collect 25 G's. Then tomorrow night bring another 24 and then another 24 the night after that and so on." As Lone Wolf said this he leaned over to pick up the duffel bag. Slinging it over his shoulder, he waved his hand towards the outline of a dumpster sitting only twenty yards away. "Set the money behind that. And that's where you'll pick up the key's. No games, no murdah, understood?"

Lone Wolf didn't wait for an answer... instead he turned and patted the roof of the car. The engine turned and the high-beams were put on... blinding the three. They put their arms up to shield their eyes from the blinding light... exactly what Lone Wolf wanted them to do. They didn't see him open the car door... thus they didn't see the inside car light come on... revealing only one other person inside.

The three watched the Probe as it slowly backed out of the ally... then pulled onto the side street... then slowly crept away.

"Who the fuck that nigga think he is?" Hollow Tips yelled as he waved his pistol around wildly. "That bitch ass motha fucka..."

"If this shit any good, that's a helluva deal," K-9 said as he turned the package over in his hand.

"Nigga, fuck that! Who the fuck this nigga..." Hollow Tips cursed, but was interrupted by K-9.

"Cuz, 25 G's for two and a half? Nigga that's half of what we're payin' Crime Boss, whenever the fuck you get through!"

"It ain't about the work. It's about this bitch made nigga thinkin' he can..."

"We's 'bouts to get paid, cuz!" B.G. Slope yelped and clasped his hands from sheer joy of anticipation.

In frustration, Hollow Tips shoved B.G. Slope... who fell to the ground. He slowly pulled himself up with fright and whispered softly, "I didn't do nothin'."

"Just shut the fuck up," Hollow Tips said as he went to pick up the other two packages that Lone Wolf tossed onto the ground.

"Let's just get to he tilt, rock it up," K-9 said as he handed Hollow Tips the third package. "If it's all good, we'll pay. If not, lock-n-load, nigga."

* * * * * *

As Lone Wolf and Murdah Man pulled away from the ally, Lone Wolf let out a long sigh of relief and let his head drop back. His body trembled from the rush of adrenaline that was pumped into his system by fear and excitement.

"Don't tell me you was scared, cuz." Murdah Man said as he took a right on 23rd Street, heading south.

"Fuck yeah, I was scared, nigga. Cuz had a pistol in my face."

"I heard you talkin' big, what you expect?"

"I had to. When you test a nigga manhood, it fucks up his judgment." Earle Feather said.

"Yeah, but why? Any motha fucka would jump on a brick for 12 stacks. All that other bull shit was unnecessary."

"Yeah, well..." Lone Wolf said as he tried to control the trembling of his body, "I had to."

Suddenly, Murdah Man howled with laughter. "What was goin' through ya mind when he pulled his strap?"

"I was thinkin'," he said as he started to grin, "'Fuck! I just bought these pants!'"

"What?" Murdah Man said turning towards Lone Wolf, his nose wrinkled. "This nigga ready to smoke you, and you're thinkin' about ya gear?"

"Its a joke."

"I don't get it."

"Of course not," Lone Wolf replied. Murdah Man eyed Lone Wolf suspiciously.

"You's a weird nigga, cuz. But I ain't trippin', you still my nigga."

"I hungry, cuz," Lone Wolf said as he watched a fast food restaurant fly by.

"You got a victim in mind?"

"Naw, nigga. I mean I'm hungry hungry," Lone Wolf said as he rubbed his stomach. "In the past two days I've only eaten a taco salad."

"A TACO SALAD?!" Murdah Man said as he began to laugh. "A fuckin' salad, cuz!"

"That was Lady's idea."

"So where you wanna go? It's 12:17, ain't too many places open."

"Drive-thrus are open all night. Let's just go to the next one we see."

"Lets just go to an after hour. You said we gonna be clubbin' tonight. They got hot-wings 'n shit," Murdah Man retorted as he eyed Lone Wolf.

Suddenly, the howling cry of an automatic sub-machine gun shot red-hot lead into the Ford Probe with a sinister crackling sound. The windshield shattered into a web of glittering crystals. Murdah Man lost control of the car as he tugged at the wheel. Spinning out of control, the sound of rapid fire and squealing tires roared like thunder in the ears of Lone Wolf as panic began to set in.

The car finally came to a rest... but the thunder of the machine gun didn't. Under heavy fire, Murdah Man slung open his door with the SKS. Hot lead ate away at the hood of the car. Murdah Man stood up partially and opened fire. Murdah Man didn't know for sure who he was firing at, nor where his adversaries stood... he just fired in their general direction.

With his semi-automatic .357 SL, Lone Wolf exited the car in a low crouch. The gun fire from the opposite end had finally ceased, but Murdah Man continued to let off round after round in the direction. "Run, nigga!" he yelled at Lone Wolf... his voice as loud and as dangerous as the assault rifle.

In his crouching position, Lone Wolf let off a few quick rounds, then dashed for the cover of a building. As he ran to his place of safety, all firing had stopped, only the sounds of their running footsteps and heavy breathing defiled the still night.

"Who the fuck was that?" Murdah Man growled as he stalked the surrounding area, his rifle leveled and ready to fire.

"Cuz, we gotta..." Lone Wolf began, but was cut short by the sounds of hissing bullets. Round after round of lead exploded on the brick building around them, sending bits of jagged stone flying into the air. Both Lone Wolf and Murdah Man ducked behind a concrete divider, they could hear the bullets thumping against the stone slab on the other side.

"We gotta split up, cuz," Murdah Man said as he pulled the clip out of the rifle. "Only seven shells left," he said as he placed the magazine back in its place. "What about you?"

"Damn near full clip," Lone Wolf said without looking.

The firing had stopped.

"Get back to the tilt," Murdah Man said, Lone Wolf nodded his head. "You ready? Go!" As Murdah Man yelled this, he stood up and let off his remaining seven rounds. The unknown assassins returned fire.

With his ears ringing, Lone Wolf let off a few rounds and was up and running. His heart raced as his legs pumped. The darkness of an ally looked promising with providing a safe haven, he ran towards the refuge of the soft darkness.

All was silent.

The cool air burned in his chest as he gasped for breath... his head throbbed. He stopped to let his eyes adjust to the darkness.

Slowly he began to make his way down the ally... the moon light had trouble penetrating the thick outgrowth of trees. The faint outline of cars and garages provided him with a wide path to follow.

Suddenly, at the end of the ally came a laughter from the darkness. It wasn't the sound of joyful laughter, but that of an evil snare. His hand began to tremble as he held on tightly to his weapon.

He took cover behind a parked car, his back resting against a fence pole. With his pistol level, he listened carefully... but the ominous silence mocked him. With his finger on the trigger, he slowly stood up. With each step he took towards the growing darkness, it seemed to Lone Wolf as if the tension was increasing exponentially. He peered into the darkest corners with intensity. The threat, unseen and unheard, lurked behind every corner... behind every dumpster... behind every car. Like a child afraid of the dark, he began to see movement out the corner of his eye... coiled and wicked. He turned with his pistol leveled... but all was calm. He felt danger lurking within every ill-defined shape... within every partial outline.

Again, the wicked laughter pierced the air. Lone Wolf gripped his pistol with an almost supernatural strength, summoned by fear and despair. "Please God, not again," he begged... whispering his fear into the night's air. His eyes were opened wide, yet his enemy remained unseen.

Suddenly, Lone Wolf lurched backwards, as if struck by a powerful blow. He landed with a loud thump against a garage, he slid down the wall until he hit the ground. There they were, the monstrous entity looming just ahead... the faces of death.

Unable to tear his gaze away from the mouths calling his name from within the shadows, his throbbing head began to burn. Pains were shooting through his entire body as the moans of the dead steady grew louder. It felt as if flames were gnawing away at his soul, yet he shivered from the intense cold. Hot tears rolled down his cheeks as he watched the faces of death inch towards him. As they drew closer, the pain increased.

Suddenly, a blinding light flooded the darkness. The light pierced the faces of death like a flaming sword, and instantly they were gone. The moans of the dead were replaced by a low squealing sound.

"Ah, man, you a-ight?" a man asked as he opened his car door to get out, genuine concern lined his voice. "You need help?" the stranger asked as he stepped towards Lone Wolf, who laid on the ground in a heap of human misery. The man passed in front of his car's headlights, then stopped in the center of one of those bars of light, sending a lengthening shadow that loomed over Lone Wolf, casting a sinister looking silhouette.

Driven by a fear induced by panic, Lone Wolf scrambled on his hands, trying to push himself away from the ominous shadow. The man noticed the Desert Eagle in his hand as it clinked against the concrete.

"Whooo!" the man yelped with surprise. "Look, man..." he started. But was stopped when Lone Wolf raised his pistol. Lone Wolf's eyes glittered in the dark... reflecting he cars headlights; he held his pistol tightly in his hand. The man returned to his car, then pulled back out into the street, leaving Lone Wolf again in the midst of darkness... in the midst of demons... in the midst of himself.

Alone in the silence and darkness, like always, thought became the monstrous entity.

"Nooo!" Lone Wolf whined as he staggered to his feet. He wanted to run from the ally... he wanted to get away... but his legs were as heavy as lead.

From the ally, Lone Wolf stumbled out onto the street. Lone Wolf felt a false sense of security under the pale yellow street-light as he stood there gasping for air. His body shivered from exhaustion. His every muscle flared from aching... his weary body felt as if it was ready to collapse... but he knew he had to keep moving. Like demonic hounds at his feet, he knew the spirits of the dead were on the prowl and despite his intelligence, he knew of nothing that would be successful at keeping the spirits of the dead at bay.

* * * * * *

Amber Faye looked at her watch impatiently, then let out a low and long sigh. "Almost 12:30," she whispered to herself. She looked up and down the main street, but saw no cars coming. On the radio she listened to slow music. Her car had that brand new smell to it that she liked. The Corinthian leather upholstery was soft and creamy.

"Cone on!" she said impatiently to the red light. "Turn green, already."

Tonight was the night she celebrated the publishing of her first book, a book of poetry... a book titled Spiritual Warfare. Although she lived far off in the suburbs, her friends wanted to celebrate with her deep within the inner city. Her first mind warned her that such a venture could only lead to trouble. But the lure of bright lights and danger called out to her... clouding her better judgment.

Suddenly, the passenger door jerked open. She gasped in terror. A man entered the car holding a pistol. There had been a rash of car-jackings lately in the streets of Omaha... but never in her wildest imagination did she believe she would fall victim to one. She began to scream... her voice penetrating deep into the quiet streets. "Please, take what you want! Please just don't hurt me!" she screamed frantically.

The man looked at Amber Faye with dead eyes... his long hair was wild... his features contorted in feral blood-lust. "Go," he said between clenched teeth, but Amber Faye was paralyzed with fear. He reached his hand out tentatively, grabbing onto her sleeve... she pulled back in terror. But something in the expression in his eyes reached into her heart with a cold chill.

"Please, go." A whisper was all he could manage. She watched the pistol slip from his hand, landing on the floor mat between his feet. He was falling in and out of consciousness... grabbing onto her sleeve made holding onto consciousness that much easier. His head fell onto her lap as he sobbed and moaned in a monotone. She felt his every muscle contract as a violent shiver tore through him.

He looked up at her and whispered, "Die-vi-lone," and his luminous eyes had gently touched her soul. His head fell back into her lap... his grip loosened and his arm became heavy. Slowly consciousness oozed out of him.

DAY THREE

Sounds of terrified screams and squealing tires filled the early morning air as the get-away car sped down a side street full of innocent children on their way to school. To the east... needles of brilliant light from the rising sun pierced the scattered clouds. The smell of gun powder, mixed with blood lingers above yet another murder scene. Children and parents alike began to slowly pick themselves up from the ground... their eyes scanning the surrounding area for any signs of danger. But the danger had passed... leaving two victims dead in it's wake. One... the intended target. The second... a girl of age 9... an innocent by-stander.

The mother of the child watched helplessly as her little baby girl's flesh was ripped apart by the hail of bullets. To the mother, it played out in slow motion... nothing seemed real. Although the early morning air was filled with screams... she wasn't able to hear anything but the racing of her own heart.

Kneeling beside her daughter... she looked down at the child's peaceful face. One could easily mistake the child for sleeping. And to the mother... this is what the little girl was doing.

"Get up, baby. We'll be late for school," she said weakly. Her dry eyes looked over the sleeping girl's small body. The wetness of blood continued seeping threw her many wounds... darkening her baby blue blouse.

"Come on, baby," she whispered in a soothing voice as she lifted her head from the cold pavement. "You can do it." Her eyes brimming with tears as she continued to encourage her daughter to wake up... but the little girl maintained her peaceful look. And now... the woman would go to her grave whispering a mother's love and comfort soothingly to an only child she will never again hold or touch.

* * * * * *

The sun... slowly spinning on it's arc, set the top of the trees on fire to the west... illuminating them from the shadows just below. The setting of the sun... less than an hour away was the national symbol for all those who lived life in the shadows. Like those legendary evil beings from ancient fables that robs from graves to feed upon it's corpse, creatures of the night were making ready for their nightly activities. For with darkness came the predators... the pimps and the prostitutes who ran the streets... the hustlers and drug fiends who dwell on every corner... in every ally. The drug dealers and the notorious Jaynes Street Gangsta'z.

"Whuz brackin', blood?" one of the young men said as they made their way up the porch steps.

"Big B-Low, whud it be like?" another said to the one sitting on the porch.

"Just bickin' back, bein' boo, blood. You know how I do it," B-Low said as he gave dap to the three men. The music of D.J. Quick could be heard coming from within the house... along with the sound of a baby crying. "What cha'll getting into tonight?" B-Low asked the group.

"That nigga U-B from Victor Block doin' a set tonight at the Lounge. He said he wanted all Dawgs there tonight," one of them answered. "Jaynes Street, Flatlands, Vietnam, they all gonna be there. So what's brackin'?"

"U-B and who else?" B-Low asked.

"Shit, U-B, Freddy Dead, Pocket Pete, that nigga Pudd. All them nigga'z will be coming," another one answered.

"Freddy Dead and Pocket Pete?" B-Low asked.

"Everybody from Dozah Mac-n-Productions. Them rickets gonna hold one next week at Fontenelle Park. We thinkin' about sprayin' them nigga'z!" the silent one spoke up.

"Psst. Let me go get ready," B-Low said as he stood up.

Just then, B-Low was struck by a barrage of lead and buckshot. A sawed-off pump spat out a foot-long flame as the buckshot tore away at B-Low's chest. He howled savagely. Three semiautomatic pistols rang out as the other three dove for cover... each one of them reaching for their own weapons. But the gunmen had vanished as quickly as they appeared... speeding off in what they thought was a tan suburban.

The three looked over at B-Low, who gave a long moaning scream. The blood gushed over his feverish fingers as he laid dying.

"Oh, hell naw, blood!" one of them moaned. From within the screen door, a woman began to scream.

"Someone call the ambulance!" they heard a neighbor call out.

"Did you see who did it?" another neighbor asked.

"Let's go," one of the men said to the other two. "The police will be here any minute," he said in a low voice... tugging at the two men. All three, with pistols in hand, slowly made their way through the gathering crowd. The youngest one looked back at the porch... where he saw the screaming woman cuddling B-Low's head against her breast... her hands were already growing crusty with drying blood. This was the last image he saw before the crowd closed... obstructing his view.

DAY FOUR

Blood colored mist was swirling around Lone Wolf as he stood alone. The crimson mist, as substantial as dust, turned the park around him into a ghostly facade... filled with sinister shapes. Beyond the swing-set laid an open field. A field bathed in the radiant glow from heaven.

Wishing to escape the murky gloom that surrounds him... Lone Wolf began to make his way towards it... but the shadows took form... grabbing him... holding him... suffocating him.

Suddenly... brilliant rays of sunlight descending from above provided an euphoria for his soul that seemed to open his mind and enhance his vision as never before. The brightness enveloped him... embraced him... comforted him... carrying him into the light of the open field. Once there, he heard the familiar voice call out, "I got cha, lil' brah."

Lone Wolf turned at the sound of his brother... his heart fluttering with joy. But his expression instantly turned to one of horror as he stared into the abyss. Around him... instead of the rustling silence of the open field of paradise... he heard nothing but the rising chants of the voices of the dead. He tried to run... to escape... but the pursuing mist was overshadowing... over powering. Screaming demons began to pour out from the swirling mist... charging towards him as he stood helplessly and afraid.

* * * * * *

Amber Faye was startled the first time Lone Wolf jerked in his sleep. She was silent... watching him from the edge of the bed as he fought tirelessly against the enemies that hunted his dreams. "I must be crazy," she whispered as she watched Lone Wolf thrash about. Every time he lay motionlessly... she would move a little so that his profile was limned by a splash of the sun's predawn glow. Here he would look peaceful... innocent. His young face glistened with perspiration... causing strands of hair to cling to his face. But the moment was always shattered by violent compulsions. His face would grimace... and his teeth would bear.

"I must be freaking crazy," she said in a harsh whisper.

She was taken aback when Lone Wolf's eyelids flew open. His eyes shone with wild confusion as he sat up and looked about the room. His bare chest heaved as he clinched tightly to the sweaty sheets. The wild confusion quickly turned evil as Lone Wolf intense dark eyes focused on Amber Faye.

"What have I done," she whispered ever-so-softly to herself as she pulled back in terror. The once peaceful, young innocent face turned hard and brutal... his full lips became a thin line of hatred.

"Who are you?" Lone Wolf asked in a hoarse, raspy voice.

"A-A-Amber, um, Amb-ber," she stammered. "Amber Faye," she finally said.

He could see the genuine fear lurking in the depths of her soft brown eyes... and it touched him. "Where am I?" he asked... trying to soften his tone... but it still came out in a low toned growl.

"M-my, um, home," she managed to whisper. "You, um, fainted in, um, my car."

Lone Wolf didn't have the slightest ideal of what she was talking about... nothing around him seemed real. He only had flashes of what had occurred in the past few days. But all was lost in the murky depths of consciousness.

"You've b-been out for, um, two days."

"What?" Lone Wolf exclaimed.

"Well, um, maybe not two days. But, um, like 32 hours," she stammered, then dropping her eyes she said shyly, "I washed your cloths."

* * * * * *

After a long, hot shower, Lone Wolf was getting dressed when he felt the heaviness of his pants pocket. Reaching in, he pulled out the pager and cell phone Lady had given him. The pager had a total of 23 pages since the night before... all belonging to the same number... Murdah Man.

"What?" Murdah Man asked... his voice heavy with sleep. This was his way of answering the phone.

"Cuz, it's me." This instantly woke him up.

"Cuz, yo a-ight?" Murdah Man asked with worrying lining his voice.

"Yeah, I'm coo."

"Where you at? I thought them nigga'z or the police got you."

"Naw, I'm, um, I'm," Lone Wolf said. Truth was, he didn't know where he was at. "I'm with some white girl, I guess I..."

"Some white girl!" Murdah Man interrupted him. "Man, there's a war goin' on. You know how many times I paged you, nigga? I thought..."

"Whoa, whoa, hold up. What cha mean, 'a war'?"

"Yeah. That nigga Ra Roz got got yesterday morning. Then that oo-lob B-Low got lit up last night. Not to mention what happened to us. Nigga, it's all out war."

As Murdah Man told of the current events... Lone Wolf sat on the toilet. "Damn, cuz," Lone Wolf moaned. "Not my homie, Roz."

"I know, huh?"

"Who did it?" Lone Wolf asked.

"Nobody knows. Some mah fucka'z thought it was me cos we was banging. But throwing them thangs or not, that's still my homie. Where you at so I can have somebody swoop by."

"I don't know where I'm at, cuz. Hold on." Stepping from the small bathroom. Lone Wolf found Amber Faye in the small kitchen. The overpowering smell of bacon ad eggs made him realize how hungry he was.

"Um, ah, what's your name, again?" Lone Wolf asked. The woman had her back towards him, and was startled by his voice.

"Amber Faye," she answered quickly as she spun around.

"Where am I, Amber Faye?"

"View Point Apartments."

"Cuz," Lone Wolf said into the cell phone. "I'm at The View Point Apartments."

"View Point? Where the fuck is that?"

"I don't know, hold on." Turning to Amber Faye, he asked, "Where am I?"

"South-west La Vista."

"La Vista!" Lone Wolf exclaimed. "Damn, cuz. You gotta come swoop me now," he said to Murdah Man.

"Cuz, the ride."

"Damn! Didn't you mess with some white girl here?"

"Sandy? Yeah."

"Tell her to come pick me up, cuz. I gotta get the fuck up outta here."

"I'll drive you," Amber Faye said stepping forward. "Wherever you need to go. I'll take you."

Lone Wolf eyed Amber Faye suspiciously. Upon closer observation... he wondered how her subtle beauty had escaped his attention. And it was then did he realize that she wasn't a white girl... she looked as if she might have been mixed with Mexican or some other Central American culture. Her golden complexion... like the rising of the morning sun... her thin, yet full lips... creating such a beautiful paradox... her thin and narrow face which seemed to protrude at the mouth. Her long, brown hair... softly curled and highlighted by beauty. It seemed to Lone Wolf that Amber Faye had a shy, yet sophisticated beauty... holding evidence of a sweet and gentle personality.

"I need to go to the north side," Lone Wolf said as he studied her eyes... which still held a hint of fear.

"Okay," she said softly... turning her eyes towards the ground.

* * * * * *

The two drove in silence the majority of the trip. Lone Wolf often felt her eyes stealing glances... as if trying to study him without his knowledge. But when he glanced her way... she would avert her eyes quickly. This made Lone Wolf uncomfortable to a certain degree... but he kept quiet, as if he didn't noticed.

"Why did you help me?" Lone Wolf said, finally breaking the silence.

"I don't know." After a moment of silence, she said slowly, "'From the sins of Prometheus, until Charon last toll. May the flames of Ash'Na, rekindle thine kindred lost soul.'" After she said this, she looked shyly at Lone Wolf, waiting for a response. When there wasn't one, she said softly, "Sorry."

"For what?"

"I don't know," Amber Faye lied. The truth was, Amber Faye had assumed that her poetry was lost to Lone Wolf. She assumed that Greek legends, as well as mythology in general were unfamiliar subjects to this uneducated thug. She felt as if displaying her superior knowledge would some how offend Lone Wolf... something she did not want to do.

"I write poetry. That was something I wrote and..." Amber Faye started to get excited, but when she looked into Lone Wolf's hard eyes, she finished softly, "I just got my first book published."

Lone Wolf turned towards the window and softly said, "Thanks for helping me, and feeding me." He waited for a response, but there wasn't one given. "And I'm sorry I scared you." After a pause, he continued, "I have issues," he said trying to make a joke, but to Amber Faye, such a justification was the ultimate understatement... she failed to see the humor in it.

The two sat in an awkward silence as they reached the downtown limits of Omaha. With each lingering moment... he became more and more uncomfortable. Now it was his turn to still glances of Amber Faye. The softness of her profile made Lone Wolf wonder why such softness would even be bothered by the likes of somebody of his character. He was threatened by the power that knowledge lent a person radiating from her. He had to remind himself that she was small and fragile... and afraid. But this knowledge still didn't ease the pressure he felt from her.

"What's your name?" Amber Faye asked softly.

"Lone Wolf."

"Oh, is that your birth name, or a street name?"

"Birth," Lone Wolf replied. He knew what questions were going to be asked next, for the questions were always the same with females that wanted to make small talk. He understands the power of a name... and how his name alone was the perfect icebreaker and it would give the woman the excuse she needed to open the doors to a conversation. But Lone Wolf underestimated her intelligence.

"Sioux?" she asked.

"What?" Lone Wolf asked, surprised. Usually the woman would first ask if he were Indian, then he would correct her by saying "Native." Followed by what tribe? What's that? And which parent was Native?

"Well," Amber Faye started, "the name Lone Wolf sounds like a name of the Plains. Although Macy is the closest reservation to the city of Omaha, they're not Sioux, they're Omaha. And being that Nebraska is located just south of the Black Hills, I figured it was safe to say you're either Lakota or Dakota. So by me asking if you were Sioux, I assume if you had knowledge of your culture you would automatically tell me what branch of the Sioux Nation you're apart of."

After she said this, she looked at him shyly... A slow and timid smile played on her lips.

Lone Wolf was very impressed by her process of elimination and by her deductive reasoning... which only threatened him even more. "Oglala," he said bluntly. He wasn't used to dealing with women of her caliber.

Amber Faye noticed the touch of annoyance lining his reply... so she drove in silence. She followed his every instruction... turning right, then left, then right again. Amber Faye looked around nervously the closer they got to their intended destination. When they pulled up up, she was on the brink of panic.

"It's coo," he said trying to sooth her. "Thanks for every thing," he said... not sure of what to say next. "I, um, well... here." He reached into his pocket and pulled out the money he had left over from the mall, and threw it on the dashboard. Amber Faye eyes were darting back and fourth nervously. It was obvious she had absolutely no experience in such settings. But the thump of the money drew her eyes towards Lone Wolf.

"No," she said softly. "I don't want your money."

"Take it," he said softly, yet firm. "It's the least I can do. You could of called the po-po's. But you took a chance with me, thank you." After he said this he stepped from the car. After re-adjusting his pistol he had tucked in his waist band, he closed the door. Slightly leaning over, he looked at Amber Faye and said, "I understand Prometheus, Charon, and Ash'Na are connected by fire, but what does that have to do with me?"

Her eyes lit up in delight. Smiling a joyful smile, she said, "Think about it, you'll understand."

Lone Wolf smiled his best smile, but knew it still was fierce, but this time she didn't flinch. Instead she returned the gesture.

"The circle of fidelity is an unfulfilled prophecy based on the nature of man," Lone Wolf stated. "So, you, um..."

"That's shallow, Mr. Lone Wolf," she said smiling... her eyes twinkled softly with mischief. "It's a little deeper than that. Think about it, you'll understand," she repeated.

* * * * * *

"Damn, cuz!" Murdah Man said as he lifted Lone Wolf off the ground in a bear hug. "You had a nigga worried, cuz!"

"If you don't put me down..." Lone Wolf strenuously said.

"Cuz, I thought you got got, cuz. For real, cuz. I was like damn, cuz. Them mah fuckin' nigga'z...." Murdah Man spat at a rapid pace.

"Hold on, cuz. I'm coo. I'm straight," Lone Wolf reassured Murdah Man. "But there's a lot of stuff we gotta talk about."

"Wait!" Murdah Man suddenly yelped holding up his hands. "Check this out." Murdah Man disappeared into the back, but quickly returned holding a navy-blue book bag. Tossing it to Lone Wolf, he said, "25 G's cuz! I still went to pick the shit up," he exclaimed excitedly. Lone Wolf opened the book bag and found an assortment of currency. From five dollar bills, to crumbled hundreds... evidence that B.G. Slope had to scrounge for it.

"You make some more sells?" Lone Wolf asked.

"Naw, cuz. The rest is still there," Murdah Man said pointing to the black duffel bag resting beside the long couch,. "The shit's hot."

"Cuz, who the fuck was that bustin' on us?" Lone Wolf asked.

"I don't know, cuz. At first I thought it was Slope, Hollow Tip and that otha nigga. But it happened right after we left them so..."

"It couldn't have been them," Lone Wolf finished his sentence.

"Yeah."

"Well," Lone Wolf said slowly, weighing every word. "Who ever it was knew exactly what they were doing. You didn't see a face, a car, nothing, huh?"

"Nope. Not even a shadow. All I saw was sparks from his choppa."

"You know what?" Lone Wolf said softly... as if not wanting to offend Murdah Man. "That sound like the work of Ra Roz."

"Nigga, get the fuck up outta here," Murdah Man said waving his arms dismissively.

"Cuz, listen, that was a straight up ambush. And a damn good one, too. It's almost like they knew exactly where we gonna be. How many nigga'z you know smart enough to pull something like that off?"

"Stop, nigga!" Murdah Man said defiantly. "Me and that nigga Ra Roz go back before us, feel me?" he said as he waved a hand between the two of them.

"On the set, that's my homie, too. But you did treat cuz like a bitch."

"Man, fuck that!" Murdah Man eyes flashed. "And nigga, fuck you!"

Lone Wolf took a step back in caution. He was well aware that there was no getting around his brutal insistence. "A-ight," Lone Wolf said softly. "Tell me about Ra Roz and B-Low."

Murdah Man spent the next thirty minutes explaining the two incidences... along with possible suspects and other rumors and theories surrounding the two murders. Nobody had the slightest clue as to who murdered Ra Roz... but everybody beleved it was Ra Roz who killed B-Low. But Ra Roz was dead before B-Low was murdered. To Lone Wolf, none of it made sense.

After Murdah Man had finished, he asked Lone Wolf, "So, what we gonna do with the rest?"

"We gonna sell it to Slope. But we gotta get there. What's up with ya ride?"

"One-time got it," Murdah Man said smirking. "By now they lookin' for that nigga Robert Smits."

"Who's that?" Lone Wolf asked.

"It was me until I burnt the ID's. Now I'm Richard Brown," he said laughing as he produced legal papers. "One of the essay's from the South Side Soma Lomaz had it done in 45 minutes. We'll just have Lady take us to get another ride. Speaking of which," Murdah Man said as he scrounged his face, "Lady came here three times yesterday looking for you. Called at least twenty. She said she was calling the celly, too. But here wasn't no answer. You better call her."

"For what?"

"Let her know you alright. She was really trippin' when I told her what happened."

"Yeah, Imma go ahead and holla at her," Lone Wolf said as he reached in his pocket for her number. "She was really trippin', huh?" Lone Wolf asked.

"Cuz, I don't know what you said to her, but she's diggin' the hell outta you."

Lone Wolf continued to search his pockets, but the only items in them were the pager and the cell phone. Nothing more. "What the hell I do with her number?" he mumbled to himself as he checked his back pockets a third time. "Damn!" Lone Wolf scoffed once he realized where the number was.

"What'z up, cuz?" Murdah Man asked.

"Lady's number is folded up in the money."

"Where's the money?"

"I gave it to Amber Faye."

"Who the fuck is Amber Faye?" Murdah Man asked.

"The woman that took care of me when I, um," Lone Wolf cleared his throat, "got sick."

"Cuz, what the fuck happened after we split up?" Murdah Man asked Lone Wolf, wrinkling his brow.

"Cuz," Lone Wolf sighed, "it's a long story."

* * * * * *

Lone Wolf and Murdah Man stood on the small porch waiting for Lady to pick them up. The hot afternoon sun hung brightly in the sky. The two wore dark sunglasses. The two weren't God's best children... Murdah Man with his long braids and black jumpsuit... somewhat short and stocky with a powerful biuld. Lone Wolf with his long hair pulled back into a ponytail... his black outfit hung sinisterly from his huge frame. Murdah Man with his box shaped 9mm Glock... and Lone Wolf with his Desert Eagle .357 semiautomatic SL. They were in fact far from God's children.

"We really should take a couple of bricks for Slope," Murdah Man said.

"Naw. We'll do that tonight. We gotta go get a car now."

"We won't have one by tonight."

"We can if it's in Lady's name," Lone Wolf replied.

"Oh, hell naw!" Murdah Man exclaimed. "She'll hold that shit over my head. You saw how she was banging on the door and screaming my name that morning she had to go to court over a few parking tickets I got in her car. Forget that."

"So what we gonna do 'til we get our ride?" Lone Wolf asked.

"Nigga you the one with a key to the city. Where's your screw-driver?"

"You know what? I'll have her get me one. I need a car anyway," Lone Wolf said.

"Don't do it, cuz," Murdah Man warned. "When she don't get her way, she's a straight up bitch."

"You know it's only a matter of time before they catch me. At least this way all won't be lost. She'll get the ride when they take me back to juvie."

"Man, fuck. Look's like your mind already made up. So..." Murdah Man voice trailed off.

"I want me a '78 Fleet-wood. Big body."

"Why all ya'll ass nigga'z into old ass car? You need ta get a sports car. Motha fuckin' drop top."

"You only a year older than me, young ass nigga," Lone Wolf said grinning.

"Nigga, I's been servin' since day one, cuz. Straight O.G. Status, young ass meat."

Just then, the '97 Lexus pulled up to the curb. Soft music seeped from behind the rolled up windows. "About time," Murdah Man grumbled. As the two made their way down the driveway, they were surprised when Lady got outta the car, and ran towards Lone Wolf. She threw her arms around him savagely, and then tried to kiss him.

"What the... hold on," Lone Wolf said as he pulled back. Looking into her soft brown eyes, he saw a flash of anger that had vanished as quickly as it appeared.

"What's wrong with you?" she ashed as she placed her hands on her hips.

"Nothing. I just don't like being, touched," Lone Wolf lied.

"But you like guerrilla fuckin', huh?" she exclaimed... disgust written on every feature of her beautiful, refined face.

"Didn't you?" Lone Wolf replied. He saw the flicker of embarrassment in her eyes before she quickly turned them away. Slowly she turned around and started walking towards the car. Lone Wolf marveled at the ampleness of her backside. "Oh, my God,'" he said to himself as he watched her walk away. He was grinning to himself, but then flinched when Murdah Man stepped in front of him. Even through the two pairs of dark sun glasses, Lone Wolf could fell the sharp stare of Murdah Man.

"What?" Lone Wolf asked, trying to sound innocent. "I told you she was excited when I called her."

"I don't believe this shit," Murdah Man said as he threw his arms up, then turned and walked away. "Man, how the fuck..." Murdah Man mumbled to himself. "This stuck up holier than thou, gold digging," Lone Wolf heard him say, but the rest was lost, for the music from the car drowned it once he opened the door.

"Hurry up!" Lady yelled out to Lone Wolf, who just stood there.

"Come on, cuz," Murdah Man said before he shut the door. Slowly Lone Wolf crawled into the back seat.

"Ya'll fuckin'?" Murdah Man asked as Lady pulled away from the curb.

"Not any more," she said as she smacked her lips.

Murdah Man turned in his seat, facing Lone Wolf he asked, "You actually fucked her? Like, for real?" Lone Wolf nodded his head. "Her?" Murdah Man asked again pointing at Lady. Lone Wolf nodded again. Murdah Man cast an inquiring glance towards Lady... who simply rolled her eyes at his question. "Cuz, yous a bad mah fucka. You know how many nigga'z been tryin' to strike that? And you know she ain't trynna fuck with anything outside a balla. And nigga, you ain't ballin'."

Lone Wolf and Lady sat in silence the entire length of the ride while Murdah Man went on and on about his disbelief.

"When this shit happen?" Murdah Man asked. "Don't say the mall." Murdah Man waited for a reply... but the two sat in silence. "Ya'll fucked at the mall?" Murdah Man said in shock. "Ya'll freaks for real, huh?" he said grinning. "I will never look at Toys-R-Us the same way again."

* * * * * *

The '97 Lexus pulled into the used cars parking lot and Lone Wolf immediately spotted the car he wanted. Towards the front sat a '64 Chevy... its dark blue paint glistening in the sun.

"Lady," Lone Wolf called out... trying to soften his voice. "I need you to do me a favor."

"What?" she said in shock.

"Just listen to what I have to say, please." He reached over the seat to tenderly touch her shoulder, but she jerked away then hastily exited from the car. Murdah Man laughed.

"You big ol' pimp, you," Murdah Man chuckled. "'Just listen, baby. Please. I love you.'" he mocked while making funny faces.

"Nigga, fuck you," Lone Wolf said as he stepped from the car.

"Fuck me?" Murdah Man laughed. "Ain't we in this situation cos you ain't any good at fuckin'?"

Lone Wolf spotted Lady on side of the small administration building. She was putting coins into a soda vending machine.

"Lady," he called out as he approached her from behind.

"What?" she snapped as she began to pound on the machine.

"Will you just listen? I need you to do me a favor." Lady ignored him as she went about pounding on the machine that had just stole her money. "You know," he started, "Being on the run I can't get nothing on my own." Lady acted as if she didn't hear him as she reached into her small clutch purse for more change. He started to become irritated. "Look, Lady, I got two G's right now, I need you to..." he was cut off by a long sigh.

She reached up to insert more coins when Lone Wolf grabbed her wrist then forcefully spun her around. The coins fell from her hand and clattered on the concrete. She looked up at Lone Wolf... her eyes flashed with fury.

"Let go of me," she said in a harsh whisper as she tried to pull away. Lone Wolf placed his right hand around her neck then shoved her back forcefully into the soda machine... it rocked back and creaked under their pressure. Pinning her right arm above her head, he leaned down within an inch of her face and grumbled, "Shut up and listen." When she tried to protest, he applied pressure to her neck... squeezing. As he tightened his grip on her neck, he felt her heart pulsating through the soft flesh surrounding her jugular vein. He could feel every labored breath vibrating in his grip. He looked at her gravely... searching her eyes for his intended reaction... but they only shone of fierce rage and boiling anger.

"Let go," she managed to gasp. But he only tightened his grip even more. Doing this caused the rage and anger to vanish instantly... being replaced by a distorted, feral lust. Her once fiery eyes now looked into his with soft tenderness. A silent smile threaten her lips. Lone Wolf removed his hand from her neck, only to place it forcefully under her chin. He pushed her head back forcefully... exposing the tender flesh of her neck. He leaned down to tenderly kiss her swollen neck. He felt the long moan vibrating in her throat.

"Don't," she whispered softly... muffled by his wavy hair. Their fingers intertwined as he passionately gnawed on her soft flesh.

"Lady," Lone Wolf whispered.

"Yes,baby," she moaned.

"I need you to do me a favor."

* * * * * *

"Nigga, dis a tight ass ride," Murdah Man said as they pulled out from the sales parking lot. "How the fuck you talk her into doin' this?" he asked as he played with the factory system. Lone Wolf causally shrugged his shoulders as he turned left on Dodge Street, heading back towards the north side. "So you going?"

"Going where?"

"Before we pulled off I heard Lady tell you to go to her crib tonight. So you going?"

"Don't know. But right now, I'm hungrier than a mah fucka. How about you?"

"Cuz, you always hungry," Murdah Man said.

"Nigga, I ate twice in four dayz. I'm ready to smash some shit." Lone Wolf reached into his pocket and pulled out his pager, it read 4:37 PM. "Damn, cuz, it's earlier than a mah fucka, huh? How long was we there?"

"Dunno. But a nigga could use some bar-ba-que," Murdah Man said rubbing his stomach.

"Skeet's?"

"Psst, coo."

* * * * * *

Pulling into the small parking lot of Skeet's Bar-ba-que Joint, they was greeted by the mouth-watering aroma of the delicious food that awaited them within. The place was alive with activities. From the sounds of music, to the sounds of cursing and laughter. A place like Skeet's wasn't for the timid.

"That shit smells good, huh?" Murdah Man said as he lead the way through the small crowds. Once inside, the two stood in the slow moving lines. Sudden bursts of feminine laughter would pierce the air as they talked nosily. Two children were playing "it tag" within the small restaurant. They ran about carefree... weaving in and out of customers standing in line.

"Tag! You're it!" the boy yelled playfully as he tagged his younger sister.

"Nah-uh, this is base. You're still it," the small girl protested.

Lone Wolf watched them as they played innocently... naively... completely indifferent to the cruel and harsh world that surrounds them... the hood. A brutal place that will one day seek to punish and destroy them. A place in which hopes, dreams, aspirations, joy, peace, love and positive interactions are fragments of some do-gooder's inexperienced imagination.

Lone Wolf envied them. For eight long years, he had been tortured by the inescapable realization of *HIS* fragmented and futile existence. With anger and bitterness as his only and constant companion, he had learned long ago that regardless of how hard one strives... one could never truly escape the iron clutches of their social class... one could never truly escape the hood.

"Cuz," Murdah Man said, bringing Lone Wolf back to reality. "I told you we should have brought a couple of bricks. Them nigga'z probably right down the street."

Lone Wolf didn't respond. Instead he turned his attention back towards the playing children, who now played with a paper sack. Watching the simplicity of their new toy held evidence to his belief that ignorance and oblivion is the only true protection from life and it's harsh realities.

The two children turned towards Lone Wolf. They slowly walked towards him... studying him. He towered over the children as they stood searching his face for a long moment. Then they smiled and ran away... resuming their joyful games.

"Get cha'll ass's ova here!" a voice roared from the other side of the restaurant. Lone Wolf flinched at the voice... for it was a voice he instantly recognized... a voice he was raised to fear. Like Lone Wolf... the two children too had grown to fear this voice... for their innocent smiles instantly turned to gapes of horror.

"Get cha'll ass's over here, now!" The man was yelling at the children... yet Lone Wolf flinched in fear nevertheless as the past came rushing back... enveloping him like an open grave in it's fetid embrace.

As the young boy drew closer to the man, he ducked his head from the monstrous blow he knew was coming.

"What the fuck is wrong with you?!" the man yelled as he threw back his fist... ready to strike the child. Lone Wolf saw the justified fear written in the child's eyes as he ducked out of harms way. Lone Wolf knew and understood the child's fears... the pain. He stood watching the man as he swung again at the child. Again the child had gotten lucky. But he knew what was to come tonight. He knew what horrible fate awaited the poor child once he was isolated in his bedroom... with nowhere to run... with nobody to witness... with no one to interfere.

The many scars on his body began to burn as he looked to the face that put them there. His old wounds burning as if liquid fire had been poured over them. On his left check, Lone Wolf had a two inch scar resembling a tear stain... although it's not easily visual unless you're looking for it... he felt it burning... glowing red against his golden complexion.

He passed his trembling hand over the handle of his .357 as he stood watching the dark face writhe and contort like it had once done in his nightmares.

"Please, not now," Lone Wolf begged the spirits... but the man's face became even more distorted... wavering... rippling... his flesh dripping from his face like sweat... revealing a sinister skull.

"Cuz!" Murdah Man yelled at Lone Wolf. His voice instantly clearing up the hallucination. Lone Wolf slowly turned toward him... his eyes were dark and hollow from fear.

"You a-ight?" he asked as he grabbed Lone Wolf's shoulders.

"Let's go," Lone Wolf said in a low voice as he turned towards the exit.

"What about the food, cuz?" he called to Lone Wolf... but he was already out the door.

* * * * * *

From across the street, the two sat in the car in silence. His eyes never left the only exit point of the restaurant. Again he felt for his pistol... passing his burning fingers over the cold steel.

"Cuz, what the fuck are we doin'?" Murdah Man asked... but Lone Wolf's face remained as hard as the cold steel of his pistol. "I'm hungry as fuck," Murdah Man whined.

Blinking against the familiar sting of unshead tears... Lone Wolf sat in silence. All his life anger had always forced away the pain... the fear... but now it failed to hold back the rising tide of childhood fears that he felt returning to him. He remembered how the man would mercilessly beat him... and how his own mother... his own flesh and blood would nod with pleasure... gloating over her boyfriend's power... smiling over her son's unfortunate predicament. He would cry out to his mother in anguish... begging for help... for her protection. But she loved her many boyfriends more than she loved her only son. So the boyfriends were free to do with Lone Wolf whatever they pleased.

Finally, the man emerged from the restaurant. Despite the warm summer air... Lone Wolf felt a shiver from deep within as it made its way to the surface... causing him to tremble. He waited for the inner demons to awaken... to stir the rage and anger... to flood his body with it's wicked venom... adrenaline. He felt helpless in the face of his childhood fears.

Lone Wolf watched the man and two children crawl into a small hatch back. He followed the small car closely as it turned right, driving north on 24th Street.

"Where the fuck we going?" Murdah Man asked. But when he looked to the eyes of Lone Wolf... he saw that they were moistening... threatening to shed a tear. Lone Wolf looked over at Murdah Man... Murdah Man nodded with ignorant understanding and didn't question him anymore.

Lone Wolf followed the car as it took a left on Lake Street. Murdah Man saw B.G. Slope already out on the corner slanging drugs. Murdah Man wanted to say something... he then thought it best to remain silent.

From Lake Street, the car took another right onto 30th Street. It rolled three miles before it took another right onto a side street. It stopped only at the second house.

As Lone Wolf slowly drove past, he watched the man and children enter the small brick house from his rear-view mirror. He could see the reluctance in the child's every step.

"Now what?" Murdah Man knew what Lone Wolf was thinking at this point. After a moment of silence, Murdah Man said, "Now's not the time."

His pager read 5:23. He knew Murdah Man was right... it would have to wait until night falls. For the child... he felt a surge of guilt as he thought of the dire predicament concerning his immediate fate. But Murdah Man was right, nevertheless. It was usually Lone Wolf who took into account all circumstances to keep them out of trouble. But now it was Murdah Man who had been the voice of reason.

"Yeah, you're right," Lone Wolf submitted.

"I saw Slope of the strip. Let's handle that. That fool back there ain't going nowhere. Let's stack that cheddar, then we'll take care of this nigga later, feel me?" Lone Wolf listened to Murdah Man as he talked. "You wanna head to the strip first? Or do you wanna go get the work?" he asked Lone Wolf.

When Lone Wolf did respond, Murdah Man reason, "the strip is closer. So let's ride out."

* * * * * *

"Man, we was waitin' for ya'll nigga'z all night last night!" B.G. Slope said as he approached the car. "Them swerves said that work was fire. We want it all."

"Some stuff came up. But you want it all, huh?" Lone Wolf asked as he put the car in park.

"Ya motha fuckin' right. But Hollow Tips got the loot," B.G. Slope said as he leaned to peer inside the car. "Where the nigga at?" Murdah Man growled, returning to his murderous facade.

"Him, um, um," B.G. Slope stuttered. Murdah Man had gotten the reaction he desired.

"Speak!" Murdah Man snapped. He grinned with satisfaction when he saw B.G. Slope flinch.

"Him, um, him gone."

Lone Wolf looked at Murdah Man and busted out laughing. "'Him, um, him gone,'" Lone Wolf mocked. "Let me handle this, cuz," he told Murdah Man. "Bringin' the child outta him," he muttered to himself as he turned back to B.G. Slope. "Where is Hollow Tips?"

"Him, um, he's, um, he'll be back soon," B.G. Slope said as he kept his eyes glued to Murdah Man.

"How much ya'll got?" Lone Wolf asked.

Feeling a little more at ease, he answered, "At first we was only able to come up with 17. But this morning cuz and K-9 holla'ed at the homies. Now we got sixty four. Tonight, we might have the whole yard."

"Hmm," Lone Wolf said as he slowly nodded his head. It really bothered him that the three had informed other members from Hill Top... this may interfere with his plan. "Who you tell um you getting it from?" he asked B.G. Slope.

"I didn't say. I can't tell them I'm messing with someone besides Crime Boss," B.G. Slope answered.

"So they still think it's coming from him?" Lone Wolf asked. It was very important that Lone Wolf's name stayed out of all drug transactions... or it would be him who would fall by the sword next.

"Naw, Crime Boss back in Cali. He should be back sometime next week," B.G. Slope said.

"All this stuff stays between us, understood?" Lone Wolf tapped Murdah Man's leg when B.G. Slope didn't answer.

"Understood, nigga!" Murdah Man roared as he pulled his 9mm Glock and took aim. B.G. Slope eyes swollen in fear and he threw his arms around his face for protection.

"Yeah, yeah!" he yelped.

Lone Wolf grabbed Murdah Man's arm, a sign for him to lower his pistol.

"Come over here," Lone Wolf said to B.G. Slope, who had pulled away in fear. "Few of us that knows about this. You, Tip, K-9. I want you to tell them fools what'll happen if they run they mouth, understood?" B.G. Slope nodded his head. "Nobody has to know." Lone Wolf looked at B.G. Slope for a short moment... his eyes full of terrible and fearful understanding. "So, how much you get from the other two?" Lone Wolf asked, trying to lighten the mood.

"We got off a quarter," B.G. Slope said.

"That's it? And you already want the other seven?" Lone Wolf asked.

"Hollow Tips said it's better to get it all now, 'cos you might find somebody else."

"Smart thinkin'," Lone Wolf replied. "Check game, cuz... I want you to have the money on you tonight. We'll swoop by sometime after nine. Need I bring the heavy artillery?" As he said this, he narrowed his eyes at B.G. Slope in a threatening manner.

"For what?" B.G. Slope asked. "At 12 a brick, ya'll robbin' ya'llselves," he said laughing.

"Murdah," Lone Wolf called. This instantly wiped the smile off his face as he looked fearfully at Murdah Man.

"H-h-hold on!" B.G. Slope yelped.

"You think this joke, huh?" Lone Wolf asked B.G. Slope. "When have you ever known me to be funny? Keep ya mouth shut and have the money tonight."

"I'm just saying, Feather man, why would I say anything to anyone when I'm dealing with you? I get it cheaper, I don't have to kick money back to the lazy fucks who aren't out here on these streets. I'm pocketing nothing but pure profit. So why would I say anything to mess that up?" B.G. Slope said nervously.

Although B.G. Slope was known for his stupidity... what he said now made so much sense to Lone Wolf. So he didn't question him any further concerning their business transactions. Instead he calmly said, "Back the fuck up."

B.G. Slope was taken aback by the sudden brashness... but still he did as he was instructed. As they drove away, Murdah Man said, "Nigga, you always jokin'. And you try to be funny, but you ain't funny at all."

"Yeah, but that idiot don't know that."

"Know what? That you ain't funny? The whole hood know that," Murdah Man said as he started to chuckle.

"I don't know how you got all these nigga'z sacred of you. But I'm glad you do. It makes my job easier," Lone Wolf said to Murdah Man.

"What you mean you don't know? Now that's funny. You know Imma killa," Murdah Man responded.

Suddenly Lone Wolf's face became grim. Instinctively, Murdah Man knew where his mind went. "The time will come. Let the sun fall. Until then, lets get something to eat."

* * * * * *

The car was silent as the two sat eating their take-out cheese burgers and fries. Lone Wolf kept looking west... waiting for the sun to set. The sky glowed with brilliant pinks and purples... the clouds looked very much like cotton candy.

"We need some beats, cuz," Murdah Man said breaking the silence. "Tomorrow lets go to Big Boy's and get a system put in. This shit right here is pathetic," he said as he played with the AM/FM stereo. He looked over at Lone Wolf, who sat silently... slowly eating... and often turning towards the setting of the sun. He knew what Lone Wolf was waiting for. Although he didn't fully understand why, he knew that whoever that man was had deeply affected him... it shone in his eyes. A sort of private sorrow was seen lurking deep within.

"You wanna kill the nigga first, or handle Slope?" Murdah Man asked.

Lone Wolf shivered at the thought of killing his once tormentor. He didn't know if the shiver was caused by joyful anticipation, or by a fear of the consequences that may follow. But it didn't matter... he knew what needed to be done in order to put an end to the spirits of the past that haunts him. "Get that nigga, now," Lone Wolf said as he tossed his remaining food from the window.

* * * * * *

Lone Wolf slowly made his way to the small brick house and knocked on the flimsy wooden door.

"Hold on!" he heard the man yell from within the house. He turned towards Murdah Man, who stood in the middle of the street... studying the opposite side of the baby blue hatch-back.

"Ya'll shut the fuck up and get in ya'll rooms!" the man barked. Lone Wolf felt for the children. Finally the man swung open the door and looked up at Lone Wolf.

"Yeah, what's up?" he asked Lone Wolf.

Then and there was a collision of the present with the past. Lone Wolf studied the eyes of his phantom... they were those of a school-yard bully. Now at the age of 34, they no longer held the youthfulness of the years when Lone Wolf had known him before.

"Is that your car?" Lone Wolf asked, swinging his hand towards the hatch-back.

"Yeah. Why?"

"I accidentally scraped the paint pulling in, man. I only have $700.00 on me now to pay for the damages."

"Huh?" the man said in confusion.

"I chipped the paint on the other side. See, it's, um, come on and I'll show you," Lone Wolf said as he made his way back to where Murdah Man stood. The paint wasn't chipped... but Lone Wolf needed the man close to his '64 Chevy.

"$700.00?" the man asked as he followed closely behind. "For a new paint job it'll cost double that," the man lied greedily.

"I kinda figured that. But that's all I have on me," Lone Wolf lied, too.

The two were stepping from the curb as Murdah Man pushed the button to pop the trunk.

"Let's see here," the man said as he walked to the opposite side of the car. "What the fuck!" the man exclaimed when he saw that the car wasn't scratched.

The man was peering down at the paint job when Lone Wolf landed powerful blow to the man's jaw. The shock of hitting bone rattled all the way up his arm. The man staggered before hitting the ground. Lone Wolf pulled back in pain. "Ahhh!" he yelled as he rubbed his knuckles. "God damn it," he grumbled. The man let out a long low howl of pain as he slowly picked himself up. Murdah Man, with his 9mm Glock, delivered a murderous blow to the back of the man's skull. The man crumbled... completely unconscious.

"What the fuck?" Murdah Man asked shrugging his shoulders.

"That shit hurt," Lone Wolf said rubbing his knuckles. "It landed wrong."

"Wow," was all Murdah Man said before placing the unconscious man into the truck of the car. "I see why you ain't no killa," Murdah Man said laughing as he slid into the passenger's seat.

Lone Wolf flinched in pain when he tried switching on the car's ignition. Murdah Man laughed again.

"Shut the fuck up," Lone Wolf said as he tried again... this time with success.

"Or what?" Murdah Man teased. "You gonna hit me with your good hand?"

"Yup, and Imma hit you in your good eye."

* * * * * *

It was completely dark as the '64 Chevy slowly circled Carter Lake. The bright yellow moon illuminated the calm waters... reflecting it's light in soft ripples. Lone Wolf's eyes darted back and fourth... searching for a place of darkness. They finally arrived on the opposite side of the lake. To their right, behind a fortress of trees stood Emply Air Port... but it's bright lights couldn't penetrate the small forest of trees. To their left... only dim house lights off in the distance held evidence that humans were around. Lone Wolf slowly backed into a shadowy nest. Murdah Man was the first to exit the car. When Lone Wolf pushed the trunk button... the man was staring down the barrow of Murdah Man's 9mm Glock. The man gasped in fear.

"Get out! Murdah Man growled as he seized him by the neck. The man fell to the ground with a heavy thump. "On your knees, motha fucka!" Murdah Man roared. With a snarling grin, Murdah Man slowly moved down upon the man... who pulled back in horror.

"Yeah, nigga," Lone Wolf said softly as he drew near with his .357 in hand. "Remember me?"

The man ducked his head, begging. "Please sir. I don't know you. Please don't kill me," the man begged.

"Look at me?" Lone Wolf said icily.

"Please, sir. Oh my god, please."

"Look at me!" Lone Wolf yelled as he grabbed the man by the back of his neck. "Do you remember me?" Lone Wolf asked in a frosty voice. He swelled with pride and joy when he saw the fear and desperation ablaze in the man's face... the same fear and desperation he had shone the man ten years earlier. "Do you remember me?" Lone Wolf repeated as he struck a heavy blow to the side of his face with his pistol. The man collapsed to the ground... curling up in the fetal position. "Remember the cord?" he asked as he landed another blow. "'Member the fire?!" he yelled as he landed blow after blow. "The box?! The cross?!" With every strike, the man cried out in agonizing pain.

"Get up!" Lone Wolf yelled. The man whimpered and grunted in pain. "I said get up!"

With violent exertions... he slowly got up. Then he collapsed. His eyes became dim as he coughed up blood. "Get him up," he said to Murdah Man... who pulled up the semi-conscious man and held him with his arms locked behind his back.

Pulling up his sleeves... Lone Wolf revealed two scars on his right arm... a four inch scar on his bicep and a two-inch scar on his outer forearm. "Remember these?" Lone Wolf growled at the man. The man's eyes were closed. "Look!" Lone Wolf yelled as he punched into the soft wetness of the man's face... the wetness of blood and tears. A gurgling shriek pierced through the clammy air. "Shut up and look!"

The man slowly raised his head. Through swollen and bloody eyes, he stared at the scars. "Remember these?" Lone Wolf said softly. The man's eye's slowly drifted from one scar to the other... then finally came to rest on the eyes of Lone Wolf... eyes that blazed with fury.

The man's eyes darkened in frightful recognition. Lone Wolf saw this. "You remember, huh?"

"Oh god, please. I'm sorry. Please, god, please."

"Shut the fuck up!" Lone Wolf roared as he punched away with his swollen hand. But as always... the anger forced away the pain. In the darkest depths of his being... Lone Wolf felt those inner demons rejoicing with hymns as he pummeled the man who once sought to punish and break his will to live.

* * * * * *

92

The sour stench of blood filled the car as they drove in silence. With the back of his hand, Lone Wolf wiped away the blood and tears that now flowed freely down his cheeks. Murdah Man saw this... but said nothing. He knew it wasn't like Lone Wolf to allow anybody to see into the depths of his tortured soul, although he was subject to display irrational burst of emotional violence. Even from all the pieces he placed together from the whole ordeal... it still didn't paint a full picture. But he still could feel the pain that Lone Wolf felt, nonetheless.

In his minds eye... Lone Wolf could see the dreadful fear written on every feature of the man's face as he beat him. As vivid as ever. In his ear he could hear the man pleading for his life as a pistol was forcefully placed against his temple. The man had felt the physical anguish that Lone Wolf had suffered as a child... so why doesn't he feel satisfied? The man had cried and begged as Lone Wolf had done as a child... so why didn't this gratify those inner demons? Why is he still hurting? Why is his soul still burning? Why can't he be happy? Why can't he find peace?

"I shoulda kilt that nigga." Lone Wolf said aloud. Murdah Man didn't respond. With his swollen hand, Lone Wolf struck the steering wheel in anger. "Ahhh," he shrieked as he struck the dashboard. "I shoulda killed um," he cried... forcing away the pain in his hand. He had left the bloody man to suffer from his own guilty knowledge... but his past actions warrant something more severe. It warranted death.

"That's not you, cuz," Murdah Man said softly. "That shit would of ate at you until it killed you."

Lone Wolf looked over at Murdah Man. He saw strange emotions lurking just beneath his murderous facade. Suddenly... he felt a tremendous surge of pride and respect for Murdah Man, and all that he had overcome. He now understood that Murdah Man's mentality was a by-product of his environment. He knew that Murdah Man was far from typical. Like himself... he knew that his spirit had been forged in the furnace of suffering. But like so many people who are raised in such brutal surroundings... the hood... he had lost his way in a world of harsh indifference and desensitizing spiritless strife.

Lone Wolf had always known that he existed in a constant state of war... a war being waged between the flesh and the spirit. He now understood that Murdah Man was engaged in the same war. Some would turn to drugs to numb the pain of their useless existence. Others would turn to alcohol to drown out their tension and sorrows. Some would turn to sex to mask their loneliness and despair. And in the midst of the absolute insanity of the streets... Murdah Man had found that an explosive temper and fear was his only ticket to a relatively peaceful existence.

He now understood Murdah Man... but when will he understand himself? He knew that we all had skeletons on our closest... living serpents of impiety that dwells in the blackness of our hearts and souls. He knew this... but knew not the origins of his own skeletons and serpents.

Lone Wolf saw Lady getting into her car as he slowly drove up the street of which Murdah Man's house stood. She was ready to pulled of when Lone Wolf tapped the horn. After he pulled the '64 Chevy int the drive-way, the two stepped from the car.

Lady slowly made her way to their car. Again she was dressed exquisitely in a DKNY skirt. Her shapely legs seemed to glisten in the darkness. Murdah Man walked past her with a grunt while Lone Wolf stopped in front of her... his eyes were bloodshot and fixed in a glassy stare. She saw traces of dried mud on his face.

"Why are you guys always so beat up and dirty looking? What are you two up to?" she asked Lone Wolf. She wanted to reach out and touch him... but she was hesitant because of the way he had re-acted earlier. Lone Wolf didn't answer... he simply walked past her. She followed close behind.

Inside the house, Lady gasped in horror once she realized the two were drenched in blood. Standing side by side in the living room... Murdah Man and Lone Wolf both looked at Lady with dead eyes.

"Oh my God, what happened?" she asked. The two men looked at each other. She watched the exchange that passed silently between their eyes. Then Murdah Man turned and walked away. Her soft brown eyes searched his dark face. Again, she wanted to reach out to him... to touch him... but didn't. "Did you kill somebody?" Her heart had fluttered strangely at the question. She felt relieved when Lone Wolf shook his head slowly. Yet his eyes remained harden in it's icy stare.

Slowly... with great caution... she took a small step forward. She felt impelled to come closer to the flame that burned so dangerously behind the eyes of Lone Wolf. She didn't know what it was about his eyes that was drawing her in... but she took another small step. Perhaps it's the wisdom that lies behind those wounded eyes? Or maybe that small flicker of sadness that excited her parental instincts? Regardless the case... she took another step forward and reached her hand up.

Lone Wolf pulled back and grabbed her wrist. "Don't," he said softly... not in anger... but with purpose. A purpose she didn't understand.

Just then, Murdah Man emerged from the back carrying the duffel bag. His cloths were changed and the blood was wiped from his arms and face. "Key," he said as he drew near. Lone Wolf still had Lady by the wrist... but quickly released her. "Imma go handle that. I'll holla at cha'll in the morning."

Lone Wolf handed him the car key and watched him as he left.

"Come with me. Spend the night," Lady said as she went to grab the shopping bags which still contained his new cloths. "You can shower at my house."

With Murdah Man gone... Lone Wolf was freighted by the thought of being left alone. Although he couldn't stand being amongst large crowds... the thought of being alone... where his own thoughts became a monstrous entity frightened him more. So he followed her out to her '97 Lexus.

* * * * * *

Inside... the apartment was not what he pictured. Everything was soft and smooth... ivory and pink... satin and silk... draped and gentle. The floor was lined with a thick Persian rug, with matching curtains that were richly patterned. With a flick of a switch... the lights dimmed and soft music could be heard playing throughout the entire apartment. Lady took Lone Wolf by the hand and led him to a bedroom that was lavish... heavy... sensual. Spread across the circular bed laid a thick satin comforter... lined with a number of pink satin pillows.

She lead him past a wall of mirrored-door closets. Inside were racks upon racks of women clothing. Below... a staggering array of women shoes. She led him into a brightly lit bathroom. To the right were shelves filled with accessories; necklaces... bracelets... earrings and the like... all custom designed. To the left were shelves of cosmetics. Tucked in the corner was a jet-stream bath. This is where she led him. Were it not for the location and outer appearance of this apartment... one could easily believe that such lavish beauty could only be found in the *Life Style of the Rich and Famous*... and not dead center in the hood.

Without saying a word... Lady walked over to a counter and opened a drawer... revealing fresh towels and washcloths. In the same silence, she turned and left the room... closing the door behind her.

After a quick rinse in the shower... Lone Wolf now sat in the soothing hot liquid of a bath. His eyes were closed as a folded towel rested on them. Soft music from a small speaker discreetly hidden in a corner above could be heard above the soft hum of the jet steams. His thoughts were of the situation that had occurred less than an hour ago. How the man had plead and cried. How he begged the two for forgiveness. In the end... the hunter always becomes the hunted... the player always gets played and karma will always claim the ultimate victory.

Being visited by a ghost of the past had caused him to think of his mother. It had been many years since he had seen her last. In the year 1991 at the age of 11 she had visited him while he was in a mental hospital. There he had cried freely and openly. At first... she didn't know how to respond. She sat there... looking over the child... not knowing what to do. Before she left she made promises to return... to go to court and fight for custody of him. She promised that one day soon the two would become a happy family. She had promised to love him... to care for him... to comfort him.

He remembered how he told of his joy to his counselor, to his doctors... to his peers. He felt as if a weight had been lifted and he was able to sleep peacefully once again. Before she left... she held him. She held him as a mother would a child. That moment had become beautifully etched in his mind. A moment to remember. A moment frozen n time.

It wasn't until a year had past did he slowly and painfully come to realize that she wasn't coming back for him. He was alone in this evil and wicked world of the flesh. And ever since that betrayal... he was afraid to love... afraid to believe. He later had found out that her visit was court ordered... that as a plea-agreement she was forced to go. If it wasn't for the courts she would never had visited him at all. He would learn from indifferent sources that she was with one man after another... drinking... partying. All the while, her only son would stagger... stumble and often crawl through the days, weeks, months and years.

As the years of his senseless existence continued... he often thought of his mother. When he thought of his mother... he thought of the happy home she had promised. And a stern, small hope remained in the heart of Lone Wolf. Even now... as he laid in the jet-stream hot tub. He knew he had to see his mother... he knew he had to try again.

Slowly his thoughts had returned to what had took place that night. Although he was emotionally confused earlier... knowing not how to feel about the incident... he now smiled in satisfaction as he looked over his swollen hand. He made a fist... then unclenched his fingers. It didn't feel as bad as it once did. It looked a lot worse then it felt.

At that moment... Lady entered the bathroom. She wore an elegant silk night-gown that fell from her fragile shoulders. Her hair was an upswept mass of delicate tendrils. She went and knelt beside the hot tub. Her well manicured fingers began to play in Lone Wolf's hair.

"You relaxed?" she asked him in a silky voice. He didn't respond. After shutting off the jet-streams... she let her hand slip into the hot water. "You want me to light some scented candles?" she asked. Again, he didn't respond. "You wanna make love?" she whispered seductively as her lips brushed gently against his ear lobe. She then began stroking his arm... her fingernails digging into his flesh just enough to cause cold shivers to pass through him despite the hot water. She giggled softly when she saw his manhood jerk and spasm below the calm surface of the water. Unable to suppress it... he laughed as well. She leaned over the tub in an attempt to kiss him on the mouth. But he pulled back... causing the water to splash onto the floor.

"What's that about?"

"Don't kiss me," Lone Wolf growled.

"What? Why not?" she asked as she leaned in to try to kiss him again.

"I said don't!" he roared as he shoved her away. She toppled backwards onto the wet floor. He stood up... the water washed over his body. "You wanna fuck, then let's fuck. But don't try to make this something more then it is."

She looked up at him angrily. But before she could protest, he had already stepped from the tub and seized her by her night gown. He then hauled her to her feet by the silk material.

"Let go of me," she demanded. But he ignored her.

He forcefully removed the first layer of her gown. At first she resisted angrily... but then gasped in raw ecstasy when he forcefully shoved his middle finger deep inside of her. His fingers were thick to begin with... she twinged in pain when he plunged a second finger inside.

"Let me get loose first," she said, remembering the pain from before. "Shut up," he said as he lifted her from her feet. Any other time she would have become angry at being at being told to shut up... but knowing what was in store... she allowed herself to be carried off.

In the bedroom, he tossed her onto the bed. She yelped playfully as she flew threw the air. "Wait! Hold on," she said as she threw her hands up. "You're wet. You'll ruin my sheets. Dry off first."

He looked at her annoyingly... but eventually did as he was told. Then... like a lion... he pounced on his prey. In a fluent motion he had her pinned down and was deep inside of her. Being that this was what she had expected and anticipated... her body was receptive. She whimpered as he dug deeply inside of her with his manhood. He pounded away at her as if he were angry... but he wasn't. The sound of flesh hitting flesh and the wet squishy noises were to him the ultimate turn-on.

Every time he pulled his full length completely out of her, he could hear a faint sucking sound... he then would plunge it back in savagely. The bed squeaked as he pumped harder... faster... deeper. Her moans and groans transformed into a shrieking cry.

Sweat poured from his body, mingling with hers. Their skin grew wet and slippery. The heat between the two rocking bodies added to the height of Lady's orgasm and she cried out again and again. Her back stiffened and every muscle in her body contracted each time. But to Lone Wolf... none of this mattered. He was beyond the realm of seduction... beyond the realm of trying to impress her. Therefore, he wanted what he wanted... and he didn't stop until *HE* was satisfied.

Both he and Lady laid quietly between sweaty sheets. Her head was on his chest... her hand gently stroking his. Despite his calm demeanor... many things were racing through his mind. Although his body was there in the apartment with Lady... his mind and thoughts were in a completely different realm... locked in his own private memories. He was so far gone... he didn't hear her as she called his name.

"Hey, you," she said playfully as she waved her hand in front of his vacant eyes. "I know I'm good, but I didn't know I was THAT good," she said giggling. "You hear what I said?" Lone Wolf shook his head weakly. "I SAID, we ended up ruining the sheets anyway. I had you dry off for nothing. Oh well, huh?" But again he was already in his self-secluded state of mind. He had not the slightest idea of what she said.

"Hello?" she said waving her hand again. "Anybody home?"

"I have to go," he said as he looked down on her. A look of confusion tinted her eyes.

"Go where?"

Lone Wolf didn't know how to answer. He didn't want her to know that what had taken place that night at Carter Lake had caused old wounds to re-open. And that now he needed to find his mother. "I have to go," he repeated dryly. "I have to check on Murdah Man," he lied.

She made a face and laughed at him. "Check on Marcus, huh? Boy please. That's the best lie you can come up with?" she asked as she laughed again.

"He had to pick up some money. I just wanna make sure it went alright."

"Trust, baby boo, Marcus will be just fine." As she said this she squeezed his injured hand. He grimaced in pain. "What's the matter with you?"

Lone Wolf slowly pulled his hand back... then held it up to where she could see the swollenness. "Ohhh. What happened, boo?" she asked. But he remained silent. "Let me take care of this."

"Look, I really gotta go."

"Hold on, boo. At least let me take care of this. It's the least I can do after what you've given me."

DAY FIVE

Dawn was spreading across the roof tops of Omaha, Ne. The sunlight was slowly finding it's way down the wide streets and avenues... down the narrow side streets and alleys... illuminating the remnants of night that still huddled in mean and grimy corners.

The '97 Lexus twisted and turned through the inner streets as the two occupants sat quietly listening to the music playing softly. Lone Wolf gazed out the passenger window... not really seeing anything at all. His thoughts were of the past four days... wondering what's to come. Wondering how it will all end.

Before they left the apartment this morning... Lone Wolf had called Murdah Man. He wanted to ask him about the pick up... wondering if everything went smoothly, but he didn't want to say anything over the phone. Murdah Man didn't sound excited or angry... so the transaction must have went smoothly.

"Lone Wolf," Lady said. The voice at his side pulled him away from his thoughts. He turned towards it with a reluctant stare. "Are you okay?" she asked... but her words were lost to him.

"Why you ask?"

"I don't know," Lady lied. "You just got so distant after we made love. You started acting strange. You know you could have stayed and slept. Or at least gotten something to eat." As they pulled in front of Murdah Man's house, she looked at him with soft eyes. "How's your hand?"

Lone Wolf raised the hand that she had carefully bandaged. "Not as bad as I thought," he said as he wiggled his fingers.

"Big baby. Well, no more guns for you for awhile," she giggled.

"Guns? I hate guns."

"Oh, yeah? Then what's that bulge right there?" she asked as she pointed towards his waist band.

"That ain't no gun. Nigga, that's pipe!" Lone Wolf said laughing. "But like a gun, it can be deadly if misused." She laughed in response.

"Boy, you are so silly. So cute." As she said this she rested her forearm on the back of his seat so that she could play in his hair. As she twisted her fingers in his long, wavy hair... she said, "That's the Lone Wolf I first met. The Lone Wolf I like."

Just after she said this, he turned towards her... his eyes slowly began to blaze with fire. "What makes you think I give a fuck?" His tone was harsh.

She looked at him... confused... amazed at the dramatic shift in his mood. "What are you talking about?" she asked as she pulled back her hand. "What's wrong with you?" she asked defiantly. Despite her elegant style... Lady had grown up in the hood. She grew up around people like Lone Wolf... so she knew how to stand her own ground. But Lone Wolf didn't respond. Instead he got out of the car... slamming the door shut before storming off. Lady watched him as he made his way up the driveway to the house... torn between the emotions of sympathetic confusion and uncaring anger. "Whatever," she said to herself as she threw the car in drive, then pulled away from the curb.

When Lone Wolf entered the house... he was immediately overwhelmed by the powerful scent of marijuana. Murdah Man sat on the black leather soda rolling blunt while smoking another. Beside him sat a woman. She sat with both legs tucked under her... the long t-shirt that she wore was pulled down over her knees. Immediately Lone Wolf could tell that she was a beautiful woman... despite the fact her long hair was dishevel wild; evident of the night that she and Murdah Man had shared.

"Nigga!" Murdah Man startled. "Bargin' in my house like that. Ever heard of knocking?" he asked as he settled... continued rolling the blunt. "You almost got shot, nigga."

"With what, cuz?" Lone Wolf laughed. "Them big ass man nipples? Fool, put a shirt on," he said as he sat on the couch opposite of the two.

"Cuz, I was about ta go to sleep before you called," Murdah Man said without looking up. "Just got done fuckin' the dog shit outta this bitch. A nigga exhausted, now."

Lone Wolf looked towards the woman to see the reaction she would give for Murdah Man's blatant disrespect. But there wasn't one. *Hoodrat,* he thought to himself.

"Who's this?" Lone Wolf asked pointing at her with his chin.

"Oh, this is Sasha. She from the block." The woman simply glanced over at Lone Wolf, then continued to watch the music video's that played on the television.

"Anyway," Lone Wolf said. "You said you was about to lay it down, what cha about to do now?"

"What's on ya mind, cuz?" Murdah Man asked.

"I was just wondering if you got that shit?"

"Hell, yeah, cuz. Them nigga'z came up on the other seven somehow." As he said this, he reached behind the couch and produced a black and brown book-bag... not the one Murdah Man left with them the night before. Dumping the money on the coffee table... Murdah Man spread the bills out with one hand while taking a long drag on the blunt with the other hand. "Who we gonna get next?" he asked in a raspy voice as he held the potent smoke in his lungs.

"I don't know, cuz," Lone Wolf answered. "I wanna know who shot at us that night. And who got the homeboy Ra Roz." As he said this he saw the expression on Murdah Man's face change. Lone Wolf knew he was still feeling the loss of one of his closest friends.

"I don't know, cuz. But in time, we will find out. On the block, them bitches will feel me," Murdah Man growled.

"I heard them Jaynes Street nigga'z said it was Ra Roz who smoked B-Low."

"Yeah, cuz. Them bitches even went out lookin' for cuz until they found out cuz was resting before the shit even happened," Murdah Man explained.

"So they don't know who got that B-Low either, huh?"

"Naw, cuz. Nobody knows shit. But cuz's funeral is next Friday. You gonna be there?" Murdah Man asked... trying to mask the bitter emotions he felt.

"For sure," Lone Wolf said softly.

"I know them Jaynes street nigga'z plan on getting a new shipment," Murdah Man said changing the subject. "If we can find out when, we can get them nigga'z again."

"Hell yeah. And you know them nigga'z can't keep they mouths shut."

"I know, huh? Nigga, we can do this shit all day every day," Murdah Man said.

* * * * * *

Lone Wolf and Murdah Man spent the majority of the morning playing sports on the video game. Both Murdah Man and the woman were smoking blunts all the while... but Lone Wolf stayed away in fear of a repeat of the incident that happened his first day of freedom. It was just past noon when Lone Wolf's cell phone rang.

"Yeah, what's up?" he said answering the phone.

"Um, h-hello?" a soft voice asked on the other end. "Is this Lone Wolf?" the voice asked softly, a mere whisper.

"You gotta speak up. I can't hear you," he said as he continued to play the video game.

"Is this Lone Wolf?" the voice repeated.

"This him, what's crackin'?"

"It's me... Amber Faye."

"Who?"

"Amber Faye." There was a long pause as Lone Wolf thought the name over. "The girl who helped you," she said softly.

"Come on, nigga. Hang that phone up so I can continue whoopin' dat ass," Murdah Man said as he reached for the phone. Lone Wolf pushed his hand away and ducked his head.

"Hold on, cuz. I'll be back." Taking the phone into the kitchen, Lone Wolf sat in one of the chairs around the table. "Hello? Amber Faye? What's up, girl?"

"Um, hi."

"I'm bad with names, my fault. I'm... I don't know."

"That's okay," she said sweetly. "I just wanted to see how you were doing, that's all."

"I'm straight. Yeah, I'm coo. Ah, how you get this number?"

"Oh, I found it folded in that money you gave me. I figure I would just try. I haven't spent any of it. It's all there."

"So? That's your money. If you wanna hold it, it's coo, I guess. I don't see the point. If I was you, I'll treat myself. Feel me?"

There was a short pause. "Lone Wolf?"

"What's up?"

"Do you think, um, maybe I, um..." she paused for a moment... then took in a deep breath and continued, "Lone Wolf, I want to see you again if it's okay with you."

"Are you fuckin' serious?" Lone Wolf asked as he chuckled to himself.

"Yeah," she said softly... shyly.

"You were scared to death last time."

"No, I wasn't. I was just nervous. I didn't know you."

"And you still don't."

"But I'm not nervous."

"You should be."

"Why?" Amber Faye asked in a curious tone.

"Fuck," Lone Wolf sighed. "A-ight. Where you wanna go?"

"I don't care."

"Remember that house you dropped me off at? Just swoop by around seven and we'll just ride."

"To that house?" she asked. Lone Wolf could sense the nervousness in her tone.

"Yeah. Just come on by."

"Um, okay," she said softly... even more nervous.

"Tell you what, why don't we just meet up somewhere?"

"Yeah, okay," she said more brightly. "Where?"

"Shit, I don't know. That's on you."

"How about Lover's Lane?"

"What? Where the fuck is that at?"

"Central Park. Is that okay with you?"

"Fuck," Lone Wolf sighed. "I guess."

"Great!" Amber Faye exclaimed excitedly. "We can meet just after dark. The water fountain is so beautiful at night. The water changes colors and there's a ferry that takes you around it. And the lights and the pathways are just so beautiful. Especially the waterfall. Oh, we'll have such a lovely time." As Amber Faye proclaimed her excitement, Lone Wolf sat rolling his eyes.

"Yeah, sounds great," he said sarcastically.

"Oh, Lone Wolf, you'll enjoy yourself. Just wait and see."

"Well. I guess we'll see, huh? I'll holla at cha then, a-ight?"

"Okay. Meet me by the slides. I'll see you then. Bye, Lone Wolf."

"A-ight," he said. After he hung up the phone, he sat there in silence... wondering why a woman like Amber Faye wanted to see him again... let alone take him to a place called Lover's Lane?

Entering the living room again, Murdah Man just looked up at Lone Wolf and laughed. "Nigga, you getting' ya ass whooped," he said pointing towards the television. "213 to 7," he said laughing.

"You really get a kick outta ya-self, huh?" Lone Wolf said shaking his head.

"Nigga, don't get mad at me 'cos you getting crushed," Murdah Man said as he scored again. "What, nigga!"

The woman shook her head at his foolishness as well, giggling.

* * * * * *

After Murdah Man and Sasha went to bed... Lone Wolf grabbed a thousand dollars from off the table and his car key and was out the door. As he drove through the streets of Omaha, Ne. Lone Wolf allowed his mind to wonder. He really didn't like being alone with only his thoughts. He played with the cars AM/FM stereo, wishing he had installed a system by now.

Unconsciously, Lone Wolf found himself driving past his childhood hangouts... the parks... the abandoned houses that had been torn down years before. His head began to fill with memories as he continued to drive sedately past the many houses he had lived in at one time or another. Slowly and painfully he came to realize that he had never truly had a home to call his own. Even before the system had taken custody of him as a child... he was always bouncing from home to home. "Baby sitters," as his mother would call the ruthless and brutal people he was often left with. Suffering at the hands of complete strangers for days and sometimes weeks at a time.

Although the memories of his past were slowly fading into a murky mist of darkness... the ones he did have were like hauntings. Hauntings that were constantly tormenting him from within. Whispering and murmuring the most negative scenarios and solutions into the most vulnerable regions of his mind. Striking blow after tormenting blow to the deepest reaches of his soul. A place where he is completely unable to fend them off. Every memory that he did have left led to another unwanted memory... bringing back waves of unwanted pain.

"Now I'm in charge," he said to himself as he rested his bandaged hand on the .357 that sat on his lap. As he continued to drive, he found himself in a place where his mother used to hang out. In front of the two story blue house, there was a sea of older people. Some sitting on a couch that sat on the lawn... others standing on the raggedy wooden porch that looked as if it were ready to collapse under the weight. Most of the people held in their hands liquor bottles... all covered in a brown paper bag.

Lone Wolf came to a complete stop in front of the house and waved over an older man. Pulling his new pin-striped Polo Rugby shirt over his pistol to conceal it... Lone Wolf placed his bandaged hand at the top of the steering wheel.

As the man drew closer... Lone Wolf could tell that he wasn't old at all. Perhaps mid 30's. He just looked tired. His tattered clothes were stained with grease... evidence of being a car mechanic. His old Budweiser baseball cap lain sloppily on top of his head. His eyes were bloodshot from liquor and his yellow teeth glistened in the warm afternoon sun.

"Whuz up, pot-nah?" he said as he leaned over the car... his breath heavy with the foul stench of alcohol.

"I wanna know if you've seen a certain woman around here lately?" Lone Wolf gave him her name. The man said the name didn't sound familiar to him... then turned to ask a small group of alcoholics standing near by. After talking amongst themselves, they too said that the name didn't ring a bell.

Just then, from the porch a woman yelled out, "Yeah, I know her." The woman looked to be around his mother's age, 35-36, but the crow's feet around her dark eyes told a story of her hard life.

She tried to sway her curve-less hips seductively as she made her way to the car. The man left without saying another word.

"Hey, honey," the woman exclaimed as she leaned inside the car. Lone Wolf pulled back... trying to avoid her hot and foul breath. "Yeah, I know her. Why you ask?" she inquired as she smiled. The few remaining teeth were heavily stained by tobacco... and her extremely dry lips were so cracked in areas that they held a hint of dry blood.

Trying to avoid eye contact, Lone Wolf simply said, "She's my mother."

"Oh my sweet Lord!" she said excitedly. "You're Lil' Wolf? Oh my God, you're so big! So handsome!" As she said this she leaned completely into the car and began to hug him. Lone Wolf became nauseated and his stomach turned as he thought of the human horror and the smile of torment which now was clinging to his neck.

"Get the fuck off me!" he yelled as he swung his arms wildly. Feeling his skin crawling, he began to scratch at his arms. She pulled back... a look of disgust etched her face. "Look, I just wanna know where my mother is, okay?"

The woman looked down at Lone Wolf as she stood with her hands on her hips. "You don't remember me, do you?" she asked.

Lone Wolf looked up at her... looking for any facial features that may jar his memory. He found none. "Naw. I don't."

"I used to baby-sit you when I lived in Hill Top Projects. It's me, Sherril." But the name still didn't ring a bell. "You might have been too young to remember. But I haven't seen your mother around here in years. You know where the Francis House is? You might wanna check there."

"What?" Lone Wolf said in disbelief. He knew that the Francis House was a shelter for the homeless. But with her beauty... he found it hard to believe that she would be staying there. He knew that she could always find a trick to take her in and provide her with shelter... so why would she be staying at the Francis House? "Yeah, Imma do that," he said as he put the car in drive. "Thanks, Sherry."

"It's Sherril."

"Whatever," he said as he pulled away from the curb.

As he made his way to the Francis House, he couldn't escape the sensations of bugs crawling on his arms. Which brought his attention to his injured arm. If his mother was here... he knew he didn't want her to see him hurt... he didn't want his mother to think of him as weak. He wanted her to think of him as strong... powerful... indifferent to the love that should have always been there. Therefore, he tore off the bandages that comforted his swollen hand.

Lone Wolf pulled his car around to the back of the homeless shelter... a place where the lost and unwanted would seek refuge. A haven for those unwanted misfits who found comfort and love amongst others like themselves.

He placed his pistol in the glove compartment and exited the car. He felt cold... shivering in the bright heat of summer as he searched the many small crowds for his mother. The many faces all looked tired... aged well beyond their years.

"Ah, homie," Lone Wolf called out to a man and woman passing by. "Can you tell me here to find..." As the man thought the name over, he looked over at the woman. "She's 35, Native."

"Native?" the man asked.

"Indian," Lone Wolf answered... not feeling like arguing semantics.

"Oh, Indian," the man said. He looked around as if someone might over-hear what he had to say. He adjusted the string that held his pants up in a nervous gesture... then said in a conspiratorial whisper, "You know a couple of days ago they found this Indian woman murdered in that lot over there."

As he said this... a chill ran down the spine of Lone Wolf. His heart pounded so horribly in his ears that he could barely hear how she was murdered.

"Yup," he said in a matter-of-factual way. "They killed her then set her body on fire in that lot over there." He pointed by lifting his chin to the right.

"That wasn't her, thou," the woman said as she patted the man's arm. "That was Gina." Turning towards Lone Wolf, she said, "That name does sound familiar. Go ask them, they'll know," she said pointing to a small group standing at the edge of an ally.

Lone Wolf followed her gesture with his eyes. And there... standing in the midst of the homeless... stood his mother.

As he drew closer to his mother, he felt the heavy lump of sorrow as it rose from his chest to his throat... forcing his eyes to blur with tears. Lone Wolf had always imagined that this moment would bring anger... hatred. He had always thought that coming face to face with his mother would bring devastating rage... but his rage was gone. And only sorrow... deep unbearable sorrow, remained.

"Mama," Lone Wolf said softly. His mother had her back to him. "Mama," he said a little louder, but she continued with her conversation. He took another hesitant step forward.

"Mama." Hearing a voice, she turned and gave the surrounding area a quick glance. Her eyes fell on Lone Wolf... but she didn't recognize him. Conflicting emotions battled valiantly in his heart as he watched his mother turn her back to him... again. Love and forgiveness fought gallantly against years of emotional fortification as he stood looking at his mother. He called out to her. She turned and looked into the eyes of Lone Wolf.

"Who you call?" she asked assertively. But he couldn't respond. *Had it been so long that she doesn't even recognize her own son?* he thought to himself. The anger towards her slowly began to rise... overcoming the feeble attempt of love and forgiveness. He wanted to curse her... he wanted to scream at her. He wanted to reveal to her his identity... to violently jar her memory so that she can witness the monster she had created.

But there was no need.

Slowly the light dawned in her eyes. But the moment of gradual recognition was shattered by the sound of erupting pistols.

On instinct, Lone Wolf dropped to the ground for safety. His hand reaching to the small of his back for a pistol that wasn't there. Full fledged panic raged in the crowd behind the Francis House. They all scrambled for cover... all except for his mother. Lone Wolf looked up at her. She glanced around... but didn't seem afraid... only desperately sad... as if she had become accustom to her dreadful surroundings.

Getting to his feet, Lone Wolf allowed himself to be swallowed up by the panic stricken crowd. He then slowly descended off into the background, his eyes never leaving his mother.

Once she realized the danger had passed, she turned back towards where her son had once stood. She searched the crowd for him. But he was gone. She began to wonder if perhaps she was delusional. It couldn't have been her son. It just couldn't. There were so many things she needed to tell him. So many things she needed to explain. Again she searched the crowd as it began to settle. Unable to locate him, she felt the all-too-familiar sting of advancing tears. They fell silently.

But from the distance of which Lone Wolf stood, he could not see them fall. For if he had, perhaps the void he has felt for so long would have been fulfilled... and a new chapter of happiness would began. Finally Lone Wolf would emerge from his cocoon of pain and misery a new creature... a beautiful one, and not the monster he had become. He would then live the life that he had always dreamt of.

* * * * * *

Question upon question raced through his mind as he stepped into his Chevy. Contradictory feelings swayed in him as he sat there. But the feeling of absolving and forgiveness soon gave way to wrath and fury... again he began to resent his mother... his only living blood. Blood that spurned and disowned him.

"Man, fuck her," he mumbled to himself as he turned the engine. "I've made it this far without her," he protested. But still... he couldn't ignore the emptiness that lingered in his heart.

* * * * * *

Amber Faye stood in the light of the crescent moon, awaiting the arrival of Lone Wolf. Her pink and white wind-breaker felt heavy in the summer's night. She watched the many couples as they walked hand in hand, each in their own little world. For many years, this hopeless romantic has longed for such love. A strong, passionate love of which she could call her own. This is why she questioned her attraction to a person like Lone Wolf. His illusive personality is not a personality that is compatible for love.

Yet it was still Lone Wolf who intrigued her. His dangerous and thuggish mentality was not created by love, yet it seemed that his dark, intense eyes were a window to something amiss within. Like a mystery to which she would never truly and fully know an answer to.

Per **REMEMBER THIS MOMENT DEC. 5TH 11:13PM** Perhaps this mysteriousness was the root of her attraction? Combined with the dangerousness and elusiveness? Or perhaps this attraction was superficial? His thuggish handsomeness combined with his Native American heritage?

It seem different... somehow exotic in a very pleasant way. Or maybe it was the spark of a promise of internal love she saw behind the fire that blazed in his eyes? A promise that was meant to be kept forever. A promise that could be hers if she could just mange to break through the barriers that his harsh life has built around his heart. Or maybe this hopeless romantic was simply delusional. Seeing things that weren't truly there?

Lone Wolf stood behind her in the shadows. He had been watching her quietly for a time, wondering what it was she was thinking about. It had been her suggestion that they meet by the slides. Yet, there she was, nowhere in the vicinity. Lone Wolf thought that perhaps the reason she stood off in the distance was so that she could observe his arrival. Scope the scene, get a sense of what she was getting herself into. He smiled to himself. "Amateur," he said softly.

"Amber Faye?" Lone Wolf called out from the shadows. She startled, then spun around. "L-Lone W-Wolf?" she called out softly. He could see her eyes cloud over with fear. He stepped from the shadows. As he drew closer he saw the fear in her eyes grow dimmer.

"I thought you told me to meet you by the slides?"

"I did," she said softly. Lone Wolf decided to spare her the embarrassment.

"You said you wanted to see me?" Lone Wolf said softly. Amber Faye nodded. "Well, here I am." She nodded again, and then stood in an awkward silence for a long time. Finally, Lone Wolf said, "Are you glad I came?" She nodded and then looked up at him with that innocent, childlike smile. "Are you sure?" he said playfully. She continued to smile her incomparable smile as her eyes danced. "A-ight. Let's walk."

Lone Wolf turned and began to walk towards the water-fountain that spat brilliant colors of water 60 feet into the air. Amber Faye stood there as Lone Wolf began to walk off. She watched after him, noticing how smooth and graceful his walk was. Lone Wolf stopped and turned towards her. "Are you comin'?" Like a child she skipped to where he stood. She looked up at him, searching his face for any signs of being humored. There wasn't. He simply turned and began to walk. This time she followed.

There was silence between the two as they made their way down the beautiful lanes. There were patches of well lit areas. Others were hidden in romantic darkness. The majority of the time they walked in silence.

When they did speak, the questions were brief, followed by an even briefer answer. Lone Wolf had learned that she was 24 years old. When she asked his age, he became illusive. He had learned that she's a career writer, she had learned nothing of his occupation. In fact, the more he said, the less she knew about him. Yet, somehow, Amber Faye was growing more and more comfortable in the presences of Lone Wolf.

"Are you okay, Lone Wolf?" she asked softly as she looked up at him. "You seem so distant."

"I'm coo," Lone Wolf responded in a distant tone. The truth was that his meeting with his mother earlier weighed heavily on his mind... plus the fact that he didn't yet feel comfortable in Amber Faye's presence. He still felt a little intimidated by her intelligence and her child-like, yet sophisticated, presence. He wanted to quickly change the subject. "You know I've never been to the Old Market before."

"Oh. And why's that?" she asked.

"I heard there's a lot of old men dressed as women in there."

"Don't be silly, Mr. Wolf. Those are called Drag Queens," she said shyly. "And they're everywhere," she said as she started to giggle... she couldn't help it.

"So, are you gonna tell me about your poem? The way I see it, you called it shallow."

"Nooo," Amber Faye sighed. The way she said it brought a glimmer of a fleeing smile to his lips... but soon it faded. "Poetry is an expression. An expression of the soul. Far from that rap-crap that you listen to," she said smiling.

"'Rap-crap?' You the one saying poems about fuckin'."

"No, I didn't," Amber Faye chuckled. "It's a sympathetic poem. Not a sexual poem, Mr. Wolf." She slurred his name to the point where it almost sounded feral. "If you weren't such a thug..." she continued playfully, "then you'll have the intelligence to know the difference." She hadn't realized how insulting her comment was until after it was said. She instantly regretted saying it. The last thing she wanted to do was anger him in any way. She still considered him hostile. She looked up at him with worry. But he didn't even break stride in his graceful walk.

"You know, I'm a lot smarter than you think. Don't let this thug shit fool you." As they continued to walk slowly, he said, "I know Prometheus was the Titan that created man and then stole fire from heaven, he gave it to man as a gift. He was punished by the Greek god Zeus for this. Charon is also Greek mythology. He tolls lost souls cross the river Styx. Sometimes Styx is shown as a fiery river. Ash'Na accidentally created the ring of fire in the Pacific Ocean. She threw her traditional marriage wreath into the sea in anger. It was known as the circle of fidelity. This wreath harbored her anger and it took root in the sea. It grew and became the ring of fire, hundreds of volcanoes. As long as the balance of good and evil remains equal, the volcanoes will lay dormant."

As Lone Wolf talked, she looked upon him with amazement, for she was very impressed.

"Your poem ended with flames sparking a soul. Am I that soul?" Lone Wolf asked. Amber Faye shook her head. "So you're that soul?" Amber Faye shook her head again. "Fuck! Are any souls being blazed?"

"It's rekindled," she sad laughing. "Not 'blazed.' And yes there are."

"Who's?"

"Now, *this* is the part you have to figure out, Mr. Lone Wolf."

Lone Wolf smiled his dead smile, but didn't turn towards her. She studied his profile in the park's light. She felt her heart stir as she watched him. He was so desperately serious, so unhappy... even when he smiled and laugh. His dark eyes and young face were well etched with worry and stress. *But worries of what?* she thought to herself. *Stress caused by what? Would I ever know?*

"Why are you always so serious?" she finally decided to ask. He slowly turned towards her and tried smiling.

"What are you talking about?" he asked.

"I don't know," she lied.

"You know..." Lone Wolf said slowly, carefully weighing every word, "I still do a lot of childish shit."

"Oh, yeah? Like what?"

"Well..." there was a brief moment of silence as he thought over his many childish habits. Looking towards the heavens, he said, "As a child I really believed if you wished on a star, it would come true. Today, I know better. But there are times I find myself doing it anyway."

"Why?" she asked softly in a serious tone.

"I don't know. Praying that one day it just might come true." Lone Wolf looked at her as she turned her body to face him. Like moonlight on water, she could see the glitter of hope in his eyes. At that very moment, she didn't feel so emotionally distant from him.

"What do you wish for, Lone Wolf?" she asked softly.

For a brief moment, his heart reached out to her through his eyes. But it vanished instantly. Again, his eyes became hard... strange. "I'm not a fuckin' dummy," Lone Wolf challenged with anger in his voice. "I know that's a planet and not a star."

"What?" Amber Faye gasped, taken aback by the sudden accusation. Dropping her eyes from his, she said softly, "I know you're intelligent, now. I must admit, twenty minutes ago..."

"That's Venus," Lone Wolf said, cutting her off in mid-sentence, his tone becoming threatening. "The Roman goddess of love and beauty. In Greek mythology, she's known as Aphrodite."

Amber Faye stood in shock silence, not sure how to react. "I'm sorry," she replied in an apologetic tone. He looked at her harshly. But something in her soft brown eyes pulled at the strings in his heart. He suddenly felt embarrassed by his little temper tantrum. He felt small in the presence of such a powerful woman.

"And do you see that?" he asked pointing towards the heavens. He tried his very best to mask his voice... to make it tender... but softness wasn't something that he was used to. "That's another planet, Jupiter. The Roman king of the gods. And that's Mars, the god of war."

Amber Faye noticed the change in his tone, and she tried to relax. He turned her towards the east. Pointing towards three alined stars just above the 60-foot colorful jets of water spraying from the water-fountain, he said, "And those three stars are Orion's Belt. Orion the Hunter." He came up softly behind her and put his arms around her waist. He felt her tense in his arms. He wondered if this was caused by fear or by the butterflies one gets when touched by love?

"Many compare the Pyramids of Giza to Orion's Belt," he said in a soothing voice. He was telling her things she already knew. But she was very impressed that this gang banging thug would know such things. "And do you see that bright star?" he asked as he pointed with his finger. "That's the Dog star, Sirius The eye of Orion's dog. There's this African civilization called the Doggone, and they have legends of an invisible star orbiting Sirius. And with modern technology, we just found that invisible star. But how did this ancient culture know it was there?" Lone Wolf pulled Amber Faye closely into his body. "We can't see all the star cos of the city lights. But it's beautiful."

They stood in silence for a long time as many couples passed them by. He held her for what seemed like an eternity. It was Amber Faye who finally broke the silence. "How do you know all these things?"

Lone Wolf didn't answer. Instead he slowly pulled away and turned her to face him. For the first time she noticed the scars on his face as he looked down on her.

"Where's this waterfall you was talking about?" he asked.

"We passed it already," she said as she giggled. She reached out and tentatively touched his face. She turned him towards his left. "Look over there. It's beautiful. Lone Wolf was indeed impressed by its beauty. The underwater lights caused the goldfish to glitter and sparkle. The glistening water fell gracefully from the man-made waterfall, which aliened the stairs. He wondered why he had never heard of such a beautiful place before.

Amber Faye tucked her hand into the crook of his arm, and the two began to walk slowly. Side by side, his tall, rugged good looks were in striking contrast to her delicate beauty. She looked up at Lone Wolf and smiled. Although he did not return the smile, she felt happy, nonetheless.

Just then his cell phone began to ring. "Yeah, what'z up?" he spoke into the phone.

"Cuz, it's time to ride," Murdah Man said on the other end of the line.

"What?"

"Me and that nigga, Lil' Insane ready to ride. We need you here."

"Right now?" Lone Wolf asked.

"Now, nigga," Murdah Man said before he hung up the phone.

"Fuck," Lone Wolf sighed to himself. "I gotta go."

"Why?" she asked softly.

"Some stuff came up." He tried his very best to smile pleasantly at her, but she saw there was a glint of something chilling and evil lurking in his eyes. He turned to walk away, but she grabbed his arm.

"Lone Wolf." she whispered, "Will I see you again?" But it wasn't a question. It was a cry... a prayer... a plea to God. He held her eyes with his for a long moment. His dark eyes saying words that could not yet be said verbally. Then he turned and left. She watched after him as he strode down Lover's Lane... and then disappeared into the shadows.

* * * * * *

The crescent moon was perched high in the nighttime sky. The stars sparkled around it... glistening against the a background. A soft and gentle wind caressed the treetops... which swayed in turn to a rhythmic beat. It was a beautiful night... defiled only by the three shadows lurking in the midst of darkness. The three henchmen were oblivious to the beauty of the scene, for their minds were plagued with criminal fantasies.

"Ya'll nigga'z ready?" the first figure asked as he lifted his assault rifle. The other two nodded their heads. The first pulled the ski mask down over his face... then vanished into the mysterious darkness of the ally. With a blue rag wrapped around his face, the second followed. In his left hand he held a TEC 9 with a Lemon squeeze, in his right hand, a MAC 11. The third figure pulled down his ski mask as well. He gave his fully loaded assault rifle a quick check over, took a deep breath, and then disappeared into the ally.

* * * * *

The door burst open with gut wrenching force. Shattered wood flew threw the air as the door was kicked from it's hinges. The first figure entered. Wild panic flared in the crowd of eleven as he unloaded three round into the stereo system, sending broken plastic flying threw the air. The second figure entered with arms open, the two sub machine guns leveled at the panic stricken crowd.

"Shut the fuck up!" the third figure roared as he entered through the broken door. The terrified screams became broken whimpers as he leveled his assault rifle at them.

"Damn, B!" a man yelled. "What the fuck is..." but his sentence was cut short as three rounds exploded from the assault rifle. Instead of words, a sickening gurgle came from deep inside his throat as hot lead plunged deep into his quivering flesh. His blood showering the huddled group that laid only three feet away.

The first figure grabbed a woman by her hair and raised her off the ground. "Where's the shit!" he roared as he forcefully shoved the barrel of his rifle into the soft flesh under her chin. Her wild eyes shone of panic and desperation. Red spots of fear were on her light complexed cheeks. To the predator holding her, it was obvious she was not on familiar terms with death.

"Where's the shit?!" he roared again as he tossed the terror stricken woman against the wall with unbelievable force. She hit the wall with a heavy thump, and then slid to the floor unconscious. "Bitch!" the first figure yelled in frustration as he unloaded his rifle into the unconscious woman. Blood and pieces of her skull splattered the wall. Her body jerked with every bullet that dug into her young flesh. Her muscles re-flexing from the shock of death.

The first figure growled menacingly as he re-loaded his assault rifle.

The third figure grabbed another woman and shoved her towards the first figure. He grabbed her by the hair with an iron grip. "Where's the shit?!" he roared at the woman. She flinched with every word.

"In there. Please don't hurt me, please," she whined frantically, pointing towards the hall. The second figure holding the sub machine guns grinned fiendishly under the blue rag. The woman resisted frantically and continued pleading as she was drug by her hair into the mysterious darkness of the hall. Seconds later, another three round burst rang out from the back of the house, followed by a gurgling shriek that slowly faded away.

"Bring the bags!" the first figure yelled from the back. On demand, the third figure vanished into the darkened hallway, while the second held the hostages at bay. Within a matter of minutes, the two figures emerged carrying two duffel bags each. Each bag was bulging from the packages of the new shipment of drugs contained inside. "Let's go!" the first figure barked as he made his way towards the broken door. The third figure followed closely behind.

The second figure slowly backed towards the door, his two sub machine guns still aimed at the hostages. Standing within the frame of the door, he removed his blue rag, baring his teeth in a vicious grin. Murder and hatred shinning brightly in his bloodshot eyes.

The two sub machine guns plunged red-hot knives into everything, living and dead, as they swept the room with a thunderous roar. The bullets ate away at flesh and wood alike. Tattering and ripping everything to shreds. Blood sprayed the walls as the bullets continued to rain. Emptying both clips, the man stood in admiration of his work. With a wolfish grin, he turned and vanished into the night like a phantom.

* * * * * *

The '64 Chevy slowly crept along the curb as the three occupants scan the surrounding area. The block of 34th and Jaynes Street was crawling with police, their lights flashing brightly in their rhythmic pattern. Yellow police tape was stretched far and wide to keep the gathering crowd at bay. Lone Wolf stopped in the distance. They watched as a stretcher was brought from the house and loaded into a waiting coroner's vehicle. The sheets were soaked in blood.

"God, damn, cuz. That nigga was left a bloody mess!" Insane said from the back seat. They watched as the vehicle closed its door and pulled away. Another vehicle took its place.

"Damn! What happened here?" Murdah Man asked rhetorically.

"Hold on, nigga!" Insane yelled, startling the two. "Ain't that the house we supposed to hit?"

After a moment of studying, Murdah Man said, "Hell yeah. Man, what the..."

Lone Wolf sat in silence, not knowing how to feel. As another body was pulled from this massacre, Murdah Man said, "Them nigga'z wasn't playing, huh?" Then turned to Lone Wolf and said, "Cuz, X this plan. They been hit. Let's ride out before po-po get suspicious."

Lone Wolf agreed and turned the key in the ignition. They had to pull up in order to turn the corner. As they took a right, Lone Wolf caught a glimpse of the bloody and tangled bodies left inside. For some reason his heart lept in his throat as both sorrow and sympathy seized him.

"God damn, cuz! You see that shit?!" Murdah Man yelled in excitement. "They put in work!"

"Ripping tons of bloody torsos," Insane chimed in in his demented way of speaking.

Lone Wolf sat in silence the entire ride back while the other two exchanged their approval for the carnage they had witnessed.

"But forget what you saying, cuz," Murdah Man said as they all exited the car, each carrying his weapon. "Whoever did that got our shit. That was our lick. And I want my shit back, understand me?"

"For sure, cuz," Insane said in agreement. "Money or flesh, Imma get mine."

As they entered the house, they saw Sasha sitting on the couch. She was still wearing the same t-shirt from this morning. Her un-kept hair was now in an up-swept mass of delicate softness. She sat with both legs under her, the t-shirt pulled over her knees. In her right hand she held the television remote, in front of her on the coffee table sat a half eaten sandwich. She simply looked up as they entered, then went back to watching music videos.

"Bitch, you still here?" Murdah Man asked as he approached her. "You ain't got no home? Why the hell you still here?" he asked as he snatched the remote from her hand.

"Psst. Whatever," Sasha said as she got up. "I'm gone," she said as she walked towards the back.

"And you paying for this sandwich, too! And leave my shirt, dammit!" he yelled after her. Turning towards the two, he said smiling, "It's the only clean one I got."

"Man, you stupid," Insane said. He was watching Sasha as she left the room. "Cuz, that girl got a big ol' fat ass on her. You see that ass, Lil' Wolf?" he said as he tapped on Lone Wolf's leg.

"Naw, cuz," Lone Wolf said shaking his head. "I wasn't even paying attention."

"Nigga, that motha fuckin' ass is fat. "I'll fuck the dog shit outta that bitch," Insane said.

"You wanna hit that, cuz?" Murdah Man asked.

"Hell, yeah," Insane said excitedly.

"Go holla at her. She a hood rat She'll let you toss." But before he could finish, Insane had already disappeared into the back.

"Cuz, why you do that?" Lone Wolf asked. "You know he gonna end up beating her ass."

"I know," Murdah Man said laughing as he began to roll a blunt.

"He might mess around and shoot her."

"Naw, he wouldn't do that," Murdah Man said waving his hand.

"Psst, he did it before. I was there when he shot his last girl in the leg."

"You was there?" Murdah Man asked. "That was awhile back."

"I know. I've known cuz for years. In fact, like four years ago cuz almost killed me."

"What?" Murdah Man said in surprise. "Cuz ain't never said ya'll went back like that. Let alone he tried to off you."

"Naw, cuz, not like that. We stole a car together. I let this crazy fool drive. Next thing I know, we behind a rec. center at Adam Park, on the football field doing doughnuts. This dumb ass nigga slams into the goal post and almost kills us."

"For real?"

"Hell yeah, cuz. After we hit, the car was still running and it was making funny noises. We thought it was gonna blow up, so we got ghost. Left the doors wide open and the car running and everything. We was some lil' thugs, too. It was about five in the morning. I bet them staff members was tripping over that shit, huh?" Lone Wolf said laughing. He looked over at Murdah Man, who was by then smoking on the blunt.

He looked over at Lone Wolf with a straight face. "That ain't funny. So why you laughing?"

"Man, forget you. I thought it was."

Just then a scream came from the back of the house. "Let go of me!" Sasha yelled.

"What I tell you?" Lone Wolf said as he got up.

"Now that's funny!" Murdah Man said as he burst out laughing.

As Lone Wolf made his way to the back, Sasha came storming out, tears streaked her cheeks. As she passed Lone Wolf she tried to forcefully push him aside, but was unable to budge such a large man. Murdah Man laughed at her feeble attempt. Side-stepping Lone Wolf, she stormed towards the front door, where she stopped and turned towards Insane, who was just emerging from the back.

"You fuckin' bitch!" she spat angrily at him.

"Who you callin' a bitch?!" he growled angrily as he lunged at her. But Lone Wolf was able to grab him as Sasha yelped and ran out the front door.

"Cuz, we got other stuff to worry about," Lone Wolf said, trying to calm him down. "Let that stuff slide."

Murdah Man was on the couch laughing hysterically.

"You shoulda shot that hood-rat," Murdah Man said in between breaths.

As the three settled on the couch, Murdah Man passed the blunt to Insane. "You know you shoulda whooped her ass. You know, if the Captain would let you," Murdah Man said as he laughed even harder.

"Fuck that bitch," was Insane's only reply.

Wanting to change the subject, Lone Wolf said, "Whoever hit them oo-lobs like that was ruthless. Ya'll sure ya'll wanna go hunting for these people?"

"Ya motha fuckin' right, cuz," Murdah Man spat. "I gives a damn who it was. They got paid. Make our shit look like shit. Forget that. We get this, we each get at east a hundred G's a piece."

"Dead nigga'z tend to have homies. They'll think it was a retaliation," Insane added. "But first we'll have to find out who it was. Psst, this a free murdah cos they'll think it was Jaynes Street."

Lone Wolf knew he was in the presence of killers, and he tried to hold back the dark tides of fear and panic by pretending to be just as excited as they were... such a deed wasn't difficult. In fact, it came easy. But despite the rage and hatred that dwelt in his heart, he knew he wasn't a killer. If caught in one of his manic depressive mood swings, he was more than capable of leaving a victim laying face down in a puddle of blood. But to kill another simply for sheer pleasure wasn't something he could do.

But without the presence of love... his heart, of course, would follow it's wicked nature. "Let's go find these nigga'z."

* * * * * *

Earlier that night... Amber Faye sat on the phone... crying to her best friend, Tonya. "Oh, it's okay, honey. You don't need that jerk-face, anyway," Tonya said soothingly... trying to console her friend.

"But I do," Amber Faye protested.

"No, you don't, Amber Faye. Don't you see what's happening? As a psychologist I've seen it a hundred times before."

"Seen what?" Amber Faye asked softly as she wiped away tears and sniffled.

"The way you described him to me and how he simply left you in the middle of a date. That's setting a pattern for a real messed up relationship. Don't you see that, girl?"

"No," Amber Faye whispered into the receiver. "He said he had something to do."

"And now you're defending him?" Tonya asked irritably. "The same jerk that left you, and now you're defending him? Amber Faye, girl, just look at the warning signs. They're all there. Show no misplaced pity for this low-life creep. Get out while you can, girl."

"But you don't know him like I do. You didn't see him."

"*YOU* don't even know him. You know absolutely nothing about him, not even his age. Amber Faye, this is not like you."

"But Tonya, you didn't see him. It was so strange having him here in my house... in my bedroom. So tired... so frightened. I want to help him. I felt so sorry for him," Amber Faye said in a low voice.

"Amber Faye, listen, I know exactly what you're going through. I've been there before, and let me save you the heart ache. I know how good it feels to throw caution to the wind and how good it can feel to step outside yourself and even do something bad. He speaks to that inner teenager. The one that knows of all the wonderful possibilities that life with him holds, if you're simply willing to take a chance. But Amber Faye, it's not worth it. I know you're thinking you can change him... that you can teach him a thing or two. But honey, you can't. It will be *HIM* that changes *YOU*."

Amber Faye sank even deeper into her chair with tears brimming her eyes as she listened half-heartedly to her friend.

"He *WILL* change you, Amber Faye. You will find yourself behaving like your own evil twin by crossing one little line at a time. You will unconsciously work extremely hard at keeping this creep satisfied. Have you had sex with him?" Tonya asked.

"Na-uh," Amber Faye said as she sighed heavily.

"Good. I know his type. He'll try to have sex with you in public, or something weird like that. Just to make you fall in love with him."

"How will that make me fall in love with him?"

"Because, you already think he's the most exciting person you've ever met. He makes you feel adventurous. Combined that with having wild, hot sex in public is like giving you addictive drugs."

"What?" Amber Faye asked... both contempt and curiosity lining her voice.

"Guerrilla sex is as exciting as drugs because it *IS* a drug. Especially when there's a fear of getting caught. There's adrenaline... um, serotonin... hormones and, um... endorphins... all running wild in your body. Your chemical balance will be thrown out of whack and you'll instantly fall in love."

"Don't be foolish, Tonya."

Tonya sensed that somewhere in Amber Faye's heart... in her mind... she had refused to see the light and face the fact. "I'm serious, Amber Faye. I've been through all of this. You're the one being foolish. You're gonna get hurt. You can't change him... no matter how hard you try."

"I want to help him. He's intelligent."

"Most psycho-paths are."

"I have faith in him."

"But faith dies in the light of evidence," Tonya said. "Have not you seen enough evidence? Hope... *FALSE* hope can be so cruel and hurtful when it comes to an end."

In her heart... she knew Tonya was right. But still... there, in that same heart there was a stern belief... a stern piece of hope that remained. And she couldn't let that faith die. "I don't know," Amber Faye said softly. "I have to go."

"No, wait Amber Faye. Promise me you'll let this one go. Promise me."

"I-I can't," Amber Faye stammered. "I have to go. Bye." Amber Faye softly hung up the phone, even as Tonya continued to speak. She reached over and grabbed her white teddy bear. Holding it to her chest, she began to sob softly. She was confused... helpless... broken and pulled. She believed that Lone Wolf was the master of an internal gift. A gift she knew deep down inside that she would never quite possess. But this didn't matter to her. She wanted to be alone with him. Alone in their own private world. A world where she could protect him from what ever haunts him.

* * * * * *

Lone Wolf parked the '64 Chevy just off the freeway exit. The three head-hunters exited the car and began to make their way on foot to the

Pleasant View Projects... located just blocks away. They moved eagerly across the shadowy fields like a pack of hungry wolves... searching for a kill... their well-oiled weapons glistening in the dim moon-light. Lone Wolf smiled slightly as he thought of himself as one of his warrior ancestors... a predatorial Native American stalking an ancient hunting ground for their elusive target.

"You sure you saw that nigga Ghost?" Murdah Man asked Insane in a hushed whisper. The question brought an abrupt end to Lone Wolf's day dream... making him realize the acute danger that accompanied this mission.

"I saw that nigga as we rode by," Insane answered. They stopped just across the street from the projects and scanned the area for any signs of danger. The projects looked strangely calm... as if forewarning of the dangers that awaited them within.

"Ya'll wait here," Insane told the two. "Imma go around the back way and see what'z crackin'." Pugnacious and warlike by nature... Insane had the reputation for his abrasiveness and psychotic behavior. At the young age of 15... his aggressiveness and ruthlessness had already marked him as a rising O.G. in the street's hierarchy. A hierarchy that is dominated by other relentless, cut-throat killers trying to reach their O.G. status. Due to his deranged mentality and his demented behavioral pattern... the people of the streets dubbed him Lil' Insane.

"Cuz, where is he going?" Lone Wolf asked.

"Ain't no telling," Murdah Man replied.

Just then, two dark figures emerged from around the buildings corner. The two head-hunters saw them simultaneously. Lone Wolf felt his heart rate began to pick up and he felt that familiar snake uncoiling in the pit of his stomach... cold and wet.

"Is that him?" Lone Wolf asked quickly. Murdah Man nodded his head. Lone Wolf fought desperately to succumb the panic that was gnawing away at him. But like any other time he committed a crime... he sought out the angry demons from within to give him strength... to give him courage. And like every other time... he felt that wicked venom flowing freely through his veins... filling him full of rage and hatred. He was now ready to launch an attack.

With their ski-masks on, Lone Wolf and Murdah Man slowly stood up and looked dead into the eyes of O.G. Ghost. Seeing them, O.G. Ghost stopped dead in his tracks. The second figure, completely oblivious to their lurch of unforeseen fate, continued to walk and talk. O.G. Ghost reached out and grabbed his partner by the shoulder. Getting his attention, his partner followed his gaze and saw the two masked assailants slowly making their way towards them.

Upon closer observation, Lone Wolf could tell the second figure was very young. Perhaps only eleven... maybe twelve. The boy's face clouded over, but O.G. Ghost simply ignored his fears. The boy gave off a small yelp as he turned to run, but his retreat was cut off by Insane, who was approaching from behind. The boy found himself looking into the dark barrels of two 9mm Glocks. He gave off another yelp as he threw his arms up defensively, taking a step backwards.

"What kind of fuckin' shit is this?" O.G. Ghost snarled at the three head-hunters. O.G. Ghost himself was a well built, ugly man with a permanent sneer on his face... and a mean look in his dark eyes. He looked at each of the hunters in turn. His eyes stopped on Insane. This is when both Lone Wolf and Murdah Man realized that Insane wasn't wearing his mask.

"Man, is you stupid?" Murdah Man asked Insane. But Insane merely grinned wickedly.

"Naw, he just suicidal," O.G. Ghost said, forcing a fiendish grin with no humor intended. In spite of his menacing predicament, his ugly face revealed an evil, yet proud defiance. The child, on the other hand, could not subdue the panic that continued to eat away at him.

"What?" Lone Wolf asked O.G. Ghost. "You ain't gonna reach for your pistol?"

"Man, this my hood," O.G. Ghost said provocatively. "What I need a pistol for?"

"For something like this," Lone Wolf said as he chuckled. Murdah Man and Insane did as well. Even O.G. Ghost parted his lips in an evil snarl. The child, however, kept a wary eye on the destructive barrel of the sawed-off shotgun that Murdah Man held in his face. He failed to see the irony and humor in what was said.

"Nigga, you know what the fuck we want," Insane barked at O.G. Ghost from behind. He pressed the barrel of his Glock against the back of his head to add weight to his words.

"It's obvious you wanna die," O.G. Ghost responded. Unconsciously, Murdah Man hands tightened around his shotgun in slow anger. Murdah Man was never one to take lightly to threats.

"We wanna know about the hit on Jaynes street tonight," Murdah Man said, teeth clenched, fighting back anger. "We know nothing happens without you knowing about it. So tell me who made that hit."

"Motha fucka, I don't know. And if I did, you think I'll tell you? You to think I'm scared?" He looked at him with a look of open defiance.

"You think this a joke?" Insane said spitting out the words, unable to subdue or disguise his own anger. "I'll blow ya motha fuckin' head off."

To Lone Wolf, it was evident from the statements and expression on O.G. Ghost's face that he could care less about the threats. But when he looked into the eyes of the child, his looks betrayed their guilt immediately. It was clear by his facial expression that they did have knowledge concerning the massacre on Jaynes Street. Murdah Man saw this as well.

"Tell me what you know," Murdah Man demanded. He grinned, wolfish and keen.

"We don't know nothing," the boy assured them, obviously trying to sound convincing, but not succeeding.

"Oh, you know something lil' nigga," Insane said as he placed both Glocks into his face.

"But I don't," the boy said softly. Then his eyes fell to the brace of pistols. He swallowed uncomfortably, then tried looking down at the floor.

"On your knees, lil' nigga," Insane instructed the boy. The child complied. "Now you gonna tell us what we wanna know."

Just then, Lone Wolf's cell phone began to ring. "What the...?" Murdah Man said as he shot an angry look towards Lone Wolf.

"Hello?" Lone Wolf said answering the phone.

"No the fuck he didn't answer that," Murdah Man said aloud. His jet-black eyes were flashing dangerously as he tried his very best to control his anger towards Lone Wolf.

"Lone Wolf, it's me, Amber Faye. I know it's late, but we really need to talk about tonight."

"Look, this is not a good time," Lone Wolf told Amber Faye.

"Hang up the fuckin' phone!" Murdah Man snapped, feeling his temper swell despite his wish to control it.

"Who was that?" Amber Faye asked.

Insane had a pistol in the boy's mouth. "You gonna tell me what I want to know, huh?" The boy tried desperately to nod his head, but with the cold, hard barrel in his mouth, he could barely manage any movement at all.

"Hang up the fuckin' phone!" Murdah Man barked again, his anger not quite at bay.

"You know who did it, huh?" Insane asked the child. The child nodded despite the deadly tube pressed against his tongue.

"We really need to talk," Amber Faye told Lone Wolf.

Insane removed the barrel from the boy's mouth and asked, "Who did it?"

"T-T-T-Roy," the boy stammered.

At the sound of the name, Lone Wolf felt an icy sensation consume his body. Like a ghost dredged from the grave... the vivid images of his brother's bloody body hitting the pavement haunted him. He felt his body go numb and his arms grew heavy. With the cell phone still in hand, his arm fell to his side.

"Hang up the phone!" Murdah Man growled.

"Who else?" Insane grilled the child.

"What's going on, Lone Wolf?" Amber Faye asked as the phone hung at his side.

Taking advantage of all the commotion, with a mighty lunge, O.G. Ghost launched towards Murdah Man before he could react. With the reflexes of a seasoned veteran, Insane raised his pistol and fired twice. The 9mm Glocks barked loudly, echoing throughout the surrounding buildings. Being in such a confined area, the roar of the pistol were amplified. Lone Wolf knew other members of the Pleasant View Mafia Gangsta'z (PMG) were sure to hear it and respond.

"Oh my God! Was that gun shots?!" Amber Faye asked frantically over the phone, but the phone still hung by his side.

The first bullet found it's way into O.G. Ghost back, the second ate away at his upper left shoulder. O.G. Ghost fell to the ground with a heavy thump. Then he gallantly rose up on his knees, but collapsed again. The blood was pumping from the two bullet wounds.

In the midst of he chaotic confusion, the three hunters hadn't realized that the child had slipped away. "They shot O.G.!" a voice in the dark shouted cynically, accompanied by the sound of running feet, moving in their direction.

"Fuck! Let's go!" Murdah Man roared. Both he and Lone Wolf turned to head for the safety of the shadowy field. Insane went to follow suit... but then stopped short. Turning back on the heap of human misery that laid before him, he smiled a smile that could only be described as the snarl of Satan. He then unloaded the remaining magazine into the back of O.G. Ghost.

Hearing the footsteps draw ever so near, he let out a hoarse wicked laughter, than turned to head in the direction of the '64 Chevy.

As B.G.'s and Y.G.'s surrounded O.G. Ghost, they saw that he was still breathing. Although the breaths were shallow, irregular, he was breathing, nonetheless. Fighting back the welling rage over seeing his O.G. in such agony, Lil' Kaloney dropped to his knees beside O.G. Ghost. "It was Lil' Insane from Hoova," Kaloney heard O.G. Ghost say in the merest whisper. "Kill him," was the last two words spoken before O.G. Ghost fell into the icy grips of death's eternal embrace.

As Lone Wolf and Murdah Man crossed the street, they heard the thunderous roar of Glocks. They knew instantly what Insane had done. From the beginning it should have been obvious to Lone Wolf what Insane's intentions were. He should of known the only reason Insane would allow them to see his face was because he intended on killing them from the jump.

Lone Wolf felt his heart grow heavy as he thought of this homicide. All his life... he had always been surrounded by death... surrounded by heartless killers. Even he, himself has lain at the very hands of death countless times... constantly living so close to death... walking amongst the graves. But no matter the truth of the surrounding influences or the predestined tragic path he would follow... Lone Wolf wasn't a killer.

As the two crossed the shadowy field, they looked back and saw the dark outline of Insane just as he crossed the street. Lone Wolf scanned the darkness for tell-tell signs of a pursuit, for he expected to see other inky shapes as well... but he saw none. Slowing their pace considerably, Lone Wolf couldn't help but to think of the name that was given by the child, T-Roy.

Could it be one and the same? he thought to himself. Could the same T-Roy that had left the carnage and destruction on Jaynes Street be the same T-Roy that had been inextricably woven into the fabric of his nightmares?

But it had only been eight years, he thought to himself. *I know my brother's life is worth more than eight years in prison,* he thought. Again, he felt the familiar tugging of his soul as his head swam in the heavy sea of haunting memories. He remembered that day vividly. On that fateful day, his life was over... and the end had began. He remembered how he looked down upon his older brother in shock and silent horror.

And how Kevin had stared back at him in a helpless dread.

Suddenly, a threatening sound shattered the quiet field... the sound of pistols erupting. As Lone Wolf turned around, he saw a finger of an orange flame spit from the barrel of Murdah Man's shot-gun... an orange flame that was slicing through the darkness. The strange ringing of distant church bells began to sound in his ears... the aftermath of the destructive shotgun blast being fired so close to his head.

Although he was unable to hear the thundering roar of the return fire, he could see their distinctive flares of blue-white sparks flashing on the other side of the field. Countless pistols belonging to PMG were firing on the three head-hunters. On instinct, Lone Wolf returned fire.

The .357 Desert Eagle bucked against his palm as he sent bullet after bullet in the direction of the brief flashes. To his right, the exploding boom of the 12 gauge continued to erupt as Murdah Man let off round after round. Even Insane, who was now less than five yards away returned fire with his second 9mm Glock. More bullets cut threw the air around them. Although Lone Wolf couldn't hear the hissing buzz of the near-miss bullets, he could feel the hot air brush against his face.

Slowly, the ringing in his ears subsides slightly, and he could hear the vengeful cries being yelled as the angry mob continued pursuit.

"Fuck! I'm out!" he heard Murdah Man yell as he continued to rack the shot gun anyway. The hollow click of the trigger being pulled somehow seemed more threatening than the bullets that rained so dangerously close around them.

"I can't see!" Lone Wolf heard Insane yell. The flashing sparks from Insane's 9mm sent little black dots dancing before his eyes, temporally blinding him.

Lone Wolf fired his pistol aimlessly, he felt a paralyzing fear slowly descend over his body as he listened to the empty click of his own pistol. Insane continued to return fire until his weapon was empty and the bolt had locked back. On the other side, the muzzle flashed both sparks and fire from pistols. The flames reaching out as if trying to touch one of the hunters. Of all the three, none of then had ammunition... the hunters now truly became the hunted.

The three made a mad dash to the side of the field that was completely wrapped in darkness. A small line of trees looked promising in providing a temporary sanctuary. Lone Wolf was first to reach the promise spot. He dropped to is knees behind some bushes, gasping for breath. The air burned his lungs and ripped at his throat. Tree roots stuck out from the ground... like bony fingers of a corpse, trying to drag him into the grave. The ringing in Lone Wolf's ear had finally faded completely, and he became aware of a new noise. The sounds of terrified screams... the sound of his name being called. "Please, Lord, please..." Lone Wolf begged, "Please not now."

Just then, Murdah Man skid to a halting stop beside Lone Wolf, followed by Insane. "Get down, nigga," Murdah Man instructed Insane in a harsh whisper. "And hang up that phone," Murdah Man demanded from Lone Wolf.

Realizing the frantic screams were coming from the phone, and not from the dead trapped in his head, made Lone Wolf want to burst out laughing from relief. But he dared not, for he knew that less than twenty yards away, there were people trying to claim his soul. So instead, he simply turned of the phone and stuck in his pocket.

They laid there for a long time. Lone Wolf bathed in the sweat of fear... listening to the night chitter and moan. They had heard foot steps running past their place of concealment no less than five minutes ago... but they knew that with orders to seek retribution for the loss of O.G. Ghost, the members of PMG would not give up the search until blood had been split.

Slowly lifting his head, Lone Wolf scanned the field, searching for any motion or indications that would alert him to danger. Murdah Man and

Insane did the same. They studied the projects off in the distance by street lights that filtered down through the trees. They saw many men, but they were no more than vague shapes. The trucks and cars in the parking lot were nothing more than black objects against the dark gray background.

"I don't see anyone, cuz," Murdah Man said breaking the silence.

"Me neither," Insane chimed in.

"You think we can make it back to the car?" Lone Wolf asked, trying his best to suppress his fears.

"Cuz, we ain't got no shells, and I know they are out there," Murdah Man said as his eyes continued to scan the surrounding area. He knew that in such darkness it would be all too easy to walk headlong into an ambush.

"Where's the punk police when you need um?" Insane said chuckling.

Although Lone Wolf knew it was a joke, he did find it odd that after so many gun shots the police still wasn't there.

"Nigga, Pleasant View's the pits," Murdah Man said, than continued as if reading his mind, "it's gonna be a few weeks before they even find out there was a murder up in there."

"Cuz, the longer we stay here, the better chance we have at getting caught, cuz," Lone Wolf said. "We gots to go."

"For real," Murdah Man replied.

"Ya'll ready?" Insane asked as he slowly stood up. "Let's go."

* * * * * *

After reaching the '64 Chevy, they all stood gasping for air. "Did you kill um?" Murdah Man asked Insane after he regained his strength.

"You know I was," Insane responded.

"I can't believe you answered that fuckin' phone," Murdah Man said to Lone Wolf with a wolfish grin on his face.

"That's some gangsta shit, for real," I said laughing. "That's the type of shit you see in movies or read in books."

"Who was it anyway?" Murdah Man asked.

"Oh girl from La Vista."

"If only she knew what just happened," Murdah Man chuckled.

"Come on, ya'll, lets ride out," Insane said as he stepped into the car.

DAY SIX

Lone Wolf laid sprawled out on the couch... unable to sleep. He tossed and turned as he thought of the name that the child had provided just hours ago. The thought of this T-Roy and the one of his past licked across his brain like the cold rasping tongue of the dead. His name alone resurrected ghosts from a graveyard of hostile and hurtful memories. His memory... alive with veritable fury... crying out for vengeance. A vivid recollection of his sinister face floating before his mind's eye. The malicious snarl he gave as his weapon bucked against his palm... sending murderous lead that ate away at his brother's flesh.

He felt the tightening of reactive anger in his chest as the explicit imagery clogged his mind.

He shook his head as if to throw the bitter memories from his mind.

Just then he heard a noise towards the back of the house. His head came up and he sat very still... listening for a repetition of the sound he had just heard. He knew he should be in the house alone, for Murdah Man had dropped him off before taking Insane home.

He pulled his Desert Eagle .357 from under the couch cushion. He got off the couch... circled around until he was pressed against the wall beside the hallway. The early morning sun had yet to rise, the entire house was still in darkness. He peered down the darkened hallway. Seeing Murdah Man's bedroom, he saw that the door was slightly a jarred on the other end.

Again, he heard the sound... the sound of two voices speaking in harsh whispers. He slowly walked towards the bedroom door... paying close attention to the dark opening of a second door... a door where deep shadows kept him from seeing inside. The hall was infused with shapes and shadows that were familiar to him in the light of day. But now...

drenched in darkness... the same shapes had taken on a hidden... more sinister meaning.

His mind raced as he thought of the possible dangers that may lay ahead. Burglars, robbers, murderers. Perhaps even one of Murdah Man's victims... a formidable foe who has returned on a mission of vengeance. *It could be nothing at all,* he told himself. But he found absolutely no comfort in the thought. Although only a hand full knew the dwelling place of Murdah Man, it was only a matter of time before people found out where he lived. Throughout his gang-banging life span, Murdah Man had created a number of victims, thus, a number of enemies, *for dead nigga'z tend to have homies,* as Insane had so delicately put it.

Now standing just outside the bedroom door, Lone Wolf clinched his weapon and held his breath... trying to listen to what's being said inside the room. But the voices turned to hushed whispers. Moving swiftly... he threw open the door and leveled his pistol; the empty room mocked him. He began to shake and tremble with the sudden release of adrenaline. His muscles jumped and twitched with useless energy, for this rush of adrenaline had nowhere to go. He felt sweat rolling down his face.

A faint stirring behind him started him violently... causing his heart to lurch violently in his chest. He reflexively spun around... aiming his .357 into the darkened hallway. But again... nothing was there... all was silent. He forced in a labored breath as he tried his best to control his shaking hands. Slowly he began to make his way to the living room.

Suddenly... behind him, from out of the darkness, a chilling cry erupted. A cry of pain... a cry of agony. The cries of the damned. He spun around aiming his pistol... but all was clear. To his right he heard a sinister snarl... to his left... wicked laughter. Spinning around... leveling his weapon... he saw with his eyes that he was alone. But he felt the cold presence of living evil all around him... the songs of the dead were everywhere.

Lone Wolf clapped his hands over his ears... but the screams... trapped within his head... mocked him at every turn. The hideous wail pierced threw the entire house... violently shaking the walls. He squeezed his eyes shut... for he knew the faces of death were coming soon. All at once he had the vertiginous sensation of the walls closing in on him.

Dropping to his knees... he was making faint whispering sounds in his throat as he tried to pray away the demons. The air burned his lungs and ripped at his throat as he tried praying out loud. The voices laughed at such a feeble attempt... but he refused to stop.

"Dear Heavenly Father..." he said with forced labor. "The fury of Satan..." but his words were cut short with the overpowering sensation of the walls ballooning outwards. Opening his eyes, he saw that the wall had expanded... the door frame stretched as if it was drawn on a rubber balloon. He watched as the walls collapsed in on him... then expand once again. The walls pulsated like a evil heart... growing in intensity before disintegrating into the infinite blackness of he abyss... not of space... but the blackness of time.

Then all at once... all was silent. Lone Wolf found himself laying on the floor in the hall... surrounded by evil silence. Drenched in sweat, he struggled to breath. His body ached with pain. Before paralyzing fear could repress his action, he got up and stumbled into the living room. Looking back towards the hall way, he felt his heart flutter. He was alone with nothing more than his thoughts... frightened by his own treacherous imagination. He had to get out of the house.

To the east, the heavens was beginning to lighten. Gray, baby blue, and pink were pushing back the darkness. Lone Wolf stood in the center of the yard with his head back and his eyes closed. The cool morning air felt like fire in his chest. Despite the burning in his lungs, the sweat that covered him dried and chilled him, but still he didn't move.

In the distance he heard the barking of a dog, the driving of cars, and the sound of singing birds... nothing more. He half expected to hear the voices of the dark... the evil laughter of the demonic forces, and the chants of the damned... but they didn't come.

Feeling the comforting weight of his .357 in his hand, he slowly opened his eyes. He knew a pistol would prove useless against the spirits of the dead... but it brought him a false sense of security, nevertheless.

With his head still tilted back, he saw the tiny stars burning in the heavens beyond the expanding sunrise... still struggling to shine. A single star in the heavens became the focal point of his vision... the focal point of his prayers... the focal point of his every wish.

"Star light, star bright..." he whispered softly into the cool air. "... the first star I see tonight." Lone Wolf knew he was being childish... foolish....

"I wish I may, I wish I might..." but he was desperate, he needed something to believe in. "... have the wish I wish tonight."

He felt so hopeless. "I wish..."

* * * * * *

Dawn had come and gone when Murdah Man pulled Lone Wolf's '64 Chevy into the driveway. The sun was slowly inching it's way towards the peek of noon. He found Lone Wolf sitting on the porch steps with his head in his hands... the pistol laying between his legs.

Stepping from the car, Murdah Man called out, "What'z up, cuz? Key didn't work?" But Lone Wolf didn't even stir. He simply sat in silence. Approaching Lone Wolf, the closer he got he came to realize that Lone Wolf's lips were moving... as if he were praying.

Stopping just in front of him, barely audible, Murdah Man could hear that Lone Wolf was singing in his Native tongue. In the past he has heard Lone Wolf both talking and chanting in the Ancient Lakota language... but each time it seemed strange; hearing this mystic language escaping the lips of such a gang-banging hoodlum. He asked Lone Wolf about it in the past. He told him that as a child he went to live with a Native American foster family. A family that had given him a home, taught him the culture and traditions of his ancestors. With this family he had learned the Lakota language and participated in many sacred ceremonies.

But despite all his efforts he had given to accept this new existence, Lone Wolf said he couldn't escape "Them." Murdah Man didn't know who "Them" were, nor did he ask. He did, on the other hand, learn that the family had gotten fed up with his thuggish ways and finally kicked him out.

"Now there you go with that 'hey-ya hey-ya' bull shit," Murdah Man snickered. A look of quick irritation flashed across Lone Wolf's face as he glanced at Murdah Man. Murdah Man went to say more, but Lone Wolf silenced him with a hard look. Although Murdah Man was an efficient killer, he knew he couldn't stand a chance when engaging in hand-to-hand combat with the well experienced Lone Wolf.

Being raised within the system, with the absent of pistols and other weapons, Lone Wolf had developed the deadly combination of speed and power efficiently. In almost every placement the system had placed him in, rather it was foster homes, group homes, mental hospitals, he was almost always the youngest. He had come to learn violence was the only way to protect himself... and he did so eagerly and skillfully. And being that the situation wasn't serious enough to involve weapons, Murdah Man decided to stand silently.

After the song was finished, Lone Wolf looked up at Murdah Man gravely. "We gotta get this nigga," he said softly.

"Who?"

"T-Roy." As he said the name, Murdah Man saw a flash of fury flicker across his brow.

"Psst, we gonna get our shit, cuz," Murdah Man replied.

"Naw, nigga, you don't understand," Lone Wolf said as he fought down the tremor of anger that was rising inside of him. "I know you heard about my brother."

"Yeah, I heard the story of Krump Dawg."

"That nigga that smoked him name was T-Roy. O.G. T-Roy from Murda 8," Lone Wolf said, his jaws clenching as he spoke.

After a brief second of thought, slowly the light danced in his eyes. "Ain't that the name that lil' nigga gave?" Lone Wolf nodded. "You think that maybe..." Murdah Man's voice trailed off. He watched as Lone Wolf's breathing quickened and his eyes turned strangely dark. "Why didn't you say something last night? Cuz, let's go get this fool," he told Lone Wolf.

Without further words being spoken, the two stepped into the '64 Chevy and pulled out of the drive way.

* * * * * *

As they slowly prowled and stalked the north side, the two sat in silence. With Murdah Man driving, Lone Wolf sat in the passenger's seat loading the two pistols and the sawed-off pump. His repression of fury was easily visible. After the weapons were fully loaded, he racked each one, putting a live round into each chamber. "This ain't enough," Lone Wolf said, his voice tight and barely audible.

"Whuz up, cuz?" Murdah Man asked.

"I said this ain't gonna cut it. From what we saw last night, that nigga got heat."

"You know what Lil' Wolf?" Murdah Man said slowly, as if deep in thought. "From what we saw, it had to be more than one person. They had to be deep in order to kill so many at once."

"What did you do with the K and the 1-7-four? If you didn't melt them down we can go get them motha fucka'z."

"Shit, I threw them in the Missouri River," Murdah Man said, his voice full of regret.

"We got the N's now. Let's go holler at Snook'ums to get some more straps," Lone Wolf said.

As Murdah Man took a left on Hamilton Street, he said, "You know what, cuz? We gotta gang of straps from those robberies. Do you think Snook'ums would trade?" Lone Wolf shrugged. "I mean, they some pretty nice pistols, huh. If not, we could slang them, huh?" Lone Wolf nodded his head.

* * * * * *

Murdah Man pulled into the driveway of Snook'ums home. Stepping past the yellow '73 Buick, they both saw that car's interior was ripped to shreds, the trunk was dented and slightly a jarred. "Cuz must be swervin', for real," Murdah Man said laughing.

As they approached the house, Murdah Man yelled out, "Ah Snook! Ah cuz!" He pounded on the front door once, then twice. "Let's go to the side," Murdah Man said as he stepped from the small porch.

As they turned the corner, a cool breeze swept across their path, tousling Lone Wolf's long, wavy hair.

"Cuz, why don't you get that braided? The way the wind hit you, that shit look gay," Murdah Man said laughing, completely oblivious to the fury that raged in Lone Wolf's heart.

In the next house over, a pit-bull barked fiercely at the two from behind a fence. It's short hair ridged down it's back. At first, it startled the two. But once Murdah Man saw that it was secured behind a well enforced fence, he began to mock the dog. And would have continued doing so if Lone Wolf wouldn't have forcefully pulled him away from his game.

"What the fuck?!" Murdah Man growled, fighting back welling rage over being snatched around so forcefully. He followed Lone Wolf's pointing finger. His anger was instantly replaced by confusion as he looked at the shattered door frame. As they drew closer, they saw the door leaning in... being held up by a single hinge. The top two hinges were completely destroyed. Another cool breeze floated at them from the northeast, and when they scented the air... they could smell the scent of rotting flesh. At once Lone Wolf knew what took place.

"Come on. Let's bounce," Lone Wolf said as he tugged on Murdah Man's shoulder.

"Nigga, what you talking about?" Murdah Man said, his confusion turning to excitement, his eyes glowing with dark amusement. "We abouts to raid this fool. Take all his shit."

"Naw, cuz. We gots to dip. Besides, you saw his car. Trust-n-believe, whoever smoked him didn't leave anything unturned. We gotta go before somebody sees us."

By any judgment of sanity, Murdah Man knew Lone Wolf was right. But still reluctant, he followed Lone Wolf back to the '64 Chevy.

As they backed out of the driveway, Murdah Man said, "We fucked, cuz. This was the only person I know who could get choppa'z and other heavy shit."

Lone Wolf knew Murdah Man was right. For the average street hoodlums, despite what the media say, it was extremely difficult for anyone to find and purchase assault rifles. One had to be either well connected to an arm's supplier, or have access to military equipment within the US Army. And in order to have such access, one would have to have rank within the military's hierarchy. Something the average street thug couldn't possibly possess.

"Stick'ums," Lone Wolf said quietly, more of a thought then a name.

"What?" Murdah Man asked.

"O.G. Stick'ums. Snook'ums older brother."

"Stick'ums?" Murdah Man said laughing. "Who the fuck named these nigga'z? Anyway, what about him?"

"It was Stick'ums who put Snook'ums on. They got another brother named Snipes. But cuz is a lot younger. He don't get down. He's trying play pro-football," Lone Wolf replied.

"Where can we find Stick'ums?" Murdah Man asked. Lone Wolf shrugged his shoulders and shook his head.

"I know Snipes from the block. He's from my hood," Lone Wolf said. "I know cuz can get a hold of him. Just head over to 37th and Grand. One of my O.G.'s gotta know where Snipes live."

After a moment of silence, Murdah Man scoffed. "Stick'ums," he said as he shook his head.

"Yeah. Stick'ums. When Snook'ums told me about him, he said that Stick'ums got his name from bein' a stick up artist back in the 70's. And Snook'ums said he got his name in Vietnam. Say he got 18 confirmed kills."

"18," Murdah Man scoffed again. "Nigga, I had 18 bodies before I was 13."

Any other time Lone Wolf would have laughed and mocked such foolishness. Although Murdah Man had indeed slain a number of people, he knew that the number was far from 18. He highly doubt if it was close to 8. Lone Wolf didn't respond to the statement because they had more important issues to discuss.

* * * * * *

The sinking of the sun had cast long shadows over the streets of Omaha. Appearing in the eastern sky was a pale sliver of moon. To the west... the sky was still laced with brilliant pinks and purples. The two were headed towards the residence of Stick'ums.

Lone Wolf could still feel the twitching churns of anger stirring in his stomach. The anger of being neglected and rejected by his own hood... his own friends... by the same men he committed crimes with side by side.

He could easily recall how less than an hour ago he was looked upon with disdain as he and Murdah Man stepped from the '64 Chevy. How as he made it up the driveway, his homeboys fixed him with mean mugs and cold stares. The members of Tré Seven sat on the porch, stood on the lawn, lingered in the driveway... and Lone Wolf could feel their eyes on him as he walked into the house. He was angrily aware that he was under mean and silent scrutiny by the members of Tré Seven.

Inside, Lone Wolf felt eyes on him from all around the smoky room. But unlike the members who dawdled outside, those inside didn't give out right hard stares; but more like sideways glances when he wasn't looking. These men were the same men who once protected him... whom he once protected. The same men who once fought side by side with against any opposition who dared opposed 37th Street. But now, these same men looked upon him with contempt... as if wondering what he was doing here.

Never in his life had Lone Wolf felt so alien to an environment. Not even when he was in the system, surrounded by racist white people.

"Oh, so now you wanna come back to the block," Lone Wolf recalled one of his O.G.'s saying to him. It was the O.G. who taught him the art of money laundering, but now he spoke down on Lone Wolf with rejection and great hostility. "You wanna make moves with this nigga, stack N's and shit. What the fuck you want with Tré Seven?"

Lone Wolf could recall how he looked over at Murdah Man. He could see that in his eyes he wanted desperately to reach for his pistol. He could tell that Murdah Man was fighting this powerful urge to lash out.

"This still Tré Seven," Lone Wolf said harshly, pushing aside the rising fear. "I've put in more work than any of the nigga'z up in this motha fucka." Lone Wolf spoke with more venom than he realized. He instantly felt the tension escalate, and he knew he was walking a thin line.

"Look, O.G., cuz," Lone Wolf said in a softer tone. "O.G. Snook'ums gone. I'm looking for Snipes. That's it, cuz."

Lone Wolf recalled how as they were leaving, Flex, a Y.G. who stared at them the entire time with impolite curiosity, approached them from the porch. "You making 40th AVE money, huh? You flipping?" he asked Lone Wolf.

At any other time, Lone Wolf would have completely lost his temper at such vitriolic accusing words... lashing out in furious anger... leaving him face down in a puddle of blood. Yet now... off balance from the whole ordeal... he could only look up defenselessly at Flex's infuriated expression.

Lone Wolf shook away the memory, irritated with himself for being so sensitive. *I shoulda whooped that nigga'z ass,* he thought to himself. *Naw, if I did, both me and Murdah Man would be dead.* But such revelations didn't ease the anger that stirred in him.

He then thought of Snipes and how indifferent he behaved at the news of his brother's death. How Snipes reluctantly gave the two directions to the house of Stick'ums. How he went on about his day with little regard to the loss of a brother.

The last rays of the sun sank below the horizon as Murdah Man pulled the '64 Chevy to the curb. As the two stepped from the car, Lone Wolf looked towards the darkened heavens, amazed at how swiftly time flies.

"We gonna get this fool. Don't even trip," Murdah Man assured him, as if knowing what Lone Wolf was going to think of next.

The two entered the screened in porch. The porch was carpeted... complete with a short couch... two Lay-Z boys, and giant house plants. Lone Wolf was impressed with the lay out; it was like an extra living room outside the house.

Just as Murdah Man went to knock on the door, the two froze in paralyzing fear as they heard the cocking of a pistol.

"You ready to die?" a voice called from behind. The voice was low... deep... guttural. With a pistol resting against his spine, Lone Wolf had already began to close his eyes... awaiting the deadly explosion when Murdah Man said, "Your little brother, Snipes, sent us." The anger was thick in his voice.

"Snipes?" Stick'ums grunted. "What for?"

"It's about Snook'ums," Lone Wolf said softly... trying to line his voice with tenderness and regret. But the fear was replaced by anger, the evidence was clear in his voice. "He's dead. Me and cuz found him this afternoon." Lone Wolf felt the pistol lift from his spine.

Stick'ums circled around them, them looked at them with a scrutinizing glance... giving the two a thorough over hauling. For a fraction, the gunman glared at Lone Wolf... hatred twisted the old man's face. He then looked at Murdah Man with his hard critical eyes. Murdah Man's face was a mask of hatred as well... but he didn't move nor speak. Lone Wolf wondered if his own face carried that same look of hatred. The look that all tenets of the ghetto seem to have.

It seem as though Stick'ums was about to speak. His lips stirred soundlessly as he tightened his grip on the pistol. His expression tautly anxious. "Did he send you?" the old man asked.

"What?" Lone Wolf asked, startled. "Who?"

"Snook'ums? Did Snook'ums send you?" he asked again.

"He said the nigga'z dead," Murdah Man grimaced with irritation.

"Is that right, young blood? My little brotha'z dead, huh? That's sad," Stick'ums replied, but without much conviction. He paused... looking at Lone Wolf with cold contempt, Stick'ums said, "That's too bad."

* * * * *

Inside the house, there were rich pools of light cast by floor lamps. But they were overshadowed by the dingy look and smell of the old couches. The old carpet was the same dirty green color as the furniture. Both Lone Wolf and Murdah Man sat on the long couch, Stick'ums sat across from them in a reclining chair. Crossing his legs the way a woman would, the old man sat the pistol on his lap and glared at the two intruders.

Murdah Man was the fist to speak. "It seems motha fucka'z don't even care Snook'ums got smoked."

"Dig this, young blood," the old man spoke in his deep, raspy voice. "That cat stiffed me one too many times, ya dig? Together, boo-coo N's was bein' dropped. The cat got grid than decided to split. Left me with squat, ya dig?"

"What the fuck he just say?" Murdah Man asked, looking over at Lone Wolf. Lone Wolf shrugged his shoulders. A chuckle sounded deeply in the old man's chest.

"It's like this, young blood, we was in business together. Then he back-stabbed me when I was nothing but righteous, ya dig?"

"That's why we're here now," Lone Wolf said. "We don't know any body else who can get a hold of the type of stuff he could. And we know it was you who put him on.

Stick'ums looked a Lone Wolf. "What you know about straps?" he asked Lone Wolf.

"A few years back, Snook'ums took me under his wing. Before he started smoking that pipe," Lone Wolf answered. It was hard for him to read the facial expression of Stick'ums. The old man had a thick frowning crease across his brow. His twisted face very much resembling a pit bull. Stick'ums picked the revolver up from his lap. Slowly he un-chambered all six rounds, then flipped the cylinder shut with a flick of his wrist. Leaning towards Lone Wolf, he handed him the weapon and asked what type of pistol it was. Taking control of the weapon, Lone Wolf briefly turned it over in his hand and instantly handed it back.

"It's a Colt," Lone Wolf replied.

"No shit. It says Colt right on the side. But what kind of Colt?" Stick'ums asked as he tried handing the weapon back to Lone Wolf. But Lone Wolf held up his hand, declining the pistol and said;

"If I had to guess, I say Colt .44 Anaconda."

"Why"

"The diamond on the handle tells me it's part of the Cold Diamond Back Series. It's too small to be a .45 Python, too big to be a .38 Diamond Back. So my guess is it;s an Anaconda."

Stick'ums slowly got to his feet with a low grunt. Slowly he made his way to the closet located on the opposite side of the room. "What about this?" he asked as he opened the door.

"God damn, cuz!" Murdah Man shouted with wicked delight, "Now that's a motha fuckin' choppa, cuz!" he said as he excitedly rapped on Lone Wolf's leg. Lone Wolf tried to silence him with a hard look, but the sight of such heavy weaponry brought out the inner child in Murdah Man.

"What's this?" Stick'ums asked Lone Wolf.

"M-60," he said as he got up and walked to where Stick'ums stood. The weapon was placed on two hooks embedded within the door. Beside the weapon hung a tripod to it's left, and to it's right, at least a thousand rounds of ammunition. All of which were placed neatly into the chain jacket that fed the murderous weapon.

Stick'ums grunted at the answer then disappeared into the darkness of the closet. Murdah Man stood beside Lone Wolf as Stick'ums tugged at the string of an overhead light. The bright light illuminated the walk-in closet, revealing two shelves packed with an assortment of assault rifles. Entering the closet, Murdah Man's eyes beamed with delight as Lone Wolf examined the weapons.

Lone Wolf could tell many of them were American made... more than likely obtained from a black-market arms dealer connected to the US army. But he also recognized some of the exotic weapons as well. Weapons from Brazil... Argentina, and Europe. And although the weapons were well groomed and in mint-condition, he realized that the few rifles he could identify were greatly out-dated. Lone Wolf ran his fingers across the M-1... the M-14... the Argentina FMK-3 sub-machine guns... a Chinese Type-50 and an Israeli Armalite. Lone Wolf wondered where in the Mid West could one find ammunition for such relics?

"This is my collection," Stick'ums said in his raspy voice. "They're only for show," he continued as if he were reading Lone Wolf's mind.

"Yeah. It's a nice collection. But we need something we can use," Lone Wolf said as he studied the MAT-49 sub-machine Uzi.

"Snook'ums stole my collection. That summa bitch!" Stick'ums yelled, shouting the name in a paroxysm of demented fury. "But if he's pushing up daises like you claim, then I think we can help each other, young blood. Give me a couple of dayz."

DAY SEVEN

Lone Wolf awoke from a thin depression of sleep. He laid upon the couch with his eyes wide open... staring into the soft darkness of the living room... awaiting the rising of the sun. For what purpose? He really didn't know. He knew Murdah Man would remain asleep well into the noon hours. Until then, he was left alone with his own thoughts... something he could not bare for too long.   Reaching over, he grabbed his pager from the coffee table. It read 4:43 AM. Replacing the pager in it's place, he laid back and closed his eyes... searching for sleep. But it wouldn't come.

In times like these, he found it necessary to keep his mind focused on positive issues. His favorite... he imaged himself as this great and mighty eagle... soaring in the heavens. Floating on the wind with his powerful wings stretched... motionless... soaring on the icy currents of celestial bliss.

But like always, such peaceful images would become tainted by self-loathing sorrow. He would began to see himself as this proud and mighty eagle drifting form one place to another... constantly seeking something vague and obscure... something he never seems to find.

Again... an old sorrow embraces him. And because of this sorrow... deep within his body, he felt the knotting heat of anger as the spirits from within mocked him. He knew the feelings well and it enraged him further that he couldn't combat it. It grew and grew until the demonic forces from within seized control and forced him to act out with great fury and murderous hostility. And then the rejoicing of the wicked spirits would be alleviated by the evil forces that sought to punish and break his will. The forces of loathing and self-hatred. Forced that generated anger and rage... emotions that feed the evil spirits within. A vicious cycle of emotional turmoil that left Lone Wolf beaten... without hope.

"Fuck!" Lone Wolf roared as he jumped to his feet. Snatching his possessions and his car key from the table, he made his way to the door. Now out in the cool morning air, he inhaled deeply before making his way to the '64 Chevy parked in the driveway. Once inside, he flipped the engine then backed out onto the street. As he switched gears from reverse to drive, he shook his head helplessly, then drove, heading south, not really knowing where he was headed.

His thoughts turned to the incident that took place in Pleasant View Projects. The name T-Roy again pledged his mind. He knew that in time he would have to resolve this constant nagging. But first he would need weapons... heavy weaponry judging from the bloody carnage he had witnessed.

With this his mind turned to Stick'ums. Lone Wolf knew Stick'ums needed time to re-establish new connections with old suppliers... but Lone Wolf's patients were wearing dangerously thin. He needed to know if the two T-Roy's were one and the same.

Abruptly, a fragment of his re-occurring nightmare floated briefly into consciousness. The thought filled him with a new... more restless anger as his foot pushed harder on the accelerator. The speedometer read 63 miles per hour. He was traveling in a 35 miles an hour zone. On both sides of him, the houses that shot by stood dead silent... the streets were still deserted due to the early morning hour. He slowed the car, nevertheless. He knew that behind any bush there could be a police squad car lurking in ambush. The last thing he needed was to be pulled over due to his foolishness... especially being that he was on the run and had a fully loaded pistol on his persons.

He was approaching the southern boarder of downtown Omaha before he realized where he was going. It was both strange and funny to Lone Wolf how his mind and body kept such information from his consciousness. Consciously, he had known only that he needed to get out of the house in hopes of escaping his thoughts. Foolish, he knows. But the information that his mind, and perhaps his heart, hid from him was that he needed Amber Faye... and this is where he was headed.

* * * * * *

The intercom buzzed long and loud within the early morning darkness. Upon hearing it, Amber Faye rolled over in her bed to see the bright digital clock on her night stand. It read 5:16. The intercom sounded again, this time longer. She scoffed at such rudeness as she passed slowly through the dim silence of the living room.

"Yes," she said into the intercom, her voice still heavy with sleep. "Who is it?"

"Lone Wolf." His voice sounded small in the speaker. But hearing his voice instantly cleared away the thick fog of sleepiness. She tapped the buzzer that unlocks the lobby door. In a hast she quickly made her way to the bedroom. Switching on the light, she had to shield her eyes against it.

Being that she lived on the third floor, she knew her time was limited, that he would be at the door any second. Without allowing her eyes to fully adjust to the brightness, she began to splash water on her face. After drying her face, she than began to pick at her hair, fluffing it in parts, trying to flatten it in others. Looking down at her night gown, she began to feel immature. Her night gown was nothing more than a white t-shirt that read "I 'heart' U" in bold red letters. The red short sleeves were laced with tiny white hearts. Instantly, she wanted to change, but her attention was drawn towards the knock at the door. "Oh, crap," she said as she made her way to the door, tugging on her t-shirt as she went.

Upon opening the door, she found the large man looming before her... looking as rough and thuggish as ever. His dark, pin-striped Polo shirt was un-tucked, hanging over a pair of baggy black jeans. His boots were untied and his long wavy hair was untamed. Despite the fact that there was something about him that spoke of pure danger, he had that kind of sad... broken handsomeness one reads about in fictional romance novels. A certain, ephemeral quality, that could never exist in reality. But here it was... standing before her.

"Come in," she said softly. After he entered, she closed and locked the door than lead him by the hand into the living room. She noticed that his hand felt unusually cold to the touch. Almost as if she was leading a walking corpse instead of a living being. *Even in the summer it can get cold outside,* she tried to justify to herself. After switching on the living room lamps she stood in front of him, studying his face. He did indeed look desperately sad. Yet, somehow, his eyes remained hardened.

"Lone Wolf, what's wrong?" she whispered. The sadness that lined his face quickly disappeared and was replaced by thin lines of anger. He didn't speak. Instead, he stared at her with a kind of almost contempt. She lowered her big brown eyes for a moment... and then... looking back up at him said, "You are so weird." She really didn't know what to expect with such a statement... but was pleasantly surprised when his expression softened. His lips even threatened to smile.

"Nothing's wrong," he mumbled.

"Are you hungry?" He shook his head. "Are you tired? Would you like to rest?" Again he shook his head. She wondered what it was that he wanted. Still holding his hand, she felt his eyes on her as she looked around the room. "Well, what can I offer you?" she asked, but he remained silent. She could feel a warm and pleasant sensation slowly spreading through her body. She felt the butterflies stirring inside. But they instantly dissolved as she thought about their last conversation over the phone. She remembered hearing many gun shots. First off in the distance... but then more shots rang out near the phone. *Were they coming from Lone Wolf?* she asked herself... afraid of the answer. But she had know.

"Lone Wolf?" she said as she lead him to the couch. Now sitting, she gently took both his hands in hers. "That night on the phone, after our date, I know I heard gun shots." She searched his body language for any tell-tell signs of nervousness... of perhaps even regret. There were none. "Is that what they were, Lone Wolf?"

After a brief pause, he said, "Gun shots? Me and my homie was just playing video games."

She knew he was lying. But for some strange reason, this did not bother her. All she wanted to know is whether or not he was responsible for any of the shooting. She recalled how they met. How the pistol fell from his hand as he slipped into unconsciousness. Who was he running from then? She remembered how as he slept that first day, how she picked up the pistol to study it. She had never held a pistol before. She was surprised at how heavy it was... how her small hands trembled as she held it... afraid it may go off by accident. She knew north Omaha could indeed be a dangerous environment... but did he really need to carry a fully loaded weapon? Or was he only adding to the problem?

"Do you have a gun on you now?" she asked.

"No," Lone Wolf lied. "What I need a strap for in Honky Land?" he teased.

Amber Faye squinched her nose at him. "You know there are African Americans here in La Vista, too," she replied.

"'African Americans?' Nigga, please."

"Yes, there are, Mr. Lone Wolf."

"So where these nigga'z at?" he continued to tease, although it was done with a straight face.

"Not only am I part Mayan, I'm of African descent, too. And I live out here."

"You part Mayan? A 'Mexican?' I didn't know that."

"My real name is Linda Perez. Linda means 'pretty' in Spanish. Amber Faye is simply a pseudonym for my poetry," she said as she twirled her fingers in the palm of his hand.

"Really? I didn't know any of this. Either way, you still can pass as white, so to me you're a white girl," he said as he giggled a little. "I'm not callin' you Linda. Cos you're really not that pretty. Well, maybe a little, for a white girl. I think they call ya'll Oreo's. Colored on the outside, white on the inside."

Amber Faye pouted at the remark, sticking out her lower lip defiantly. The face that she made reminded Lone Wolf of Dr. Doolittle's 'Who Ville'. He smiled to himself inwardly... for with her protruding face... she would fit in nicely.

"I'm not an Oreo," she said. Then her smile became playful, "But I am just as yummy."

Again Lone Wolf looked as if he wanted to smile... there was a slight turn in the corner of his lips. At that moment his heart softened... against his will.

"But you know what? I knew you had some black in you. That's the only thing that would explain that pretty ass hair of yours." He then lapsed into a strong silence... quietly looking over the exquisite beauty that is Amber Faye... the exquisite beauty that is Linda.

"I had fun with you last night." Lone Wolf finally said. "Lover's Lane was just as beautiful as you said it would be."

"That wasn't last night, Lone Wolf," she said laughing. "That was two days ago."

"You know, I wouldn't mind going back with you," he said matter-of-factually.

"That'll be great. But this time can we go into the Old Market?" she asked excitedly.

"A-ight, coo."

Then she looked at him mischievously and said, "We can go see some drag queens."

Lone Wolf couldn't suppress a laugh. As he laughed, she could sense something different in him now, too. Something strange. Almost like some current of electricity flowing between their entwined hand. A current that had not been present before. Or perhaps it had been... but had for some reason laid dormant.

"Lone Wolf?" she said softly as she looked up at him. The way she said his name tugged at his heart... sending a tingle of raw pleasure throughout his body into his manhood. Looking into his eyes, she too felt the stir inside. A tremor raced down her arms and legs as she reached out and touched his face. "Do you want to be with me?" she asked as she tenderly stroked his cheek.

At the question, Lone Wolf felt himself flinch. Something deep within his heart began to flutter... a feeling that he had never experienced before. He felt somewhat disturbed by this strange effect she was having on him. The sensation began to grow. Looking into the murky depths of his own heart... he looked her in her eyes and replied honestly, "Amber Faye, there's a lot of stuff about me you don't know. I ain't well. Some may say I'm a little sick in the head."

She looked at him for a moment. Then her lips parted into a slow smile. The doubtfulness that lurked in his eyes was evident that she could change him, for if he questioned it, she know there was room for belief.

Leaning forward, in a silky voice, she asked, "how about for just now?"

Lifting up from the couch, Lone Wolf loomed over her. Amber Faye looked up at him in confusion. Lone Wolf ignored it. Placing a hand around her neck, he forcefully shoved her back onto the couch. The confusion that had once been in Amber Faye's eyes turned to raw fear.

"What are you doing?" she asked, her voice brittle. He straddled her and held her down by the shoulders. "Stop it! Get off of me!" she demanded as she tried to kick free. Again her cries fell onto def ears. Instead, he reached into her long, curly hair, grabbing a fist full, he began to pull. The softness of her neck was then exposed. He leaned over and began to gnaw at the softness... feeling the silken flesh in between clenched teeth.

"Stop it!" she wailed. "You're hurting me!"

The ring of sincerity in her quivering voice caused him to hesitate. He rocked back and looked into her face. Her eyes were moisten... freshly fallen tears-stains ran out the corner of her eyes. As he looked over her, she whimpered and cried. The sounds of her whimpers were like white-hot needles piercing at his heart.

"You said you wanted to be with me." He tried to sound apologetic... but it came out demanding... accusing. She flinched at his words. It was at that point did he truly realize that his voice was so stringent... so devoid of warmth; that it was a harsh, sterile voice of a hoodlum that had lost all touch with the sensitivity of humanity. The by-product of being raised amongst the enemies of the state.

An unusual surge of guilt touched his heart as he looked down at Amber Faye. She hid her face from him... her slender shoulders convulsing from crying. He reached out to touch her... to hold her... to comfort her... but she pulled back in justified terror.

"I'm sorry," Lone Wolf said softly. But again, he could sense that his voice was devoid of compassion. In frustration, more at his own insensitivity, Lone Wolf turned from her and made his way to the front door. He gave her one last worrisome look before he left out the door. Her shoulders continued to shutter.

As Amber Faye heard the door opening, she looked up... her face was wet with tears. Just as he crossed the thresh hold, she tried to call out to him... but the words were frozen in her throat... clogged by fear. It wasn't until after the door was closed did she manage to mutter, "Don't go, Lone Wolf. I understand."

* * * * * *

Lone Wolf sat behind the wheel to his '64 Chevy, tensed and remorseful for his foolish display of senseless transgression. He flipped the engine and backed out of the parking space. Images of her tear-filled eyes played his mind... the whimpers of helpless terror that escaped from her throat echoed in his ears. The feelings of shame and self-disgust took a hold of him completely as he pulled from the lot.

Heading north, he cursed himself again for his stupidity. He couldn't shake this overpowering feeling of callus brutality. For eight torturous years, Lone Wolf had known nothing but hell. A harsh and brutal existence that he had grown to somewhat accept. It wasn't until Amber Faye, this Linda, came along did he realize that there was a possibility of happiness for him. He knew this Linda had the power to employ love and overcome the hell created by his evil and wicked ways, and she would love him to the bitter end, and back again as he continued to live his life in sin. He knew that this woman could have rescued him from the evil clutches of his own character.

Again, the sight of her crying flashed before his mind's eye. At the thought, he felt the wet softness of a single tear as it slowly rolled down his cheek. He felt his heart moving into the realms of unfamiliar emotions... emotions that had been forgotten long ago.

Then the fury came... breaking his heart loose from the enchanting emotions that was so strange to him. The recognizable and comforting fury coursed his veins like a hot current of acid. He had became use to rage and fury... just as much as he became well acquainted with apprehension and fear. He knew in a flash of angry revelation that he could never return to Amber Faye.

For his stupidity he balled a fist and smashed it into his own face. Stars danced before his eyes as he delivered another powerful blow to his eye. Driven by shame... he smashed his fist into his face until he felt the warmth of blood flowing from his nose. He could taste it in his mouth... and this brought him some comfort.

"Just as well. Fuck that bitch," he growled to himself as he instantly transformed the self pity onto Amber Faye. "What the fuck I need her for?" he tried to reassure himself... but the war that raged in his heart held on firmly to hope.

* * * * * *

As Lone Wolf pulled onto the street of which Murdah Man lived, he instantly spotted the '97 Lexus parked in the drive way. He looked at his pager, the time read 7:13AM. *She's early,* he thought to himself. Pulling up to the curb in front of the house, he stepped from the car and began to make his way to the door. Just as he reached for the knob, the door came open. Standing in front of him was Lady. Her face lit up in joyful delight and her eyes danced.

"Hey sweetie!" she said joyously as she stepped from the house. She stopped just short of Lone Wolf, shocked at the swollenness and redness of his face. "Oh my God, Lone Wolf! What happened to you?" she asked as she went to touch his face... but stopped instantly. She looked up at him... debating rather or not she should. She looked into his eyes, they were black... distant... so she decided against it. "What happened to you, Lone Wolf?" she asked with what seemed to be a genuine look of fondness in her eyes.

Then she let off a little chuckle. "Both you and Marcus are all beat up, face swollen and eyes black. What the hell do ya'll be getting into?" she asked as she giggled.

Lady was dressed exquisitely... elegantly. Her tight fitting Armani dress hugged her gentle curves. A large oval opening, resembling a giant tear drop, revealing her back from her neck to her waist; her ebony skin glimmering tastefully. Her black suede open toe high-heels left her brightly polished nails visible. He allowed his eyes to run along her curving hips slowly.

She knew he wasn't going to tell her anything... so she thought it best to let well enough alone. "You know you can come by anytime," she said in a satin tone, trying to change the subject. Her luminous brown eyes promising the delights that could be his.

Lone Wolf rested his eyes on hers. Lady was indeed a gorgeous woman, but the fleshly desires of her beauty and lust impelling features no longer held his fascinating interests. Now, instead of pure lust, when he looks into her eyes, he now only feels contempt. He wondered why this was.

"I'll be there tonight, a-ight?" Lone Wolf lied.

"I'll be ready. You take care of yourself, okay, Lone Wolf?" she said as she raised her hand to caress his face, her intricate diamond signet ring caught the early morning sun, gleaming and glistening as she stroked his face. When she turned to walk to her car, Lone Wolf didn't even turn to watch the enticing sway of her hips, he no longer found it alluring. Instead, he headed for the house.

Just as he was about to cross the threshold, Murdah Man emerged. "Nigga, you seem to be always disappearing." Lone Wolf grunted in answer. "Lady's about to take me to get my new ride, cuz. It's time to floss," he said as looked at Lone Wolf. "Damn, nigga, what the hell happened to you? Who whooped your ass?" Murdah Man said when he looked into the face of Lone Wolf.

"I did it to myself," he answered bluntly.

"You know what, I can believe that," he said as headed towards the Lexus. Looking back, he said, "Then we gonna finish that game, know what I'm saying?"

At once, Lone Wolf knew he was speaking on the manhunt for T-Roy, a hunt that hadn't strayed too far from his forethought.

"We gonna get this fool, trust 'n believe, cuz," Murdah Man said as he continued make his way to the Lexus. "Just hold ya-self together."

He watched as the Lexus backed out from the driveway, then disappeared in the distance. Again, Lone Wolf was alone with only his thoughts. "Fuck," he growled to himself.

Just as he was entering the empty house, his cell phone rang. "Yeah, what'z up?" he answered.

"It's me, young blood," the low and raspy voice responded. "Come holla at me," he said before he hung up.

Lone Wolf stood in the silence of the living room. He wondered if it was possible that Stick'ums had re-established himself so quickly. Or could it be possible that he had already been turned down for some unexplained reason? Whatever the situation may be, he was more that willing to go. Anything that served to occupy his mind from the destructive nature of his own thoughts would be just fine with him. He didn't want to think of T-Roy... or Amber Faye... or Kevin... or his mother. He only wanted to think of nothing but peaceful thoughts. As irony has it, this peace of mind comes from the purchasing of weapons. Lone Wolf smiled to himself as he stepped from the house.

The old man seemed excited when he opened the door. "Young blood," he smiled in greetings as he ushered Lone Wolf into the house. His pit-bullish face took on an odd contorted shape when he smiled.

"Ya face, should I ask?" the old man questioned. When Lone Wolf didn't respond, he continued with his train of thought. "I was on this shit all night last night, ya dig?" he told Lone Wolf as they entered the dining room. "From what the mugs was telling me, Ol' Snook'ums was basing and all that bull-jive, coming up short on the duckets. If Ol' Snook'ums wouldn't of cashed in, they would of snooked um, ya dig? So they was more then happy when Ol' Stick'ums came around."

After saying this, Stick'ums held up a hand, signaling Lone Wolf to wait, then he disappeared around a door frame. Within seconds, he emerged carrying an assault rifle in each hand. After setting them on the dinning room table, he shoved them in front of Lone Wolf. Lone Wolf instantly recognized the AK-47, the second took a little studying before he could recall it's model.

"Check game, ol' school," Lone Wolf said as he toyed with the second weapon, "We can't do shit with an Armalite. Something like this would have ATF all on our asses."

"And a AK wouldn't?" the old man accused.

"Psst, you can get AK's anywhere. For this Armalite, you need direct ties with the Middle East." The AK was indeed the most popular assault rifle amongst organized street gangs. Although it is extremely difficult for the average street hood to possess any type of heavy fire power, the few that did have assess to such weapons could always find an AK at a relatively cheap price. These weapons are used all across the globe... therefore to trace it's source of origins would be next to impossible. Where an Armalite on the other hand, they are rarely, if ever used, in America. And the distinctive mark of this weapon would attract the attention of not only the ATF and the FBI, but of the CIA as well.

"Don't sweat it, young blood. These were given to me. Kindda like a appreciation gift. Tell me what you need and I'll have it in three days. *If*, of course, you have the duckets." As he said this, he took a La Finca Corona from his shirt pocket. After biting off the end, he lit it, then inhaled deeply, forcing the potent smoke deep into his lungs. Lone Wolf wrinkled his nose at it's disgusting smell.

"Whatever's needed, huh?" Lone Wolf asked. The old man nodded his head. "You know, every since them South Family nigga'z ate up that punk police with them choppa'z, every nigga from every hood trying get they hands on some heat."

"I know, young blood," the old man responded.

"Together we can stack chips, if you can get it like that." The old man smiled in response. "Psst, let's do the damn thing."

In less than a half an hour, Lone Wolf had compiled a list of weapons. Stick'ums looked over the list with admiring approval. "But you know what? I never did understand why ya'll young cats use shot-guns. Especially when you saw them off. If it ain't at point blank range, the sawed-off pump is useless."

"It's more of an intimidation thing," Lone Wolf said as he played with the AK-47 that sat in front of him. "It's meant to scare people more than anything."

"Yeah, ain't nothing more scarier than be-bees bouncing off you," Stick'ums said, making no effort to conceal the sarcasm in his voice. "But you know, young blood, all these weapons gonna cost a pretty penny, ya dig?"

"Psst, I got this, understood?"

"If you say so," the old man said as he stuck the list in his pocket.

"Why don't you let me take this off your hands?" Lone Wolf said, referring to the AK.

"You got the N's?" Stick'ums asked. Lone Wolf nodded his head. "On you?" Lone Wolf nodded again then pulled a large sum of currency from his pocket. "Then yeah."

"Yesterday, I saw a Chinese Type-50 in your closet. What you want for that?"

"Oh young blood, I can't sell that. I got my first body in Nam with that. Took it straight outta the Chinks hands and killed him with his own weapon," Stick'ums said smiling, reminiscing about his days spent fighting in the Vietnam War. "After that, I dumped my M-16 and rolled with that."

"What about the M-16 that's in there?"

"The M-16, huh?" Stick'ums grunted. "You know most of my sticks are show guns, right? It just so happens that you picked the one that isn't. I guess I can let that go," he said as he re-lit the cigar that had went out long ago. Almost instantly Lone Wolf was hit with another wave of nauseating pains to his stomach. He couldn't stand the smell of the cigar.

"Three days, huh?" Lone Wolf asked, blinking against the smoke that drifted into his eyes.

"Three days."

"Then it's on and cracking."

"Come share a drink with me," Stick'ums said as he stood up.

"Naw, I'm straight, old school."

"In the Asian culture, a man can lose his life, turning down hospitality," Stick'ums said, his raspy voice sounding even more guttural. Lone Wolf knew that he shouldn't drink, because he knew that once he started, he couldn't stop. At the age of 12, Lone Wolf was a stone cold alcoholic. But going against his better judgment, he lifted the shot glass of Bourbon and downed it... grimacing as he swallowed.

He coughed and his eyes watered. Slowly the burning heat of the liquor expanded in the pit of his stomach, and then slowly reached the rest of his body. He hadn't known exactly how tense he was until the strong liquor entered his system. Slowly, almost stealthily, he felt a strong relaxing sensation consume his body. As he continued to drink, he felt this sensation expanding... enveloping... leaving him caring less and less about his foul and trivial existence.

* * * * * *

His pager read 11:37AM when he stepped from the house. The blazing afternoon sun almost blinded him when he emerged from the darkened interior of the small house. A small sliver of pain began to gnaw away in his skull as he reached his hand up to shield his eyes. The alcohol that sat in the pit of his stomach began to exacerbate... causing him to become nauseated. The strap to the dirty-green duffel bag that contained the rifles began to dig into his shoulder.

He repositioned the bag before he stated his slow ascend to his '64 Chevy. The bag slapped heavily at his legs as he stumbled with every step he made. "Damn," he growled to himself. "I knew I shouldn't had drunk that stuff."

Lone Wolf knew he had an extremely low tolerance for alcohol. He was well aware of the fact that a single shot could seriously impair his judgment... leaving him vulnerable and open for an attack at every point; physically, mentally, emotionally, and to his utmost dismay... psychologically. He now began to wonder how he withstand an attack from the demons within after having three shots?

While drinking... it was easy for him to forget the reality that's been forced upon him... almost like a safe haven where he could escape his own mind. But when it was time to return... he knew what awaited him. In the beginning, it's the first murmur... the first whisper... the first utterance... followed by an onslaught of emotional torment spewing from deep within like the molten lava overrunning the brim of a volcano. If unchecked, the voices of the dead would consume him completely... bringing with it all it's attendant miseries. And then again he would find himself trapped in a padded room within a psychiatric institution. This is why he vowed never to allow these inner demons to triumph ever again. And thus far... he has been successful at maintaining a certain degree of this vow.

Of course they would come... bringing pain... hallucinations... misery... but they have yet to completely triumph.

Lone Wolf kept waking slowly, yet determinedly, towards the car... trying to rid himself of the cold and frightening restlessness of his gut. He cursed himself for being apprehensive, cowardly, for the demons didn't always come. But if they were to this time... could he protect himself from their sinister persuasion?

Now holding onto the car to support his wobbly legs, his throat tight and convulsed, his hands shaking without control.

"Damn that was a long walk," he said aloud as he looked back. The distance from the house to the car was less than ten yards... but to a man teetering on the brink of drunkenness, it felt like ten blocks. At seeing the short distance he traveled, he couldn't suppress laugh. "Yeah, I'm on one."

* * * * * *

The ride back to Murdah Man's slow and strenuous. Lone Wolf was sure to stick to the back streets, paying extra attention to each and every sign, and keeping a close eye on the speedometer. The last thing he needed was to be pulled over by some overzealous police while transporting two assault rifles.

When he finally reached the block of his intended destination, he noticed the white drop-top '95 Mustang sitting in the driveway. *Must be Murdah Man's new ride,* he thought to himself. He parked the '64 Chevy at the curb in front of the house. After grabbing the army bag, he exited the car and made his way to the house. This time the trek wasn't so laborious.

The effects of the alcohol must be wearing off, he said to himself. *And soon will be the moment of truth,* he told himself bitterly. Thus far, the demons have remained in their lair... the deepest, darkest trenches of his soul. But their treacherous ways were so unpredictable. He wondered to himself rather it's possible to be analytical of such occurrences? If so, he might be able to calculate the approximate time of their arrival. But could such methods be truly relied upon? Thus far his intelligence has gotten him nowhere when dealing with these inner demons. All the knowledge he's accumulated over the years in the system couldn't put out the fire that raged in his heart. There was even once a time when he felt this desperate need to believe in a higher power; God, Takashila, Allah, Jehovah, Yahweh... whatever His name may be. But even then, during times of prayers, he would feel a twinge of self-reproach... as if he may began mocking his own prayers.

Maybe one day the fire will die on it's own, he would often tell himself. But 'one day' could never come fast enough. The demons were responsible for this fire; it's the fire that releases that wicked venom into his system... seeping into his veins. And it's this venom that fills him with rage and hatred... in turn, causing him to lash out.

Upon entering the house, he was greeted by Murdah Man and his execrating words. "Nigga, what I tell you about knocking?" he said as he sat back down on the sofa... but his voice was so distracted and devoid of resolve that it completely undid the harshness of his words.

Lone Wolf didn't respond. Instead he shrugged off the heavy army bag and placed it in front of Murdah Man on the coffee table. "What's this?" he asked. But the second his finger tips touched the stainless steel through the clothe, he instantly knew.

"Oh snaps! Where you get these from?"

Lone Wolf spent the next ten minutes explaining their new ventures of dealing with weapons. He told him how Stick'ums could get them any weapon of their choice within a matter of days. He then explained how he wanted to become the main source of weaponry and how they would go about it. Murdah Man listened as he played with the AK.

"And you know what, cuz?" Murdah Man asked Lone Wolf. "If this works out, we could be the new King Pins up in this piece. Slanging dope and straps, man who can mess with us?"

"It'll be lovely if we had a plug for yay. But we don't. We get our stuff from robberies," Lone Wolf said.

"And we can keep getting our shit from 2-11s, cuz. Think about it, we ain't paid a dime for them keys we been slanging. And we won't never have to with these." As he said this he worked the lever on the AK... the metallic click of the rifle added emphasis to his already menacing words.

"In that case, we gonna have to sell keys to other people besides Slope dumb ass. Cos if him and them other two idiots start balling outta control, but not getting work from Crime Boss, then he'll know something up. So we gotta spread our work out," Lone Wolf responded.

"Or we can rob these bitch made nigga'z, too. Then sell them back they own dope!" Murdah Man said laughing. "Then we'll only need a couple of keys. Rotate them mah fucka'z like Dayton's."

"Cuz, you crazy as hell. But it might work," Lone Wolf replied.

At that moment, Murdah Man stood up and approached Lone Wolf. He eyed Lone Wolf suspiciously as he leaned over him. "Cuz? Are you drunk?" he asked as he eyes him curiously.

"What?"

"Cuz, you faded. Eyes all blood shot. I thought you didn't drink?"

"I don't."

"Psst, I smell it on your breath. But you hide it good as hell. But with your face all beat up and shit, I guess it wouldn't be too hard to hide. But you love fighting, huh? Even when it's with yourself," Murdah Man said laughing.

"All bull shit aside, I did have a couple of drinks earlier with Stick'ums. But I'm straight." At that moment, the image of T-Roy flashed across his mind. It drove a fiery bolt of rage through him.

"Damn, cuz. What the hell was that?" Murdah Man asked, noticing the drastic mood swing within Lone Wolf's eyes.

"T-Roy," Lone Wolf said between clenched teeth. Murdah Man didn't respond. Instead, he sat back on the sofa, his facial expression bleak. Then

Lone Wolf said, "We gotta see if it's him. That's the only reason I got these two now." He pointed towards the assault rifles with his chin. "Cuz, we gotta wait until night falls," Murdah Man said slowly, as if he were evaluating every word. "'Til then you should get some sleep."

"Sleep? Nigga, is you serious?"

"Cuz, just think about it," Murdah Man said as he slowly shook his head. "You one of the smartest people I know. But sometimes you step outside yourself and do stupid stuff. Now just think about it."

He didn't need to think about it long before he realized Murdah Man was right. Already his body was feeling weary... strained. Lone Wolf often had to be reminded to eat and sleep. He would go days with little rest and little food. His body would slowly disintegrate and his work would suffer. But his mind would be too deeply involved in whatever to notice the evidence before his eyes.

"You can crash in my bed, cos I ain't gonna be quiet out here. You know how I get when I play Mortal Combat. It'll be quieter back there."

"Man, I ain't sleeping in that nasty ass bed," Lone Wolf chuckled. "Ain't no telling how many hood-rats you done had in that bed."

"Pull the sheets off then. Flip the mattress. And when Lady comes back, I'll send her back."

"Lady's coming back?" Lone Wolf asked.

"Yeah, when she's done. She had to go somewhere fancy. You didn't see her all dressed up?"

"Yeah. But I just thought that was her style."

"When she took me to get my car she told me she'll be back as soon as she's through so she can see you."

"To see me? Did she actually say that?" he inquired.

"I know I bull shit a lot, but real talk, how did you get her wrapped around your finger like this? I mean, I've seen nigga'z literally through diamonds at her, and they get shot down. What's so different with you?" Murdah Man asked as he looked confusingly at Lone Wolf.

"That's your cousin, you sure you wanna know? It might piss you off."

"Psst, nigga please. She a grown ass woman. You might teach me something. So what'z up?"

"A-ight, it's like this," Lone Wolf started, speaking slowly, as if choosing his words very carefully. "Lady is just that, a Lady. But she's also one of us, a thug. That elegant shit is just an act, trying to escape who and what she truly is. And nigga'z fall for that elegant act. She not really soft, or tender. Deep down inside, she just as rough and rugged as we are. But nigga'z try to handle her with kid gloves. I got to her because I touch that ruggedness deep within her. Does any of this make sense?" he asked as he read the confusing look on her face. "Basically, nigga'z throw diamonds at her, and I throw rocks at her, because that's all I know."

Murdah Man wrinkled his nose at the statement. "Psst, whatever works, man."

* * * * * *

Lone Wolf startled with a furious lurch that almost knocked him from the bed. The hand that rested on his arm snatched back and vanished. In panic, he jerked from the bed and stared with sleep clouded eyes across the bedroom... his heaving chest pulsing with quickened heart beats. Heart beats so powerful it looked and felt like a maniac's fists banging on a dungeon's wall.

The dark form before him recoiled against the wall as Lone Wolf's hoarse cry ripped open the silent darkness. Cold fear poured through his veins as he stared at the moving shadow; he clawed desperately for his pistol. He should have known the demons within would never let him be. He survived the alcohol without incident... slept without nightmares... only so that evil fate could deliver him into the shadow's dark embrace.

Suddenly, the light switch was flicked and Murdah Man voice filled the room. "What the hell going on back here?"

"I-I don't know," feminine voice replied. Her voice was shaky... thickened by the disturbing aberration she had just witnessed.

The fear and panic began to subside as Lady's face came into gradual focus. Lone Wolf's heart was pounding so heavily... so powerfully... it seemed as if it would drive through his chest cavity. Breath shuttered in his lungs and his flesh felt numb and cold. He could fell the trickle of icy sweat on his forehead... he wiped it with a shaking hand.

"Girl, don't you *EVER* sneak up on me like that! *ESPECIALLY* when I'm sleeping!" Lone Wolf cried in anger, trying his best to mask the true depths of his emotions.

"I-I'm sorry," she said as she too tried to battle her own fears. "Marcus told me to come back here, that you were expecting me." Then her expression turned angry. "And don't yell at me!" she snapped.

Half-formed curses sounded in Lone Wolf's throat as he sat on the bed; his legs were still shaking. "You know you lucky, right? You lucky I couldn't find my strap, or 'Marcus' would of got you lit the fuck up."

"What did you just say?!" Lady yelled as she approached Lone Wolf. The fear she once felt now completely gone.

Lone Wolf looked up at Lady, her eyes were fiery. He than looked over at Murdah Man... his chest shuddered with repressed laughter. "This shit's really funny to you, ain't it?" he snapped at Murdah Man. Murdah Man could no longer suppress the urge, he busted out laughing.

"What did you say, Lone Wolf?" Lady was now looming over him. "Repeat what you said! I ain't one of these nigga'z out here! I ain't scared of you!"

Lone Wolf placed his head in his hands. "Will you just shut up, please? God damn." His voice was low, but forceful.

"Who you tellin' to shut up?!" Lady said as she poked Lone Wolf in his head.

"Fuck! That's it!" Lone Wolf growled as he grabbed his .357 and stood up... towering over Lady. Her soft brown eyes filled with terror and Murdah Man grew silent. Lone Wolf felt a stir of pleasure at the alarmed expression crossing her face. "I'm leaving," Lone Wolf said as he turned to walk away.

At his words, Murdah Man howled with laughter and Lady's eyes flashed with unbridled anger.

"Don't be doin' that stupid shit!" Lady curse at Lone Wolf, but he ignored her and walked into the living room, amused at his game. Lady followed him into the living room, cursing him as they went. Murdah Man continued to laugh off in the back ground.

"Lady, look, I apologize. Damn! What more you want me to say?" Lone Wolf asked in frustration.

"You must of done some foul shit to a lot of people to be so scared," Lady accused.

Spinning on his heels, Lone Wolf seized her by her arms in an iron grip. He jerked her body against his, then leaned in towards her. "You think that maybe some people done some foul shit to me?" he whispered harshly in her ear so that Murdah Man couldn't hear. He then pulled back then looked her deeply in her eyes. "I said I was sorry," he said aloud.

Her eyes were no longer angry. Again they were soft... sympathetic. Her whole demeanor completely different.

"What he say?" Murdah Man asked as he approached them, the hint of amusement still in his voice. "Don't let that fool lie to you. He did the same thing to me," Murdah Man said in a chuckle. "If I were you, I'll smack the hell out of him."

* * * * * *

The sun had long dropped below the horizon when the three emerged from the house. Murdah Man was careful not to reveal to Lady what was in the green army bag. Which wasn't difficult, for her mind was preoccupied by the presences of Lone Wolf. Lone Wolf on the other hand had already began to withdraw.

About ten minutes before they stepped from the house, he had began to think of T-Roy, and again the nagging doubt began to anger him. He knew he had to be reclusive for this anger would undoubtedly dictate his actions. And while angered, he knew he couldn't withstand another confrontation with Lady without physically lashing out at her. And he couldn't reveal his emotions nor his plans to her, for she would interfere with their hunt for T-Roy. Therefore, he thought it in their best interest to say as little as possible to her. She was absolutely oblivious, or perhaps indifferent to his mental aberration.

"So, you coming by tonight, Lone Wolf?" Lady asked, her voice softened to a confidential whisper.

"He already know we've tossed. So why you whispering? It ain't a secret," Lone Wolf asked.

"I know he knows. But still..." her voice trailed off. "You gonna spend the night with me?"

"Yeah," Lone Wolf lied. "As soon as we take care of this bidness, a-ight?"

* * * * * *

The '95 Ford Mustang slowly crept threw the north side, it's two occupants on the prowl... searching for the man who has thus far lead a massacre on 34th and Jaynes Street. Lone Wolf sat on the passenger side, the fully loaded AK-47 resting across his lap. His eyes scanning every face... every car... every shadow for the man that's the cause of his nightmares.

The stereo system played C-Bo, but the music was barely audible. The two sat in silence... each wrapped up in their own thoughts. They had concluded that Tommy Rose Garden would be the logical location to began this man-hunt, for these "wooden" projects were conquered by Murda 8 in '93 after a bloody and vicious street war.

As the Mustang slowly drew near, Lone Wolf felt the muscles of his abdominal closing in, like the tightening of coils. He didn't know if these knots were from apprehension or from the anticipation of vengeance. He did indeed feel a tingle of excitement.

Simultaneously, they spotted a group of young men standing beneath the paleness of a street light, their red outfits taking on an orangeish color in it's yellow light. Murdah Man gently applied pressure to the break while shutting off the headlights. Lone Wolf turned off the stereo completely. The group was totally unaware of their presence. They continued to shout and laugh, shadow boxing in the street lights. It wasn't until the group was approached by a drug addict did Lone Wolf realize they were out selling drugs, however ineffective their selling methods may be. The corner of which they stood received little car traffic, let alone people walking on foot.

"You know any of these fools?" Murdah Man asked, pulling Lone Wolf away from his thoughts.

"Naw. But the dude with the red Dope Man's kinda look like Trigg, huh?"

After closer observation, Murdah Man chuckled. "He does, huh? Kinda younger."

"Do you think they'll know who we are?" Lone Wolf asked.

"They look like some young ass B.G.'s, so probably not. Why?"

"Because..." Lone Wolf said slowly, still deep in thought. "It look like they working. If they don't know you, we can just roll up like we swerves looking for a fix."

"Nigga, I ain't no hype."

"Naw, man. I'm saying, if we swerving, they might tell us who they O.G. is."

"I got a better way," Murdah Man said as he placed the M-16 between his legs with the barrel pointing towards the heavens.

"Yeah, but that might stir up too much shit. You forget, them nigga'z put in work," Lone Wolf said. Murdah Man grunted in response. "Better yet, we can say we looking for a dub. If it was T-Roy that did that hit on Jaynes street, you know all these fools is sitting fat and wanna get rid of it as quickly as possible, feel me?" Murdah Man didn't respond. "We ain't' wearing blue. Just don't say my name and I won't say yours. They won't know what hood we from."

"Psst, whatever's clever," Murdah Man said as he turned on the head lights and pressed on the accelerator, headed towards the group.

"Ah! Ah, homeboy! Let me holla at you real quick!" Lone Wolf yelled towards the group. He wasn't talking to anyone in particular, but knew whoever the unspoken leader of the group maybe would automatically step forward. The group eyed the vehicle suspiciously. Many of them reached towards the small of their backs as if to draw their weapons. "Ah, playboy, we just looking, right? You on?"

"Yeah, blood. What you need?" one of them called out.

"We looking for a dub. Can you stand it?" Lone Wolf said, his voice getting lower in hopes the young man would approach the car to hear what was being said.

"Like what? Quarters?"

"Psst, man, I'm talking about a couple of zips," Lone Wolf said, his voice steadily declining in tone. And it worked, for one of them approached the car. The young man's eyes were dark... his expression was one of hard suspicious and readiness.

"Nigga, you po-po?" he asked accusingly as he leaned over the car.

"What!" Lone Wolf shot back. "Motha fucka, do I look like the punk police?"

The young man first glared at Lone Wolf suspiciously, then turned his eyes towards Murdah Man. "Naw, blood. We ain't got it like that," he finally answered.

"Then who does?" Lone Wolf asked as he pulled out a large sum of cash form his pocket. Lone Wolf could see that in his eyes, greed and loyalty were battling for supremacy, both throwing sensibility and caution to the wind.

"How much you working with?" he asked Lone Wolf.

"Like I said, we looking for zips and zones. My homie just moved here from Cali..." he said pointing a thumb towards Murdah Man. "And we looking for a plug. Man, we trying ball outta control, understood?"

"Peep game, let me go holla at one of the O.G.'s. Swing back in about 30 of um," he said as he turned to leave.

"Hold on, playboy," Lone Wolf called out to him. "30? Man, we trying clock. We ain't got time to be wasting. Who you dealing with? Let me holla at him."

"What, blood?" the young man said in disbelief. "ya'll nigga'z one-time?" he accused again as he reached to the small of his back.

"Ah man, what I say about..." Lone Wolf started to get loud, but Murdah Man tugged on his arm.

"Nigga, who the fuck you..." he snarled as he produced a semi-automatic pistol.

"Man," Murdah Man said to Lone Wolf. "Let's just go."

"Yeah, you better ride the fuck on," the young man spat.

As Lone Wolf watched he man cock the pistol, fury poured through him like a current of white-hot acid. He wanted desperately to reach for the AK-47 which rested under his feet. Sensing so, Murdah Man tugged on his arm harder. "Let's just ride out," Murdah Man said in a feeble attempt to subdue the fury that raged in Lone Wolf.

"Yeah! Get the fuck on! And don't let me see you around this motha fucka again!"

"Smooth move, Shaft," Murdah Man laughed sarcastically.

"Man, fuck you," Lone Wolf said bitterly, the wicked venom still coursing through his veins.

"I'm just saying, cuz," Murdah Man said laughing. "It was a brilliant ideal. Lets just walk up to some drug deala'z and ask them who they working for. I mean, it's just genius. It's good thing the police ain't picked up that method."

Lone Wolf shot him a murderous look, rage glittering in his cold black eyes. Upon seeing the expression in Lone Wolf's eyes, Murdah Man toned down the sarcasm. After a brief moment of silence, Lone Wolf asked, "Cuz, you been drinking?"

"What? Naw, man."

"You high?"

"High? Naw. Had a fat ass blunt earlier. Why you ask?"

"Cos, you starting to act goofy," Lone Wolf said. "You know what we came here to do. Don't mess this up." Lone Wolf's voice took on a dangerous, quiet note. "We on a mission to see if this nigga smoked my brother. This is real, cuz. I need you, cuz. I can't have you acting like a goof troop."

"Ahhh," Murdah Man said slowly, nodding his head. "So you plan on smoking a sucka, huh?" Lone Wolf didn't respond. "I didn't think you had it in you, young Wolf. But I guess this'll push anybody over the edge, huh?" Again, Lone Wolf sat in silence. "Well... we tried it your way. Now let's try mine."

* * * * * *

Their footsteps click in broken rhythm on the pavement as they ran down the street, making sure they stuck to the shadows. With their deadly weapons in hand and blue bandannas wrapped around their faces, the two head-hunters stopped within a block's radius of the targeted group. Slowly... stalkingly, they ascended ever-so cautiously towards their victims; stopping after reaching 30 feet from them. They scanned the distance only to see the group bragging about how they pumped fear into the hearts of Lone Wolf and Murdah Man. The two head-hunters sneered sinisterly in dark and demented amusement.

"You ready, cuz?" Murdah Man asked Lone Wolf in a harsh whisper. But at that very moment, a '97 maroon Blazer pulled up. Both Lone Wolf and Murdah Man darted towards the safety of some over-grown hedges. Peering through the shrubbery, they tried to get a glance at the driver, but the yellow street light reflected off the windshield.

"What'z up, blood?" one of the group members called out as he approached the car. "What'z brackin'?"

The driver of the truck responded, but the two henchmen couldn't hear his voice.

"Psst, same ol' thang, bickin' back bein' boo, you know," the young man told the driver. "It's all about the 8."

Again, the driver said something, but nothing was heard by Lone Wolf. The young man started laughing. He then turned towards he group and yelled, "Ah, Dione! O.G. said keep your dick outta them hypes. He wants all his money."

"Psst. It only cost a dime a pop," the one called Dione responded "A nick a lick if it's a slow night," he said laughing, the group laughed as well. The driver responded, and the young man relayed the message.

"He said do what you do, just don't eat the pussy then think you gonna hit his blunt." The group howled with laughter.

Lurking within the cozy nestle of shadows, Lone Wolf continued trying to see who the driver was... but it was to no avail. The thought of the possibility that T-Roy was the driver began to plague his mind. The fiery acid of vengeance began to scold his heart as he tightened his grip on the AK. In his mind he could visualize himself launching an attack at that very moment. Emerging from the shadows with his fully automatic weapon blazing bright tongues of flames stretching outward through the smoke of the barrel; fire piercing through the smoke like a true vision of hell.

Slowly the Blazer began to pull away. It's triple-gold Dayton's spinning ever-so slowly. A final comment was made by the driver, causing the group to howl with laughter, and then the Blazer began to pick up speed. As it made a u-turn in the middle of the street, it's headlights flashed briefly on their place of concealment. Lone Wolf was caught off guard, he couldn't duck in time. The flickering illumination made his shadow billow on the house behind them.

"Get the fuck down!" Murdah Man barked at Lone Wolf as he forcefully tugged at him, pulling him to the ground. Fortunately, the group was completely unaware of any activities that surrounded them. Lone Wolf saw the driver. It wasn't the image of T-Roy that Lone Wolf remembered.

"Man, is you stupid?" Murdah Man cursed Lone Wolf. "You telling *ME* not to fuck up." Lone Wolf didn't respond, his mind was engrossed with the driver of the truck. His name was Ty-Bud, the shy and nerdy brother of a woman Lone Wolf once messed with. The sight of him jolted Lone Wolf, but not enough to drive away the murderous fury in him.

Once the Blazer disappeared into the distance, Lone Wolf asked Murdah Man, "You ready for this?"

"You already know," Murdah Man responded.

The two hunters emerged from the shadows, their assault rifles poised and ready, their eyes gleaming of rabid hatred. A woman was the first to spot them. A faint, involuntary cry escaped her throat as she shrank back in fear. The man standing next to her followed her gaze. Instantly he was frozen in the icy grip of paralyzing fear that strikes one rigid... turning him into an up-right corpse. The remaining group didn't realize what was going on until the head-hunters were upon them, shouting demands for them to relinquish their drugs, money, and weapons.

"You know what the fuck this is!" Murdah Man growled. "Empty your motha fuckin' pockets."

With his AK leveled, Lone Wolf searched the crowd for it's weakest link, the one that will lead him to T-Roy. He had his eyes on a small and petite woman, standing no taller than 5'2". She remained silent and still. He made the grave mistake of judging an adversary solely on their appearances... he mistook that stillness as immobilizing fear.

"You! Come here!" he barked at the small woman. She looked up at the much larger Lone Wolf... sudden, naked rage blazed in her expression. "Oh man," Lone Wolf said to himself. He knew that defiance at a time like this, from a petite and fragile woman like her, could incite courage and bravery within the group... causing them to do something stupid... leaving Murdah Man with no choice but to slay them all.

"Not you," Lone Wolf told the woman in an attempt to clean up the mess. "Him! You!" he said pointing with his AK to the man standing to her left. "Come here!" Lone Wolf let out a sigh of relief at the strangled sound of horror he made. The woman seemed to calm somewhat. *Phew, that was close,* he thought to himself. As the man reluctantly drew closer, Lone Wolf snatched him up by his shirt, placing the short barrel of the AK in the softness of his neck.

"Where the stash?" he growled maliciously... applying pressure to his throat to add emphasis to his words. The man's throat had become clogged by fear. So even with the absence of the pressure from the barrel, he still wouldn't have been able to speak. He could only stare in wide-eyed fear while producing compulsory animal sounds.

"Where's the stash?" Murdah Man barked. The man whimpered and ducked away.

"Ah!" a strangers voice called out to them. "Ya'll on?" Lone Wolf turned to see a drug addict approaching them, totally oblivious to what was taking place. "I need a twomp," he said as he continued to walk head-on into danger.

Murdah Man spun on his heels, leveling his rifle at the approaching drug addict. "Oh, snaps," the man said, the surprise creeping into his voice.

"Get cha ass over here," Murdah Man growled, the man slowly complied.

Still holding onto the cowering man, Lone Wolf said to Murdah Man, "We gotta take this some place else." Murdah Man agreed.

The two armed men shepherded the crowd to a more secluded area less than 50 feet away. Once in between the safe confinement of two project buildings, the two head-hunters forced their captures to lie face down on the ground.

"Not you," Lone Wolf said to the man he had in his grip. "Where's the motha fuckin' stash, nigga?" Lone Wolf demanded as he added more pressure to his victim. A sissified scream strangled in the man's throat.

"You too, bitch. Get cha ass on the floor!" Lone Wolf heard Murdah Man roar. Lone Wolf saw that he was speaking to the petite, yet defiant woman. Lone Wolf was anticipating trouble.

"Who you calling a bitch?!" the woman yelled frantically. "Let me find out who you are, I'll have my cousin Pumpkin Pete fuck you up. Now, bitch!"

"Is she threatening me?" Murdah Man asked as he turned towards Lone Wolf, a hint of sinister amusement glittering in his eyes. "Is she seriously threatening me? Did I miss something here? Do you see this gun?" Murdah Man asked as he planted the stock of his M-16 into the woman's face... she fell to ground with a soft whimper. "Do you see this gun?" he asked the unconscious woman. "This ain't no little fuckin' gun, neither. This will hurt you."

Turning back towards Lone Wolf, Murdah Man said, "We got the straps and they threatening us. Can you believe this?"

Lone Wolf didn't respond, instead he turned his attention back to the man in which he had in his grip. The look he directed at the man chilled the man's blood. It was a look of murderous hostility and dire impatience. "Go," he growled at the man.

"Hold on, cuz. Go where?" Murdah Man asked.

"Stay here. This bitch-ass mark take me to him," Lone Wolf replied reassuringly.

"Naw, cuz, you ain't going at this by yourself," Murdah Man said with an intense flash in his eyes; hot... overtly defiant. "You messing with killa'z. Like you said, you need me, cuz."

"I got this, cuz. I *NEED* to do this by myself," Lone Wolf said as he shoved his hostage in the general direction. Murdah Man looked after them until the two disappeared around the corner of a building. He knew the rage and hatred in Lone Wolf's heart was strong, but he questioned whether or not it was strong enough to do what needed to be done.

Slowly, reluctantly, Murdah Man turned his attention back towards the group that laid before him. He looked down upon the unconscious woman. "Damn, she gotta big ol' booty, huh?" Murdah Man said out loud as he chuckled sadistically. With the toe of his boot he lifted up the red Chicago Bulls jersey that obstructed his view. "She got a juicy booty on her. Ah, cuz..." Murdah Man said giggling to the man laying closer to her, "When she wakes up, would you snitch on me if I touched it?"

* * * * * *

With the barrel of an AK resting against his spine, the man stumbled across the parking lot. Images of T-Roy falling before the dazzling flash of fire spitting murderously from the AK plagued Lone Wolf's mind. His heart began to race, the wicked venom began to seep into his veins, and the murmurs of the dead began to chant their unending hymn of the damned. Lone Wolf knew he was ready. He has suffered for far too long. Tonight... the demonic spirits of the dead will find their peace.

"I-I-In t-there," the man whimpered as he pointed weakly towards an opened door. The screen door was missing it's screen, the metal frame was bent beyond repair.

"Is T-Roy in there?" Lone Wolf snarled as he thrusted savagely with the barrel. The man's lips stirred soundlessly, as if to speak. To Lone Wolf this meant the lie was frozen in his throat. Trembling in anger and frustration,

Lone Wolf rested the assault rifle against his neck and looked deeply in his eyes, "Is T-Roy in there?"

The man instantly lowered his eyes, obviously unable to withstand Lone Wolf's hostile and questioning gaze. In a swift motion, Lone Wolf lashed out angrily with the stock of his AK. The wicked venom that was coursing through his veins gave him an almost supernatural strength. The forged metal connected solidly with the man's jaw. The gruesome sound of shattering bone was almost enough to break the murderous hypnotic state of which Lone Wolf was in. Almost.

In swift, long strides, he crossed the parking lot. Without hesitation, he swung aside the ragged frame of the door and entered the apartment. Heavy marijuana smoke defiled the entire apartment; the music was playing softly.

He first spotted a lean, light complexed man wearing a tank top. He was sitting on the floor in between the legs of a woman who was braiding his hair. On the opposite end of the couch sat another man, his low and defined brow gave him the look of a stereotypical gang-banger. His Afro was wild, with a bright red pick protruding from the left side. He was playing video games with a third man. This third figure had his back to Lone Wolf. But as he took a long pull from the 40oz bottle of Old English, Lone Wolf could tell from his profile that it wasn't T-Roy.

The woman was the first to spot Lone Wolf, the sound of a panic induced scream gurgled in her throat. Knowing he couldn't reveal his true intentions, Lone Wolf roared, "Come up off your stash!" To add emphasis to his demand, he racked the AK, sending a live round sailing threw the air. The metallic click of a bullet being chambered is always enough to pump fear into the heart of any sane person.

The man that had his back to Lone Wolf tried to get to his feet. In two long strides, Lone Wolf was able to cross the room and delivered a powerful blow before he could stand fully erect. He then spun the rifle on the man with the Afro. With the AK mere inches from his face, he asked in a low growl, "You wanna die, nigga?" The man didn't budge.

The man who had felt the heavy hand of Lone Wolf stirred on the floor. The coughing that came from his throat had a liquefied sound to it. Under his blue bandanna, Lone Wolf smiled to himself.

"Who else in here?" he asked as he stepped towards the couple. The woman shook her head in an exaggerated manner. "Don't lie to me. Is anybody else here?" he barked as he lunged at the two with his rifle.

"No, no! I swear!" she wailed in fear.

Turning back towards the three men, he asked, "So ya'll the Murda 8 O.G.'s, huh? Ya'll the bitches running the show? Where's the work at? No, no, no, wait, first off, who the fuck is T-Roy?" When nobody answered, he delivered a powerful kick to the man that sat on the floor getting his hair braided. The kick landed in his side, he doubled over in pain. "Who is he?" Lone Wolf roared.

"He's the one calling the shots," the man said with tremendous difficulties, he was still holding his side.

"Where is he?" When the man didn't answer, Lone Wolf went to deliver a second kick, but the man pulled and retorted sharply;

"He's on the south side. He pushing some work. He's leaving for Lincoln tonight."

"Damn, blood!" the gangster-looking man with the Afro pick grumbled. "Why don't you tell this fool every thang?"

"Like what?" Lone Wolf demanded as he repositioned the rifle at him. Lone Wolf knew he wouldn't respond. So without delay, he planted the broad side of the handle into the side of his face. "Ya'll got a death wish, huh?" he asked the group. "Ya'll really wanna die or something?"

He turned the rifle back on the couple. Knowing he had to continue concealing his main objective, he once again demanded money and drugs. He forced the woman to place the item in a dirty pillow case. Some intuition told him that there was more in the house, there had to be, but Lone Wolf was here to uncover the true identity of T-Roy. A mission he had yet to accomplish.

"Where did T-Roy come from?" Lone Wolf asked the woman as she was placing the seven kilo's of powder cocaine into the pillow case.

"He just got out of prison," she said softly.

At her words, Lone Wolf felt the nauseating swirl of demons as they stirred anxiously, trying to escape from within. Lone Wolf clenched his stomach as the wave of nausea seized his body.

Sensing a moment of weakness, the man with the Afro launched an attack. Lone Wolf's most primal instinct came into play when he saw the man coming towards him. Through reflexive response, Lone Wolf swung the rifle in his general direction and pulled the trigger. The three round burst echoed loudly within the apartment, completely drowning out the soft music that was being played. The man's body spent backwards under the heavy impact of the bullets.

Fortunately for the man, he only suffered from flesh wounds. Grimacing from the pain in his bleeding shoulder, side, and arm. The man slowly sat up... gripping one of his wounds.

"Man, you shot me." His voice was horsed... thick with pain.

Outside, Lone Wolf could hear the commotion began to pick up. Neighbors began to slowly emerge from their apartments... scanning the surrounding area in an attempt to find the source of the gun shots... asking each other questions, revealing what little information they may have.

"Damn," Lone Wolf growled to himself. "Shut up," he warned the man. Lone Wolf knew he couldn't wait for the woman to finish finding the money to place into the bag, and he knew there had to be weapons in the apartment... but he also knew that time was running dangerously short. Snatching the pillow case from the woman's hands he turned and bolted towards the door.

Before entering the apartment, Lone Wolf hadn't realized how cool the night had grown. A rush of cool air flushed his face as he passed the broken screen door. A somewhat large crowd had gathered towards the end of the parking lot. With the spoils in hand, he raised the AK towards the heavens. The night was torn open by the exploding fire. Panic flared within the crowd and they all scattered in every direction. As Lone Wolf made a mad dash through the parking lot, he could hear the curses of other gang members.

"That nigga just came from Scoop's crib!" he heard one of them yell, followed by the rhythmic echo of pursuing feet. Again Lone Wolf sprayed the heavens with bullets, they pursed no longer. He turned one corner after another. After rounding the final corner, Murdah Man came into view, he was pestering the hostages. "Get ghost, cuz!" he yelled out to Murdah Man.

After hearing his warning, Murdah Man turned the M-16 on his hostages, he laughed wickedly as he fired his weapon just above their heads. The bullets ate away at the bricks, causing jagged pieces of concrete to rain on the terrified group. "Trés, bitch!" he yelled hysterically before he unloaded more rounds into the wall. When the firing ceased, he laughed in a way only a maniac could, then spun on his heels to follow in the direction of the fleeing Lone Wolf.

* * * * * *

In the safety of the '95 Mustang, Lone Wolf's head fell back as he gasped for breath. The cool air burning in his chest. The spoils laid on the floor in between his feet while the AK rested on his lap.

"What's in the bag?" Murdah Man asked in between breaths. Unable to answer, Lone Wolf lazily handed him the pillow case. But Murdah Man was too tired to look inside. "Was he there?" Murdah Man gasped. With great effort Lone Wolf shook his head.

Finally Lone Wolf was able to ask, "Why the hell you park so far away?"

"We the ones with the heavy artillery. I didn't think *WE'LL* be the ones running. So T-Roy wasn't there?" Lone Wolf shook his head. Murdah Man began to shift through the pillow case, then added the contents of his pockets to it. "Didn't get much from them nigga'z. Couple of ounces and about 700 in cash. I did get two straps, thou." As he said this he produced two small caliber pistols.

"Only two? Damn near all them nigga'z was acting like they had heat."

"Them bitches was perpetrating. You know how some nigga'z do it," Murdah Man replied. He then looked over at Lone Wolf and asked, "Now what?"

INTERMISSION

For two and a half weeks, both Lone Wolf and Murdah Man flourished prosperously. The means of obtaining the merchandise needed to remain operational within the drug trade was simple; they would rob one drug dealer and sell the spoils to the next. Within this time span, not a single drug dealer was safe... and very few went unscathed. Lone Wolf was right in predicting them having to sell to other buyers besides B.G. Slope and the other two. Becoming flamboyant with his new connection, Murdah Man had to silence Hollow Tips... and in the process had accidentally slain two innocent by-standers.

B.G. Slope and K-9 was sitting on 27 kilo's before Lone Wolf decided the time had come to find new customers. He and Murdah Man had formed silent alliances with Murder Town Gangsta'z (MTG) and 4-4 AMG. They provided these two sets with both narcotics and heavy weaponry in exchange for foot soldiers. These soldiers would serves the two masterminds as head figures, as puppets, drawing all the attention to themselves for the purpose of providing a smoke screen so that the two masterminds could continue their treacherous ways of dealing drugs without being the least suspicious. Such deception and manipulation had caused MTG to lose six of their members... and AMG lost two of theirs... both to the graves and prison. But the O.G.'s who had formed this secret alliance with the two thought this was an acceptable loss for their new found source of commodities.

Insane would often participate in these drug heists. But only with the intent on making a quick dollar. He had no intentions of becoming an active member within the organized crime syndicate, he wanted to remain wild and independent.

Stick'ums was true to his word. He provided Lone Wolf with every weapon that was asked of him. Lone Wolf would then sell the weapons to the South Side Soma Lomas, a Mexican gang. They would then transport the weapons back to the north side, selling them at a healthy profit. Such arrangements were necessary, for secrecy was crucial if the two wanted to maintain their weapon connection and their methods of obtaining narcotics without becoming targets.

With his new found wealth, Stick'ums quickly opened up an after hour joint where he employed drug addicts. Not only were they a cheap labor force, they would also provide Stick'ums with information concerning shipments of drugs. If he thought such information was both reliable and worthy, he would then relinquish such information to Lone Wolf at a low cost... who would then set up their next sting.

Under the alias of James Johnson, Lone Wolf obtained his own apartment... not even Murdah Man knew where he lived. Lone Wolf was petrified of the thought of being alone... so many women came and went... but Amber Faye never truly strayed too far from his thoughts. A few times he was temped to contact her, but the thought of being rejected was more than he could bare. But still, he thought often of her.

Lady began to slowly fade away into the background. Sensing the change in attitude towards her... she thought it best to leave Lone Wolf be. Their last encounter was nothing more than a head nod as the two passed in the night.

The voices of the dead were all but suppressed. He could still hear them within... their murmuring and chanting... their prowling and stalking... their anguish cries and snarling... and their fighting amongst themselves. These imprisoned spirits... bound in dungeons of frail mortal flesh.

Within this two and a half week period, he had suffered only twice from hallucinations, despite his heavy drinking. Each time the faces of death emerging from the darkness. Depicting figures that were demented... leering... darkly distorted and flushed... staring lasciviously with maniacal blood-lust.

Lone Wolf and Murdah Man both were well on their was to reaching half a million apiece. All the while searching for the ever-so-elusive T-Roy. But living life in it's fastest lane would always come at a great price. A price that Lone Wolf should have seen coming by any means of sane judgment. But Lone Wolf's lack of insight-fulness only serves to verify his mental aberration.

DAY TWENTY-FIVE

The sun was now close to the horizon. Shadows crept towards the east... stretching out... concealing the streets with it's shadowy embrace. Lone Wolf sat in his '64 Chevy just outside the new establishment of Stick'ums, named "The Blue Note." The custom designed system was pumping Bone Thugs-N-Harmony as he sat waiting the arrival of Murdah Man. He lifted the 40oz bottle of Magnum to his lips... allowing the bitter tasting fluid to fill his mouth before swallowing. He had been buzzed all day... fighting the unyielding urge to become fully intoxicated.

Stick'ums had phoned the two late that afternoon, telling them to drop in, for he had urgent information to provide them. Lone Wolf wondered what the information may be, and why it was so important that the two had to be called in. The next shipment of weapons were not due to arrive for another couple of days; *so that couldn't be it,* he thought to himself. Perhaps he had knowledge concerning the arrival of another drug shipment? But such information was usually given to Lone Wolf alone, and when he went to retrieve the weapons. Maybe an unforeseen problem had arise with Stick'ums connection? This couldn't be, for Stick'ums wouldn't have phoned them. Instead he would act ignorant when Lone Wolf came for the shipment in an attempt to keep clear of any wrong doings. If Lone Wolf was to approach him inquiring about weapons, Stick'ums would act as if he didn't know what Lone Wolf was talking about. So what could be so important?

Question upon question raced through his mind as he stared blankly through the windshield, completely unaware of all the activities outside. He was startled when there was a tap on the window.

"Ahh man, get away from my car!" Lone Wolf cursed as he rolled down the window.

"Whoo! Hold on, pimp," the man yelped as he threw his arms up in mock surrender. "I'm not lookin' for problems. I just wanna know if you on?"

Lone Wolf looked the man over as he stood there, staring back at Lone Wolf with blank, obsidian eyes... his expression hollow and drugged. "Naw, homie," Lone Wolf replied as he relaxed again. "I don't get down."

The man expression churned as he took a step back to get a full view of the '64 Chevy. Glitter was sprinkled lightly over the pine green paint-job... which sparkled as brightly as the gold rims, despite the darkness that began to settle over the streets of Omaha.

"Come on, pimp. I ain't no police, man. And all I need is a dime," the man said as he stepped back up to the car.

"I told you I don't fuck around. You see them fools over there?" Lone Wolf said as he pointed with his 40oz bottle. "They slanging. Go bother with them."

"Aw, come on, dawg. I just..." but the man stopped abruptly when he saw Lone Wolf reaching towards the floor board. "A-ight! It's coo, it's coo."

The crimson sun had dipped blow the horizon long before Murdah Man pulled up in his '95 Mustang. "Been here long?" he asked Lone Wolf as he pulled the car up beside the Chevy.

"Not really," Lone Wolf responded.

"What the hell is this about?" Murdah Man asked. Lone Wolf shrugged his shoulders in an exaggerated manner. "Hold on, I'll be back," Murdah Man said as he pulled off. He made a U-turn in the middle of the street, obstructing the traffic in both directions, then pulled the car in behind Lone Wolf.

Grabbing his .357 from under his seat, Lone Wolf exited the car and met Murdah Man at the front entrance of The Blue Note. The two entered and was greeted by the sounds of BB King singing the blues. In one section... the dim illumination of the walled blue light barely held the darkness at bay. But the second section was brightly lit by a single florescent light which hung above a single pool table. Behind that was a '70s fashion jukebox, which played old records of forgotten blues composure's. People were sitting in the scattered chairs and tables... drinking and smoking cigarettes and cigars.

Lone Wolf's gaze wondered around the smoky room until his eyes fell on Stick'ums. He sat behind a cage, one of the dreadful La Finca Corona hanging from his lips.

"Young bloods," Stick'ums said in his usual raspy voice when he saw the two approaching. "About time ya'll showed up. I got some intel that'll split ya wig, ya dig?" Turning towards the woman standing next to him, Stick'ums told her to watch the cage while he's gone... then lead the two towards the back. The room he lead them to was brightly lit, it's pale blue walls covered with photos of naked women posing. In the center was a metal office desk... complete with a business style chair and two chairs sitting in front of the desk.

"Taking this business look a little too far," Lone Wolf said laughing.

"I am a business man," Stick'ums said as he sat behind the desk. "I called ya'll in cos I heard about this cat coming in from the left coast tomorrow night. Bringing with his 150 key-lo-G's."

"What!?" Murdah Man involuntarily called out, unable to control his excitement.

"Believe you me, young blood. Got this hit this afternoon from this cat who's head maintenance in the warehouse they'll be at tomorrow." Stick'ums could see the grim anticipation growing inside of Murdah Man.

Lone Wolf on the other hand sat quietly... fighting the first twinge of nervousness growing inside of him. Lone Wolf knew that anybody moving that much merchandise would not only be heavily guarded, but well connected on the street level. So an attempt at robbing this individual would quickly be known, and the perpetrators would easily be pointed out and eliminated.

"So *MURDAH* Man, how much is this info worth?"

"Nigga, don't be fuckin' with me!" Murdah Man roared. Stick'ums jolted in dismay. "Is this shit for real?"

Stick'ums smile was quick... distracted. "As much as I done for ya'll, have I not always been righteous?" There was an undertone of resentful mortification in his raspy voice. Murdah Man bared his teeth in a derisive grin.

"Naw, homie, we can't do nothing with this," Lone Wolf spoke up. Murdah Man turned towards him, glaring at him with cold, dark eyes. And in them, Lone Wolf saw something he did not expect to find; contempt... resentfulness... hostility... all directed towards Lone Wolf.

"Cuz, think about it," Lone Wolf told Murdah Man. "Only one fool has that much weight. And he's from Cali. And we knew he'll be coming back any day. Now, who do you think it is?" Lone Wolf asked. Murdah Man regarded him with demoniacal glee.

"Yeah. And if we take this bitch out, we'll be the new motha fuckin' Crime Bosses. Ain't that what we been working for?" Murdah Man asked. "We get this lick, cuz, we'll be running this city," Murdah Man said, but there was something gone from his eyes as he said it. Lone Wolf felt the sense of dark alarm within him growing steadily. He slowly shook his head, he knew Murdah Man's mind was made up.

He looked back at Stick'ums, who was now obviously pleased. His posture was now different, the anger and resentfulness for Murdah Man's harsh words now cleansed from his eyes. "We talking about 150 keys, young blood. Now what ya'll do is ya'll bizness, I can care less. But ol' Stick'ums ain't no fool. I know what ya'll do. A little advice from this ol' fool... make this 150 the last one and quit the game."

"Nigga, is you stupid?" Murdah Man asked Stick'ums., his voice lined with resentful agitation. "A lick like this can set us up to roll with the big dawgs. We take this fool out, we take over his territories. People will have no choice but to come to us."

"Ya'll young cats have done a damn good job at keeping a low profile. But if ya dig off in his territories, your names will be out there," Stick'ums said with logical certainty.

"So motha fuckin' what?" Murdah Man snapped.

"All those other cats ya'll be robbing..." Stick'ums said with a derisive smirk, not having to even finish the statement.

"Nigga'z know we got heat. They know we some killa'z," Murdah Man said, speaking mainly about himself. "And they know that any nigga try to test nuts will get ghost. Especially wit the M-60 choppin' away at they flesh."

A deep and resonated chuckle sounded in Stick'ums throat, in correspondence with the raspiness of his voice. "You still trynna get me for that, huh?"

"Hell yeah," Murdah Man replied.

"Maybe one day. But listen here, you two, ya'll got far, fast. But don't press Lady Luck. She can be a bitch, ya dig?" Stick'ums was now speaking mostly to Lone Wolf. He held his eyes with an intense stare. "You get this 150, ya dig? Sell it to the same cats ya'll been messing with. But not at once. Spread it out, over time and none would be the wiser. You try to sell it all at once, they'll know it was you who got this cat from Cali. But you keep doing what you been doing, they'll think nothing's changed. After that... go legit." After a pause, Stick'ums said, "Quit the game. That simple."

Lone Wolf looked over at Murdah Man, conflicting emotions rising in him.

"First off, old ass nigga," Murdah Man said as he pulled his Glock .40 and cocked it. "There's only one way out the game. Second, keep your comments to yourself, 'ya dig?'"

Stick'ums eyed Murdah Man with cold hostility. "Do what ya do," Stick'ums answered in a tightly restrained voice. "I'm just telling ya'll what I'll do. What I'm going to do."

"What you mean, ol' school?" Lone Wolf asked.

"Psst, young blood, Ol' Stick'ums gonna have the only cat-house in Omaha. You two got me here. But it's time for me to step back, ya dig? Go legit."

At the statement, Murdah Man looked over at Lone Wolf, then looked back over at the old man. "Are you fuckin' serious?" Murdah Man spat at him. "What we gonna do about heat? Huh?"

"You took care of Ol' Stick'ums. Now Ol' Stick'ums gonna take care of you," the old man said, but his words failed to reassure Murdah Man. "But back to the matter at hand, I called ya'll in for a reason. So let me know something, ya dig?"

* * * * * *

Far off in the distance, the two could hear thunder resonating through the heavens. The over cast looked as if threatening to rain. Lone Wolf sat in Murdah Man's Ford Mustang. "I don't think we should, cuz. I mean, we got everything we could ever need. We really should let this shit ride," Lone Wolf had spoken. His voice was calm... quiet with resignation.

"Naw, nigga. Forget that, cuz. We hit this fool, take um out, then *WE* calling the shots," Murdah Man replied, his voice heavy with unrestricted tenacity. "You really think we could stop now, huh? You already in too deep. You know it's only a matter of time before these dummies figure out it's been us all along. If we stop now, we open ourselves up to become targets. But we do this, get out on top, we'll be outta they reach. It's the only way. Ain't no turning back. We ball 'til we fall, now."

It was impossible for Lone Wolf to comprehend the suicidal folly of such an unachievable mission. Murdah Man thought he was impervious to injury. Such thinking makes him a liability. It was obvious to him that Murdah Man intended on killing Crime Boss and his henchmen... placing him in a position to obtain ultimate control and power over any and all drug transactions in Omaha. He wanted to become the sole provider to every drug dealer.

Stick'ums thought this as the final resolution. The single hit that can set a person straight for life. Lone Wolf thought it a foolish idea altogether... for he had witnessed Crime Boss's display of raw power. He knew that his henchmen were well trained killers; and such a mission could back fire... leading both him and Murdah Man to an early grave.

"So what's cracking, cuz? We gonna do this?" Murdah Man became frustrated when Lone Wolf didn't respond. "Peep game, cuz. I know you wanna leave this game alone, and that's coo. But we do this right here, not only will we be balling outta control, nigga'z and bitches will know for sure they can't get with us."

Lone Wolf turned towards him. He saw a look of ruthless animosity etched on Murdah Man's face. He began to wonder if maybe he had some personal vendetta against Crime Boss... and this is why he wanted to either kill or be killed. It was the only rational explanation for his willingness to even consider colliding with Omaha's most notorious drug lord. "Cuz, we got everything."

"Naw, nigga, I want it all."

"Let me think about it, cuz."

"Yeah, a-ight. You sleep on the this. But remember this nigga, with or without you, I'm going. Imma try this fool."

DAY TWENTY-SIX

The tortured cry of Lone Wolf's name ripped him from his sleep. He shot up in his bed, his chest heaving for air. Instantly he knew it was a dream... a dream he once again could not recall. Only the echo of his name being cried out rang in his ears. His gaze wondered aimlessly around the room as he awaited the sleep fog to clear. His eyes fell upon a woman that laid asleep next to him. He looked upon her with disgust and contempt.

"Ah. It's time to get up," Lone Wolf said, his voice still heavy with sleep. With her eyes still closed, she turned towards his voice with a slow smile. The smile gradually faded as she fell back into a shallow sleep. "Ah! It's time to get up, girl!" he said a little louder as he poked her in the forehead with his middle finger.

"Ow," the woman languidly groaned, lazily rubbing her forehead. She looked up at Lone Wolf, her eyes blinking sluggishly. "Ummm..." she moaned softly, seductively as she stretched. "Good morning, baby boo."

"You a-ight?" Lone Wolf asked.

She smiled up at him them answered, "A little sore. But that's how I like it."

"Sore, huh?" he asked, knowing she was speaking on their sexual escapade. "Can you still walk?" She nodded her head yes as she stretched a second time. "Good," Lone Wolf said softly. "Get out."

"What?!" she said in shock, the sluggishness and sleepiness instantly gone.

"You gotta go."

"For what? Why?" she asked lambently, as if she was hurt.

"What's my name?" he asked the woman. She looked at him confusingly. "Tell me my name and we can do this the right way. The way lovers do. If not, get the fuck out." The woman stared at him without blinking... the mixture of hurt and anger shown in her eyes. "Yeah, get out," he instructed her as he reached over and grabbed a bottle of Christian Brothers that sat on the night stand.

The woman smacked her lips and crawled out of bed. Still naked, she crossed the room, picking up articles of clothing as she went. He could hear her cursing him under her breath, but he could care less. "Where's my bra?" she spat angrily as she shuffled through her belongings, then searched the floor again. Lone Wolf sat in bed nonchalantly... searching for that small zone of comfort.

Finally the woman turned to him. Defiantly, she demanded, "What's my name?"

He looked at her confusingly. His lips then parted into a slow grin, he knew what game she was trying to play. Lone Wolf not only answered her question, he went on as far as telling her her age, her place of employment, and even an aspiration she wishes to fulfill within the next two years. The woman was dumbstruck. "How am I suppose to get home?" she asked.

Lone Wolf reached over to the night stand and grabbed the money that laid beside the pistol. After peeling back three twenty dollar bills, he threw it at her.

"Call a cab," he replied dryly.

"Where did all this come from?" she asked, her eyes threatening to shed a tear. "Why all of a sudden you acting like this?" He didn't respond. He couldn't respond. He watched her as she stormed from the room... seconds later, the slamming of a door.

Lone Wolf sat in silence, sipping on the mixture of Coke-cola and Christian Brothers... the question of, *where did all this come from?* being repeated in his mind. The truth was, he didn't know where it came from... nor why he felt the way he did.

He started to unlock the heavy gates of consciousness as he concentrated on the question. He thought that maybe the answer lies in the past... in some obscure crevice of memory. Perhaps it was his mother's many, many relationships that influenced his current judgment? Leaving him unable to settle. At the thought, he felt a twinge of resentment. He was nothing like his mother, if circumstances were suitable, he was capable of love. Thus he rejected the thought immediately.

"I'm nothing like her," he assured himself. "If given half a chance." With this, his thoughts turned to Amber Faye. He knew beyond a shadow of a doubt that he could find love with her. *So why don't I?* he asked himself. *Maybe I am like her?*

"Hell naw," he said out loud. "It's gotta be something else."

Perhaps it's his total absorption in fulfilling a contradictory mission? A mission of protecting himself from ALL outsiders while seeking the protection of another. Perhaps this mistrust played a role in his inability to allow Amber Faye in? He wants nothing more then to follow his heart. Unfortunately... emotional circumstances dictate otherwise. Such matters seemed to be an enigma beyond solution. And the more he thought about it... the more despondent he became.

"Man, forget this," he growled to himself, giving up his search for the answer to her question. His gaze moved lingeringly around the room, the quietness buzzing loudly in his ears. Knowing what was to come next, he jumped to his feet and dressed quickly. In a matter of minutes he was fully dressed, money, pager, cell phone and pistol in pocket, and out the door. He wouldn't allow himself enough time to fully realize he was alone.

* * * * * *

After ensuring there was a live round in the chamber of his Glock .40, Murdah Man stepped from his '95 Mustang. The morning was gray and dreary... heavy clouds covering the heavens completely. All morning there had been mist and rain... a thin veil of moisture covering the earth. The air was wet... clammy. Murdah Man made his way up the sidewalk leading to Stick'ums front door. As he reached the steps to the screened-in porch, he heard the raspy voice of Stick'ums.

"What's up, young blood?"

His voice had caught Murdah Man unaware. He jumped in a flash of startling.

"Ah man, don't be doing that shit!" Murdah Man cursed as he made his way up the steps. From the outside, one couldn't see into the screened-in porch, no matter how hard one would try. But from the inside, concealed within the darkness of the porch, one could see outside clearly. "Mess around and get shot up in this piece," Murdah Man continued. Stick'ums chuckled in response.

"What brings you by, young blood?" Stick'ums asked as Murdah Man stepped through the screen door.

"I came to see what's up with the heat," Murdah Man replied.

"I thought Feather's took care of that end. And you, China White?"

"Naw, homeboy. We's partners. We do this together," Murdah Man lied. Although it was true that the two were in fact partners, it was Lone Wolf who controlled all issues concerning weapons, while Murdah Man handled every aspect of the drug trade. Such arrangements were set in place so that one could not interfere with the commission of the other's duty. Therefore, when it comes to weapons, it was Lone Wolf who dealt with Stick'ums; and Stick'ums dealt strictly with Lone Wolf. Everything was done on a need to know bases... the way Stick'ums preferred it. Therefore, Murdah Man had not the slightest clue that Lone Wolf was expecting a shipment the following day.

"Ain't no happenings, ya dig?" Stick'ums lied. He was well aware of their business arrangements. "Waiting for the cat ta hit me now."

Murdah Man studied the old man... hatred flaring in his eyes. Seeing this, a flicker of uneasiness oppressed Stick'ums.

"What's up with that choppa?" Murdah Man asked, his voice dropping low... taking on a dangerous note.

"What about it, young blood?" Stick'ums asked defiantly.

An overshadowing mask of ruthless animosity crossed the face of Murdah Man as he glared at the old man.

"I'm here to take it. And every other strap you got up in here," Murdah Man said. Stick'ums eyed the young killer, but he was far from impressed. Stick'ums chuckled, low... raspy... guttural. "You think this a fuckin' joke, old ass nigga? Ya thinking' I'm fuckin' bluffin', nigga?!" Murdah Man roared as he pulled his Glock from concealment. His words and actions cut to the quick... but Stick'ums fear and apprehension didn't show on his bull dogfish face.

"I've lived a long life, ya dig? Truth be told, I should died a few times in Nam. This shit ain't nothing' but borrowed time, ya dig?"

Instantly, a rush of cold resistance from hot lead slammed against the old man's chest. The gunshot barked loudly within the screened-in porch. The impact of the bullet flung Stick'ums back in the recliner. He sat there gripping his wound. His face remained a taunt, truculent mask of determined resistance against the pain that swelled in his chest. As Murdah Man stepped forward with his pistol leveled, he heard the slow and shallow breathing of the old man. With sporadic, liquefied sounds, Stick'ums began to cough up blood. The coughing slowly turned to a low chuckle.

"Nigga, you still think it's a joke?" Murdah Man asked as he placed the barrel of his pistol against Stick'ums left eye. Defiant to the end, Stick'ums chuckle turned into a weak and strained laugh... followed by the coughing of more blood.

"Let me tell you something', young blood," Stick'ums said in between forced breaths. "Those gats in there is useless. Even the M-60. They're show guns. None of them work... none of um have firing pins." With this said, he began to laugh again, it being more labored. Sounds of gurgling blood was evident in this laughter.

Anger mounted suddenly in Murdah Man. His Glock jerked as he pulled at the trigger, sending a bullet through the left eye of Stick'ums. The lead found its way out the back of his skull, spraying the back of the recliner with its insides. Although dead, Stick'ums sat twisting and jerking helplessly... his hands slowly opening and closing.

* * * * * *

As Lone Wolf exited the corner store with a half-pint of Christian Brothers and a bottle of Cola, he felt a single rain drop fall onto his face. Looking up towards the skies, the heavens were gray and bleak. He felt the cold wetness of a second drop hit his flesh.

After reaching the '64 Chevy, he instantly began blending the liquids. Sitting back, he took a long drink of the bitter-sweet mixture. Closing his eyes, he savored the taste as he swallowed slowly... seeking to douse the fire that was raging in his stomach.

Just as he opened his eyes, a black hearse rolled into view. A long line of cars crawled slowly behind the hearse as it rode mercilessly onward. Lone Wolf recognized the symbol on the side of the limos. It was the insignia of Salem's 1st Baptist Church... the church of which held the services for the funeral of his brother, Kevin.

Turning over the engine, unconsciously Lone Wolf fell in line with the rest of the mourners as the hearse solemnly lead the way. Subconsciously he knew where they were headed... to the cemetery of which held his brother. This is why he followed.

The hearse came to a gradual halt outside the iron gates of the cemetery. The long lines of cars followed pursuit. Beyond the iron gates one could see countless head-stones... along with large statutes with eerie looking crypts lurking here and there.

Slowly, the heavy gates were pulled open and the black hearse pushed grimly onward. Gentle mounds of green, bordered by bright flowers, dotted the landscape. So many markers... so many names... so many forgotten people... so many unfulfilled dreams. Lone Wolf began to wonder how long it would take for his memory to fade, fading into darkness... like the setting of the sun? How long will it take for his name to die out like the billion upon billions of people that had died before him? Names that will never be spoken again?

It had only been eight years for his brother, Kevin... yet he is now nothing more than a playground legend... a legend that's slowly dying a second death. Soon he will be forgotten by all. All except for Lone Wolf. Kevin now rests here in this cemetery... alone... in the midst of strangers. The same as Lone Wolf will one day.

With this, Lone Wolf began to think of his own immortality. If he were to die tonight, who would hold his hand in comfort as he struggles to breathe? Who would stand by his side as he takes his last breath? Who would mourn his death? Who would attend his funeral? Who will keep his memory alive? Lone Wolf knew if he were to die tonight... he would die cold and alone. He would become one of these lonely green mounds... a name of complexity on a simple marker... surrounded by strangers... and then quickly forgotten.

He watched as the line of cars came to a rest. A casket was lowered from the hearse... a plain and simple wooden box. The inexpensive casket was eerily reminiscent of Kevin's arrival eight years earlier. Slowly his eyes began to water.

Again he found himself blinking against the familiar sting of unshead tears.

He remembered vividly how only three people attended the funeral of Kevin. Himself, and his two new foster parents. Foster parents who were completely indifferent to the child's pain and loss. They had only brought him because it was ordered by the courts. It had seemed to the child that even the minister and the six Paul Barriers were indifferent.

Lone Wolf continued to watch as the mourners followed the casket to its final resting place. He watched as a mother broke down, screaming the name of her daughter... a daughter who will soon be nothing more than a green mound and a headstone. Beside the grieving mother stood two small children, her grandchildren, perhaps. They stood rigid... grasping tightly to the black dress of the crying woman. The smaller of the two, the little girl, stood confused... unable to fully comprehend what was taking place. Her slightly older brother stood beside her... crying softly... clutching tightly to his little sister's hand.

"We're leavin' mommy here?" the little girl asked innocently as she looked up at her brother. "I don't want to. We can't leave her here by herself," she said as she began to cry.

The heavens opened its heart and bled more tears.

The boy stood in silence... caring nothing of the rain... capable of only looking upon the casket which embraced his mother. The boy looked to be only eight years old. He knew how the child felt. How strange it felt to leave a loved one here in a plain wooden box... left alone out in the rain.

With the pain soothing mixture in hand, Lone Wolf exited the car. Slowly he began to make his way to the resting place of his brother. He took one last glance over his shoulder to where the two children stood. The little girl looking up at her big brother... her tiny hand intertwined with his. The boy's face wet with tears and rain... watching as his mother is lowered into the ground.

On the verge of drunkenness, Lone Wolf made it to Kevin. Hot tears blurred his vision as he stood listening to the vast, enveloping silence of the cemetery. Coldness swirled around him; the clinging wetness caused him to shiver. Time and time again he drank the mixture... praying its warmth would overcome the coldness of the rain. It had yet to prevail.

He could recall warm and sunny days when he and Kevin would play in the front yard. And how Kevin had sworn to protect his little brother whenever times got hard.

"'Birds of a feather flock together,' ain't that what you told me?" Lone Wolf whispered into the rain... wondering if his words could be heard. Another tear fell as he thought of his present position... alone in a cemetery... abandoned in chilling, mucilaginous mist and rain... sunk in abject sorrow.

His thoughts turned towards the ever so evasive T-Roy... the source of his relentless misery. He and Murdah Man had searched extensively for him... yet somehow he had remained elusive. The two head-hunters would show up mere minutes after his departure. However hard Lone Wolf had tried to keep his intentions under wrap, he was sure T-Roy knew he was a marked man.

Maybe that's why T-Roy keep leaving town for two to three days at a time, Lone Wolf wondered, *kinda like his own personal game.*

The realization drained his waning confidence even further. He pulled the Desert Eagle from the small of his back then sank down onto the cold, wet grass... inert and miserable.

* * * * * *

In the process of ransacking the house of Stick'ums, Murdah Man's cell phone began to ring. Although reluctant, he answered. "What?!" he asked in his usual manner of answering the phone.

"What's cracking, cuz," Lone Wolf replied softly. "Where you at?" he asked Murdah Man.

"Nigga, where YOU at?" There was an acrimonious note to his response, but it was too fleeing for Lone Wolf to grasp.

"I'm at the cemetery."

"The cemetery? What for?" Murdah Man asked. Lone Wolf was hesitant to reply.

"Cuz, we gotta get this nigga T-Roy, for real, cuz. We gotta kill this nigga." Lone Wolf tried his best to conceal the shakiness of his voice... but his attempt was unsuccessful.

"Don't even trip, cuz," Murdah Man reassured him. "We's bound to catch this fool slipping. But for now, we gotta focus on tonight, feel me? I mean, that is if you gonna be there for a nigga."

Lone Wolf sat silently on the other end of the phone. Murdah Man knew that he could count on Lone Wolf to be there despite this reluctance. He knew that Lone Wolf wasn't the kind to leave a friend to fend for himself... especially when the odds are stacked so dramatically against him. Besides, the time has come for Lone Wolf to claim his first soul. And by the murder of the infamous drug-lord, Murdah Man will be left in a position to kill two birds with one stone. This was his true intent.

"We gonna need heat," Lone Wolf finally said.

"That's what I'm working on now," Murdah Man said as he worked the lever of the M-60. He pulled on the trigger, but he didn't hear a click. When Lone Wolf didn't respond, he asked, "What the hell is a firing pin?"

"Huh?"

"What's a firing pin?" Murdah Man repeated.

Due to his current state of mind, Lone Wolf didn't want to get into details. So he simple replied, "It's what shoots bullets."

"So a strap won't work without one?"

"No," Lone Wolf said dryly.

"Man, damn!" Murdah Man roared as he flung the assault rifle across the room. He picked up another rifle, squeezed the trigger, listening for a click. There were none. "I gotta go, cuz," Murdah Man said into the phone. "I'm abouts to whoop this dude ass."

After hanging up the phone, Murdah Man stormed out onto the porch. Looming over the lifeless corpse of Stick'ums, he shoved the relic of an M-14 into his face. "What is this, huh?!" he roared at the dead body. "Make it work, motha fucka!" he yelled frantically as he grabbed Stick'ums by the back of the neck... his head rolled and his arms swung lifelessly. "Make it work!" Murdah Man demanded as he pried the dead man's eyelids open. "You think I'm bluffing!" he roared in words that sounded demonic in their fury.

When Stick'ums didn't respond, Murdah Man flew into a blind rage. He dropped the corpse and commenced to beat it brutally with the frame of the assault rifle. "Ohh, you gonna make these work," he grumbled as he dragged the carcass into the house, where the vicious assault continued.

* * * * * *

Lone Wolf lowered the cell phone... his hands trembling from both anger and inconsolable sadness. To keep his composure while speaking to Murdah Man was harder than expected. But he knew Murdah Man was right. For the time being, their main objective is to stay focused on that night... mindful of the dangers inherited in such a mission.

But still... to detach himself from the harness of the indignation which has both haunted and enslaved him for far too many years seemed unfeasible. To remain optimistic while on bended knees in the heart of a cemetery would be difficult for anybody... especially with the imprudent obstacles which lies ahead. He wanted to cry out in frustration... in anger... in agony. Rain drizzle and tears mingled on his taunted face... it was difficult to tell where one ends and the other begins.

"I'll be back," he whispered as he touched the headstone of Kevin. He slipped the phone back into his pocket and picked up the consoling mixture. With his .357 still in hand, he slowly raised to his feet. He knew the time has come, with the life he led, he knew it was inevitable. "I'll be back," he promised again. He knew it was now do or die. "One way or another, dead or alive, I'll be back."

* * * * * *

Lighting split the dark heavens in mad flashes... followed shorty by the crashing volley of thunder. Thunder that seemed to mimic the destructive storm that brewed in the heart of Lone Wolf. But such a display of celestial intensity was a misrepresentation of the rain... for it was nothing more than a light drizzle. The two head-hunters sat in Murdah Man's Ford Probe just outside the N. 16th Warehouse. In spite of their mission, their arsenal of weapons were nothing more than three handguns.

All that day Lone Wolf tried again and again to get a hold of Stick'ums... for he knew to successfully undertake such an extreme task, they would need heavy weaponry. But his many attempts to contact Stick'ums were to no avail.

After reassuring his twin Glocks were fully loaded, Murdah Man turned towards Lone Wolf, "What's up, cuz? You about ready for this here?"

"Cuz," Lone Wolf said slowly, not fully understanding why he was so willing to partake in such a suicidal mission, "I'm down for whatever. I just wish we had more heat. You know they gonna be suited and booted."

"I tried to get some choppa'z earlier today. But the fool was on some bull. In fact, that's where I was at when you called," Murdah Man said.

"Yeah, I've been trying get a hold of Stick'ums all day. He got a closet full of heat. Even though he don't like it, I think I shoulda just stopped by, huh? Damn!" Lone Wolf growled the last part.

"That fool dead somewhere," Murdah Man said as he laughed manically. "If he ain't dead, then he only got one good eye," he continued as he laughed hysterically. Then all at once, he stopped. "Let's go," he said to Lone Wolf as he quickly stepped from the car.

Lone Wolf watched him as he exited the Mustang... there was something eerie in Murdah Man's words... a truly demented ring in his voice... something truly amiss. In his dark eyes, a glimmer of something too fleeing to be captured by the glancing eyes of Lone Wolf. After he checked the live round in the chamber, Lone Wolf exited the vehicle as well.

The two hunters quickly hopped the security fence then dashed swiftly across the open lot in a low crouch. Their footsteps echoing unnaturally loud in the ears of the nervous Lone Wolf as they ran threw puddles of water. The night had grown cool, the heavy mist that clung to his face sent a serpentine chill lashing down his spine. They headed towards the building's edge, seeking the security that the shadows held.

They crouched among the unattended bushed and ferns. Lone Wolf's palms were slippery from nervous perspiration and drizzle. After drying them off on his pants leg, he gripped the Desert Eagle with resolved determination.

"This fool got guards on point," Murdah Man said to Lone Wolf, his voice light from dark amusement. "Like he really a King Pin or something"

Lone Wolf followed Murdah Man's gaze. Two armed guards stood just outside the rear entrance. He instantly recognized the curved magazine on the AK-47's frame. Again he felt the surging chill racing along his spine. This time it was caused by the inadequacy of his own pistol.

"How we gonna get past them?" he asked Murdah Man. He became uneasy when Murdah Man didn't respond. "Damn, I shoulda went by Stick'ums," he said regretfully.

"What for?" Murdah Man asked. "We got two new choppa'z right there." As he said this, a tight venomous smile formed on his lips. "How many Steven Seagull movies have you seen? Just like in the movies, this it'll be easy, cuz."

Lone Wolf couldn't believe what he was hearing. Although he had anticipating such a derange and demented response, he still found it unbelievable. His lips twitched and stammered with unspoken words.

"We gonna do this like G's," Murdah Man said as he began to wrap his blue bandanna around his face. He then turned towards Lone Wolf.

Lone Wolf's face assumed his usual mask of false calmness. "Lone Wolf's down for whatever," he said trying to sound as confident as possible despite the grinding churn of nausea seizing him from within. He then pulled his own blue bandanna from his back pocket and wrapped it around his face.

As if trained in the art and tactics of guerrilla warfare, the two head-hunters slowly made their way towards their intending targets. Once they were in range, Lone Wolf saw Murdah Man lifting his two pistols out the corner of his eye. He raised his own .357. His heart seemed contracted in an icy claw as thoughts of committing his first murder flashed across his mind. Those inner demons who sought for so long for this moment were now stirring anxiously. The wicked doxology of the damn sounded loudly in his ears. The chant had drowned out Murdah Man's Twin Glocks as they spat bullets in the direction of the armed guards. Although he couldn't hear the barking of the pistols, he saw the strobing flash in his peripheral vision. Lone Wolf followed suit.

As Lone Wolf squeezed the trigger, the Desert Eagle .357 semiautomatic SL roared and bucked against his clammy palm. The thunderous roar of three pistols caught the two guards completely by surprise. The first went down in a hail of hot lead. Due to the demonic chants in his ears, Lone Wolf didn't hear him scream like a wild animal as bullet after bullet dug into his chest.

The stuttering burst of an AK ripped opened the night as the second guard returned fire. Such a display of superior fire power instantly silenced the voices trapped in Lone Wolf's skull. As he dove towards the wet ground, he could hear the bullets buzzing overhead... like a nest of angry hornets. His short life began to flash before his eyes.

In the beginning, he knew it was idiotic to undergo such an impossible task, that it was delusional to truly believe that three hand guns could truly overpower two assault rifles. Even with the element of surprise working in their favor, such a mission was still impossible.

Suddenly, there was silence. An eerie, omnipotent silence.

"What, nigga?!" Lone Wolf heard Murdah Man roar. "Ya'll nigga'z can't fuck with this!" Murdah Man yelled towards the warehouse as he laughed wickedly. Lone Wolf raised his head, only to find Murdah Man swinging his arms about wildly... pacing madly back and fourth... cursing the dead guards and the warehouse building. His blue rag no longer concealed his face. A look of vicious triumph etched on every feature of his face. If ever there were a living being that looked more cruel... demonic... more Satan-like, it was Murdah Man at that very moment. His dark eyes shone of pure wickedness in the scattered street lights.

Slowly, Lone Wolf got to his feet, his black hoodie now dark and heavy from puddle water. He watched as Murdah Man stood over the two corpse, he still cursed the dead bodies. With his two Glocks, he began to unload the remaining clip into the head of the second guard. Lone Wolf watched as his body jerked with convulsive shudders as the merciless bullets dug into his skull. He then picked up the man's AK and worked the bolt, making sure a live round was chambered. With an evil snarl of satisfaction, he tossed the assault rifle to Lone Wolf, then picked up the second.

Not expecting to be thrown a fully loaded rifle, Lone Wolf caught it clumsily, almost dropping the Desert Eagle in the process. "Nigga, what the hell is wrong with you?!" Lone Wolf barked at Murdah Man. "Don't be throwing me no loaded choppa!" When he looked up, he saw that Murdah Man's face was cruel and emotionless.

Their attention was then drawn towards the warehouse, where inside a man was yelling. His voice boomed. It was a voice accustomed to authority and giving commands.

"That's him?" Murdah Man asked. The truth was that although he had seen Crime Boss a few times, Lone Wolf had not the slightest clue of what he sounded like.

"That's him," Lone Wolf answered in a matter-of-factual way.

"Then what we waiting for?"

The sound of running feet drifted towards them on a light breeze. Lone Wolf struggled with the overpowering urge to retreat. In an instant, Murdah Man was gone, disappearing inside the warehouse entrance.

Driven by greed... Murdah Man was a warmonger with an unquenchable thirst for war. Although Lone Wolf wanted to flee, he tucked his .357 into his waistband, than reassured that the AK was operational, then followed Murdah Man into the shadows of the unknown.

* * * * * *

Sounds of gunfire and yelling filled the warehouse. Angry bullets ate away at tattered wood. The bursting pulse of AK's flashed and twinkled like mini strobe lights, illuminating flickering sparks, closely resembling an underground rave. Shattered glass and empty shells raining down, tinkling like a hundred tiny bells. Nothing seemed real, as if being played on a video game. People falling and dying.

In a flare of panic, a man stood and sprayed an area with his AK until his weapon was empty and the bolt locked back. More bullets cut threw the air, ripping into the flesh of the standing man. The putrid odor of fresh copper and gun powder hung heavily in the air.

One by one, the guards fell before the flashing strobe of the muzzle. Soon Crime Boss was left alone. His mask of invincibility vanished almost immediately... replaced by uncontrollable apprehension. His eyes grew round as the two invaders slowly approached, like two deadly vipers stalking their prey. He turned to flee, but hot pain raked saw-toothed nails through his thigh as burning lead pierced through his flesh.

He tumbled to the ground. He clawed at the concrete, trying to escape, dragging his bloody and useless legs behind him. A boot came down on his neck... pinning him to the ground. A single shot rang out, it found it's way into his back... embedding itself within his breast plate. Pain ebbed and swelled in his chest as he struggled to breath. The boot lifted from his neck, only to be placed under his shoulder, then it flipped him over onto his back. Wave after wave of nerve-clutching pain coursed through his body as the boot came down on his chest. He tried to cry-out... to scream... but the blood that was accumulating in his lungs prevented him from doing so.

Through a misty veil of pain, Crime Boss found himself looking into the eyes of the most demoniacal form he had ever seen. A wicked and sinister snarl plastered on his cadaverous face.

"This one's yours," the man with the dead eyes and cruel grin said aloud. The second viper who stood off to the side now approached, slowly. He discarded the AK and pulled a semi-automatic pistol from his waist band. He slowly lowered the pistol... taking precise aim in between the eyes of Crime Boss. He pulled the blue rag down from around his face... revealing a young... yet brutally vindictive face. It was the last face Crime Boss would ever see.

* * * * * *

The wet of the night air clung to Lone Wolf's flesh as he and Murdah Man stepped from the warehouse "Wait here," Murdah Man instructed him before he left for his Mustang. Zipping up his black hoodie, Lone Wolf placed his .357 in the small of his back. Doing this, he felt a shiver from deep within as it made it's way to the surface... causing him to tremble.

As he stuck his hands in his pockets... he wondered if the trembling was caused by the heated metal or by the fact that eight dead men laid sprawled out just behind the warehouse door. One of them being Crime Boss. He felt unusually calm despite the circumstances. He didn't feel the anticipated surge of guilt... nor the overpowering joy for surviving such an impossible task. He didn't feel anything. Just a powerful sense of tranquility.

He stood gazing vacantly into the air. He now turned his attention towards the heavens. The overcast sky was heavy with the promise of more rain. In fact, off in the distance, he could barely hear the low growl of rolling thunder. He then looked at the surrounding area, the warehouse was in deep shadows, here and there were scattered pools of light, cast by low hanging street lights. Hundreds of rain puddles that were spread out on the wide lot glistened in this light as well. All the rest was dark. He stood wondering how long they were in the warehouse. He glanced down at his pager, 3:58AM.

Just then, Murdah Man slowly pulled up in is Mustang. He backed the car up all the way to the door, then popped the trunk. In less than five minutes they were able to load all 150 kilo's of powder cocaine.

Pulling out of the warehouse's lot, Murdah Man turned to Lone Wolf and said, "I just got hit on the pager. This yea-brick from the south side looking for 15 zones." His voice was completely void of emotions. "We abouts to go handle that."

"Psst, we can't ride around with all this work. We should drop it off first and get rid of these guns, feel me?" Lone Wolf responded.

"Naw, homie, we gonna handle this now," Murdah Man said, his expression was flat when he said it. Again he turned towards Lone Wolf and said, "Nigga, this a new game. Only the strong survives." His voice was low and it carried a sharp note in it.

Looking at Murdah Man, Lone Wolf could see that there was something missing from his eyes. Although they had always been cold and dark... evil and sinister... he could tell that something was gone, replaced by something he could not completely comprehend. But before he could respond, Murdah Man had already taken a left on the freeway, heading south.

* * * * * *

The rugged and raspy voice of Bushwick Bill was playing on the stereo system as Lone Wolf watched the houses fly by off in the distance. Looking at these homes, he wondered if it's occupants were happy. A happy home is the dream of every outsider... especially to him. His mind instantly turned to his mother. He thought of their last meeting behind the homeless shelter... and how she didn't recognize him.

How long ago was that? he thought to himself. *One week? Two? Perhaps three?* He couldn't recall exactly. Memories were evasive to him now... uncertain in time and content. So many things has happened to him within the past month. Besides, when you're living life in it's fastest lane, time becomes irrelevant. Now, only vague memories of his mother could be played in his mind. He could only remember the physical pain. These memories were strong... vivid... felt.

As they crossed the Kennedy Freeway, he looked down on the cars and people below. Wondering where it was they were headed to at such an early hour. *Probably a booty call,* he thought to himself. Thinking this caused him to think of Amber Faye. It has been a couple of weeks since the "incident." This last encounter was a disaster. The desire to contact her has always been strong. But somehow he's managed not to succumb to this unyielding urge. *She probably hates me now,* he thought to himself, which made resisting calling her easy.

Even before then, he knew that she despised his life style... his mentality. She would often tell him that she could see something great in him, but he didn't believe it. He was indeed highly intelligent. But years in lock-up with nothing but books to occupy one's time could do that to anybody. She would often say she believed he was bound for greatness. *But how could this be when he wasn't even good enough for a mother's love?* he thought to himself. Amber Faye didn't know him, and what little she did know of him, she despised. So how could she believe in him? "None of this matters now, she hates me," he said between his teeth, just loud enough for only he himself to hear.

* * * * * *

At that very moment... unable to sleep, Amber Faye sat at her desk... staring blankly at the note pad that laid before her. She was surrounded by wads of balled up paper. She was dressed in only a blue t-shirt that Lone Wolf had left behind. It was five sizes too big for her small and petite frame. But it was her favorite shirt. She wore it as a night gown every since he left it. It was always this time of night when her every thought was of him. That vulnerable time of night when she knew she was inescapably alone.

Picking up her pen, she tried to focus on the few words that she had written down, the start of a new poem, the physical manifestation of written expression. "The ways of love... From a thugs point of view," she read out loud.

She knew that if she could only complete this poem, she would have a better understanding of Lone Wolf. This is what she was seeking. But how could she complete it? Before him, she has had absolutely no experience with the likes of him.

Her life had been nothing more than a legacy, a tradition created by the hands of many generations. She didn't have to do much to maintain the cocoon of comfort that had been spun by these generations. But despite this legacy, despite her lifestyle... she was all too familiar with neglect... with loneliness. And although she hadn't been destined to suffer as Lone

Wolf had, she still had a quiet fire that burned in her soul... a private kind of sorrow, if you will. And she knew that if only she could douse the blazing fire of pain and hatred that raged in his soul with the fire of loneliness in her own heart, she could spark and rekindle the flame of eternal love that will burn forever. She believed in this from the beginning... and her faith in this remains strong. Each night she prays that he will return to her... or at least call her... for she misses him dearly.

Again she tried to focus her eyes on the notepad. "The ways of love... From a thug's point of view," she read aloud for the twentieth time. But still she had nothing to add... again she found herself incapable of conceiving such a twisted and warped mind-set. In frustration she tore the page from the pad and balled it up.

After setting down her pen, she simply listened to the soft hum of the refrigerator and continued to think of Lone Wolf. She drew her knees up and pulled her t-shirt over her legs. Crossing her arms over them, she rested her chin on her upraised knees and began to slowly rock back and fourth. She shivered. *It's chilly,* she thought to herself. She stared at the unmade bed. *If only Lone Wolf were here,* she thought, *he could lie beside me; not for sex, just for warmth.*

* * * * * *

"This fool said he'll be in back of that old club up behind the stock-yards. Know where that's at?" Murdah Man asked without taking his eyes from the road.

"Yup," Lone Wolf responded, not catching on to the fact that business was done on a pager, so such information could not have been easily relayed.

After so many turns, Murdah Man pulled into an empty lot and got out. "Come on," he told Lone Wolf. An opaquing alarm began to pull at the soul of Lone Wolf as he stepped from the car. This subtle warning seemed to settle in the hollowness of his stomach as he searched the area for sign of danger. He had his trusty Desert Eagle tucked into his waist band, he also had Murdah Man there. But although he was well protected by his pistol and Murdah Man, he still couldn't ignore the snake he felt slithering in the pit of his stomach.

After turning the corner of the old, condemned brick building, Murdah Man yelled out, "Cool Breeze! Where you at?!" But the only answer he got in return was silence. "Coo' Breeze!" he yelled a second time, but again he got the same response. Turning towards Lone Wolf, he said, "Forget this. Let's just ride out."

Turning back towards the Mustang, Lone Wolf was leading the way when suddenly he felt the heavy blow of stainless steel across his neck. Dropping to his knees, he felt a second blow on the crown of his head... a solid impact that shot a white-hot sliver of pain throughout his body. Stars danced behind closed eye lids from yet another blow... followed by another, but a blow not of the stainless steel frame of a pistol, but the blow of a well placed kick. His eye lids were growing heavy as a grayness... like a mist at dawn, filled his consciousness. He felt warm blood tickling down his face as he fought to stay conscious. He tasted blood in his mouth as he endured blow after blow.

On the brink of unconsciousness, he was engulfed by excruciating pains more terrible than he had ever known before.

Those inner demons sought out desperately for energy within his drained body so they could launch an attack. But none was found. Pain flared in almost every place on his body as he fought to clear his vision. Through a red haze of pain, he found himself looking down the barrel of Murdah Man's pistol. He tried reaching for his own weapon, but Murdah Man kicked him onto his back.

Murdah Man's lips were moving, but the only sounds Lone Wolf could hear was the chants of the dead, and the pounding of his own heart. He watched as Murdah Man's finger tensed on the trigger, and he knew that with just a little more pressure, his suffering would end. Not just the fleeing physical pain that he was feeling now, but the pain that have had him praying for death night after night. With just a little more pressure and there would be no more pain... no more sorrow. He will be at peace by his brother's side.

With this thought, images of Kevin played his vision. Now it was Kevin he saw standing behind the trigger. He stretched a bloody hand up towards his brother... with eyes pleading for help... pleading for protection. But the agonizing pain of his body wouldn't allow his hand to touch his brother. Nor would it allow his eyes to stay open much longer.

Suddenly, a radiant light pierced the darkness behind Kevin. As Lone Wolf's eyes looked towards Kevin's smiling face, he saw that the gun had vanished, leaving only a hand. A hand that beckoned to him, palm opened and the fingers slightly curled. Lone Wolf cried out to Kevin in a tiny voice spurred by pain. He tried reaching out again, but was plunged into darkness.

* * * * * *

Lone Wolf didn't know how long he had laid unconscious before he returned to the agonizing pain of his unfortunate predicament. He laid immobile, groaning at the waves of terrible pain that filled him. He tried looking at his pager, but the pager was busted, and his cell phone was as well.

Staggering to his feet, he grimaced against the pain that throbbed in his entire body. In a pain induced daze, everything around him was hazy at the edges. The only things that had any clarity was those he looked directly at, as if he was looking through a parting mist.

He was holding onto conscious only with the most intense exertion of will. The lot of which he stood was emerged partly in shadows. With careful deliberation, and moving like a drunken man trying to maintain his balance, he slowly made his way across the lot; heading towards a green neon sign that read, "Bar and Grill."

The ravaging pain of his body forced him to stop. Standing there, he could feel himself sinking gradually into a half-conscious, yet fitful reverie. He stood wondering who could he turn to? The pain grew and grew until it was too much for him, and he slowly dropped to his knees. Again he wondered who could he run to to ease the pain.

On his knees in the dark of a rain swept night, he contemplated his disastrous fate and the sequence of unfortunate events that had lead him to this miserable situation. The betrayal of his closest friend, Murdah Man. The thought drove an icy needle into his heart. He reached to the small of his back and was surprised to find that he still had his weapon. Lone Wolf wanted to cry out in anger... in pain. Instead, he clutched the pistol firmly... feeling the comforting weight in his hand.

Again, Lone Wolf staggered to his feet with great effort. With his pistol in hand, he concentrated his thoughts... his emotions... his entire being on a single purpose... revenge. As he rolled this feeling over in his heart, he felt the demons within began to stir. It gave him warmth in the cool of the night. It gave him strength in spite of the weariness of his body. It gave him a faint sense of pleasure despite the state of misery.

Reaching the Bar and Grill, he saw a pay phone in the soft glow of a street light. With his body now completely sapped of it's energy, he stumbled towards it. Picking up the receiver, he began to push the numbers needed to place a collect call. He listened as it rang once, twice, and then three times. On the fourth ring the phone was answered. In a small and fragile voice lined with sleep, she said, "Hello?" It caused his heart to flutter.

"Um, Amber Faye?" it took an effort of strength and will to keep his voice from faltering. "I need you."

DAY TWENTY-SEVEN

Amber Faye turned her gaze towards the heavens. The skies were too pale to be night, but too dark to be dawn. She shivered in the crisp morning as the temperature seemed to penetrate her body. She wrapped her arms around herself for warmth... wishing it could be Lone Wolf who kept her warm instead. She let out a long low sigh as she thought of Lone Wolf... wondering why he wanted to meet her here, and especially at such an early hour. She could smell the faint scent of rain floating on a gentle breeze. *The Midwest got some strange weather,*she thought to herself.

Just then she saw Lone Wolf slowly approaching her, staggering with every step he took. His face a mask of hopeless dejection.

"Lone Wolf," Amber Faye cried out to him as she ran towards him. "Are you okay?"

Bloody and tired, he looked upon Amber Faye with his dead eyes. "I'm so tired," he said softly. There were so many questions Amber Faye wanted to ask, but instead, she threw her arms around him to keep him from losing his balance.

"Let's go home," she said softly, and she helped him to her car that was parked less then twenty feet away. Once inside, Lone Wolf took his pistol from his waist band and held it. Amber Faye watched it as it slipped from his hand onto the floor. It reminded her so much of the night he first came crawling into her car... crawling into her life... seeking her help... her protection... her love.

During that first encounter, she could sense an evilness about him that she could not completely grasp. But in time, despite his many flaws... she has come to learn that this evilness was nothing more than loneliness. A loneliness that was very much akin to her own. A loneliness she could destroy... if only he would allow her to.

She watched him as he leaned back... closing his eyes as the gentle vibration of the car lulled him into the twilight realm of the Sandman. *What a world of mixed emotions in those eyes,* she thought to herself. Distrust... fear... hopelessness... anger... all etched and well hidden in the endless depths of his harden eyes.

She could tell he was fighting off a wave of sleep. Too many nights without sufficient rest had began to take it's toll. She wondered what it was that had brought him back. An answered prayer? She also wondered why he was bloody and exhausted? She did indeed know it was of a criminal element... but nothing more. "Well, every soul has it's demons," she whispered softly to herself.

As she drove, she would often look over at him. Only after she was certain that he was asleep did she reach out to touch his face... gently... passionately... lovingly. She wondered where the blood was coming from, or even if it was his. Like every other time, she felt an ache rise in her heart as she watched him sleep. *How sad he looks,* she thought, *even now.*

Dawn's first light had pierced the scattered clouds over head. As the sun's early morning rays descended upon his face... she felt something deep down inside of her die again. Looking at him, she could imagine herself as Wendy in her favorite childhood story, "Peter Pan." He's the leader of the Lost Boys... a motherless child roaming the streets aimlessly... so far away from home.

After the La Saber pulled into the View Point Apartments, she reached out attentively to arouse the sleeping Lone Wolf.

"Baby, we're home," she whispered softly, but to no avail. "Baby?" she said. This time he jerked awake. His eye lids flew open and his body tensed. Amber Faye too, was startled, but it was something she has come to expect. "We're home, baby," she whispered as she stroked his head.

"I must've dozed off," he mumbled in a raspy voice, shaking his head to clear it. He grimaced in pain from his throbbing head.

"Baby, what's wrong?" she begged for answers. With his head bowed down, she was able to see that certain spots of his hair was matted thickly with blood. "Oh, my God!" she cried. "Baby, you're hurt. We have to get you to a hospital," she cried frantically. "You fell asleep! You could have died!"

"Please, no hospitals," he said with his teeth clenched... fighting off the pain.

"But baby, you're hurt," she protested.

"I said no." Lone Wolf tried to growl, but the pounding of his head was more than he could bare, in a softer tone, he said, "Amber Faye, please. I just need some rest."

After Amber Faye helped the large man into the apartment, she gently laid him in bed. He fell instantly asleep. "You have to stay up," Amber Faye whispered as she placed a hand under his neck. "You can't go to sleep," she said as she arose the sleeping Lone Wolf.

"I just need to rest. That's it."

"But your injuries? You might have a concussion."

"If I did I would have died last night."

Amber Faye laid Lone Wolf's head upon her lap... and soon he was asleep. Gently cradling his head, with a wet wash cloth, she nursed his wounds as best she could. She found two deep gashes on the crown of his head. As she gently cleaned the crusted blood from his head, she wondered what it was he was doing. She wondered on who had inflicted these wounds on the man she loved.

Loved! She flinched at the thought. *I barely know this man,* she thought to herself.

Suddenly, his body jerked and his muscles tensed. She pressed her palm against his heaving chest. Tiny beads of perspiration began to form on his face. Leaning over him... she gently kissed away the sweat from his forehead. His flesh felt extremely hot under her lips. Just then, his eye lids flew open. His hollow eyes shone of intense desperation and wild confusion. "It's okay, baby," she whispered softly, smiling down on him. "You're safe. I won't let anything hurt you," she said as softly as a gentle breeze. "Now sleep, honey," she said as she gently stroked his cheeks.

His eye lids were growing heavy, but he fought hard to keep them open... obviously terrified of what haunted his dreams. "I'll protect you," she promised him... knowing he wanted nothing more than to close his eyes and sleep in blissful silence. This was all he needed to hear. He closed his eyes and was asleep within seconds. She sighed as she watched him sleep peacefully. Despite her promise... she felt helpless in the face of his fears.

Perhaps it was because she didn't understand them... or even know them, for that matter. But she would do her best to protect him nevertheless.

* * * * * *

The sun came over the tops of the hills... bathing the streets of Omaha in golden shafts of dawn's early light. The sweet smell of soft rain moistened the air, combined with the smell of freshly tilled earth and cut grass.

Murdah Man stepped from his drop-top Mustang. Making his way to the back, he lifted the trunk, then shifted through the many weapons that laid unceremoniously inside. Pushing aside the assault rifles, he decided to go with the sawed-off Mosh-berg pump. He thought it would be easier to conceal than a rifle. After making sure it was fully loaded, he tucked it under his arm and pulled his black leather coat over it to conceal it. Once the trunk latch was closed, he began to make his way across the street, heading towards the golden brown duplexes.

* * * * * *

With the thick curtains closed... the smoke of marijuana fouled the air in the dimly lit living room. Insane sat on the sofa, watching a woman who swayed her hips to the rhythm of the rap music that played softly in the back ground. She was scantly dressed in Daisie Dukes... her baby blue tank top was cut to mid-drift. She danced provocatively in front of Insane, often reaching out to playfully tug at his baggy jeans.

After taking a long and hard pull from the blunt, he then passed it to the woman. Despite his repetition, the woman was now feeling completely at ease in the presence of Insane. This is why she made the mistake of reaching for the 40oz bottle of Old English that he held.

Reading her intentions, Insane pulled back the hand that held the bottle and shot a fist into her face with his free hand. The blow had caught her just below her left eye. It sent her tumbling to the floor. "Bitch, don't you ever put your nasty lips on my forty," Insane said calmly and then he took a long drink from the bottle. "I know where your mouth been," he chuckled to himself.

Just then there was a slight knock at the door. "Go answer that," he told he woman as he picked the blunt up from the floor. She looked up at him... almost defiantly in spite of the rapidly swelling of her eye. She watched him as he nonchalantly took another pull from the blunt. There was a second knock, this time slightly louder.

"Answer the damn door!" Insane barked at the woman, she flinched at the harshness of his tone.

After getting to her feet, the woman made her way to the door. "Who is it?" she yelled as she put her eye up to the peep-hole. But there wasn't an answer. "Who is it?" she tried again. "Move your hand so I can see," she said as she stared into darkness. Turning towards Insane, she said, "Whoever it is got their hand over the hole. I can't see who it is."

Just as she was returning her eye to the peep-hole, there was a heavy explosion of a shotgun... followed by the door being kicked in as Murdah Man entered the duplex. The destructive blast blew the shattered glass and metal of the peep-hole point-blank into her face, leaving nothing recognizable.

Once her body landed three feet away, it spasm and kicked, the heels of her bare feet dug into the plush carpet as she tried to lift herself up. Although she was no longer living, the part of her brain that wasn't exposed was still functioning, sending conflicting orders that caused her to kick and try to lift herself up.

Still sitting on the couch, Insane leaned back and went into convulsions of laughter. A laughter that was cold... chilling... frightening. He found humor in how she was trying to escape despite the fact that she no longer lived.

Than all at once... he stopped his hysterical laughter. He looked up at Murdah Man with his cold dark eyes... studying him icily.

"So it's like that now, huh?" Insane asked coldly, his anger showing in his voice. Murdah Man pulled on the rack to his shotgun, sending the empty shell flying while chambering another round. Insane then found himself staring into the dark, round barrel of the sawed-off pump.

"Aw, you oh bitch ass nigga, you kill me you gonna have all of HCG on your ass," Insane warned, his voice like a rasp across cold steel. "And if you think you getting my stash, nigga, you got life all fucked up."

Murdah Man grinned at him fiendishly. "Motha fucka'z know you smoked Ghost. You come up dead, they'll blame Pleasant View. Then Imma take your stash," he whispered savagely... making a show of tightening his grip on his weapon.

Blind with rage, Insane cursed, "Nigga, fuck you!" and clawed for the pistol that laid beside him. Murdah Man pulled on the trigger. The flame from the barrel lanced out. Touching the chest of Insane. The buckshot hit his chest with a wet slap... sending him sprawled out on the couch.

"See you in hell, *cousin*," Murdah Man said, grinning humorlessly. The fire in his eyes were equal to the flame that spat from his weapon. Slowly... nonchalantly... he began to gather the drugs and money. Then quietly stepped from the duplex, ignoring the many eyes that watched him step into his car, and pull away.

DAY TWENTY-EIGHT

Cool after noon breezes lifted the thin white curtains away from the open windows, making them flutter, then drop lifelessly when the wind died down. Amber Faye laid in bed... holding the sleeping Lone Wolf in her arms. She had come to learn that the only time he would sleep peacefully is when she held him... babied him... protected him. And all the while soothing him... endlessly cajoling... pouring soft words into his unconscious and frightened mind. But the second she left his side, he would convulse... shaking feverishly... fighting tirelessly against the unyielding demons that haunts him in his sleep.

She tenderly stroked away strands of hair that clung against his forehead. Than she passed a finger along his broken body. She lovingly stroked his hands, destined by cruel and brutal fate to pull triggers. Causing death and destruction, she was sure of it. *I could teach these hands to love,* she thought to herself.

"The start of another poem," she said aloud, but then shook her head despairingly. For far too long, Amber Faye has had nothing but words to keep her warm. Looking down at Lone Wolf, she became determined to fulfill that ultimate quest of love through him. She knew that it would take great and valiant efforts to pull him back from the edge of the emotional abyss of which he lingered still. But in her heart... she knew he was worth it.

As if on some virtuous cue, Lone Wolf began to stir, then slowly opened his eyes. He looked up at Amber Faye briefly, then winched in agonizing pain from the head-ache that racked his skull. Not only from this pain, but also from a pain that reaches far beyond the physical, a pain that seemed to intensify every day. She held him tighter. "Shh," she said in a soothing voice. He buried his head in between her breast. The soothing rhythmic beat of her heart some how seemed to ease his pain.

Lone Wolf tried to stretch, but his aching body protested vigorously. "How long was I out this time?" he grunted in pain.

"Not long enough," she said, a note of sorrow thickening her voice. "Lone Wolf?" she said softly. After a brief moment of silence she asked, "Are you going to tell me what happening?" She knew the question was a long shot, but she also knew she had to ask. "What about that night on the phone, Lone Wolf? What happened then?"

She felt his body loosen as he inhaled deeply. She thought he was going to speak, but the words never came.

"Please tell me something, Lone Wolf," she plead. "Did you kill somebody?"

"I was talking to you, remember?" he said in a tired voice.

It was true, he was indeed talking to her when the first two shots rang out. But what about the numerous shots that followed?

"Have you ever killed anybody?" Her voice was low... almost inaudible... as if she was afraid of the answer that he may give.

Lone Wolf tried to laugh at the question, but the pain caused it to sound more like a growl. "I'm not a killa," he finally said. She wanted desperately to believe him. But with the little facts she knows, and with his evasiveness, she was hard pressed.

"Will I have to love you through bars an concrete?"

"Love me?" Lone Wolf asked as he sat up on his hands. He felt a strange sensation fall over his body as he asked her. Amber Faye slowly nodded her head. For a fleeing moment, she saw a softness in his eyes. But then she saw his eyes grow hard.

"I wrote a poem," she said quickly, trying her best to keep him from slipping back into a state of self-seclusion. "I wrote it while you were sleeping. You want to hear it?" Lone Wolf settled onto his forearms, a more comfortable position. Still looking up at her, he nodded his head. "It's called 'I Believe,' Okay?" Again, Lone Wolf nodded.

"I believe in the sun, even when the sun cease to shine.
I believe in your love, even though your love isn't mine.
I believe in the day when you'll say it's my love you're needing.
But 'til that day comes along, I got to stay strong, and keep on believing.

I believe in the stars, even when the stars can't be seen.
I believe fairy tales not only dwells in hopes and dreams.
I believe that one day you will say it's my love you're needing.
But 'til that day comes along, I got to stay strong, and keep on believing.
I believe in true love, for this love will set you free.
From these chains, form your pain, from your current state of misery.
I will pray for the day, you will say it's my love you're needing.
But 'til that day comes along, I got to stay strong, and keep on believing.

After she finished, she waited for Lone Wolf to respond. When she realized that he wasn't going to commit, she asked, "So what do you think?"

After a moment of thinking it over, he smiled and said, "You actually get paid for that? That sounded like a rap, or lyrics to a love song. Maybe I can be a poet."

"Ohhh, I hate you," she said as she playfully pushed him back. Lone Wolf grimaced in pain. "Oh, I'm sorry, baby," she said quickly after she realized she had forgotten about his injuries.

"I'm coo," he said. Lone Wolf smiled his dead smile. Only his mouth smiled, but the smile never touched his cold, dark eyes, never. He had forgotten how to smile with his eyes and heart many years ago.

"Your eyes are so dark, Lone Wolf. So cold," she said softly. "Even when you laugh, they are hard. Try to make them kind... soft... gentle."

"And how am I supposed to do that?"

"By letting me love you," she said as she caressed his face.

"But you don't know me."

"No, I don't," she said as she lowered her eyes. But then she raised them with a hopeful gleam and said, "But I know what you need. Our needs are one and the same. And maybe that's why I feel compelled to break down your walls."

"Really?" he said simply.

"Did you know that sometimes you cry out in your sleep? I know about you mother, and her many boyfriends. But who is Kevin?" As she said the name, she saw his eyes flash dangerously. But only momentarily. Now, within his wounded eyes, she saw that there was a kind of wisdom there that he had gained from loss and pain. But it stayed only in the deepest... most secluded depths of his eyes, behind the hatred. It was a private kind of sorrow... a window to something amiss within.

"I'm sorry, baby," she whispered as she leaned forward to kiss him. She kissed him with a soft hunger and passion that gently fanned the small flame of love within.

Suddenly, Lone Wolf pulled back. "I gotta go," he said softly as he edged from the bed.

"What? Huh?" Amber Faye said in shock. Her bewildered expression caused him to hesitate.

"Naw," Lone Wolf whispered, shaking his head. "I really do have to go."

As Lone Wolf dressed, Amber Faye sat quietly on the bed. Her legs were crossed with her hands folded in her lap... her head was bowed and tears fell silently. When she looked up at him, her huge luminous eyes plead with a nostalgic yearning that was too powerful for words. Seeing this played on his consciousness.

"Look, Amber Faye," he said as he sat beside her on the bed. "There's so much shit I wanna tell you. There's so much going on in my life right now, it's hectic."

"Then why don't you?" Amber Faye asked... wanting to understand.

"Why don't I what?"

"Why don't you tell me something? I am a lot stronger then I look, Lone Wolf. I've suffered too, you know." Something dim overshadowed her face; a shade of memory. She looked up at him with bleak, tortured eyes. Something he hadn't noticed before. It was a painful look look of lost akin to his own. A painful look of misery and loneliness only Lone Wolf understood.

He wondered why he hadn't noticed it before. Until now, when he looked into the eyes of Amber Faye, he saw only kindness... gentleness. A zest for life that he knew he could never truly experience. But now, he saw the reflection of his own bitter emotions within her pain-filled eyes.

"No!" Lone Wolf roared with involuntary intensity. The sudden outburst startled Amber Faye. Seeing her jump in fear caused a tremendous surge of guilt to pass savagely through his heart. "Amber Faye," he said softly, trying his very best to sound apologetic, but controlling the hardness of his tone was something he had yet to master. Again, it came out demanding... forceful. "For eight years now... I've turned my eyes away from God. I've been living an evil life and I've tried to hide myself from His sight because of these evil deeds. I wouldn't be able to endure His gaze for all the stuff I've done. Especially within the past few days."

"That was beautiful. so... poetic," Amber Faye said softly.

"Amber Faye," Lone Wolf said, ignoring her statement. "You don't know what I've been through. One day I'll tell you everything. But for now, Amber Faye... baby..." he felt strange as he called her an affectionate name. "I'm in too deep. And that's why I have to go." As he said this he stood to his feet. With his Desert Eagle in hand, the young man now looked every bit the image of a street warrior. Amber Faye just knew he was out for revenge.

* * * * * *

The two sat quietly for the majority of the ride. Although he had told her where to take him, she still felt lost. She wasn't too familiar with the north side, it was a place where she was warned to stay away from many times. *If only I would have listened,* she thought to herself. *I wouldn't be in this predicament.* She glanced over at Lone Wolf, who stared vacantly out the window. She wondered why she was putting up with his antics... his silly games.

What am I doing here with a man who completely lacks emotional involvement with anything but himself? she asked herself. *He's selfish, mean, with an abrasive personality that's difficult to endure.*

But it's not his fault, she assured herself. *He's simply a by-product of his environment. Lone Wolf did once tell me that pessimism is a survival trait for those who live life on the streets. There's so much wisdom in this young man, I can see it. I can take him away from these streets... I can take him away from here... putting an end to his misery. We can go to California,* she thought to herself. Her heart longed to see the beauty of the ocean.

She looked over at him again. She could see the swolleness of his head wounds, even through the thickness of his hair. She wondered what had happened. *Why is he being so rash? So insensitive?* she asked herself. *It can't be me, I didn't do anything. I was careful not to mention what had happened the last time we were together, how he hurt me, not only physically, but mentally and emotionally as well. But it's not your fault, Lone Wolf.* She wanted to say this out loud. She wanted to assure him that she held no ill-will towards him for that. That she understood why he would think she would enjoy him like that.

What am I doing? Why am I thinking this? she wondered. *Why am I absolving him? He hurt me. Tonya was right. Everything she said was true. He has done nothing but hurt me. Despite my willingness to give my all, he has not the slightest regards or appreciation for all I've done. And like Tonya said, I'm crossing line after line just to make him happy; but he doesn't care.*

Again she looked over at Lone Wolf. This time she glared at him with justifiable anger. But the anger vanished almost instantly when he looked back at her. His eyes were moist... as if threatening to release a tear.

Quickly he turned away, as if ashamed to show any signs of weakness. *Perhaps another survival trait acquired from the streets,* she thought to herself. Suddenly, in a wave of sympathetic comprehension, she finally understood him. She could see right through the facade to what truly lies within. On the surface, his thuggish ways was nothing more than a mask... an illusion he wanted the world to see... an illusion that mirrored his environment. But underneath this threatening exterior laid despair... harrowed anguish and suffering. Beneath it all he was defenseless as a child... very young and very frightened. And because of this fear, he was very angry... extremely hostile.

She reached over and placed her hand over his... and beneath his hand, on his lap, laid his Desert Eagle. He didn't look up. Although the signs of her revelation has always been there, only now has the truth been so transparent. *I can change him,* she thought to herself. *All I have to do is take him from here. Then I can cherish and protect him... guard and guide him. I know it can work.*

Amber Faye slowed the car to a gradual stop. Looking over at Lone Wolf she could sense the nervousness. His hands clenched tightly around

217

his pistol, his eyes darting back and fourth... very much like the first time she acted when she first dropped him off. She wanted to say something, but was at a loss for words. Finally she said, "How can I get a hold of you now? You know, with your cell and pager broken." He looked over at her, but didn't respond. "I guess I won't need this number anymore." As she said this, she reached into her pocket, then produced a large amount of money. He instantly recognized it as the money he had first given her. Inside the folded money was the number to the cell phone.

"Damn. You still got that?" he asked, referring to the money.

"I told you I wasn't going to spend any of it. It belongs to you." Again Lone Wolf didn't respond. "But I was just thinking. Maybe I will spend it. On us. Use it to buy us plane tickets out of here. Would you like that, Lone Wolf?" Immediately after she said this, she could visibly see a violent tremble tear through him. He hid his face from her, his hand clinched the pistol restlessly. "I don't know what's going on in your life, Lone Wolf. And I can not fathom why you're so reluctant to reveal it to me. Either way, Lone Wolf, we can leave it all behind. Just me and you," she told him sincerely, with a trace of a tear in the corner of her eye.

After a pause, he finally said, "It's not that easy. But soon it'll be over, I promise."

She wanted so desperately to believe him, but something in his words had driven fear deeply in side of her. His words were dark, almost cryptic, like it hid some demented threat. It chilled her blood. She began to cry.

At this, Lone Wolf tore from the car in anger, slamming the door as he left. But this time Amber Faye didn't jump, she wasn't afraid. She now understood him. She knew that he would never intentionally harm her physically again, despite his hostility.

She didn't watch him go. Instead, she sat crying. But behind the tears there was still hope. The hope that she would never let go. Slowly her whimpers subsided, like the beats of a dying heart.

* * * * * *

Lone Wolf's eyes darted back and fourth as he made his way into the ally. He held his pistol with a solid grip, poised and ready. This apprehension was caused by the fact that Murdah Man knew where he had parked his car. It was he that had suggested to Lone Wolf that they take only one car, leaving the '64 Chevy parked in an ally.

Reaching the car, Lone Wolf's eyes surveyed the surrounding area. Although the sun was shinning brightly in the warm afternoon sky, an ally was the perfect strategical sight for a well designed ambush.

Detecting no signs of danger, Lone Wolf then studied the car. He wasn't sure rather or not Murdah Man had any knowledge of explosives. But it wasn't a risk he was willing to take. He then began to wonder if perhaps he was over reacting. If Murdah Man wanted him dead, he would not be standing here. On the night of the betrayal, he had Lone Wolf in the prime position to commit an execution style murder. All the elements were in play to ensure that Murdah Man would have gotten away scott clean. He had Lone Wolf isolated in the far south... in the dead of night, in an empty lot. Not to mention that Lone Wolf still had on him the murder weapon that was used in the slaying of a notorious drug lord. This alone indicated a number of people with motives to want Lone Wolf dead. From a gang-land retaliation to a drug trade gone horribly wrong. Either one would have left Murdah Man in the clear.

As these things raced through his mind, Lone Wolf realized that he still had the murder weapon in hand. He then decided that the disposal of this weapon would become his prime objective. Followed by the necessity of locating heavy artillery... something more then just pistols.

As he stepped into the Chevy and switched the ignition... something dark and sinister began to squirm in the most secluded recess of his mind... a treacherous solution that was edging itself towards the light of consciousness. A solution that had some how averted revealing itself despite the grinding headache that ailed him still. The solution should have been obvious... for it was the way of the streets and it's many gangs. Eye for an eye... tooth for a tooth... retaliation is a must.

It had always been said that the first murder is always the hardest. This is a theory he will soon challenge. His only problem... he has yet to decide who will fall victim to this age old street ideology first... the source of his misery, T-Roy? Or the treacherous Murdah Man for his betrayal?

* * * * * *

After removing the firing pin, Lone Wolf threw the Desert Eagle .357 semi-automatic SL into the Missouri River... the final destination for perhaps hundreds of other murder weapons. He then headed towards the Blue Note, where he half expected to find Stick'ums. He wasn't surprised at all when he learned that the after-hour joint was closed during this time of day. He cursed himself for being foolish.

His drive to the residence of Stick'ums was a brief one. So brief that when he had pulled up to the curb, he hadn't decided on the type of weapon he wanted. At his own apartment he had a number of pistols and a .410... but he knew he needed a fully automatic assault rifle for his mission. But it's made and model... he had yet to decide.

"Old school!" Lone Wolf yelled as he knocked on the screen door. He yelled a second time when there wasn't a response.

Entering the screened-in porch, he was greeted by a soft putrid smell. A scent so subtle that it didn't register to him that it was the smell of petrified blood. He noticed the fly infested recliner and the dark spots that defiled it, but it didn't dawn on him that he was looking at pieces of fragmented skull and dried tiny chunks of brain.

Stopping at the front door, he knocked only once when the door became slightly a jarred. The sour stench became strong. "Old school!" he yelled as he pushed on the door. The rancid smell caused his stomach to churn as he passed the threshold. Instantly he saw the living room had been over turned. The couch was tattered, ripped cloth and cotton were scattered on the floor.

He then saw the closet of which stored Stick'ums many weapons. The door was opened and the light was on. Even from across the room, he could see that the space was completely emptied. The situation had eerily reminded him of Snook'ums and his unfortunate demise.

Suddenly, a wave of nausea seized him as he instantly understood the truth of the matter. The subtle smell was that of rotting flesh... the body of Stick'ums, who was probably stuffed in the dark and damp basement. The empty closet that once held his arms collection... the room that had been torn apart. *But who?* He wondered.

"Murdah Man," he said out loud unconsciously. He felt the full force of the facts as he said his name. The nauseating pang grew. He recalled how Murdah Man had asked bout firing pins... the ghastly joke about

Stick'ums missing an eye. Murdah Man didn't possess any knowledge of weapons. His knowledge was limited to loading and firing... nothing more. He couldn't have possibly know that show-guns were in-operable.

Another wave passed through him as he thought of Snook'ums. *But could Murdah Man have killed him as well? The look of confusion that first crossed Murdah Man's face when he saw the door of Snook'ums kicked in... could that have been an act?* he wondered. The way he teased the pit-bull... the way he tried to anxiously rush into the house despite Lone Wolf's warning... could Murdah Man be clever enough to act completely ignorant during the entire ordeal. Lone Wolf searched his memory... trying to see if he could recall anything out of the ordinary that day.

He could not. But he knew one thing... he needed to get out of there. He tried to recall rather or not he had touched anything while in the house. Although he wasn't positive, he began to wipe items off nonetheless.

* * * * * *

Lone Wolf had always assumed that Murdah Man didn't know where he lived. With this assumption, he casually strolled into the apartment complex. As he ascended up the stair- way he heard the menacing grind of metal against metal... the sound of a pistol being racked. In paralyzing fear he froze... his heart contracting in his chest. The sudden burst of adrenaline felt like ice in his veins as he heard the familiar low tone growl of Murdah Man's snarl.

"You done got caught slipping, cuz," Murdah Man laughed his evil and sadistic laugh. He then circled Lone Wolf. "Now what if I wanted you ghost? Huh?"

Lone Wolf stood in silence, icy beads of sweat forming across his brow.

"What'z up, cuz? Lil' Wolf?" Murdah Man asked with what sounded like genuine concern, his Glock .40 hanging loosely in his right hand. "Where you been, cuz? We gotta make this money." When Lone Wolf didn't respond, he chuckled sinisterly. "Oh cuz, I know you ain't tripping over that bull shit. You mad? Huh? You mad at me?" he said as he waved his Glock under Lone Wolf's nose.

Lone Wolf found himself looking into eyes that had completely lost their sanity. For the last couple of weeks, he had sensed a gradual change in Murdah Man and had witnessed the signs of his deteriorating emotional state... but never would he had ever believed that it would come to this. He now wished he never got rid of his .357. He was now standing face to face with a man that had left him for dead without a pistol.

"Don't trip on that petty stuff, cuz. That night was your night, cuz. Feel me? You got put on. Like when you joined Tré Seven, remember you got your ass whooped by all your homies? It's like that, cuz. Except now yous a killa. You got quoted. And *I* put you on." After he said this he lowered his pistol to his side.

Although Lone Wolf stood in shocked fear... it didn't show on his face. He wore the conventional mask that thugs wear... especially in times of tension and distress. The mask of a vicious mean mug. "Nigga, you pistol whipped me, nigga," Lone Wolf growled.

"I had to, cuz. You know I can't mess with you throwing hands. You know I can't fight as good as you. I had to use a weapon. But it don't matter cos we the new Crime Bosses, huh?!" Murdah Man said. "I ain't made no moves since that night. I waited for you. Now, you ready to do this, cuz? You ready to take over the city?" As he said this, he tried to hand Lone Wolf the Glock... handle first.

Lone Wolf eyed the pistol, then looked into the eyes of Murdah Man. He didn't know what to think. His pessimistic instinct impelled him to reach for the pistol... only to turn it on Murdah Man. But what Murdah Man had said seemed logical in it's own demented way. Had he wanted Lone Wolf dead, his flesh would be decaying on the south side at that very moment. And why would he hand over his pistol knowing it could be turned on him?

But *what about Stick'ums?* he thought to himself. He had always known Murdah Man was mentally unstable... but weren't they all? This was the main reason he found comfort in his presence. Such a mentality was familiar to him... like seeks like. But was he crazy enough to bite the hand that provides them with weapons? To Lone Wolf that seems more like an issue of stupidity than insanity. Either way, it was a question that needed to be answered.

Lone Wolf took the pistol from Murdah Man's grip. His hand shaking visibly as he did so. Murdah Man noticed, but didn't speak on it. Trying to regain his composure while looking confident, Lone Wolf said, "Stick'ums dead. I just came from there. I have no way of getting chopppa'z now."

"What? Man, you bull shittin'?" Murdah Man responded. The ring of sincerity in his voice seemed to sound authentic to Lone Wolf. "What the hell happened?" he asked Lone Wolf.

Lone Wolf told him what he knew, but revealed nothing of his suspicious towards him. After he finished, Murdah Man stood shaking his head slowly. "Damn, cuz!" Murdah Man roared as he pounded both fists into the wall. The plaster gave way slightly. "What we gonna do now, cuz? Where we gonna get heat, now, huh?" Murdah Man asked, but Lone Wolf didn't respond.

Lone Wolf was still debating rather or not he should lash out physically on Murdah Man in the form of retaliation. His head still throbbed lightly from the inflicted injury. In hand-to-hand combat he knew he could defeat Murdah Man. Albeit the victory would not come easy, he would over come Murdah Man, nevertheless. And Murdah Man knew this as well. So the question taunted him still... why would he hand him a fully loaded pistol, leaving himself defenseless if what he was saying wasn't true?

In a low and regretful tone, Murdah Man said, "Insane's dead. I got word last night, cuz. Him and some hood-rat caught buckshot."

Hearing this shook Lone Wolf right to his very core. A veil of sorrow descended over him as his knees grew weak, causing him to stumble. He placed his hand against the wall to support his failing legs... while his hand that gripped the pistol wiped at his face. "Bull shit, cuz." Lone Wolf challenged, but his resolve was weak.

"It seem s like fools is dying all around us, cuz. But you know what, cuz?" Murdah Man said attempting to succor the sentimental atrocity. "Now that we running this city, that bitch made nigga T-Roy ain't got no choice but to come to us." At the sound of the name, it became the focal point of Lone Wolf's every thought. "He might even come to rob us," Murdah Man chuckled sadistically. "In time this fool will come to us. But for now, I'm getting O.G.s from every hood to meet with us tomorrow night so we can start moving shit. We meeting at Chubbs. I need you on point, cuz. I got some choppa'z I need you to look at for me. I'll be back tonight so you can check them out for me, a-ight?" After he said this, he turned and began to walk down the stairs.

Despite Murdah Man's efforts, Lone Wolf still felt the animosity towards Murdah Man for what he had done. Lone Wolf raised the pistol and took precise aim. He fought the grisly urge to pull the the trigger... sending a bullet into the back of Murdah Man's skull.

"We gonna run this city, Lil' Wolf!" Murdah Man yelled without turning around. "People will bow to us." Then Murdah Man disappeared out the door into the bright sun of day.

* * * * * *

Entering his apartment, Lone Wolf sat his keys and newly acquired pistol on the coffee table, than sank onto the couch with a heavy sigh. Leaning his head back, he rubbed his face with both hands tiredly and inhaled deeply. Confused... he pondered the perplexity of the situation with intense scrutiny. Nothing made sense to him anymore. The death that had been incorporated into his already brutal and worthless existence only served to aggravate the situation further. First Ra Roz... followed by Snook'ums and Stick'ums... and now Insane. He recalled how Murdah Man had causally put an end to Hollow Tip's life... but what would be gained by the murder of the people that provided from them?

He then thought of the look in Murdah Man's eyes. The look of complete insanity... the look of a mad-man that had lost touch with reality. Such a look caused him uneasiness, but the greed that was steadily growing in his heart hindered any rational judgment. It did feel nice having his own things... his own apartment... designer clothing... and a '64 Chevy Impala that's envied by most.

He was utterly opposed to Murdah Man's original plan to rob Crime Boss. He still believe that there will be consequences and repercussions... but not that they have a chance at being prime drug lords... why not take advantage of such a rare opportunity? Lone Wolf decided what's done is done, and the time has come to reap the benefits of such a hard-earned victory.

With this decision being made, he retrieved a custom designed brief case from the back of the closet. Inside the brief case laid an assortment of pistols. He removed each weapon from it's cove and looked it over. His weapon of choice was his Detonics Mark V.

After securing the lock on the brief case, he got up to retrieve a 40oz bottle of Old English. Again, he sat pondering the complexity of the immediate circumstances. He didn't know how long he sat there contemplating... drinking on yet another 40oz bottle of the consoling liquid... but the shadows within the apartment began to take shape. Without hesitation, he got up with a pistol in one hand, and the alcohol in the other, and headed for the front door.

* * * * * *

With a 40oz bottle of Old English in hand, Lone Wolf took another step towards the building's edge. Looking threw blood shot eyes, he cast his gaze down upon the massive grave he calls home. A grave dug especially for him. Lifting the bottle to his lips, he allowed the bitter tasting substance to settle in the pit of his stomach. Then in anger and frustration, he hurled the bottle out towards the open space... the remaining liquid inside raining down upon the city.

Throughout his 16 years of roaming this wicked world of the flesh, he had experienced death and pain time and time again. Life was nothing more than a burden... a tribulating trial which gave absolutely no promise of improvement. He thought of how Insane was now with his brother. As for himself? Here he stood on a building's edge... with no future... and a virtually hopeless presence.

Once upon a time, he was afraid of death, but still willing to face it. But here and now... his heart and soul desired the day that will be his last... for it will be his first in a more peaceful existence. An existence where Murdah Man and his treacherous ways would be irrelevant. An existence where the pain caused by T-Roy would become obsolete... for it will be an existence where he, himself, too would be with his brother.

He took yet another step closer to the edge as he tried desperately to understand the present and accept it on it's own terms... but it was to no avail. He looked far below at the tiny cars as the slowly crawled by. *I can end it all here. No more pain... no more sorrow. Just one more small step... and my suffering will end.* With unseen enemies lurking in every shadows... around every corner... with evil demons and foes constantly trying to hurt him... knowing not who to trust... he knew no other way to ease the pain.

Allowing the wind to comb threw his long, wavy hair, he drew in a deep breath... then slowly released it into the nights warm air. *Just one more small step.*

Closing his eyes, his thoughts turned quickly from suicide as he thought of Amber Faye. As images of her filled his mind, he began to marvel at her strength... her beauty... her courage. Again, he felt moved by her passion. *This is truly an amazing woman,* he thought to himself. Even as he struggled with the meaning of love and devotion... Amber Faye refused to give up on this street thug. Her love was without question. Even as he tried desperately to comprehend the definition of loyalty and faithfulness... Amber Faye stood fast... ready to protect him and love him with a love devoid of regret and bitterness. And in return for this love... he had given her nothing but mistrust... heartache.

Maybe she can ease my pain, he thought to himself. God knew the thought of suicide had been mounting in his heart for many years, now... increasing with each day that passed. Perhaps this act of betrayal by Murdah Man was a blessing in disguised... for without it he would have never contacted Amber Faye... and he would of never known he could depend on her in his darkest hour.

In sorrow and in despair... he called out to her... and she answered. In pain and in misery... he reached out to her... and she came running. While healing and recovering... she nursed and protected him. Even when he was nothing more than a stranger... she looked beyond the physical and heard the crying of his heart... the yearning of his soul.

"Yes," he said aloud, "... she can take me from here." And with this new revelations... he decided the time had come for him to quit the game... to lay the past to rest.

* * * * *

Amber Faye sat out on the balcony over looking the other apartments. Her knees were pulled into her chest as she gazed at the full moon. She sighed heavily as she felt the gentle breeze blowing threw her long, beautiful hair. As she thought of Lone Wolf, she realized she had no faith of her own remaining... she could only cling to his and his promise that it would be over soon. But this faith was as powerful as her own. She just wishes she knew what her faith was in... she knew that such blind faith could either lead her to true love and happiness... or plunge her into the dark trenches of loneliness and despair. She shuttered at the thought... but her faith remained solid... strong... powerful. Again she sighed helplessly.

From inside the apartment, she heard the phone as it rung once... then twice. Slowly she raised to her feet... then went to answer the phone.

"Hello?" she said softly into the receiver.

"Amber Faye... it's me."

"Is it done? Is it over?" Amber Faye asked anxiously, trying to conceal the quivering in her voice.

"Yeah... it's over. It's done. I'm done."

"What did you do, Lone Wolf?"

"I didn't do nothing. I'm just so tired. So fed up with it all."

"Can we leave now?"

"Yeah," Lone Wolf said softly.

"Tonight?"

"Tonight."

"Oh Lone Wolf, I love you so much. I knew you'll come around, I just knew it. Let's not take anything with us. Let's just go, just ourselves. Just our hopes and our dreams, but nothing more."

Lone Wolf sat quietly on the opposite end of the line, thinking over what was being said. It was difficult for him to believe in her words... it seemed too good to be true. All his life he had known nothing but adversity and disappointment... but his faith was in her. "Where we going?"

"Wherever the next flight takes us, Lone Wolf. We will be on that next plane... and wherever it takes us, there we will began to build a new life... together." As she said this she couldn't keep the tears of joy from falling... finally she will have the opportunity to fulfill that ultimate quest. The ultimate quest of love... true immaculating love.

"I need to go home first, get my ID and some money and stuff. Why don't you meet me there, then we'll leave together."

"Okay. But where do you live?"

After Lone Wolf had given her directions to his apartment, the two sat in silence, each thinking about the drastic changes their lives will now endure. Between the two... they had no reason for staying. Neither had family nor any other obligation. They now had only each other... and dreams of the life they will build together.

"I love you, Lone Wolf," Amber Faye said softly... trying to disguise the shakiness in her voice.

"I know you do. You've shown me. You ready to do this?" he asked.

"Yes, I am, Lone Wolf," Amber Faye said. "And I know you love me, too. You don't have to say it."

With every word she spoke... he felt the barrier around his heart growing weak. Like the protective wall around a castle under constant attack. Her words of love were like projectiles of a catapult... destroying the shielding wall, brick by brick. Soon he will be left exposed... vulnerable... and the thought frightened him.

"Look, Imma go now. Meet me at my tilt. I need to get some money and grab my other ID."

"Other ID?" Amber Faye said.

"Yeah. I'm on the run. You didn't know that? Been so for awhile, now."

Amber Faye sat in silence... stunned at this new revelations. "On the run?" she repeated. "What did you do? Is it bad?"

"What? Naw. Just some bull." Lone Wolf didn't want to reveal his young age to her... therefor he couldn't explain the pettiness of him being on the run. Instead, he simply said, "On the plane I'll explain everything, a-ight? I promise."

"Okay," Amber Faye said softly. "I'm leaving now, Lone Wolf. I'll see you in twenty minutes, okay? I love you, Lone Wolf," she said again. But again Lone Wolf didn't respond.

After she hung up the phone, she lowered her head... feeling conflicted and pulled. She wanted nothing more than to run away with Lone Wolf... but the many skeletons that he harbored made her feel uneasy. *Perhaps I am making a mistake,* she thought to herself, *and I'm crossing another line that Tonya had warned me about. It doesn't matter, I'm going to be with him. We'll make it work,* she assured herself as she allowed a silent faith to fill her. A faith that the two would prevail.

With the decision being made... she clasped her hands in sheer excitement. Whatever obstacles they would face... they would face together. And now there was nothing that could tear them apart.

* * * * * *

As Lone Wolf pulled into the parking lot, he noticed the '95 Mustang belonging to Murdah Man. "Damn," he grumbled to himself. He had forgotten that Murdah Man had told him earlier that he would be back with assault rifles for him to inspect. He wanted to pull off, leaving Murdah Man and his quest for power behind. But he knew Amber Faye would be on her way.

"Where the fuck you been, cuz?" Murdah Man asked Lone Wolf as he stepped from his car.

"Nigga, where the fuck *YOU* been?" Lone Wolf responded as he drew near. Murdah Man scoffed at the response.

"Peep game, cuz. I got some heat for yo ass, cuz. I just need you to do your thang. See if you can fix them. We may need them tomorrow night when we meet with the O.G.s." Murdah Man then turned and led the way to the Mustang.

As Lone Wolf followed, he wondered how he was going to tell Murdah Man that he was finished with the game. He than decided that the best course of action was to be blunt... perhaps maybe even a little forceful. This was the only thing Murdah Man understood.

As they drew the Mustang, something tugged at Lone Wolf's peripheral vision. He turned just as Trigg emerged from the shadows. "Whuz up, cuz?" he said to Lone Wolf.

"Where the hell you come from?" Lone Wolf asked.

"Taking a piss," Trigg answered.

Lone Wolf could hear the underlining resentment in the tone of his voice, but he thought nothing of it. He knew that Trigg was a coward at heart... and the only time he was "hard" was when he was in the presence of one of his homies. Which is why him and G.C. were so compatible.

"Why you rolling with this busta?" Lone Wolf chuckled. He heard Trigg scoff at the question, but again he ignored it.

"Imma put the fool on," Murdah Man said over his shoulder. "Imma make this busta a killa tonight. Pop the trunk, motha fucka," he told Trigg. Trigg followed the order. "Check this out," Murdah Man said as he lifted the trunk.

At once, Lone Wolf felt his heart lurch into his throat. The constricting snake gripped his chest as he looked down upon the M-60 that belonged to Stick'ums. Beside it was the tripod and the jacket. Under it was other assault rifles he had saw in Stick'ums storing space. Instantly, all was clear. "What the fuck is this?" he asked Murdah Man.

"What it look like?"

"Where you get these from?" Lone Wolf asked as he ran a finger across the cold steel. Murdah Man chuckled in response. Lone Wolf felt a shiver tear threw his body, he backed away from the car.

"What, nigga? You surprised? You know you dealing with cut throats. We do what we need to do to stay ahead."

"Are you for real?" Lone Wolf asked. "Are you serious?"

"Cuz, we need this thang to work. Let fools know, that if they mess with us, nigga we cutting they fucking body in half."

"Naw, cuz," Lone Wolf said softly as he slowly shook his head. "This ain't right. This don't even make sense. All you had to do was tell me you wanted one."

"I wanted this. And now I got it."

"Yeah, but it messed everything up. *YOU* messed everything up," Lone Wolf replied.

"So be it. But for now, we gotta get this working. Like I once said, we may need it tomorrow." As Murdah Man said this, he reached into the trunk to retrieve the M-60.

"Naw. I'm done, cuz."

"What?" Murdah Man asked as he turned to face Lone Wolf. "What you mean 'you done'?"

"I mean I'm done. I'm out." Despite the rising fear in Lone Wolf, his words were deterrent and determined.

"Oh, you think it's that easy, huh? You think you could just leave? You may have been able to walk away from your own hood, turn your back on your own homies. But like I told that old ass nigga before I kilt him, there's only one way out this game." As he said this he produced a Glock .40 from the small of his back. A pistol identical to the one he had given Lone Wolf earlier that now laid in his waist band.

Lone Wolf's felt the overpowering fear take control of his body. He knew the greed in Murdah Man's heart was insatiable, and that he would not distinguish the ones he hunts from the ones that stands in his way. But in spite of the overpowering fear, Lone Wolf knew now was the time to make his stand. "I said I'm done," he said with a determination that belied the fear that pumped in his heart.

"What?" Murdah Man chuckled. "Is this fool for real?" he asked Trigg, who simply stood there watching things unfold. "You really think yous a killa, huh?" he asked Lone Wolf. "A killa don't care who he kills," he said as he racked his weapon. "Just ask that nigga Insane. Or even Ra Roz. Oh, you can't. I almost forgot, I smoked them both." As he said this, an evil snarl formed on his lips.

"You bull shitting," Lone Wolf challenged.

"Am I? But don't feel bad for that fool Ra Roz. You know he did bust on us first. You remember? That night you met that white girl from La Vista." When Lone Wolf didn't respond, Murdah Man chuckled, "Yeah, you remember. Cut-throats. But none of this matters now. What matters is that you make each one of these choppa'z work," he said as he pointed towards the truck with his Glock.

At that moment, so many things were racing threw the mind of Lone Wolf. Thoughts of Kevin... of T-Roy... of his mother. Thoughts of his past... of his current predicament... and what the future may hold. But the thought that triumphs over all... were the thoughts of Amber Faye.

"I can't live like this no more. I'm leaving town tonight. Like I said, cuz, I'm done."

"Trigg? Ah, cuz. Can you believe this fool? You know what? Remember when you and G.C. Was robbed?" Murdah Man laughed. "Guess who it was that went up side your head?"

Again Lone Wolf felt the constricting snake as it coiled in his chest. He remembered how Trigg had reacted when he and Murdah Man arrived that night... how he lifted the pump-action shotgun and fired without hesitation. He now awaited for Trigg to reach for his weapon.

"So that was you?" he asked as he took a step closer to Lone Wolf. Lone Wolf could hear Murdah Man snickering in the background. "That was you who robbed me and smacked me with that strap?"

The rage and hatred in his heart began to seethe in his veins... pushing aside the fear that was present. "Look, I said I'm done. Cuz, I got you this far. You can do the rest without me."

"*YOU* got me this far?! You done lost ya motha fuckin' mind, cuz. I'm the reason for your entire existence. You wouldn't have shit without me.

Ain't none of them bitch made nigga'z from Tré Seven was with you when you didn't have shit. I made you, nigga."

As Lone Wolf thought about his "friends" from 37th Street... he came to realize that in this massive world... there was only one person he could truly depend on. When the world had turned it's back on him... there was only one person that truly believed in him. And she believed in him even when he didn't believe in himself. Now... this is all that mattered to Lone Wolf. No longer will he fall victim or be used by the world of the flesh... or by the dictatorial forces that has for so long controlled his every waking hour.

"Fuck all them jealous, bitch made, playa hating ass nigga'z!" Lone Wolf said as he turn to walk away.

"Young cuz! You don't know who you messing with!" Murdah Man yelled after Lone Wolf... but he continued to walk away. The acid of hatred began to scold the heart of Trigg as he watched him leave.

"Nigga, ya digging ya own grave, nigga!" Trigg called out to Lone Wolf.

But Lone Wolf didn't respond. He simply continued to walk with solid determination.

Before Lone Wolf even heard the first shot... he felt the hot breath of a slug as it tore past his ear. Many more shots followed as he scrambled to avoid being struck. In his ear he could hear them demons from the fiery pits of hell laughing... calling his name. Hearing this... the wicked venom in his heart made it's way threw his body as the rage and hatred claimed an easy victory over love and peace.

The smell of blood and burning flesh filled his nostrils as he felt something tugging at his shoulder. He looked down at his body just as another bullet ate away at his flesh... but the pain and darkness of death never followed. Slowly dropping to his knees... he felt the agonizing pain as it slowly crept threw his body. Another bullet ripped at the flesh of his side, forcing his body to spin forcefully before hitting the pavement.

He heard the echo of footsteps as Trigg and Murdah Man began to flee from the crime scene... leaving Lone Wolf alone.

A deathly silence mocked his ears.

He took a shuttering... painful breath as he reached for his side wound. Desperate hope and fear were working together as he staggered to his feet... but the excruciating pain caused his body to crumble. Laying in a bloody heap... he knew death was on the prowl... ready to pounce at any moment.

Deep within his wicked heart he knew he couldn't die... for he was bound for the darkest trenches of hell. All he could visualize were cemeteries as the painful grimace of death flooded his every thought. Knowing his next breath could be his last... he tried desperately to cry for help... but the pain almost blinded him. Every breath he took felt like a burning stake being driven deep within his chest.

As he struggled to breath, he could hear his heart pumping rapidly in his ear... along with the terrified screams of the dead. Feelings of hot blood on cold flesh sent shivers threw his body as bitter memories flashed before his wounded eyes.

Slowly... a blackness crept into the edges of his field of vision... causing a sort of tunnel vision. Holding his side wound, he felt the sticky blood seeping threw his fingers. The fear of the unknown and the feelings of increasing agony became overwhelming as his soul crawls closer to the grave. He felt the icy fingers of death taking a hold of his soul.

Slowly yielding to death's cold, yet burning embrace... he said in a weak and thin voice, "Forgive me Father... for I have sinned." His every bitter memory turned to his mother just as he plunged into darkness.

* * * * * *

As the darkness slowly lifted... all Lone Wolf was aware of was the increasing nearness of heaven. A place where he felt safe... a place where he felt a sort of freedom from fear and pain. His soul was enveloped with a kind of love and peace at a depth of which he would have never imagined. Gasping in delight, he looked into the sky as a blinding light from above parted the clouds. Closing his eyes... he felt his soul drifting as if it were on a gentle breeze... as if sleep walking on clouds. For once in his life... he was feeling at ease.

As his spirit was rising... he heard a cry from below. Turning to see where this cry was coming from, he found himself looking at his own lifeless body... with Amber Faye holding his head in her lap. Tears streaked her cheeks as she put her hands over his... applying pressure to his side wound. She cried for help as blood seeped threw her fingers too... but her pleas for help fell on deaf ears.

"Baby, don't die! Please, baby!" Closing her eyes... the tears continued to flow as she lifted her head towards the heavens... begging the Lord for His help.

With blood stained hands... she began to tenderly stroke his cheek.

From above... Lone Wolf watched while his corpse lay in the arms of love. She rocked back and fourth... speaking softly to his soul. Looking into her eyes... he saw an inner strength and a faith that she refused to let go. A faith that the love she felt for him will pull him through. Feeling something tugging at his soul... he turned and found himself looking at the house of his mother.

With a rush if confusion... he turned to find the scene of his corpse had fallen into complete darkness, he felt his soul being pushed towards the house... he tried to stop... but his efforts were pointless. His soul was being pulled into the living room... where his mother was sitting on the couch... holding an object in her hands.

"What the fuck!" Lone Wolf cried out in anger as he looked down at his mother. The once obsolete hatred now flooded his heart in one massive wave of rage. "You bitch! How dare you abandoned me?" he cried with rage. Feeling an evil spiritual presence... he continued to curse his mother. "Why couldn't you love me the way a mother should love her only son? All I had was my love to give! What, bitch?! Wasn't enough?!"

With a heart full of rage... he began to punch towards his mother... but his ghostly arms only went threw her. "I hate you! Why did you leave me?!" he cried as he continued to punch. "Fuckin' bitch!" But nothing he said or did pulled her attention away from the object that she held in her hands.

Lone Wolf watched as his mother closed her eyes... hugging the object that she held in her hands... shaking her head slowly. "No," she said weakly as her bottom lip began to quiver. He watched as a tear escaped from under her eyelid and made it's way down her cheek.

"That's what you get," Lone Wolf said as he felt a wave of pleasure washed over his soul. Smiling down on her he watched as many more tears followed the first... falling on the object she held in her hands. "How that feel?" he said with a smirk on his face.

But then something was said that hit Lone Wolf with a powerful blow. Her lips parted as she whispered softly into the air... "Please God... let my son know that I love him." As she said this, the object fell from her hand and landed face up on the floor. The feeling of guilt shot through his soul as he stared in disbelief at a picture frame. In it... his baby picture that shows her holding him as they both smiled up at the camera. On the glass frame... traces of tear-stains held evidence that his mother loved him.

An overwhelming emotional feeling of guilt swept through him as he dropped to his knees at his mother's feet. He felt the heavy lump of sorrow as it rose from his chest to his throat... forcing his eyes to blur with tears. As Lone Wolf looked up into the face of his mother... something in the expression in her eyes reached into his heart with a cold chill. The anger and hatred that he once felt for his mother was turned into guilt and tears... tears that fell silently down his cheek.

Hugging herself... she began to cry his name out loud... she could no longer stop her tears from falling... neither could Lone Wolf. He reached up to hug his mother... to comfort her... but again his ghostly arms only went through her body.

"Oh my God, Lone Wolf... please know that I love you." The pain and misery in her voice were all too clear. He had to comfort his mother.

"Here I am, mama! Mama! I'm right here! Beside you!" Tear after tear ran down his face as he sat and watched his mother cry. Having outburst after outburst... crying his name. But there was nothing he could do.

Her body began to tremble as she dropped to her knees and bowed her head in prayer... "Dear heavenly Father... I'm not very good at this... but please God... let my son know I love him."

With both of them on their knees... at a moment so emotionally strong... that when he said, "I know you love me, mama," she heard him... she felt his presence. She jumped and opened her eyes in disbelief.

"Lone Wolf? Is that you, baby?"

Once again confusion clouded his mind. His mother jumped to her feet, looking around, trying to find her only son... for there were a lot of unspoken words that needed to be said. Somehow Lone Wolf knew his time was limited... so he just allowed his heart to do the talking...

"Please don't cry... dry ya eyes... cuz mama it's hard to bare.
And I swear... I'll be there... living off in your prayers.
Can you still feel the love we share... dwelling in your heart?
With every breath... remember not even death... can keep
us apart.

Just close your eyes... and then try... to feel my presence in your arms.
In the air... everywhere... protecting you from harm.
No need to explain... your pain... I can hear it when you call my name.
Through the years... smeared tears... showing clear on my picture frame.
Even thou... I had to go... I know I left a scar.
But late at night... we both might... be wishing on that same star.
I know it's hard... but when you feel like crying, fight it!
Cuz one day soon you and I will both be reunited."

Opening his eyes... Lone Wolf found himself soaring and floating on a substance towards heaven. Suddenly... something began to pull him back towards earth. And the pain became a river... a river carrying him away to a sea of agony. He believed he was now headed to his place of anticipation... hell. Wave after wave of torturous pain shot through is soul as he cried out in agony... begging the lord for forgiveness... begging Him to deliver him from such lacerating pain.

Closing his eyes... he felt his soul sinking into what felt like a blazing fire. As enraged flames ate away at his soul... he opened his eyes to a blinding light. Hearing a familiar cry... Lone Wolf turned to look from this light and found Amber Faye at his side.

"Hold on baby, it'll be okay."

Seeing such a beautiful and lovely face, he realized that he was back from the grave. With a sigh of relief... and the knowledge he was not bound for hell... he fell peacefully into unconsciousness.

DAY TWENTY-NINE

"All ya'll nigga'z up in here know each other, right?" Murdah Man asked as he took his place at the head of the table. "And all ya'll know me. Ya'll know I don't fuck around. I called ya'll here cos, nigga, we abouts to get paid."

The warehouse in which the meeting was held was dark and grimy. The large oval table that sat in the center was surrounded by nineteen of Omaha's most notorious O.G.s, both Locs and B-Dogs... each a representative of their own sect. The age of the group varied greatly... ranging from Slithers, (a representative of Victor Block) at the age of 52... to as young as Tru Blue, (a representative of Small Street) at the age of 24. Murdah Man was by far the youngest at the table... but his reputation was one that dared to be challenged... even by those that are egregious cut throats, themselves.

"I know Crime Boss was running shit. But he was foul for leaving motha fucka'z out on they own. Picking and choosing who he deals with. But fuck that nigga, cuz. It's a new era. All that set-tripping and gang-banging bull shit stops here. Ya'll nigga'z understand me?"

On cue, Trigg emerged from the shadows. The well-oiled M-60 glistening in the dim light. Only he and Murdah Man had knowledge that the malicious looking weapon was inoperable. But it served it's treacherous purpose, nevertheless.

"Before I lay out the plan, I wanna know who's against me?" As Murdah Man said this, his eyes went from one ruthless leader to the next... his glare offering a silent challenge. A challenge that went untested. "Any ya'll nigga'z got beef in this room, it stops here. And if one of your B.G.s fuck up, it's gonna be taken out on your ass. So keep them lil' nigga'z in line. We all about the money for now on. We gonna run this city, understood?"

DAY THIRTY-ONE

Lone Wolf was unable to move as the pain engulfed him completely. He tried to open his eyes to escape the darkness... but was unsuccessful. He tried to move his hand, but his limbs felt detached. He wanted to cry out in pain... but he could scarcely breath as the serpent of fear wrapped its coils around his neck... contracting ever so tightly. Every breath he inhaled sent a bolt of pure, white-hot agony through his body. He felt helpless and dejected. He could do nothing. Nothing but struggle with the pain... suffering beneath the merciless foray.

In his ear... he could hear over his own sporadic breathing the snickering and sneering of the evil forces that resides within. Again he tried to scream... but the serpent was unyielding... relentless... unremorseful.

He saw a shadow pass before his closed eyelids... and he felt an immoral being just mere inches from his face. It seemed as if, or something, was standing over him. An evil and demonic presence that regarded him with cold and sadistic pleasure. Pleasure derived from the sight of his desolated and ravaged form. Relishing maliciously over the fact that Lone Wolf lain in helpless mortal distress.

Again, he tried to move, to break free from the bondage of pain that kept him incapacitated. He felt his arm jerk... then raise slowly... painfully. An overwhelming surge of pain jolted him as he felt his arm fell again. The pain was more than he could endure. Like the setting of the evening sun, he felt the light of consciousness slowly slipping away... being replaced by the lengthening shadows of obscurity. Unable to withstand the pain, he allowed himself to fall into the shadowy embrace of the abyss... a place he prayed he could escape his misery.

* * * * * *

"Oh, my God! Lone Wolf!" Amber Faye cried out involuntarily. Her shouting had drawn the attention of a nurse who stood just outside the door.

"Ma'am, are you okay?" the nurse asked as she entered.

"He moved!" Amber Faye exclaimed excitedly. "His arm! I saw it move!"

"Okay, Mrs. Johnson, calm down," the nurse said as she lain a consoling hand on Amber Faye. "Your husband will be fine. The anesthetic should be wearing off soon, so he'll be moving a lot more. He'll be up and around in no time."

"I'm sorry, ma'am. I just got so excited. To finally see him move."

"Well, you'll be seeing more of it. I just hope you don't go screaming every time he does," the nurse said playfully. "But please be sure to let me know when he comes to. The detectives need to talk to him as soon as possible, see if we can't get descriptions of the perpetrators that robbed him."

"Okay," Amber Faye said weakly. The nurse then flashed Amber Faye a bright smile, then turned and walked away, leaving her alone with Lone Wolf. Again she looked down helplessly at him, wondering if he was being tormented by the nightmares that seem to never go away. She laid a hand on his arm, the bowed her head in silent prayer.

DAY THIRTY-TWO

Lone Wolf slowly opened his eyes. The slow and steady throb of pain seemed to pulsate throughout his entire body. He laid there staring at the hospital's rough ceiling plaster for several minutes... grimacing against the pain. For these moments he was clinging to consciousness only through sheer iron will. He tried to move, but his aching muscles protested vigorously. The source of the pain seemed to be coming from his abdominal area. Then, in a flash of remembrance, he recalled watching the bullet passing threw his side... tearing at his flesh.

"Oh my God, baby! Are you okay?" a sweet and lovely voice called out to him. "Can you hear me?" Amber Faye asked as she leaned over the bed.

Lone Wolf tried to focus his eyes on her beautiful face, it was a strenuous task. "Where am I?" Lone Wolf asked. His voice was faint, brimming with pain.

"The hospital," Amber Faye said weakly. Lone Wolf looked down at his body only to see that most of his upper torso was wrapped in bandages. There was tubes stuck in his arms and a heart monitor that beeped away with a kind of steady rhythmic undercurrent.

"Baby, listen," Amber Faye said as she dropped to a confidential whisper. She scanned the room to reassure that the two were alone. "You're at the hospital. I told them I'm your wife, Sara Johnson and that you were robbed. There's two detectives waiting for you in the lobby. They want to ask you some questions. Baby, I know you're on the run, but I just don't know what to do." As she said this, her eyes began to brim with tears.

"You did good, a-ight?" Lone Wolf assured her, but his voice was hollow... nothing more then a lifeless mutter. "How long was I out *THIS* time?" Lone Wolf asked in a feeble attempt to lighten the mood. Amber Faye's chuckle was enervated... strained.

"Oh, the usual amount of time. Almost two days." Again her laugh was forced. "Can you move, Lone Wolf? They said all four bullets went straight through. No vital organs were hit. They said you are extremely lucky, but you'll be sore for along time because there were a lot of muscles that was torn. Here..." she said as she reached for the book bag that served as her purse. "They gave me some pain killers for you. And they said they would advise against traveling, especially by air. But baby, we can still leave by train." As she said this, her eyes plead with Lone Wolf, begging him to leave with her. But Lone Wolf didn't respond. "We'll talk about it later. But first, we have to get you out of here."

Lone Wolf tried to sit up, but the pain that flared through his abdominal was more than he could bare. "Damn," he growled to himself.

"Try rolling out of bed," Amber Faye said in a voice lined with genuine concern... but Lone Wolf couldn't repress a laugh. "What's so funny?"

"Nothing. I just..." but his voice trailed off.

It took great effort and a test of will for Lone Wolf to get out of bed. After he tore the tubes and wires from his chest and arms... Amber Faye helped him dress in an outfit she had brought with her. He removed most of the bandages... revealing two bloody strips of gauze. She dressed him slowly... carefully... making sure she didn't pain him further. She wanted to rush, in fear the nurse would return, but she fought this urge. He then crossed the room with great difficulties.

"Wait here, Lone Wolf. I'm going to see where the detectives are. There's a stair case just down the hall, can you make it?"

"Do I got a choice?" he asked as he smiled falsely.

"I guess not. I'll be back." Amber Faye left the room in a stealthy manner. She was gone only but a moment, but to Lone Wolf, it felt like an eternity. Finally she poked her head into the room and summoned him to follow.

The fragile Amber Faye helped the large Lone Wolf down the flight of stairs, baring most of his weight, for his legs were physically frail. Although the task was strenuous, Amber Faye refused to give up. The strength that she displayed touched him so deeply... so profoundly... that he felt his heart flutter in a way that it had never done before.

At the bottom of the steps, she offered him the opportunity to rest. Lone Wolf didn't respond. Instead he pulled her to him and embraced her in a way that he had never held anybody before. Amber Faye had saw the need in his eyes before. The need to know that he is loved. Not through hollow words... but through simplistic deeds. But it still touched her to know that finally he understands that her love is real... pure.

It was Amber Faye who finally pulled away, "Baby, we have to go. I parked just outside the side entrance. I knew we would have to sneak away." Again Lone Wolf found himself marveling at her strength... her intellect... her courage. He wanted to say something to her... he wanted to hold her forever... but he knew she was right... they did have to leave, quickly.

Through the sterile halls of the hospital they crept... keeping a watchful eye out for those that would have him incarcerated once again. Slowly, Lone Wolf found his strength coming back... but the pain in his stomach was unrelenting. Amber Faye continued to support him by baring his weight when his legs would falter, but even she noticed his strength was returning.

"We're almost there, baby. Just a little further."

The closer they got to their destination, the more crowed the halls became. Finally, the side entrance came into sight. "Girl, this the Emergency Entrance," Lone Wolf said as he watched an ambulance stop in front of the glass doors.

"I know," Amber Faye said in a hushed whisper. "It was the only door that wasn't heavily guarded. Besides, it was the only place where I could park close."

Just then, a swarm of nurses came rushing towards them. They were headed towards the ambulance that had just arrived. The guard that stood at the entrance was preoccupied with the new arrival.

"Come on, baby, hurry up," Amber Faye urged him soothingly as she lead him by the hand. Fighting against the pain, he quicken his step. His mind was so involved with the pain that he didn't hear the nurses as they communicated loudly to each other. As a stretcher was unloaded, one nurse began to cut the patents shirt off while another took his vitals. It wasn't until the stretcher was wheeled past him did he realize he knew the person lying on it.

"We have two gun shot wounds to his chest..." a nurse called out. "His vitals are dropping rapidly. We need two units of LYB in room 107, and stat!"

"He's lost a lot of blood!" another called out. "Contact EPM and tell them we need the machine, ASAP!"

"We're losing him!" was the last words Lone Wolf heard clearly as the swarm disappeared behind two metal swinging doors.

Almost there," Amber Faye whispered, completely oblivious to what Lone Wolf had witnessed. His mind raced as he thought of who he saw lying in the stretcher. He smiled sadistically to himself as he thought of Karma and her mysterious ways. The thought seemed to ease the pain. He knew instantly who had shot the victim that now laid at the very hands of death... tittering on the brink of eternal darkness.

But his smile faded as he thought of the fate that Karma had in store for him. He knew the life he led was foul, and that in time he would have to account for each and every sin he has ever committed against another. This time he was lucky to survive. He could have easily been unfortunate. Like Trigg... who would soon embrace the darkness of the abyss. But he knew no other way to live. *Perhaps Amber Faye could lead me down the path I've been looking for,* he thought to himself. *I guess time will tell.*

* * * * * *

Amber Faye stopped Lone Wolf just outside the apartment. "Wait right here," she said as she went to unlock the door. "I have a surprise for you." She then looked over her shoulder at him and now there was a playful gleam in her eyes... "I mean, if you can handle it." She then disappeared into he darkness within.

He stood there in the stillness of the hall... the silence seemed to buzz loudly in his ears. Minutes ticked away before Amber Faye finally stuck her head out the door. With a mischievous smile on her face, she motioned for him to follow.

When Lone Wolf stepped into the apartment, he was met with the scent of something sweet and sensual that lingered in the quiet space. When he made it into the living room, he found that it was dimly lit; the walls were lined with scented candles. Soft music played in the background. Amber Faye stood in the center, a red robe was draped softly over her slender shoulders. Her eyes sparkled brightly as it reflected the soft flames of the candles. In her hand, she held a single rose. It's color matching the comforter that laid spread on the floor.

"Many say that love is the ultimate pain killer. Like I said, if you think you can handle it." Amber Faye narrowed her eyes at Lone Wolf. She caressed her face gently with the soft rose petals as she beckoned him with an intimate stare. Feeling out of place, Lone Wolf lowered his eyes. She stepped forward and grabbed his hand.

"I love you, Lone Wolf," she whispered in his ear. He felt the fluttering of butterflies as they stirred restlessly inside. The tingle of raw pleasure ran along his spine as Amber Faye pressed her body against his. She stood on her toes and went in to kiss Lone Wolf... but he pulled back.

"I don't know what I'm doing. I'm lost." Lone Wolf admitted. He wasn't used to the sensuality of love making. Even then, he was fighting the barbaric urge to fuck her... for this is all he's ever known.

"Just follow my lead," she purred as she began to kiss his neck. As she embraced him, she reached her hand up to gently massage his shoulders... completely forgetting about his injuries. He flinched in pain.

"Ohh, I'm sorry," she said as she tensed.

"Don't stop, Amber Faye," he whispered as their lips brushed each others. "A little pain brings a lot of pleasure."

"No, Lone Wolf. Please don't hurt me," she wined, remembering their first sexual encounter. "Let's take it slow... soft... gentle," Amber Faye sighed as her lips pressed gently against his neck, "The way lovers do."

Their lips met for a second time, their tongues playing in each others mouths. Amber Faye felt a warm sensation began to spread slowly through her body, anticipation of his hardness slowly sliding deep inside of her. Again, Lone Wolf pulled away. He lowered his eyes... but then looked up at her lovingly... passionately... shyly. He lifted his hand and gently caressed her face. She closed her eyes and her bottom lip trembled. Her heart was beating faster and faster as she slowly grind on his stiffness. Their fingers were intertwined, with closed eyes and opened minds. Again forgetting about his injuries, she went to run her fingers threw his long wavy hair... accidentally brushing against his head wound. He grimaced in pain.

"Oh God, Lone Wolf. I am so sorry. I keep..." But he silenced her with a gentle kiss. Without speaking further, she slowly began to undress him. She winched slightly at the sight of the gauze that was soaked in dry blood. But his imploring eyes assured her he was fine. Her moves were gentle... careful. His moves were shy... timid. They were both afraid of hurting each other.

He laid her down gently on the comforter. His teeth gnawing gently on the soft skin of her neck... followed by soft kisses. What they shared, she was sure of, was a deep romantic love in spite of his unwillingness to expose his gentler side. *In due time,* she thought to herself.

His body slid in between her legs. With her eyes closed, her face grimaced with passionate pain as he slowly entered her. Again, he was fighting the urge to impale her as he watched her wince with each slight movement. But he didn't want to hurt her.

Gradually the grimace on her face changed to that of growing ecstasy as he rotated his hips slowly. His movements where still small... timid. She lovingly wrapped her arms around his neck as a groan of pure satisfaction escaped her barely parted lips.

He buried his manhood deep inside of her and left it there... knowing she would love the feeling as it throbbed and pulsated. It quivered and spasm inside of her... evoking a groan of raw pleasure that came from her throat. As his tempo steadily increased, she opened her eyes and looked deeply into his eyes. Her eyes were blazing with unbridled passion as she bared her teeth. At that instant, she froze. Her spine arched off the floor as her body stiffened in the height of pleasure.

But Lone Wolf didn't want to stop... he wanted to keep her in this steady state of pleasure. He pulled out of her despite his powerful need to cum. But he wanted to make this moment about her. He started by kissing Amber Faye behind her ear... then slowly made his descent down her body.... kissing and licking as he made his way down. Periodically he would pull back to blow gently on the wetness his tongue left behind, her body shuttering in ecstatic delight each time.

Kissing and licking... he slowly made his way down... rib by rib, his big hands caressing her body as he went.

Finally, the tip of his tongue touched her sacred place, her hands pulled at his hair as his tongue probed inside of her. She dug her nails into his shoulder as she felt it slithering wetly around within her inner most regions. Lone Wolf flinched in pain at her hands being so close to his bullet wound, but Amber Faye was so far gone she didn't realize the pain she was causing him.

As the tip of his tongue played inside of her, gently flicking her clit, he slipped a finger into her. Slowly he worked it back and fourth, making sure his tongue didn't lose contact with her swollen clit. Then he worked in a second finger.

Amber Faye's passion grew and grew as he stuck his tongue as deep as he could inside of her... loving the whimpers that escaped her lips as he let it pushing around inside of her. He didn't want this moment to end. He wanted this moment to last forever.

Slipping a finger back inside of her, he wiggled his finger, as if he was telling someone to "come here." This summoning motion drove Amber Faye over the edge. Again she came. Now feeling confident that Amber Faye was satisfied, he now began to focus on his own fulfillment. Sliding his extra hard manhood into her, he made sure the bulging vein on his manhood never lost contact with her ever so swollen clitoris.

Simultaneously, they both reached the peek of ecstasy. His drained body collapsed onto her... his head falling onto her chest. Amber Faye was making small whimpering noises as she tried to catch her breath. Still inside of her, he pulled back... looking at her face. Dewy perspiration beaded her beautiful face as she fought to open her eyes. "Are you coo? Did I hurt you?" Lone Wolf inquired. Amber Faye, still unable to speak shook her head weakly and tried to smile.

Amber Faye finally drew in an extended, quivering breath, and then was still. Slowly she opened her eyes. Looking up at Lone Wolf she saw that his long hair was clinging wetly to his forehead and cheeks... a tiny, pulsing aura of candlelight reflecting from his sweaty face.

Oh my God, she thought to herself, *this can't be the same Lone Wolf. He's so gentle... so passionate.* The hatred was cleansed from his dark eyes, finally they were soft... trusting. Never had she ever felt so close to another as she felt towards Lone Wolf at that very moment. She could tell by the look in his eyes that he had felt the same way as well... perhaps for the very first time ever in his wretched life.

DAY THIRTY-THREE

Lone Wolf slowly opened his eyes. For the first time in many years, he slept with complete abandonment. Amber Faye laid in his arms asleep. He gazed down lovingly at her. Her face... childlike in response... seemed radiant from the soft shafts of golden sunshine that beamed across the floor. He held her tight... ignoring the throbbing pain in his shoulder.

At his movements, Amber Faye began to stir. She purred as she buried her head into the hollowness of his arm. With her ear against his chest, she could hear his heart's every beat, and hearing it caused her to giggle tiredly.

"Oh, you're up? I didn't mean to wake you," Lone Wolf said as he held her even closer. Amber Faye purred in response. "What was you laughing about?"

"Oh nothing. Just your heart beat."

"What's so funny about that?"

"I don't know. It's silly," she said as she looked up at him sweetly, placing her chin on his chest. "I was just thinking that if the Tin Man could get a heart, then why can't my Lone Wolf?"

"Oh. I thought you was laughing at my swipe," he said as he brushed her hair.

"Your what?" she asked naively.

"My swipe. My dick."

A wave of embarrassment washed over her face as she buried it in his chest and giggled. "Why do you call it that? And why would I be laughing at it? I'm not a very big woman, Mr. Lone Wolf. Something like that could hurt a petite woman like me." He laughed in response. "Besides, I like the way it feels against my thigh. Like it's lost, looking for a warm place to borrow into," she said laughing.

"What? Are you talking dirty?"

"No. I'm just saying," she said softly as she pulled the comforter up over her bare shoulders. "Did you have fun last night, Mr. Lone Wolf?" He nodded his head. "Yeah, me too. I never thought you could be so soft."

"What? Nigga, is you trying get beat up this early?" Lone Wolf asked playfully.

"I don't think so, Mr. Softy."

"Nigga, I ain't soft. I'll still bathe in a nigga'z blood. I'm still a motha fuckin' gangsta."

"I know. But I also know you'll never hurt me."

"And how you know that?"

"Because, I'm your protectress. I will never hurt you, and I will never let anybody hurt you."

As Amber Faye said this, Lone Wolf felt a violent tremor rip through his soul, causing his body to shutter. A response she didn't expect to get... but was a welcomed reaction.

"How the fuck you 'spose to protect me? Yous just a little motha fucka." Lone Wolf could hear the gentleness in his voice subsiding... returning to it's usual hostile tone. Sensing this, he tried to soften his voice. "It's gonna be me protecting you."

"I can protect you if need be. But Lone Wolf, I was talking about protecting you here." As she said this she tapped him on his chest with her finger... just above his heart. Again he could feel the trembling inside... and again he fought against it.

"How you know I won't turn on you? You know I can't be trusted," Lone Wolf said dryly.

"I trust you. But just in case you try something funny..." as she said this she reached to where his belongings laid. Reaching under the black hoodie, she produced Lone Wolf's pistol. He small hands trembled as she took control of the weapon.

"And what you gonna do with that?" he playfully challenged.

"I'm going to blow you into smithereens," she giggled childishly.

"'Smithereens,' huh? How? It ain't even loaded."

"Oh yeah? So I guess you wouldn't mind if I pointed it at you?" As she said this she waved the pistol in front of his face... but the barrel was pointed towards the heavens... and never directly at him.

"You can point it, pull the trigger. Like I said, it ain't loaded." He then put his hand over hers, he could feel her hand still trembling as she held the weapon. He guided her hand so that the barrel was pressed against his temple. "Go ahead, pull the trigger. It ain't loaded." When he said this he could feel her hand shaking even more.

"I don't like this, Lone Wolf," Amber Faye said, her innocent demeanor completely gone. She tried to pull away, but Lone Wolf's grip kept her hand and pistol in place.

"How can you protect me? You can't even pull the trigger on a strap that ain't even loaded." He laughed as he said this. He then removed his hand. She kept the barrel pressed lightly against his temple for a brief moment... debating rather or not she was willing to protect him. But then she allowed the pistol to slowly drop to her side.

"Why do you do that?" She asked as the tears fell. "Why do you act that way?"

"Act what way?" Lone Wolf asked as he reached for the pistol.

"Why are you so mean? So cruel?" she asked as she anxiously relinquished the pistol. Lone Wolf didn't respond. Instead, he held the pistol up, then hit the release switch. The fully loaded magazine slid from the handle, landing heavily on the red comforter. Amber Faye's eyes became round with fear. He then racked the pistol, ejecting the live round that lay in the chamber. Amber Faye began to cry and shake uncontrollably.

"What the hell is wrong with you?" Lone Wolf asked as he laughed sadistically.

"I could have killed you," she said in between sobs. "Why do you do that? Why do you have to be this way? Do you want to die?"

"Look, Amber Faye, I knew you wasn't going to pull the trigger. That's why I did it."

"But what if I did, Lone Wolf? I believed you when you said it wasn't loaded. What if I did?"

"Then you would of had a lot of explaining to do to the po-po's," Lone Wolf laughed.

"That's not funny, Lone Wolf." As she said this, she cried even harder. "Why are you anxious to die? I don't want to lose you. I just found you."

"Lose me? What the hell are you talking about?"

"I don't know," she said as she wiped away the tears... her sobs slowly subsiding. "It's just that I'm always praying for you... always. You just don't know, Lone Wolf. Now-a-days... all I do is cry and pray. Pray that you'll come around and realize what you have. Not only what you could have with me... but what you have in yourself. And it just tears me up inside when you do these self-destructing things. Almost like you don't care about life... about yourself. Well, I do. I care."

Lone Wolf sat quietly... listening to every word that was being spoken. And he knew that very word she said was true. He had heard her prayers. He could recall how he looked down on his lifeless corpse as it lain in the arms of Amber Faye. He remembered how she had cried out his name in complete agony... in complete misery... in complete pain. The recollection of watching her tears fall as her cries went unheard began to pierce his heart... in the same way the bullets ate away at his flesh. A new wave of pain washed over him. An unfamiliar pain. But such emotions could not be read on his face.

"Are you listening to me, Lone Wolf?"

"I heard every word you said," he said drily. Again, he realized his tone was devoid of warmth... devoid of the sensitives that one associates with new-found love. And again he tried to soften his tone. "And I believe you. I saw you hold me and cry."

"What? When?" she asked as confusion over-shadowed her face.

"If I told you, you'll think I'm crazy," he said laughing.

"I don't think, Mr. Lone Wolf... I *KNOW* you're crazy," she said smiling through tear-filled eyes. Lone Wolf wanted to disclose to her what he had witnessed on his brief journey amongst the graves... but decided against it, for such disclosure would only verify to Amber Faye his unstablness.

"It doesn't matter," he finally said.

"I guess it doesn't," Amber Faye said as she settled back into his arms. "All that matters is that we leave as soon as we can. How are you feeling?"

At the question, Lone Wolf noticed the slow and persistent vibration of pain. A physical pain that was almost forgotten.

"Do you want your pills?"

"Naw. I want something to drink."

"You need some water?" Amber Faye asked as she went to get up.

"Naw. I need a 4-D of Old English. That's what I need."

"I don't think that's a good idea, Lone Wolf. Just take a couple of pills, then you can rest because I know they'll make you drowsy." When he didn't respond, Amber Faye reached for her robe, then went to retrieve the medication, a glass of water and some fresh bandages. Once she returned, she fed him the pills then held the glass so that he could drink from it. She then set the glass to the side and began to change the dirty bandages over his wounds. Once completed, she then nestled back into the warmth of his arms. "Now, is that better?" she asked as she placed her head in the crook of his arm... but he didn't respond.

"You told me you would tell me everything once we were on the plane. But since we're not leaving for a few days, can you tell me now?"

"Tell you what?"

"Tell me everything. There's so many things I want to know. I don't even know where to begin. I guess you can tell me how you got shot. Do you know who did it?"

"No," Lone Wolf like. "Like you said, it was nothing more than a robbery."

"Why are you lying to me, Lone Wolf?"

"What? Ain't nobody lying to you."

"If it was a robbery, then why did you still have your money and your gun?"

"Because, when they rolled up, I showed them I had heat. I guess they started panicking and just started blasting. And next thang you know, I'm laid up."

Amber Faye sat silently... saying nothing about the doubt she had. Instead, she said... "I guess that makes sense, kind of. Well..." After a brief pause, she asked, "Who's Kevin?"

At the question, she felt his body tense under her. His muscles jerked and popped. Instantly she regretted asking the question, for she believed he would now become hostile and reclusive. She was pleasantly surprised when he answered.

"Kevin's my nigga..." he said slowly. "The only nigga I've ever trusted."

"Where's he at now?" she asked slyly, afraid she was pressing the issue beyond the realm of comfort. After a moment of silence, Lone Wolf said, "Sometimes I go to Hope Hills just to think."

"Where's Hope Hills?" Amber Faye asked. But Lone Wolf continued as if he didn't hear the question.

"Sometimes I walk around aimlessly. You know, just thinking of shit. And somehow, someway, I always seem to find my way to Kevin. Sometimes, I just..." but his voice trailed off... and then he grew silent. Amber Faye was desperate to know more... but feared the repercussions that may ensue.

"Remember that night on the phone, Lone Wolf?"

"Yes, I remember. And, no, it wasn't me," he said irritatingly.

"Dang, I'm just asking. I don't know what else to ask without worrying about a reaction. I mean, you wear secrecy like armor. But you don't have to be defensive around me."

"Yeah, I know. It's just that sometimes I..." he said quietly... but again his voice trailed off. And again he grew silent.

"You know what, Lone Wolf? It doesn't matter. None of it matters because soon it'll all be behind us, huh?" she asked. When he didn't respond, she looked up at him and found that he was fighting off a wave of sleep. "It's okay, Lone Wolf," Amber Faye whispered. "Let your medications take you. I'm not going anywhere. I'll protect you." She believed in her words with every single fiber of her being. She didn't know how... but she knew she was ready and willing to protect him.

* * * * * *

Amber Faye was asleep when suddenly she felt Lone Wolf jerk underneath her. She sat up to find his chest heaving laboriously as sweat rolled from his face. "Shh," she cooed soothingly in an attempt to calm him... but his face grimaced, then snatched away. She placed a hand on his chest while the other combed threw his hair. "It's okay, baby. I'm here." she assured the sleeping Lone Wolf... speaking softly to his soul.

She watched as he fought gallantly against the demonic forces that seemed relentless in their pursuit to hunt his every dream. She listened to every incoherent utterance that escaped his trembling lips. She cried and prayed silently as she watched in helpless dread... knowing not what to do.

Suddenly, Lone Wolf cried out in anguish. *That name again,* she thought to herself. She tried again to console him... but her efforts were unavailing. She listened as he mumbled that second name... T-Roy... his face then grimaced in pain. His body jerked and twitched. His lips stirred... as if trying to speak. His forehead crease as she stared at him... feeling lost and helpless.

Suddenly, he sprung up... his eyes were wild with anger and fear. She felt a lashing flame of fear overcome her as she looked into the cold, dark eyes of Lone Wolf. His face, the mask of rage and hatred. The very emotions she wished to one day cleanse from his heart. She watched with apprehension as he dressed quickly... and then finally grabbing his pistol. She flinched as he slammed the magazine into the handle with the palm of his hand... then racked it forcefully.

She wanted to cry out to him... to stop him... but her throat was clogged with fear. He looked down upon her... his eyes... dark and sinister. She looked up at him... staring at the mask of hatred through gelatinous tears.

"Please, don't go, Lone Wolf," she said softly as the tears flowed freely. She saw something change in his expression. His dark eyes seemed to be pleading. Not for sympathy... but for something more akin to understanding. There was then a glimpse of the fleeing guilt that passed quickly through him. But then his face instantly resumed it's murderous facade.

"Murdah Man," he growled viciously before he turned towards the door. He grabbed Amber Faye's car keys then stormed from the apartment.

"Baby, please!" Amber Faye cried frantically. With her red robe wrapped around her body... she followed him down the stairs and then out into the cool wetness of the night's air. "Please don't go!" she cried after him. She sank to her knees on the cold wet grass. She watched as the tail-lights grew smaller and smaller as he descended into the night.

Thunder split the heavens above... but it didn't faze Amber Faye as she sat crying. Light rain fell from the skies... mingling with her own tears. She wondered where he was headed.

"Hope Hills," she whispered into the rain... praying it was true. *Where is this?* she though to herself. "It doesn't matter," she said aloud. "He needs me. I have to find him."

* * * * * *

Lone Wolf felt the wicked venom pumping strongly through his veins as he sped through the wet streets of La Vista... heading to the north side. The unyielding pain of his wounds began to aggravate him. The pain...

that eddying pain that he could not escape. Lone Wolf knew what he had to do. This was a mission of vengeance... the same mission that he once vowed to complete. But his resolve was weak. Such weakness had led him to his current state of misery... recovering from the wounds of a Glock .40.

"Nigga, fuck this shit," he growled to himself as he pressed on the accelerator... picking up speed. He knew what he had to do... and this time Murdah Man will fall victim to the same ideology that he himself abides by... retaliations a must.

DAY THIRTY-FOUR

Drizzle sprinkled the windshield as Lone Wolf sat restlessly outside the residence's of Murdah Man. His hand sat on top of his weapon as his eyes scanned the dark and wet streets. He knew not how long he sat there fantasizing about the demise of his recently acquired archenemy... but he knew his resolve was strong. He refused to suffer the same fate as his brother by allowing his adversary the opportunity to claim his soul. He knew the treacherous Murdah Man would try again... this is why he sat waiting for his return.

It wasn't until 5:37AM when Lone Wolf saw the '95 Mustang slowly creeping along the curb. After reassuring a live round was chambered, Lone Wolf quickly exited the car.

Murdah Man pulled into his driveway. Then parked the Mustang at a slanted angle. Lone Wolf watched from the shadows as Murdah Man stumbled from the car... in one hand he held a 40oz bottle... in the other... a pistol.

Keeping to the shadows... Lone Wolf made his way quickly and stealthily towards Murdah Man. He watched as Murdah Man unscrewed the 40oz cap... took a long pull from the bottle, then replace the cap back o the bottle.

Lone Wolf crept up slowly behind Murdah Man. He gripped his pistol firmly as he went to deliver a blow to the back of Murdah Man's skull. The hollow thump rang loudly in the quiet morning as the metal connected solidly with bone.

At the point of impact... Murdah Man accidentally let off a round from his own weapon. But his pistol fell from his grip as he fell towards the ground.

With the toe of his boot... Lone Wolf flipped him onto his back... then took precise aim. Murdah Man's eyes were wild... but then came into gradual focus. He found himself in the very position he held many a victim... which only invoked a sadistic snarl from the lips of Murdah Man.

"Somebody hit me. Was that you?" he chuckled to himself... completely oblivious to the lurch of detestable fate he now faced.

"You ready to die, nigga?" Lone Wolf asked as he forcefully pressed the barrel to his temple. Again, Murdah Man laughed wickedly... his breath was heavy with liquor.

"Why you wanna kill me, huh? After all I've done did for you?" Murdah Man went to pick himself up... but the heavy boot of Lone Wolf came crashing down onto his chest.

"You tried to kill me. You tried to leave me for dead," Lone Wolf growled as he repositioned the pistol.

"What? Nigga, that's bull shit. It was that nigga Trigg. He tried to kill you, not me. You shoulda seen what I did to that fool for that, too," Murdah Man said as he laughed to himself. "I told him, 'you fucks with my nigga, Lone Wolf, Lil' Wolf, you fucks with me, cuz.'"

"Nigga, you think I'm stupid, huh?" Lone Wolf asked as he delivered a blow to he side of his chin. He felt the bone shatter under the forceful blow. Murdah Man took the pain in stride. Blood stained his teeth as he smiled up at Lone Wolf.

"You oh bitch ass nigga," Murdah Man said in a voice filled with anger. "Nigga, you better kill me, nigga."

"Psst, Think I won't?" Lone Wolf asked as he raised his pistol... taking aim in between the eyes of Murdah Man.

"Wanna know something messed up?" Murdah Man chuckled. "You know that fool T-Roy?"

At the name... Lone Wolf felt the sudden rush of anger wash over him.

"Me and that fool been doing business since the day he got outta prison. Ain't that shit funny?" Murdah Man said laughing. "I just came from his house."

In a second rush of anger, Lone Wolf delivered yet another blow with the broadside of his pistol. "Where is he?" Lone Wolf demanded as he pulled Murdah Man up by his collar. Murdah Man grinned fiendishly up at Lone Wolf.

"Where the hell you think? You know, for a smart nigga, you sure are blinded sometimes." Murdah Man said as his mouth filled with more blood. "How's the gut?"

At the question... the devastating rage that pumped through his veins impelled him to pull the trigger. The deadly explosion was loud... but it failed to drown out the sickening sound of the bullet that penetrated Murdah Man's skull. His head snapped back from the heavy impact... and his legs kicked and twitched.

Again, Lone Wolf anticipated the sounds of those inner demons rejoicing at the display of unbridled hostility... but they remained confined in the murky depths of his besmirched and sinful soul... quiet and subdued.

In the distance, Lone Wolf heard the barking of a dog... and then the murmuring of people as they tried to hush them. He knew that soon they would emerge from their houses in an attempt to investigate the source of the gunshots... so he knew his time had come to leave.

Rising to his feet... Lone Wolf looked down upon his once best friend. Murdah Man's face no longer seemed hostile or murderous. Instead... in spite of the soft glistening of blood, he looked peaceful in the early morning street lights... the polar opposite of what he truly was. Guilt began to consume him as he stared at the young and peaceful face of Murdah Man... thinking that perhaps his resolve had gone too far.

"Play pussy, get fucked," he finally said to himself as he remembered the excruciating pain he had suffered at the hands of his closest friend. "I didn't start this war."

Hearing the opening of front doors... Lone Wolf turned to walk away, but stopped short when he remembered the pain consoling liquor that Murdah Man held before the ordeal. Locating the 40oz bottle... Lone Wolf retrieved it, then disappeared into the shadows.

* * * * * *

Making his way through rows and rows of head stones... Lone Wolf felt the alcohol from within as it fought against the pain that was well known to him. Staggering with every step he made... he shivered in the crisp morning air as the temperature seemed to penetrate his body.

Tears blinded him as he finally came to the resting place of his brother. With what was left of Murdah Man's 40oz in hand... he took another gulp of the bitter tasting fluid, then slowly dropped to his knees. He pressed his cheek against his brother's headstone and closed his eyes; he felt a chill race up his spine as the damp concrete touched his face.

The early morning sun hid behind a thick blanket of gray clouds. All morning there had been mists and rain. The day was as bleak as the soul of Lone Wolf.

Taking another gulp of the pain numbing liquid... Lone Wolf allowed his mind to wonder back to the days when he and his brother would play in the park... but his past had became so vague and hazy... he hardly understood anything anymore. Even the present and it's hectic chaos became as dark and murky as his past. Living his life full of violence... with those inner demons always trying to escape from within... hearing in his mind the chittering screams of the dead... living his life in constant fear, for he could feel on his face their morbid breath. He knew his dying day was on it's way... and soon he would join the screams of the dead, for the number of his adversaries is constantly growing. Tears of pain slid from beneath closed eye lids. He knew he would join the tormented moans, for his heart and soul was tarnished by the grime and soot of a sinful life.

"I knew I'd find you here."

Lone Wolf was startled by the soothing voice. By natural instinct he instantly reached for his pistol. Amber Faye gasped and pulled back as she found herself looking down the barrel of the Detonics Mark V. After he saw who it was, his tensed trigger finger slowly relaxed. Finally, he allowed the pistol to fall to his side.

"Go away," he mumbled as he let his head fall back onto the headstone.

Dropping to her knees beside him, she lain a consoling hand on his shoulder. She felt his muscles contract under her gentle touch. "Lone Wolf?" she whispered softly. "Talk to me, Lone Wolf. Please." But he said nothing.

After a moment of silence, he finally asked, "How did you find me?"

"I remember you saying something about Hope Hills. So I took a cab to get your car. So here I am... I knew you needed me." Her eyes fell upon the headstone of which Lone Wolf gently caressed. "So this is Kevin?" she asked in the merest whisper. Again she felt his muscles tense at the mention of his name. She sat silently as waves of guilt surged towards her throat for her asking.

Little did she know that at that very moment, a strange wave of relaxation and regret had passed together through the body of Lone Wolf. The kindness in her voice triggered a fresh burst of tears. He hid his face from her... but she felt his shuttering under her touch. From the first day they had met... Amber Faye had given him her all. Since that first night she was determined to protect him... to guard him with the zeal of a young lioness guarding her cubs. She saw his talents... she saw his potential. She saw his strengths... and she believed in him. She knew there was a hollowness in his icy heart... an emptiness only her love could fill. She knew there was a war going on inside of him. And she knew her love could tip the balance, if only he would allow her to love him.

Lone Wolf had long stopped shuttering and the silence was growing heavy between them. Sitting back on his heels... he looked at her with an anguish that tore at her heart. She suddenly found herself staring at him from across an abyss. She wanted to hold him, to ask him... to comfort him... but she dared not cross the threshold. Instead, she searched his bloodshot eyes... and there... in the midst of the hatred and the darkness... she saw the truth once again... she saw the pain.

"I love you, Lone Wolf." It was the merest whisper... spoken as much with her eyes. It wasn't the first time she had said it to him. But this time it was different. This time it pierced through the protective layers of iron and steel and warmly caressed his icy heart. Again, the tears began to fall.

"I remember along time ago..." he said softly in that far away voice he got whenever he spoke about the past. "I was with my brother and his friends. We were playing football out in the middle of the street."

Long buried memories fought for acknowledgment as he spoke softly. "We was playing football and it was my turn to catch the ball. I was so happy, so excited. Then out of nowhere I saw a car rushing straight towards me. I remember I was so scared I couldn't move. All I could do was stand there, waiting to get hit by his car, waiting to die. Then I felt someone lift me up out of harms way. It was my big brother. It was Kevin." His voice was barely an audible whisper at the last. He looked up at her... her eyes full of terrible understanding and tears.

"From that day on, I knew that my big brother will always be there to protect me. I just knew he would never leave me. But he was taken from me. He died in my arms and it's all my fault. If only I would have left when he told me too, he'll still be here. I was in the house dicking around, wasting time. If only we would have left when he first told us to, he would still be here. And now I'm haunted by them, and there's no escape."

After a long moment of silence, Amber Faye fought to find her voice. "How?" she asked in a tiny voice... as if she was afraid of his answer. Again she felt his every muscles contract as the image raced through his mind. The bullets piercing the body of Kevin. The sound of his body hitting the pavement. The sound of his last cry.

Suddenly, Lone Wolf pushed her with the force of a possessed demonic being. It paned his wounded shoulder... but the anger instantly drove it away. She flew backwards, landing against another headstone. Lone Wolf swept up his pistol and 40oz and stood above her.

"Baby, please don't." Here words were spoken softly and her eyes seemed to grow large as this huge man loomed over her. She had never felt smaller or more frightened then she did at that very moment. As Lone Wolf looked down at her... something sinister and wicked jumped at her from his dark, bloodshot eyes. She began to tremble visibly and had to fight not to cry out. She looked at him with despair blending into desperation.

"Give me my keys," he growled at her. Her hands shook as she relinquished the keys.

"Please, Lone Wolf, no," Amber Faye whimpered.

Lone Wolf turned and threw the 40oz against the headstone of Kevin. The quiet stillness of the cemetery was now defiled only by the shattering glass. But when Lone Wolf turned back towards her, she saw that behind the anger and hatred was that hurt and pain again. And again, a great anguish tore at her heart. She wanted desperately to reach out for him... but all she could do was look at him with helpless horror as Lone Wolf threw her keys at her then turned and stalked off.

Less than twelve hours ago she laid in his arms... fantasizing about the wonderful life they will share together in a new city. Less then twelve hours ago she gained strength from him despite his injuries... his words took her every doubt away. But now here she was... left alone in this cemetery... laying beside the burial sight of his brother... clinging desperately to a fading hope... praying for the redemption of Lone Wolf's soul, for she knew what he was about to do.

* * * * * *

The '64 Chevy splashed along the back streets of Omaha as the heavens continued to wash the city clean. With the sleeve of his hoodie, he wiped away the tears and rain from his face as he inhaled deeply. He now wished that he never busted his 40oz... his strength... his comfort. He wished he had a blunt... or some pills. Anything that served to alleviate the pain and the stench of his fucked up existence would do just fine. Instead, he had nothing. Nothing but a fully loaded Detonics Mark V that rested heavily on his lap. That, and an undeniable notion that somebody had to die.

Making twists and turns through the rain swept streets... Lone Wolf made his way to Tommy Rose Garden... the notorious hangout for those belonging to Murda 8. Stopping just outside the parking lot, he exited the car and placed his pistol in his waist band. Feeling the cold steel pressed against his warm flesh caused him to shiver. Flipping his hood over his head, he began to make his way towards the projects. Despite being on a main street, the parking lot was eerily quiet... as quiet as the cemetery he just came from. The cars stood in rows like coffins... awaiting their place below earth. As he drew closed, he could feel his primitive instinct of survival slowly rise. His heart began to pump it's venom and the inner demons began to stir.

Once at the door... he could hear the music of Mack 10 seeping from within the apartment. He knew there had to be other people in there, but how many? His most primal instincts had now been fully aroused as he reached for his pistol.

With weapon in hand... Lone Wolf felt a chilled wind press against his cheek. It felt like the back of a corpse's hand. His breath became labored as he stood looking at the door. Lone Wolf had never felt so alone... so isolated as he did right now. Lone Wolf loved his brother with an intensity that words could never describe. And now his murderer awaits just beyond this door. The voices of the dead urged him on. The screams of the damned rang in his ear. The moans of his brother echoed in his mind. Without the presence of love... his heart followed it's wicked nature.

With a well placed kick, the door crashed open with unnatural force. The two women inside jumped in horror. Sounding off with terrified screams. Entering the apartment, Lone Wolf raised the pistol and let off two rounds. With the adrenaline pumping... his muscles jumped and his hand shook terribly, completely throwing off his aim. The two bullets found it's way into the wall just above the head of a screaming woman. She threw herself to the ground as she was showered by wall plaster. The voices trapped in his head had completely drowned out the woman's screams and the blasting music.

His vision became blurry.

He got the feeling of intense desperation as he made his way through the apartment... firing his pistol at every ill-defined shape... at every shadow... at anything that even remotely resembled a man. But they were all illusions, only the two women and T-Roy was in the apartment. It was in the last room where Lone Wolf found T-Roy.

His vision instantly cleared and the screaming in his head subsided.

T-Roy stood motionlessly in the center of the room... unaffected... unafraid. Lone Wolf found himself looking into the eyes that took away his brother. A clear and vivid image of Kevin's fall flashed in the mind of Lone Wolf. He figuratively shook his head in a feeble attempt to clear these horrific images from his mind.

T-Roy held Lone Wolf's eyes firmly with his own icy stare. The hardness of his face held evidence of his years spent in prison... along with the muscles protruding from beneath his tank-top.

Lone Wolf raised his pistol and took a step forward. In a low, deadly voice... he asked, "Do you remember me?" But T-Roy's eyes remained hardened. Lone Wolf had seen heartless and stone cold killers whose eyes had never shone as much as a flicker as they killed. He now wondered if they all behaved in the same manner as they lay at the very hands of death. Instead... it was Lone Wolf who fought back the fear... the tear.

"You kilt my brother!" he yelled frantically as he delivered a heavy blow to the side of T-Roy's face with his pistol. His head snapped sideways... but his body didn't budge. T-Roy slowly raised his head and looked at Lone Wolf. His eyes were fiery... blood trickling from his mouth. He grinned fiendishly and spat blood.

"You can't kill me, nigga," T-Roy said in a low, icy tone... as icy as death itself. "I've been dead, nigga."

Lone Wolf found himself staring at Satan reincarnate. He is familiar with the hell created by the "correctional" system... and he knew that the only creatures that could survive the fiery pits of hell were demons. Now here he stood... face to face with the demon of his past... the root of his own personal hell which began on that fateful day. His hands shook as he slowly raised his pistol and took precise aim at his head. T-Roy's facial expression remained the same.

"You ain't no killer," T-Roy laughed wickedly as he took a step forward. The blood continued to drip from his mouth. "You can't kill me. You ain't got it in you." Like a coiled snake launching it's venomous attack... T-Roy sprang forward with his fists clenched.

The last image Lone Wolf saw before closing his eyes was the blood-dripping face of Kevin... his brother... contorted in agonizing pain. But before Lone Wolf could pull the trigger... the air was split by the exploding thunder of a pistol erupting. He opened his eyes just as T-Roy fell before him... his skull was shattered and parts of it's insides were exposed. He stood there... staring at the gory sight. He waited for the wails of the tortures... but they were hushed. He waited for the screams of the dead... but they were silenced. He awaited the memorized scream of Kevin... but it came no more. He heard nothing but a soft whimper coming from behind him.

He slowly turned. Lone Wolf found Amber Faye standing in the door frame. Her hand shook profusely as a pistol fell from them. Her face was frozen in a mask of helpless incapacitated dread as she stared at her victim. She had never killed before. She had never even fathomed the thought. The very act shook her to her very core. Slowly, tears began to fall down her soft face.

Outside... the menacing whine of police sirens grew louder and louder. Lone Wolf took a step towards Amber Faye... but she couldn't tear her eyes away from the carnage she had caused. "Let's go baby," he said softly.

Slowly, Amber Faye looked up at Lone Wolf. Through tear-filled eyes she said, "I will always be here to protect you."

Just outside the apartment door... the police squad cars came to a screeching stop. He knew it was too late for them to make their escape.

He drew Amber Faye into his arms and embraced her. He felt her body shaking uncontrollably... but still he held her. "I love you, Linda," he said weakly... but his resolve was strong.

And there they stood... embracing amid the ashes of their dreams.

FROM THE SINS OF PROMETHEUS...
UNTIL CHARON'S LAST TOLL...
MAY THE FLAMES OF ASH'NE,
REKINDLE THINE KINDRED LOST SOUL.

BALANCE OF POWER

BY

EAGLE FEATHER

SYPNOSIS

With the murder of Crime Boss, Omaha's most notorious drug lord, the street wars are raging as each gang fights to gain control of the ever-elusive drug trade. After ten years of incarceration... OG Tav is finally set free. Using tactics of deception, manipulation, and brute force... OG Tav quickly ascends the street's hierarchy. On his rise to power... Tav is forced to engage in physical and psychological warfare against the most ruthless criminal masterminds. WitH the fleeting nature of power... he must now tread the treacherous path of with he had carved out for himself.

THE CAUSE

Their well oiled AK-47's glistened dimly in the pale aqueous light that filtered through the tiny windows... windows of translucent glass that was perched high above in the warehouse. As the five armed guards paced the inner perimeter, their eyes scanned the dark corners which laid in deep shallows. The dusty warehouse was filthy with the grime and soot of years of non-usage. Crime Boss stood in the center, barking orders with the causal arrogance of a man accustomed to command. He stood over the three street thugs as they obediently unloaded wooden creates from the U-Hal rental truck.

"Now, open them," he ordered.

With crowbars in hand, the three men complied. After prying the wooden lids from its place, each man swung open its door, revealing boxes marked "Coffee Maker." Crime Boss then gave the order to remove the continents within the boxes, and to place them on a metal table. He surveyed the continents, mentally taking inventory of what was being placed in front of him.

Suddenly, outside the warehouse, the night seemed to explode with fire. At first he heard the single shots form the intruders semi-automatic pistols... followed by the shuddering burst of assault rifles as his armed guards returned fire.

The sharp report of the AK sent the remaining guards into full alert. Each one of the henchmen racked the bolt action lever to their assault rifles... chambering a live round. They then turned towards the Crime Boss... awaiting their instructions like trained killers. Crime Boss smiled sadistically to himself.

Then all was silent. Crime Boss just knew his henchmen had slain the foolish intruders.

"Go help clean up the mess," Crime Boss said with a cold smile. "You three," he said to the thugs, "Put this shit in duffel bags and let's ride out."

Just then, an unfamiliar voice roared from outside the warehouse. "What nigga?!" the strange yelling taunted. "Ya'll nigga'z can't fuck with this!"

"What the fuck you waiting for?" Crime Boss roared ed at his guards. "Go kill..." But his words were interrupted by a volley of gun fire and a wicked laughter that pierced the air.

"Uh-oh, Mr. Crime Boss," the evil voice continued mocking the drug lord. "I gots me a AK. You done fucked up now," it said as it chuckled wickedly.

The Crime Boss felt the anger grinding in the pit of his stomach as he thought of the two guards he had posted outside. He knew they were dead. "I want that nigga dead. You hear me?!" he ordered harshly. "I want that nigga dead. I want that motha fucka'z head! And I want it now!" As Crime Boss spoke, his voice rose with the power of his conviction.

His henchmen were running towards the entrance of the warehouse, but stopped when they saw two sinister shadows emerging from out of the darkness. Both sides opened fire simultaneously. The air became alive with relentless lead as the automatic weapons snarled in unison. The three thugs took up arms and engaged in combat as well.

Bullets buzzed angrily threw the air as Crime Boss dove for cover. From this new position, he watched as bullets were exchanged between the two opposing groups in a stunning visual display of raw fire power. A bullet pierced the throat of one of his men... he watched as the man dropped his weapon and gripped his wound with both hands. Blood seeping threw his fingers as he grasped for air.

The intruders spayed the wooden crates that Crime Boss used for cover with wild bursts of fire. Splintered wood showered him as he ducked even lower. "Kill them nigga'z" he shouted angrily. He relaxed somewhat as he heard the answering burst of AK's as his hit men obeyed their orders. This fire redirected the attention of the intruders, for they now fired upon the guards. Crime Boss peered into the direction of the two shadows... but saw nothing but the pulsing lights of assault rifles spitting demonic flames from the darkness. He watched as another one of his men was hit by the merciless lead. The thick bullets tore half his face off as the heavy impact spun his upper torso around. The sickly sweet stench of fresh blood and the acid sting of gun powder was thick in the air.

Crime Boss then witnessed another one of his thugs fall victims to the destructive shadows. He watched in utter horror as his body was viciously ripped apart by the flesh eating lead. The bloody and tattered body fell before the Crime Boss. He became acutely aware of his own vulnerability as he laid just mere inches away from, the twitching corpse. He pried the assault rifle from the dead man's grip and tried to rack the loading mechanism. He felt a resurgence of the cold fear slithering in his gut as he realized the weapon was jammed. The breach of the rifle had been struck by the on-coming fire... rendering the weapon useless. He glanced around wildly... his eyes searching in vain for another weapon.

As quickly as it began... the fire fight had ceased. Only the sound of a man drowning in his own blood could be heard in the silence. The dying man coughed... then gurgled... and then was quiet. The drug lord watched in stunned horror as the two shadows stood triumphantly amongst the ruins of ruble, and bloody and tangled bodies.

The deadly silence seemed to buzz loudly in the Crime Boss's ear as panic gripped him in it's icy fists. His blood ran cold as he heard the evil and sadistic snarl coming from the shadows. He realized he was the last one left. The last one waiting to die.

Again his eyes scanned wildly abut the warehouse... seeking desperately for a weapon... for an escape rout... for anything that could aid him. But he saw nothing but blood soaked bodies. He heard nothing but the beating of his own heart... the blood pounding relentlessly in his ears like a deafening symphony of unbridled terror.

In a feeble attempt to escape the gruesome carnage, he turned to run... but the three round burst from the assault rifle ripped threw his legs... tearing muscles and shattering bone. In a blacken haze of pain, he fell to the ground. The once powerful drug lord found himself frantically trying to crawl away from the exploding pain that throbbed in his legs. On the verge of losing consciousness, he crawled a few more feet... leaving a bloody trail.

He spotted an AK-47... like promise of salvation, almost within reach. He tried reaching a shaky hand out for the weapon when he felt the sharp bite of a slug as it buried itself into his back. The bullet pierce through his back and lodged in his chest. He felt as if he was drowning as blood began to fill his lungs.

The pain in his back was so great, he didn't feel the heavy boot of the warmonger as it pinned him down by the neck. Fiery pain shot wave after agonizing wave through his body as the boot lifted from his neck and flipped him over, then came crashing down on his chest. The boot forced the gathering blood from his lungs and out his mouth. The blood he spat was thick... viscid.

He looked up at the intruder with a defeated gaze. The face he saw didn't seem real... didn't seem human. More like a demonic creature that roams the fiery pits of hell. He watched in sheer horror as the creature's lips turned down into a satisfactory snarl. Blood seeped from under his boot as the predatory intruder stared down upon his victim. "This one's yours," he announced to his partner.

The Crime Boss could dimly see the hazy outline of his death as the second figure slowly approached... the shadows seemed to cling to him. He tossed aside the AK and produced a Desert Eagle .375 semi-automatic SL and took direct aim. With a slight tug... the blue rag slipped from, his young face and the hatred appeared... as vivid and sinister as the first creature.

The Crime Boss saw the sparks from the pistol... but didn't feel the lead as it pierced his skull... tunneling a hole... then exploding out the back. All that he had... all that he gained threw hard fought battles... now meant nothing as he slowly slipped into the darkness depths of hell.

THE EFFECT

DAY ONE

The prison alarm sounded off as the heavy gates began to open. On both sides of the barbed-wire fence stood two guard towers. Men armed with fully automatic assault rifles slowly prowled along the catwalk... stalking with overbearing arrogance and self-delusional trait of power inherited by most prison guards. The prison alarm sounded a second time as the gate came to a halt.

"One coming out!" an armed guard shouted... then motioned the convict to continue.

The afternoon sun was blazing as Tav stepped from the shadows of the penitentiary. The sun was glistening off his shaved head. His massive shoulders bearing the light weight of a duffel bag containing all his worldly possessions.

OG Tav... a man of silence... of dominance... a singular icon of brutality and death. He slowly made his way towards the gates of freedom... glaring at the armed guards with a kind of demonic glee. His face was that of perpetual scorn... and his jet-black eyes shown that of unharnessed hatred. At the age of 27... for ten years he had known nothing but prison and its attendant miseries. For ten years he had known nothing but to survive the living hell that is known as prison. And for ten years he had awaited this fateful day. A day where the gates of hell would be thrown open... and crawling from the swarming pit of the living dead would be Tav... re contrived into the image of his hellish surroundings. Again he glanced at the prison guards... is lips turned down in an evil snarl.

The armed guard gripped the assault rifle unconsciously as he watched the convict. His face clouded over as he caught a glimpse of the terrifying entity that he "correctional" system had created. A monster that will be set free into society... unabated and untamed... baring years of pint up anger and hostility. "When will the administration learn?" the guard grumbled to himself as he repositioned his weapon. But he knew redemption and rehabilitation was a thing of the past... such matters were beyond his control. He could only watch as this jaded convict stepped threw the gates into a society that wasn't prepared for such a monster.

"Closing gate twelve!" he yelled as he pressed the button. Again the alarm sounded and the heavy gate began to close.

Printed in the United States
By Bookmasters